Once

"Once upon a time"

IS TIMELESS WITH THESE RETOLD TALES:

Includes:
BEFORE MIDNIGHT
GOLDEN
WILD ORCHID

CAMERON DOKEY

Simon Pulse

NEW YORK   LONDON   TORONTO   SYDNEY   NEW DELHI

SIMON PULSE

An imprint of Simon & Schuster Children's Publishing Division

1230 Avenue of the Americas, New York, NY 10020

This Simon Pulse paperback edition February 2012

Before Midnight copyright © 2007 by Cameron Dokey

Golden copyright © 2006 by Cameron Dokey

Wild Orchid copyright © 2009 by Cameron Dokey

All rights reserved, including the right of reproduction in whole or in part in any form.

SIMON PULSE and colophon are registered trademarks of Simon & Schuster, Inc.

For information about special discounts for bulk purchases, please contact

Simon & Schuster Special Sales at 1-866-506-1949 or business@simonandschuster.com.

The Simon & Schuster Speakers Bureau can bring authors to your live event.

For more information or to book an event contact the Simon & Schuster Speakers

Bureau at 1-866-248-3049 or visit our website at www.simonspeakers.com.

Designed by Mike Rosamilia

The text of this book was set in Bembo.

Manufactured in the United States of America

2 4 6 8 10 9 7 5 3

Library of Congress Control Number 2011926585

ISBN 978-1-4424-2283-4

ISBN 978-1-4424-3995-5 (eBook)

These books were previously published individually by Simon Pulse.

Contents

BEFORE MIDNIGHT

For Delaney

One

WHAT DO YOU KNOW ABOUT YOURSELF? WHAT ARE YOUR
stories? The ones you tell yourself, and the ones told by others.
All of us begin somewhere. Though I suppose the truth is that
we begin more than once; we begin many times. Over and over,
we start our own tales, compose our own stories, whether our
lives are short or long. Until at last all our beginnings come
down to just one end, and the tale of who we are is done.

This is the first story I ever heard about myself: that I came
into this world before my time. And that my coming was so
sudden, hot, and swift, it carried everything before it away,
including my mother's life.

Full of confusion was the day of my birth, of portents, and

of omens. Just at daybreak, a flock of white birds flew across the face of the sun. Its rising light stained their wings bloodred. This was an omen of life taking flight.

At full noon, every single tree in every single orchard on my father's estate burst into bloom at once, in spite of the fact that it was October. This was an omen of life's arrival.

At dusk, a great storm arose, catching everyone by surprise. My mother was in her garden, the one she planted and tended with her own two hands, when two claps of thunder, one from the east and the other from the west, met above her head in a great collision of sound. The earth shook beneath her feet. Crying out, my mother tumbled to the ground. What this portended nobody ever did decide, because it was at precisely this moment that I declared my intention to be born.

Fortunately for my mother, she was not alone. The healer, Old Mathilde, was with her, as she often was when my father was away from home. Just how old Old Mathilde is, no one really knows. But no matter what her years, she was strong and hale enough to lift my mother up and carry her indoors—through the gate in the garden wall and around the side of the house, up the steps to the front door, and across the great hall. Then, finally, up a wide set of stairs from the great hall to the second floor. By the time Old Mathilde reached my mother's chamber, it was storming in earnest, and she, herself, was breathing hard. The wind wailed like a banshee. Hailstones clattered against the roof with a sound like military drums.

Old Mathilde set my mother gently on the bed, paused to catch her breath. Then she summoned Susanne, who worked in the kitchen, instructing her to bring hot water and soft towels. But when Mathilde went to stir up the coals, the wind got there first, screaming down the chimney, putting out the fire. Not content to do this in my mother's room alone, the wind then extinguished every other fire throughout my father's great stone house by the sea, until not so much as a candle remained lit. All the servants quaked in fear. The women buried their heads beneath their aprons, and the men behind their arms, for nobody could remember such an event ever occurring before.

And so it was first in shadow, and then in darkness, that Old Mathilde and my mother strove to bring me into the world. Just before midnight, I arrived. At my coming, the storm ceased as suddenly as it had begun. A great silence filled the great stone house. Into it came the loud voice of the sea, and then my mother's quiet voice, asking Old Mathilde to place me in her waiting arms. She asked this just as the clocks throughout the house began to strike midnight: the only hour in all the world that begins in one day and ends in another. This was the moment I knew my mother's touch for the first and only time.

And this is the story Old Mathilde has told me each and every time I asked her to: that, with my green eyes, I gazed up, and with her green eyes, my mother gazed back down. She ran one hand across my head, her fingers lingering on my bright red hair, for this, too, was the exact same shade as her own. Then

7

she bent her head and pressed a kiss upon my brow. I carry the mark of it to this day, the faintest smudge of rose just at my hairline.

"Mathilde," my mother said then, and with the sounding of her own name, Old Mathilde understood what my coming into the world before my time would cost. For she recognized the sound my mother's voice made—a sound that was both less and more than it had ever been before.

No one is better at understanding the world than Old Mathilde, at being able to see things for what they truly are. This is what makes her such a good healer, I suppose. For how can you mend a thing, any thing, if you cannot truly see what is wrong? Some things, of course, cannot be healed, no matter how much you want them to be, no matter how hard you try. Old Mathilde was not a magician. She was simply very good at helping wishes come true.

"Will you hear a wish?" my mother asked now.

Just for an instant, Old Mathilde closed her eyes, as if summoning the strength to hear what would come. For my mother was asking to bestow the most powerful wish there is, one that is a birth and death wish, all at the same time. Then Old Mathilde opened her eyes and gave the only answer she could, also the one that was in her heart.

"I will grant whatever you wish that lies within my power, Constanze, my child."

Constanze d'Este. That was my mother's name.

"I wish for you to be my daughter's godmother," Constanze d'Este replied. "Love her for me, care for her when I am gone, for I fear her father will do neither one. When he looks at her, he will not find joy in the color of her hair and eyes. He will not see the way that I live on. Instead, he will see only that she came too soon, and that her arrival carried me out of this life.

"Besides, he is a man and a great lord. He wished for his first child to be a boy."

"What you wish for is easily granted," Old Mathilde said. "For I have loved this child with all my heart since she was no more than a dream in yours. As for Etienne . . ." Etienne de Brabant. That is my father's name. "I suppose a man may be a great lord and a great fool all at once. What shall I call her, while I'm loving her so much?"

At this point in the story, Old Mathilde always does the same thing: She smiles. Not because the circumstances she's relating are particularly happy, but because smiling is what my mother did.

"Call her by whatever name you think best," she replied. "For you will raise her, not I."

"Then I will give her your name," Old Mathilde said. "For she should have more of her mother than just the color of her hair and eyes, and a memory she is too young to know how to hold."

And so I was named Constanze, after my mother. And no sooner had this been decided, than my mother died. Old Mathilde sat beside the bed, her eyes seeing the two of us together even in the dark, until my mother's lips turned pale, her arms grew cold, and the clouds outside the window parted to reveal a spangle of high night stars. Not once in all that time, so Old Mathilde has always claimed, did I so much as stir or cry.

When the slim and curving sickle of the moon had reached the top of the window, then begun its slide back down the sky, Old Mathilde got up from her chair and lifted me gently from my mother's arms. She carried me downstairs to the great open fireplace in the kitchen. Holding me in the crook of one arm, she took the longest poker she could find and stirred up the coals.

Not even such a storm as had descended upon us that night could altogether put out the kitchen fire—the fire that is the heart of any house. Once the coals were glowing as they should, Old Mathilde wrapped me in a towel of red flannel, took the largest of our soup kettles down from its peg, tucked me inside it, and nestled the pot among the embers so that I might grow warm once more.

As she did, I began to cry for the very first time. And at this, as if the sound of my voice startled them back into existence, all the other fires throughout the great stone house came back to life. Flurries of sparks shot straight up every chimney, scattering into the air like red-hot fireflies.

In this way, I earned a second name that night, the one that people use and remember, in spite of the fact that the name

Constanze is a perfectly fine one. Nobody has ever called me that, not even Old Mathilde. Instead, she calls me by the name I was given for the coals that kept me warm, for the fires I brought back to life with the sound of my own voice.

Child of cinders. *Cendrillon.*

Two

Two weeks to the day after I was born, my father came home, thundering into the courtyard on a great bay horse ridden so long and hard its coat was white with lather as if covered in sea foam. Where he had been on the night of my birth, where since, are tales that, for many years, would remain untold. But he was often sent far and wide on business for the king, so Old Mathilde sent word of what had happened out from the great stone house knowing that, sooner or later, the news would find my father and bring him home.

Just at the counterpoint to the hour of my birth he came, full noon, when the sun was like an orange in the sky. Around his neck, beneath his cloak, he wore a sling of cloth, and in this sling there was a baby boy. My father pulled the horse up short, tossed the reins to a waiting groom, threw his leg over his horse's neck, and slid to the ground. Even at his journey's end, my father's desire to reach my mother burned so hot and bright that the heels of his boots struck sparks from the courtyard cobblestones. He tossed off his cloak, pulled the sling from around his neck, and thrust it and the burden it carried into Old Mathilde's arms.

"Where is she?" he asked.

"In her garden," Old Mathilde replied.

Without another word, my father took off at a dead run. Around the side of the house, he sped through the gate in the stone wall, and into the place my mother had loved best in all the world, aside from the shelter of my father's arms: the garden she had planted with her own two hands. Surrounded by a high stone wall to protect it from the cold sea winds, it was so cunningly made that it could be seen from only one room inside the house: my mother's own bedchamber, the same room in which I had been born.

Old Mathilde had buried my mother beneath a tree whose blossoms were pale pink in spring, whose leaves turned yellow in the autumn, and whose boughs carried tiny red apples no bigger than a thumbnail all through the winter months. It was the only one like it on all my father's lands. My mother had brought it with her as a sapling on her wedding day as a gift to her new husband, a pledge of their new life. Now the mound of earth which marked her grave was a gentle oblong shape beneath its boughs, as if Constanze d'Este had fallen asleep and some thoughtful servant had come along and covered her with a blanket of soft green grass from her head to her toes.

My father fell to his knees beside my mother's grave, and now a second storm arose, one that needed no interpretation, for all who saw it understood its meaning at once. This storm was nothing less than my father's grief let loose upon the world. His rage at losing the woman that he loved. The trees in the orchards tossed their heads in agony; the clear blue sky darkened overhead, though there was not a single cloud. At the base of the cliffs upon which my father's great stone house sat, the sea hurled itself against the land as if to mirror his torment.

My father threw his head back, fists raised above his head, his mouth stretched open in a great O of pain. But he did not shed a single tear, nor make a single sound. He threw himself across my mother's grave, his fists striking the earth once, twice, three times. As his fists landed for the third and final time, a single bolt of jagged lightning speared down from the cloudless sky. It struck the tree which sheltered my mother's grave, traveled down its trunk, up into all its limbs, killing the tree in an instant, turning the new green grass beneath it as brown as the dust of an August road. At that moment, the storm ceased. And from that day onward, even when every other living thing on my father's lands prospered, on the grave of my mother, Constanze d'Este, not so much as a single blade of grass would thrive.

At last my father got to his feet, turned his back upon my mother's grave, left the garden, and went inside. He climbed the wide stairs, two at a time, until he reached my mother's bedroom door. He pushed it open, slammed it behind him, turned the key in the lock with a sound that echoed upstairs and down. Then, for many hours, there was silence as he stayed in my mother's room alone.

Just as night was falling he emerged, locked the door behind him (from the outside this time), then climbed a thin and winding set of stairs to the very top of the house. There, a stiff sea wind blowing in his face, he threw the key to my mother's room as hard as he could. It was still flying through the air when he turned away, and made the climb back down. All the way to the kitchen and Old Mathilde.

"Show me the infant," my father said, and, in spite of herself, Old Mathilde shivered, for never had she heard a voice so cold. The kind of cold that comes when the heart gives up on itself and abandons hope, a cold no fire on earth could ever warm. But Old Mathilde had not grown old by frightening easily.

"You may see both babes for yourself," she said. "For there they are, together."

And sure enough, in a cradle by the fire—for the soup kettle was not big enough for two, and besides I had outgrown it two whole days ago—the baby boy my father had brought with him from who-knew-where and I were lying, side by side. My hair was as bright as a copper basin; his, as dark as cast iron. My eyes, as bright and as green as fresh asparagus; his, a changeable and tumultuous gray, like the sea beneath the sky of a winter storm. For a time Old Mathilde did not even try to measure, my father stood motionless, gazing down at us both.

"She has the look of her mother," he finally said, and the pain in his voice was as bright as a sword.

Old Mathilde nodded. "That she does."

Etienne de Brabant exhaled one breath, and then another, as if his own body was struggling with itself.

"I should have been here!" he finally burst out. "If I had been with her, things might have been different."

"Some things most certainly would have been," Old Mathilde replied. And now she inhaled one quiet breath of her own, for she knew my father would not like to hear what must follow. "But your presence would not have changed the outcome. Not even I could do that, Etienne. Some things are beyond my power to heal."

My father spun toward her. "Your power!" he exclaimed. "You have none. What good is power if you cannot use it as you wish? You are nothing but a powerless old woman. You let Constanze die."

"Do you think I would not have saved her, if I could?" Old Mathilde asked. "If so, then you are wrong. And you forget that every kind of power has its own boundaries, Etienne. That is how you know its strength and its form.

"I cannot summon up things that must not happen. That

which must take place, I cannot stop. All I can do is to help make the wishes that lie between come true. My power must stop at the boundaries of life."

My father began to laugh, then, and the sound was bitter and wild. "A wish?" he exclaimed. "Is that what you want? You expect me to bestow a wish upon this child that has robbed me of so much?"

"It is what Constanze would have wanted," Old Mathilde said, "and what she herself did. If you cannot bring yourself to do it yet, try starting with the boy. You must have brought him to me for a reason. Therefore, there must be some wish you would bestow."

But by now, father was nodding his head in agreement, as if Old Mathilde's words had recalled to his mind a task that he had left undone.

"I wish the boy to be raised as a member of my household," he said. "Give him no special honors, yet treat him fairly and well. But on pain of death, he is never to be permitted to leave my lands, not even when he is grown. Not unless I send for him."

"By what name shall I call him?" Old Mathilde asked.

My father shrugged. "By whatever name that comes to mind. What he is called is not important."

This is sheer nonsense, of course. If what we are called is not important, why bother with a name at all? But Old Mathilde had also not grown old by being stupid. She knew when to hold her tongue and when to speak her mind. She had named one child. She could name another.

"And your daughter?" she asked softly. "You must wish something for her, Etienne. Constanze is dead, and it is your right to grieve for her. But you and your daughter are alive. With every beat your two hearts make, each of you wishes for something, for to wish is to be alive. This is a fact you cannot escape."

"Not even if I wish to?" my father inquired.

"Not even then," Old Mathilde replied.

"Then hear the wish I will bestow upon my daughter," my father said. "I wish that I might never see her again, unless the sight of her can give back the peace that she has stolen. As I imagine that day will never come, matters should work out well."

"Matters often do that," Old Mathilde said. Here she reached to tuck the blanket more securely around me for, at the sound of my father's wish, as if struggling to be free of a burden, I had done my best to kick the blanket aside. "Though rarely in the way that men suppose. Still, you have wished, and I have heard you. I will do my best to see your wish is carried out in its own good time."

My father turned away then. Away from the unnamed baby boy and me and toward the kitchen door. He put his hand upon the latch, then paused.

"I do not think that we will meet again, Mathilde," he said.

"For I will never come back to this place, if it lies within my choice."

"I imagine we shall both have to wait and see about that," Old Mathilde answered, her voice ever so slightly tart. "I cannot see the future any more than you can, Etienne. The difference is, I am content in this, and you are not."

"I will never be content again," my father said. "Not in this, or in anything else."

He lifted the latch, pushed open the door, and stepped out into the world without looking back, letting the door swing closed behind him. That was the last anyone in the great stone house saw of him for a very long time.

Three

AND SO WE GREW UP TOGETHER, THE BOY WHOSE FIRST beginning nobody knew, and the girl who came into the world before her time. Old Mathilde named him Raoul, and it was easy enough to figure out why. More often than not he reminded us all of a grumpy bear, so it seemed only right that he should have a name to go along with it, one that sounded like a growl.

Not that he was mean-spirited, for he was not. It was more that there was never a moment, except, perhaps, for when he slept, that Raoul did not carry the mystery of his beginning like a burden on his back, a mark upon his soul. Even I knew more about myself than he did, never mind that most of what I knew was painful. Sometimes it is better to know an unpleasant thing than nothing at all.

We made quite a pair together as we grew. But then we always had, from the moment Old Mathilde first placed us side by side. Raoul with his dark, storm-cloud looks, I with my bright ones, the sun coming out from behind the cloud. I cannot claim that this meant I was always good-natured. My temper could run as hot as the color of my hair, and come on as suddenly as my unexpected entrance into the world. But I always spoke my feelings, right out plain, while Raoul often held his inside and left them to smolder.

Old Mathilde honored the wish my father had made the night of Raoul's arrival. He was always treated fairly and well, no differently from any of the rest of us, including me. I might be the daughter of the lord of the house, but nobody paid much attention to that fact. My father had made it quite clear he didn't want me. I was hardly in any position to pull rank, even if that had been the way my nature was inclined. Besides, nobody who lived in Etienne de Brabant's great stone house by the sea had any time to put on airs. We were too busy working to stay alive.

The lands of my father's estate were beautiful and fertile. But, as if the lightning bolt that struck my mother's grave had somehow planted the seed of my father's unrest within our soil, what our fields and orchards might yield could never quite be predicted ahead of time.

One year, every single squash plant grew tomatoes. We made sauce until our hands turned red, then carried our jars to the closest town on market days to barter for what our fields had been unwilling to provide.

Some years our apple trees actually gave us apples. But their limbs were just as likely to be weighed down by cherries or plums. For three years running we had pears instead, followed by three straight years of oranges, a fruit which had never been known to grow so close to the sea before. After that, things seemed to settle down, as if the earth and what my father had called down to strike it had reached some sort of truce. How long it would last, only time itself would show.

And then there was the great stone house itself: huge, drafty, gorgeous. Rising straight up from the center of a great sheer cliff of stone so pale you could see your hand through it on a piece cut thin enough. Even in the darkest hours of the darkest night, the house seemed to give off its own faint glow. Veins of color ran through it, red and green, and a gray that turned to shimmering silver just as the sun went down. One bank of windows faced outward, toward the sea. A second, back toward the land that sustained us.

We were not an easy place to sneak up on.

This was fortunate since, for as long as even the oldest among us can remember, even on the brightest and sunniest of days, the country of my birth has lived under the shadow of war. In most ways, and on most days, we look like everybody else. We get up in the morning, wash our faces, put on our every day clothes. We till our fields, bake our bread, take afternoon naps with our cats or dogs when the sun grows too hot to work outdoors.

But even as we sleep, we have one eye open, one ear cocked, to discover if trouble is coming, carried on the back of the sea, or stirring up dust as it marches down the road. The desire for peace fills our hands with purpose during the day; the fear of war haunts our dreams at night.

There is one place, one land, we fear most of all. A place we do not even name aloud, for to do so is considered bad luck, as good as a summons for disaster to arrive. It lies two days' hard riding on horseback to the north of the great stone house. One day's sailing if the wind is right.

Some say our conflict is only natural. That those with common borders always fight. Others, that it is personal, the result of an incident so bitter and terrible, to speak it aloud is as good as shedding blood. I do not know the truth of things, myself. But I do know this much: We watch the sea in the great stone house. For there is a prophecy that proclaims it is the sea that will carry our salvation, or our doom. In the helpful way that prophecies sometimes have, it further proclaims it may be difficult to tell the two apart.

So I kept my eyes on the sea one autumn afternoon, the day before I turned fifteen. I squinted a little beneath the brim of my straw hat as I worked my way down the first row of the pumpkin patch, for the day was crisp and fine, and the sunlight on the water quick and bright. I was hoeing weeds, trying, without much success, not to think about what might happen when my birthday actually arrived. For on that day, as was traditional, I would make the second most powerful kind of wish there is: the one you speak silently, to your own heart alone, on each and every anniversary of the day that you were born.

For at least ten years now, my wish had been the same: that something I planted on my mother's grave might thrive.

Over the years I had tried many different things. Pansies that showed their brave faces through even our bleakest winters. Scarlet runner beans. Bee balm. Several times I had coaxed what I had planted into reluctant life, but none of them had ever thrived. No matter what I planted, no matter when I planted it, when I went to my mother's grave on the morning of my birthday, it was always to discover that every single thing I planted there had died.

It had absolutely nothing to do with the weather; of this I was certain. Nothing to do with what happened above the ground. It was what lay beneath that doomed my efforts to failure, year after year, time after time. There, the rage and grief my father had called down into our lands still held on and would not let go.

I reached the end of the row of pumpkins, reversed direction, my back now facing the sea, and started up the row beside it. The pumpkin patch was in the farthest corner of the kitchen garden, at the very edge of the great cliff on which the great stone house sat. If I went too far, I could tumble straight off the land and into the ocean.

I jabbed the hoe downward, slicing through the roots of a thistle. *This year will be different,* I thought. Tomorrow morning, I would awaken to find that what I had planted on my mother's grave was still alive and well. Because finally, I had chosen a plant so sturdy and obvious, it was literally staring me in the face: pumpkins.

Out of all the things that grew on our lands, the pumpkins were the most reliable. Though you might plant one variety and end up with another, you always got some sort of pumpkin. This year, we had the most abundant crop any of us had ever seen. Fat ones and tall ones, small ones and large. Pumpkins with skin as pale as ghosts growing alongside those with skin as vivid as orange rinds.

But the most beautiful ones of all were the ones I'd planted on my mother's grave. They'd come up almost at once, producing great curling vines. The pumpkins were squat and fat as if, each night, a family of well-fed raccoons had snuck into the beds and sat upon them. Their skin was an orange as bright as newly polished copper. Thick ribs curved down their bodies from top to bottom, some as wide across as my forearm. Surely pumpkins as bright and sumptuous as these would still be alive tomorrow morning. And if they were, then my wish had come true. I would have broken the curse my father's grief had laid upon us.

In which case, I would need to make an entirely new wish.

The only problem was, I didn't have the faintest idea what it should be.

"You're thinking about tomorrow, aren't you?" Raoul's voice suddenly broke into my thoughts. I realized that I was standing with the hoe straight out in front of me, extending into the air. I brought it back to earth with a *thump*.

"How could you tell?" I inquired dryly.

Raoul smiled. "I think it was the angle of the hoe," he answered. He cocked his head. "Aren't your arms tired?"

"As a matter of fact, they are," I said, and at this, he laughed aloud. Raoul hardly ever laughs. It's simply not the way he's made. As if to make up for behaving in a fashion totally unlike his usual self, he snatched the hoe from my hands, elbowed me aside, and began to work on the weeds himself.

"Why is it that a good crop of anything always brings a good crop of weeds as well?" he inquired after a moment.

I gave a snort. "Please," I said. "Remember where you are." We continued moving along the row in silence for a moment. "Have you made up your mind what to wish for tomorrow?"

"The same thing as always," Raoul replied. He made the hoe bite deep, pulled it back with a jerk. All trace of laughter was gone from him now. "Unless some traveling storyteller arrives to tell the tale of my birth between now and midnight."

Raoul had wished for the same thing every year too: to know who he truly is, the beginnings of his story.

"I'm sorry," I said suddenly. "It was a thoughtless question. Give me back the hoe, Raoul. This is my job, not yours."

I reached to tug it from his hands. Raoul held on tight. "Leave it alone, why don't you? It's not a thoughtless question. It's a perfectly sensible one. It just should have been mine, not yours. You're the one whose wish is about to come true."

"It's not tomorrow yet," I replied. "Now give that to me. You're doing it all wrong."

"All I'm doing is killing weeds, Rilla," Raoul said, using the nickname he'd bestowed upon me when we were both small. But he relinquished the hoe. I worked my way to the end of the row, started down the next one. Raoul kept pace beside me. We were facing the sea once more.

"Do you remember the first year we made wishes?" Raoul asked.

"I remember being tempted to wish you would go back to wherever you came from," I replied with a smile. "Old Mathilde gave you every single day of the year from which to choose a birthday, and you selected the same day as mine."

"It wasn't so unreasonable," Raoul protested. "We're so close in age we might have been born on the same day, for all anyone knows."

I gave a snort. We had been over this before. Ever since Raoul had first announced he intended to muscle in on my birthday, we had bickered with each other about it. Some years with good nature, other years not.

"That's not the reason you did it, and you know it," I said.

"No," Raoul replied. "It's not."

I stopped hoeing, on purpose this time. "Then why?" In all the years we had teased each other, we'd never quite gotten down to the reason for his choice.

Raoul dug the dirt with his toe. "It's simple enough," he said. "So simple I would have thought you'd have figured it out by now. You had everything else I wanted, so I thought I might as well have your birthday, as well."

I let the head of the hoe fall to the earth with a *whump*. "What do you mean I had everything you wanted?" I asked.

"*Have,*" Raoul corrected. "Not much has changed, not even in ten years." He moved his arm in a great sweep, as if to take in everything around us. "You have all this. You know who you are and where you come from. You have a home."

"This is as much your home as it is mine," I said, genuinely unsettled now. "Besides, I'm not so sure knowing who I am and where I come from makes me any happier than you are. It's not a very nice feeling to know your father blames you for your mother's death and plans to never forgive you for it."

"At least you know who he is," Raoul answered. "His name, and the name of your mother. It's more than I know."

"But don't you see?" I asked. "The fact that you don't means that you can hope. You could be anyone, Raoul. Your possibilities are endless, while mine are already sewn up tight. And even if you never find out, you'll still be whatever you can make of yourself."

Raoul made a slightly rude sound. "You sound just like Old Mathilde."

I made a face. "I do, don't I? I suppose it could be worse. She's right more than half the time."

"Actually, I think it's more like three quarters," Raoul replied. "That doesn't make this any easier, Rilla."

I put a hand upon his arm. "I know," I said softly.

Raoul reached up, put his hand on top of mine. Even in the depths of winter, Raoul's hands are always warm. I think it's because of all the fires he keeps, banked down, inside himself. He gave my fingers a squeeze, then let his hand drop away. I picked up the hoe, ready to get back to work.

"Rilla," he said suddenly. "Look up."

Before me stretched the great blue arm of the ocean. The surface of the water flashed like fire. I sucked in a breath. Beneath the brim of my sunhat, I lifted a hand to shield my eyes.

"What is that?" I asked, and I could hear the urgency in my own voice now. "Something's not right. The sea glitters like . . ."

"Like metal," Raoul's voice cut across mine.

I let the hoe slip through my fingers then, never heard it hit the ground. I could think of just one reason for the sea to do that.

"Soldiers," I said. "Armor. How many ships are there, can you tell?" I could not, for my eyes had begun to water.

Raoul took my hand in his, then our feet stumbled in our haste as he tugged me to the end of the row. Half a dozen more paces and we could have jumped right off the edge of the land.

"Seven," he said. "Five hulks and two galleons."

"Five hulks," I whispered, and just speaking the words aloud brought a chill to my heart.

Though the double-decked galleons with their glorious sails were the undisputed masters of the sea, it was the ungainly, flat-bottom hulks with no sails at all we feared the most. These were the ships that could bring the greatest number of soldiers to our shores. Five may not seem like such a great number to you, but the ships were large and our land is small. And there had been no soldiers for nearly twenty years now.

"What flag are they flying, can you see?" I asked, as I dashed a hand across my cheeks in annoyance, hoping to clear the water from my eyes. *Maybe they're not coming for us at all,* I thought. *Perhaps they're going somewhere else. Somewhere far away.*

Raoul was silent for one long moment. "A white flag," he said at last. "In the center, a black swan with a red rose in its beak, and a border of golden thorns."

"No," I whispered, as the earth seemed to sway beneath my feet, for this was the one we feared most of all. One not seen in our land since before I was born, since the marriage of our king and queen had taken place to put an end to bloodshed. "No."

"I can see it clear as day, Rilla," Raoul said, and I took no offense at the sting in his voice. I knew all too well that it was not for me.

"Will they try to land here, do you think?"

Raoul shook his head. "We are not important enough a place, and our shore has too many rocks. They will make for the capital, the court, and go farther down the coast."

"I wish all this would stop," I exclaimed fiercely, the words out of my mouth in the exact same moment I thought them. "I wish that I could find a way to stop it."

This is the third most powerful kind of wish there is: the one you make unbidden, not to your heart, but from it. Only knowing what it is you wish for as you hear own voice, proclaiming it aloud.

No sooner did I finish speaking than I felt the wind shift, blowing straight into my face, tickling the long braids I wore tucked up beneath my sun hat, then tugging at them hard enough to make the hat fly back. With a quick, hard jerk, the leather chin strap pulled tight against my throat.

"So do I," Raoul said softly.

At his words, the air went perfectly still. Raoul and I stood together, hardly daring to breathe. Then, ever so slowly, the wind began to shift again. Its force became strong, picking up until my skirts streamed straight out to the left, flapping against my legs. Below us, the surface of the water was covered with white-caps. Galleons and hulks alike bucked like unbroken horses.

"The wind is blowing backward," Raoul said, his voice strange.

"It can't do that," I answered. "It never blows in that direction off our coast, not even when it storms."

"I know it," Raoul said. "But it's blowing in that direction now. We wished to find a way to make the fighting stop, and now the wind is blowing backward. We did that. Did we do that?"

"I don't know. But I think we should get out of the wind. It has an unhealthy sound."

"Old Mathilde will know what to do," Raoul said.

Hand in hand, pumpkins and weeds both forgotten, we turned, and raced for the great stone house.

Four

By the time Raoul and I reached the house, Mathilde was gathering each and every living thing and shooing it inside. The rabbits were put into their hutches, the chickens onto their nests, the dogs summoned from the courtyard. Being out in such a wind could do strange things to living beings, Old Mathilde called over its unnatural voice. The wind blowing backward can make you forget yourself.

Once we were all safely indoors, I worked with Old Mathilde and Susanne, who ran the kitchen, to make a fine dinner of chowder and cornbread from the last of our fresh ears of corn. All the rest had already been dried, in preparation for the winter. By the time the meal was ready, the sun was setting. We gathered around the great trestle table in the kitchen for supper—all but Raoul, who took his out to the stables, announcing his intention to stay with the horses until the wind died down.

As if to make up for the fact that he was not always comfortable with people, Raoul was good with animals of all kinds. Perhaps because it had been a horse which had carried him to us in the first place, he loved the horses best of all.

Well into the night the wind blew, until I longed to stuff cotton into my ears to shut out the sound. None of us went to bed. Instead, we stayed in the kitchen, our chairs arranged in a semi-circle around the kitchen fire. Old Mathilde worked on her knitting, her needles flashing in the light of the coals. Susanne polished the silver, as if there might yet come a day when someone would arrive who would want to use it. Her daughter, Charlotte, darned socks. Joseph and Robert, the father and son who helped with the orchards and grounds, mended rope. I sorted seeds for next year's planting, wondering what might actually come up.

The clocks struck ten, and then eleven, and still we heard the wind's voice. As the hands of the clock inched up toward midnight, a great tension seemed to fill the kitchen, causing all the air to back up inside our lungs. Midnight is an important hour in general, but it was considered particularly significant in our house. But it was only as the clock actually began to count up to midnight, *one, two, three, four,* that I remembered what the voice of the wind blowing in the wrong direction had pushed to the back of my mind.

When the clocks finished striking twelve, it would be my birthday, and I would learn whether what I wished had come true or not.

Seven, the clocks chimed on their way to midnight. *Eight. Nine. Ten.* And suddenly, I was praying with all my might, with all my heart. *Please,* I thought. *Let the wind stop. Don't let it blow backward on the day of my birth.*

Eleven, the clocks sang throughout the house. And then, in the heartbeat between that chime and the next, the wind died down.

Old Mathilde lifted her head; the hands on her knitting needles paused. Susanne placed the final piece of silver back into its chest with a soft *chink* of metal. *It is just before midnight,* I thought.

Twelve, the clocks struck. And, in that very moment, the wind returned, passing over us in its usual direction, making a sound like a lullaby.

"Oh, but I am tired," Susanne said, as she gave a great stretch. One by one, the others said their good nights and departed. Within a very few moments, Old Mathilde and I were left alone.

"I should go and get Raoul," I said.

Old Mathilde began to bundle up her knitting. "Raoul is fine. He sleeps in the stable half the time anyway. But you may go and get him, if you like. That way, you can both go together."

"How did you . . . ," I began, but at precisely that instant, Raoul burst through the kitchen door. In one hand, he held the lantern he had taken out to the stable.

"Why are you still just standing there?" he asked. "Are we going or not?"

By way of answer, I dashed across the kitchen and, before Raoul quite realized what I intended, I threw my arms around him, burrowing my face into the column of his throat, holding on for dear life. I felt the way his pulse beat against my cheek, the way his free arm, the one that wasn't busy with the lantern, came up to press me close. We stood together for several seconds, just like that.

We look so different, Raoul and I, but in our hearts, we are so very much alike. The same impatience for what we desire dances through our veins. The same need to have our questions answered, our wishes granted. To understand, to know.

And so Raoul had known what I would want to do, now that the wind was running in its proper direction and the clocks had finished striking twelve. He had known that I would never be able to wait until the sun came up to discover if my birthday wish had been granted after so long. More than this, he had given me the greatest gift he could have bestowed. With one short walk from the stable to the house, he had set his own disappointment aside.

Raoul knew already that his wish had not been granted. He knew no more about who he truly was now than he had a year ago, or than he had on the day my father had first brought him home. But still, he had come to find me, knowing I would want to visit my mother's grave, even in the middle of the night.

During the long hours we had waited in the kitchen, the moon had risen. The cobblestones of the courtyard gleamed like mother of pearl; the great stone house shimmered like an opal in the moonglow. The three of us went across the front, then around the corner and along the side opposite the kitchen garden. At last we reached the end of the house and the beginning of the stone wall, just higher than a tall man's head, that marked the boundaries of my mother's garden. Above our heads, surrounding the moon like a handful of scattered sentinels, the stars burned fierce and blue.

"I am afraid," I said suddenly.

"There is no need to be afraid, my Cendrillon," Old Mathilde replied. "Either what you wish for has come true, or it has not. If it hasn't, you must simply try again. Some things must be wished for many times before they come to us."

"Happy birthday, Raoul," I said, as he pushed the gate open.

"And to you, little Cendrillon."

"I'm not little," I said. "And I bet I can still beat you in a foot race."

And with that, we were off and running. I knew every inch of my mother's garden, even in the dark. The rose bushes, espaliered along its walls, the stands of lilies that bloomed in late summer. The daffodils in the spring, the surprise of autumn crocus. A carpet of chamomile was springy underfoot.

There was mint, pungent and sweet. Oregano, brusque and spicy. In the very center of the garden stretched my mother's grave. The limbs of the blasted tree still raised stiffly above it, a silent testimony to my father's rage and grief. Nobody, not even Old Mathilde, had ever been able to bring themselves to cut it down.

Please, I thought, as I raced forward. Please was my word of choice that night. *Please let what I wish for come true.* I reached the edge of the grave, skidded to a stop. A split second later, the light from Raoul's lantern shone down upon the oblong of my mother's grave. I fell to my knees beside it, just as my father had done.

"No," I cried out. "No, no, *no!*"

The vines I had planted were still there, and so were the gorgeous orange pumpkins. But now the vines were withered, as if a killing frost had wrapped its icy fingers around them. The pumpkins were split open. Inside, their flesh was black, the pale white seeds gleaming like fragments of bone. From the moment they had come up, all the while that they had grown, their beautiful outsides had all been concealing the very same thing: Inside, they were festering and rotten.

"I can't do it. I won't ever be able to do it, will I?" I sobbed. "He hates me too much. What can grow amid so much hate?"

"Just one thing," Old Mathilde answered quietly. "Only love."

"*Love!*" I cried. I flung myself forward then, onto the grave, digging my fingers deep into the flesh of the nearest pumpkin. I brought my hands back up, dripping and disgusting. A great stench filled the air, one of unwholesome things kept in the dark too long.

"This," I said, as I flung the first handful from me with all my might. I scooped up more, flung it away, in a desperate frenzy now. "This and this. This is what my father thinks of me. It has nothing to do with love."

"All the more reason that what you wish for should, then," Old Mathilde said, and now she knelt down beside me to take my hands in hers, horrible as they were. I jerked back, but she held on tight. "There are two things in the world you must never give up on, my Cendrillon. And those two things are yourself and love."

"Who said anything about giving up?" I said, as I finally managed to snatch my hands away. "I'm not giving up. I'm just tired of wishing for what I can never have, that's all."

"Then wish for something else," Raoul said without heat.

"You make it sound so simple when you know it's not," I said, the words bitter in my mouth. "But since you request it, then this is what I wish. I wish for a mother to love me, a mother for me to love. And perhaps some sisters into the bargain. Two would be a nice number. That way, perhaps there will be a chance that one of them might actually like me."

"For heaven's sake, Rilla," Raoul exclaimed. "You know you're not supposed to speak a birthday wish aloud."

39

"What difference does it make?" I flung back. "It's not going to come true anyhow."

"You don't know that for sure," Raoul said. "Now come inside and get cleaned up. You smell disgusting."

"Thank you very much," I said. "For that, you can help me up."

Raoul reached down and pulled me to my feet. But when I expected him to let go, he held on. "I am sorry, Rilla," he said. "You see why I think hope is such a tricky thing?"

"I do," I nodded.

"Come," Old Mathilde said. "I am an old woman, my bones ache, and there will still be chores in the morning. Let us go back inside."

After the others had gone to bed, I stood at the kitchen sink, scrubbing my hands till they were red and raw. But the scent of my father's hate could not be washed entirely away. It clung to my skin, a faint rotten smell. At last, I gave up. I climbed the stairs to my room, curled up in bed, and pressed my face against the windowpane, gazing out at the stars.

One wish, I thought. *That is all I want. Why is that so very much to ask?*

And now I had thrown my birthday wish away. Even worse, I had thrown it away in anger. *You are your father's daughter, after all, Cendrillon*, I thought. *Tonight, you've proved you're no better than he is.*

Like him, I had chosen anger over love.

I began to weep, then, great, hot tears. I hate to weep, even when I know I have good cause. It makes me feel like I have failed, as my wish had failed that night.

At last, I put my head upon my pillow and cried myself to sleep, an act I had never performed before. Not even on the night that I was born.

Five

BUT IN THE MORNING, IT WAS NOT JUST CHORES AS USUAL. For in the morning, there was a soldier at the kitchen door.

Susanne had just finished the daily ritual of setting the morning's bread to rise. Now, she and Old Mathilde were bustling about together, setting out ingredients for two birthday cakes. I wasn't sure how much stomach I would have for mine. In spite of the fact that I had wept myself into an exhausted sleep, I had not slept well. It seemed to me that my dreams were filled with the cries of desperate men. I had been up at the sun's first light.

"Would you like me to gather eggs?" I offered now. Usually, this was among my least favorite of the daily chores. I could never rid myself of the notion that the hens resent the way we snatch their eggs. Raoul tells me I'm being ridiculous, of course—which irritates me because I know he's right.

"That would be helpful. Thank you, Rilla," Old Mathilde replied. We had not spoken of the events of last night, but I saw the way she looked at me with careful, thoughtful eyes. Not surprisingly, I found this irritating too. All in all, not one of my better mornings, birthday or otherwise.

I took the egg basket down from its hook, tucked it into the crook of my arm.

"Make sure you bundle up," Susanne advised. "It's cold out this morning. You mark my words, we'll have a hard frost before the week is out."

I took my shawl down from its peg, wrapped it around my head and across my chest, then tucked the ends into the waistband of my apron as I reached for the kitchen door. I pulled it open, then faltered backward with a startled yelp. I was staring straight down the length of a sword into a pair of startled, desperate eyes.

Old Mathilde was beside me in a flash. In one hand, she held the longest of the fireplace pokers. I heard a bang from across the courtyard, realized it was the sudden slam of the stable door. And then, over the soldier's shoulder, I saw Raoul running toward me, full tilt. Above his head, he swung a leather lead, making it sing like a whip.

"Raoul, be careful!" I shouted, just as the soldier heard the sound himself and began to spin around. I don't know whether he lost his footing, or whether the legs that had carried him this far now abruptly refused to hold him any longer. But, in the next minute, before Raoul could even reach him, the soldier went down. Toppling over like a storm-felled tree, his head struck hard against the cobblestones. Raoul skidded to a stop even as Old Mathilde thrust the fireplace poker into my arms, then elbowed me aside to hurry down the two steps from the kitchen to the courtyard. She knelt beside the stranger, placed her fingers against his neck.

"He lives," she said shortly. "Help me get him into the house."

"Wait a minute," Raoul exclaimed. "You're going to take him in?"

"I took you in," Old Mathilde replied.

"But—," Raoul began.

Old Mathilde straightened up, and looked Raoul right in the eye. "If we treat him like an enemy, that's all he'll ever be," she said. She turned around to look at me in the open kitchen door, where I still stood, hesitating. The expression in her eyes made up my mind. I set the poker aside, put aside the egg basket, and walked down the steps to join her.

"For pity's sake, Rilla," Raoul protested.

"For pity's sake," I said. "That's absolutely right. We wished for the fighting to stop, Raoul. You wished it just as hard as I did." I knelt at the soldier's feet, saw, with horror, that his boots were cut to ribbons, his feet bleeding and torn. "This is our chance to do something more than wish. Now come and help us get him into the house."

Raoul swore then, a thing he almost never does. But even as he did so, he was moving toward Old Mathilde and me, scooting her aside to slip his hands beneath the soldier's shoulders and so take the heaviest part of the body himself.

"I really hope you're right about this," he said. "On three." He counted out, and when he hit the number three, the three of us lifted the soldier from the cobblestones. By the time we made it up the kitchen stairs, Susanne had dragged the cot out and placed it near the fire. We settled the soldier onto it. Then Raoul and I stepped back as Old Mathilde set about discovering the full extent of his injuries.

"Go ahead and fetch those eggs, Cendrillon," she instructed. "You go along with her, Raoul."

"Even if we did the right thing," Raoul murmured, as we made our way to the henhouse, "I reserve the right to say *I told you so* if anything goes wrong."

The soldier ran a fever for a solid week, after which time he was so weak he could hardly hold up his head. His hands had been as torn and bloody as his feet. His clothing had been icy and soaked, as if he had been tossed into the sea, thrown ashore, then been so desperate to get away from the water he had not even bothered to look for a path, but simply climbed straight up the cliff to reach our kitchen door.

Old Mathilde, Susanne, and I took turns caring for him, changing the dressings on his wounded hands and feet, keeping an eye on him while he slept, ladling chicken broth down his throat when he awoke. The day he announced he feared he was sprouting feathers was the day we knew he would recover. That was the day he graduated from the cot to a chair.

It was also the day he told us who he was.

His name was Niccolo Schiavone, a minor nobleman's youngest son, born and raised in the land we did not name. He was only about a year older than Raoul and I, and not a soldier, in spite of the sword. He had taken it from the body of a dead comrade in a moment of desperation, certain he would not meet with a shred of kindness upon our shores. The voyage on which he had embarked was his first at sea, his first outside his homeland. He had been sent as a courier, carrying information to the queen herself.

"What kind of message requires warships to send it?" Raoul demanded one night after several weeks had gone by.

Raoul, Old Mathilde, Niccolo, and I were sitting together in the kitchen. During Niccolo's recovery, the days had slid from October into November. It was full winter now. The sea outside our windows was gray, a mirror of the dull and glowering sky; the wind blew hard and cold. But at least it was still blowing in its usual direction. As Niccolo had grown stronger, he had begun to demonstrate his gratitude for the fact that we had rescued him by performing various tasks around the great stone house.

His first feat had impressed us all, but particularly Susanne, and it was this: He revealed his ability to chop onions without crying. Then he graduated to meat, and finally to wood for the kitchen fire, great piles of which were now stacked neatly outside the kitchen door. He re-caned Susanne's rocking chair. When Old Mathilde discovered he had a talent for drawing, she set him to work making sketches of new and bigger cold frames to use in the spring. We had all carefully refrained from mentioning the reason Niccolo was available to perform these tasks in the first place: He had as good as been part of an invasion force.

But the subject of Niccolo's message could not be put off forever, and it was probably inevitable that it would be Raoul who finally brought it up. He might have gone from believing Niccolo intended to murder us all in our beds to grudging acceptance, but he was still a long way from trust. In this, though I don't think either of them realized it, he was no different from Niccolo, himself.

"I think that I must give you a true answer," he finally said in response to Raoul's question. "Though there are many in my land who would say that I should not.

"The news I was bringing to the queen is this: Her father is dead. Her brother now sits upon their country's throne. For twenty long years, brother and sister have waited for this moment. Now that their father is dead, his will can no longer hold them back from what it is that they desire: a return to the ways of war."

"But why?" I cried. "Why did our two countries ever start fighting in the first place? Do you know?"

Niccolo's dark eyebrows rose, and I could tell that I had taken him completely by surprise.

"Of course I know," he said. "Or I suppose, in fairness, I should say I know what I've been told." He paused for a moment, gazing at each of the three of us in turn. "You truly do not know?"

"We do not speak of it," Raoul said softly. "We do not even name the place you live aloud, for to do so is considered as good as inviting your soldiers to march down our roads."

"Please, Niccolo," I said. "Tell us what you know."

Niccolo rubbed a hand across his face. "To speak the truth," he said, "there isn't all that much to tell. In the land of my birth it is simply said that the conflict between our peoples began with a wish for love, ended in hate, and that in between run rivers of blood. Only when true love can find the way to heal hate's wounds can there be a genuine peace between us once more.

"It is for this reason that our late king married his only daughter to the son of his greatest foe. He hoped that love might grow between them and so put an end to the seemingly endless cycle of war."

"Well, that certainly didn't happen," Raoul said with a snort. "We may have stopped fighting for the time being, but everybody knows that what our king and queen feel for each other is a far cry from love. We're about as far away from court as we can be in this place, and even here we hear rumors of the queen's constant plotting.

"They say it has divided the court. The king has food tasters, to make sure he isn't poisoned. Soldiers sleep at the foot of his bed, and outside his chamber door. And he sends Prince Pascal away from court for months at a time. It's the only way to keep him safe, and from becoming his mother's pawn. They say she will never be satisfied until the first son of her heart and blood sits on the throne."

"Which makes no sense at all," I said. "For Prince Pascal is an only child. Of course he will inherit the throne. All the queen has to do is to wait."

"And the longer she waits," Niccolo said. "The older her son will become. Your king is young, still in his prime. He should live for many years yet. Years which will see his son grow to full manhood. The queen's chance for influence diminishes with every year that goes by. But if her husband were to be killed in battle, and her son came to the throne before he turned eighteen . . ."

"Then he would need a regent," I said. "Someone to help guide him, and who better than his loving mother?"

Niccolo nodded. "That is so."

"So the ships we saw were what they appeared to be," Raoul said. "An invasion fleet. Now that they are destroyed, what will your new king do?"

Niccolo shook his head. "I do not know."

"And you," I said quietly. "What will you do?"

"I have been thinking about that," Niccolo answered slowly. "Much as I might wish to stay here, I don't think I have a choice. I was charged with bringing the queen news of her father's death. I must carry out my charge."

"Someone else has probably brought the queen the news you carry by now," Raoul said. "You've been here almost a month."

"True enough," Niccolo acknowledged. "But I have a duty to perform. Ignoring it would bring dishonor to me, and to my family. They probably think I'm dead by now. If for no other reason, I should go to court to send them word I'm still alive."

"When will you go?" I asked.

Niccolo rubbed a hand across his face for a second time. "There's no real reason to put it off," he said. "I could go as early as tomorrow."

"It's a long walk from here to the capital," Raoul observed, but I caught the flicker of a smile. During the days of Niccolo's recovery, a genuine affection had sprung up between the three of us in spite of our initial mistrust.

"Oh, Raoul, for heaven's sake," I exclaimed. "You know better than to pay attention to him when he talks like that, don't you?" I asked Niccolo. "He knows perfectly well we will loan you a horse."

"Give is more like it," Raoul replied more somberly. "Even if Niccolo wants to come back, he's not likely to be able to, once he gets to court. He'll be set to carrying messages for someone else. Either that, or be sent back home."

"Why don't you come with me, to ensure the horse's safe return?" Niccolo proposed. "It would be good to have a companion on my journey."

Raoul's face flushed. He stood up so abruptly the stool on which he had been sitting toppled over with a crash. "I thank you, but no. Speaking of horses, it's time for me to see to them. Good night."

He turned and went out without another word, cold air swirling through the room as he opened and closed the door.

"Well," Niccolo said, after a moment. "It's pretty clear I said something wrong. Either of you care to tell me what?"

"Raoul is forbidden to leave de Brabant lands," I said, as I stood to right the upturned stool. "By order of Etienne de Brabant himself."

"De Brabant lands," Niccolo echoed, and I turned toward him at the astonishment in his voice. "These lands belong to Etienne de Brabant?"

"They do," I acknowledged.

Niccolo clapped his hands together, like a child who has just solved a knotty puzzle. "Oh, but surely this explains everything," he cried. "Why did you not speak of this before?"

"It didn't occur to me it was important," I said. I shot a glance in Old Mathilde's direction. "I'm not sure I understand why it is now."

"It explains why you would take me in and nurse me back to health where others would only see an enemy," Niccolo replied. "Etienne de Brabant supports the queen. He is the leader of her faction at court. If these are de Brabant lands, surely you, too, must be sympathetic to her cause."

"We wish for our two countries to be at peace," Old Mathilde said, when it became clear that I could not speak at all. I had never heard of any of this before. "Nothing less, and nothing more. We have no time to concern ourselves with court intrigues in a place such as this."

Niccolo's face clouded. "I'm sorry," he said. "I didn't mean—"

"Why?" I burst out.

Niccolo turned back to me, the confusion he was feeling clear upon his face. "Why what?"

"Why does Etienne de Brabant support the queen's cause?"

"I don't know the details," Niccolo admitted. "For it happened many years ago. He was loyal to the king, or so they say, until some service he performed while in the king's service brought him endless sorrow. After that, he turned his back on all that he had been before. He has been the queen's man ever since."

"Ever since," I echoed quietly, though my heart was thundering in my ears like a kettle drum. I turned my head, and met Old Mathilde's eyes. "Since the day he received word of my mother's death," I said. "Since the day that I was born. That's the day his endless sorrow began, don't you think?"

Niccolo jerked, as if Old Mathilde had jabbed him with one of her knitting needles.

"Wait a minute," he exclaimed. "You're saying you are Etienne de Brabant's daughter? I did not know he had a child!"

"I am the child of Etienne de Brabant and Constanze d'Este," I said. "My mother died the night that I was born, while my father was far from home, on the king's business, or so it now seems. My father does not forgive, nor does he forget, what happened the night that I was born. That's why you've never heard of me. My father does his best to pretend I don't exist."

"Then he is a fool," Niccolo said. "For you are a daughter of which any father would be proud."

I felt the blood rush to my face, the sudden stab of tears at the back of my eyes.

"It is kind of you to say so," I said. "But I—"

Old Mathilde got to her feet, dropping her knitting into her basket with a rustling sound.

"We have had enough of questions and answers for tonight, I think," she said in a firm yet quiet voice. "You will need a good night's sleep, Niccolo, if you truly intend to go tomorrow morning. It's a long journey. You should start at first light."

Niccolo stood up in response to her words, but I felt the way his eyes stayed on my face. "You are right," he said. "I will say good night. But I . . ." He paused and took a breath. "I would be sorry to think any words of mine had caused unhappiness," he went on. "Particularly after all your care."

"They haven't," I said. "You took me by surprise, that's all. Good night."

"Good night," he said.

The kitchen was silent for many moments after he had gone.

"It's too bad Raoul can't go with him," I remarked at last. "They would make a good pair."

"Indeed they would," Old Mathilde replied. "Perhaps they will get their chance yet."

"What do you wish for, Mathilde?" I suddenly inquired.

"That the wishes of those I love come true," she replied. "No more questions now. It's time for bed."

Six

THAT WINTER WAS THE COLDEST ANY OF US COULD RECALL.
The ground froze solid, though we had no snow. Day after day,
the sea outside our windows churned like an angry cauldron. If
you put your bare hand on the outside of the house, you could
burn the skin on your fingers, it was so cold. The only thing
that never seemed to change was the surface of my mother's
grave. It was as bare and brown as always.

December came and went, and then January. In February,
the clear cold abruptly loosed its grasp. The sky filled with
clouds and the rains came down, swelling the rivers with water,
choking the lanes with mud. Then, one morning, beneath the
bare branches of the rose bushes in my mother's garden, I saw

that the tenacious green shoots of snowbells were beginning to push their way up through the waterlogged soil. The wood hyacinths in the orchards were right behind them. The first flowers bloomed on the first day of March.

On the second day, Niccolo came back to the great stone house.

He rode into the courtyard in the strange and beautiful gleam of twilight, just as the sun came out from behind a cloud. Its rays struck the house, lighting up all the colors within the pale white stone. I was in my mother's garden, trying to prune the last of the rose bushes before the light expired. I saw the way the house abruptly blazed with color, heard the clatter of horses' hooves, Raoul's shout. And then I was up and running, pushing the gate from the garden open with both hands, dashing along the side of the house and into the courtyard.

Niccolo was still on horseback, on the sleek dappled gray that had been Raoul's choice. Raoul had one hand in the horse's mane, the other on Niccolo's leg as it gripped the horse's flank. As I rounded the corner, the horse lowered his head and pushed against Raoul's chest, hard enough to knock him back five whole steps.

"He is glad to see you," I heard Niccolo say. "He's been doing his best to pull my arms from my sockets ever since we sighted the house."

"It's on top of a hill," Raoul said. "You can see it for miles."

Niccolo laughed. "Believe me, I know." He saw me then. "Cendrillon!"

He tossed the reins to Raoul, slid from the horse's back, and crossed the courtyard with quick and eager strides to twirl me around in a great rambunctious hug. The kerchief I wear upon my head spun loose and my braids went flying.

"I am glad to see you," he said.

"And I you," I replied. "Welcome home."

"I have seen all the beauties of the court," Niccolo went on as he set me on my feet. "Not a single one of them can compare to you."

"Oh, ho," Raoul said with a laugh from where he still stood beside the horse. "He has come back to us a silver-tongued courtier. You had best watch your step around him, Cendrillon."

I retrieved my kerchief, bound my hair back up. Unbraided and brushed out, my hair falls almost to my knees, but I always keep it covered. Loose hair only gets in the way when I'm working, and I have never quite forgotten the day, when I was twelve and beginning to feel the first stirrings of vanity, that Raoul claimed its color was so bright it kept the villagers awake at night.

"So," I heard Old Mathilde's voice say. "The traveler has come home."

"And I bring news," Niccolo said, his expression sobering. "News I must share quickly, for there isn't much time. Etienne de Brabant is married again. His new wife and daughters follow close behind me."

"Married!" I exclaimed. I put a hand out, as the world began to whirl, and felt Niccolo's hand grasp mine. "My father is married? When did this happen?"

"Just last week," Niccolo said. "Chantal de Saint-Andre is your stepmother's name. She is a wealthy widow, and a ward of the crown. None may marry her but by the king's command."

"And now the king has married her to my father?" I said. I knew I sounded stupid, but I could not seem to get my brain to function. "But why?"

"That," Niccolo said succinctly, "is the question to which all the court would like an answer. Your new stepmother and stepsisters most of all."

"Stepsisters!" I cried. "I have stepsisters?"

"Two," Niccolo answered. "Their names are Amelie and Anastasia."

"I think," I said faintly, "that I would like to sit down." In fury and desperation, I had wished for a mother and two sisters. And now my father was married, and his wife and two step-daughters were on their way to my door.

"I can't tell you more. I'm sorry," Niccolo said. "I'm afraid there isn't time. They should be here any minute. I only rode on ahead to try and give you some warning."

"Why did you bring them?" I asked. "Do you serve my father now?"

"Because I was convenient," Niccolo answered. "I knew the way, and besides—"

"You are from the queen's home country," I filled in. "No matter what the king commands my father to do, you may be relied upon to keep the queen's interests in mind."

"Something like that," Niccolo acknowledged. "Cendrillon, there is one other thing that you should know."

But before he could finish, there was a great clatter of hooves as a coach swept into our courtyard. The spokes of its wheels were coated in mud; great spatters of it rose halfway up the doors and sides. Even the coachman was covered in the huge clumps tossed upward by the horses' hooves. He pulled back hard on the reins and brought the two broad-backed horses to a halt at the bottom of the steps that led to our front door. Their hot breath steamed in the air; curls of steam rose up from their backs and flanks.

Niccolo released my hand, and moved toward the coach at once. Raoul stayed beside the dappled gray. Old Mathilde made a gesture, and together we moved to stand at the top of the steps, a welcoming committee of two women, one young, one old. That would be all Etienne de Brabant's house could offer his new wife and daughters. Mathilde pulled one of my arms through hers, tucking my fingers into the crook of her elbow. I held on for dear life.

Carefully, so as not to tumble fresh mud on the occupants inside, Niccolo opened the coach door. He unfolded the steps, then extended one hand, his body bent at the waist in a bow. And it was only at this moment that I truly understood

59

what should have been obvious to me at once: My new step-mother was of noble birth. She and her daughters would be unlike anything the great stone house had seen in a good long time.

I wonder if they will have seen anything quite like us, I thought. And then I ceased to think at all. For just then, a hand emerged from inside the carriage, its fingers encased in a supple leather glove. It grasped Niccolo's, held on tightly, then was followed by the rest of the arm. A head emerged, neck bent down so as not to knock the top of it against the inside of the door. Next, a pair of shoulders, wrapped in a dark blue cloak. And now, finally, one foot was upon the carriage steps and the woman inside the coach was straightening up. At this, my mind came flowing back.

Oh, but she is so beautiful, I thought.

My stepmother's skin was as pale as our best porcelain dishes. Peeking out from beneath the hood of her cloak, her hair was midnight dark. Her eyes were the same deep blue as the hood which framed them. At their expression, I felt a strange feeling in my chest, as if a great hand was squeezing it, tight. So tight I couldn't quite get a full breath of air.

So beautiful and so unhappy, I realized. And absolutely deter-mined not to give way to what she felt. Gazing at my new stepmother's face, I had a sudden vision of a stream in early spring, just before the final thaw. On the surface, a thin sheet of ice. But beneath the surface, the current was racing, swift and strong. Where it might carry us, I could not say. Perhaps not even Chantal de Saint-Andre herself could say.

"My lady," Niccolo said, just as my stepmother's foot touched the cobblestones. "Welcome to the end of your long journey, and your new home."

"Thank you, Niccolo," she said, and at the sound of her voice, I felt a shiver move down my spine. There was absolutely no expression in it, no hint of what she might be feeling at all. "You have cared for us well and I am grateful for it."

She cocked her head then, as if she saw something unexpected in his face. "You are happy to be back in this place, I think," she said, her voice warming ever so slightly.

"Lady, I am," Niccolo said. "In this place I found . . . a surprise. I hope that you may do the same."

"I have no doubt I will," my new stepmother replied, and now her voice was dry. I saw her blue eyes sweep up and outward to take in the great stone house. If she thought it beautiful and was surprised by this, she gave no sign. I knew the moment she spotted Old Mathilde and me, for at last Chantal de Saint-Andre's lips curved in something that might have wished to be a smile.

"We have some welcome, I see," she said.

"A small one, as yet," Old Mathilde said, and she descended the steps, her hold on my arm pulling me along beside her. At the bottom of the steps, she stopped and bobbed a curtsy, once again obliging me to follow suit.

"We are not many here, and we had no word of your arrival till Niccolo came to tell us the news himself, just now. Still, we know what we are about. I am Old Mathilde. And this is Cendrillon."

"Cendrillon," my stepmother echoed, and I felt her gaze on me, and me alone, for the very first time. Not unfriendly, but cool and remote. And suddenly I knew the truth, knew what it was that Niccolo had been trying to tell me when the arrival of the carriage had interrupted him. My stepmother had no idea that her new husband had a child of his own. No idea that I was now her stepdaughter.

"I have never heard such a name before," Chantal de Saint-Andre went on.

"I don't think anyone else has it," I somehow managed to reply. *Fool, idiot, nincompoop,* I thought. *Your father has never acknowledged you, not once in all these years. Why did you think he would do so now?*

But still, I felt the pain of his denial slice straight through my heart. In my simple, homespun dress, my stepmother had mistaken me for a serving girl. And who could blame her? When my own father denied me, who was I to tell Chantal de Saint-Andre the truth of who and what I was?

"The villagers say that, because I am called the child of cinders, the fires in our house will always start, and never go out until I give them leave to do so," I went on.

All of a sudden, my stepmother smiled. A real one this time.

"That's the best news I have heard since we set out," she said. "We have been traveling for more hours than I care to count, and all of them cold ones."

"Then you must come inside and warm yourselves at once," Old Mathilde said. "We will have your rooms prepared before you know it."

"Thank you," Chantal de Saint-Andre replied. "I believe that is as warm a welcome as any stranger could wish for."

"Oh, but you are not a stranger anymore, my lady," Old Mathilde said, her voice soft but as unyielding as the stones upon which we stood. "You are now the mistress of this house. I hope you will not mind becoming acquainted with the kitchen first. With so few of us, it's the only place we always keep a fire going."

"The kitchen!" exclaimed a sudden voice. "I most certainly will not!"

And that was the moment I realized that I had been so caught up in my new stepmother that I had let all thoughts of her daughters slip my mind. They were out of the carriage themselves now, standing beside it in the courtyard, bundled in cloaks up to their chins, one forest green, the other a deep and fertile brown. Both had their mother's fine pale skin, her dark and lustrous hair. One had blue eyes, and the other brown ones. The blue-eyed girl was a little taller, more angular than her sister, and I thought her cheeks were flushed with anger rather than with cold.

So you are the one who is not fond of kitchens, I thought.

She stomped her foot against the cobblestones as if she had read my mind.

"I have not traveled for hours in a dark and freezing coach to sit in the kitchen like some serving maid," she proclaimed in a bright, clear voice. "I will stand out here if I have to, until a proper room is prepared. Till then, I will not set a foot inside."

"You'll just be cold longer," the girl beside her said, her voice exasperated but not altogether unkind. "Can you not make things easier instead of more difficult, just this once? It's only a kitchen, Anastasia. It's hardly the end of the world."

"This whole place is the end of the world," the girl named Anastasia announced. "And I am not going in until my own room is ready. Do you hear me? I am not!"

"As you wish," her mother finally said. "I agree with Amelie, but by all means stay outside, if that is what you want. I only hope you and your pride don't catch cold together."

"I know what you are doing!" Anastasia cried out, her voice as petulant as a child's. "You're trying to scare me. It isn't going to work. I will not sit in a kitchen like some common girl."

"I don't see why not," her mother observed, her own voice cool and careful. "When you have no problem behaving like one. Still, you have made your choice, and you may now abide by it. I will send Cendrillon to fetch you when your room is ready." She turned to Old Mathilde. "If you will be so good as to show those of us who wish to go in the way?"

"You cannot make me!" Anastasia cried, stamping one booted foot upon the cobblestones. "You can't! Haven't we all been made to do enough?"

What her mother might have answered then, I cannot say, for Anastasia stamped her other foot as well. And at that, as if startled from dreams of a clean, dry stall and a pile of fresh hay, the closest of the carriage horses suddenly screamed and reared straight up. Its great front forelegs pawed the air. Within an instant, the second horse had reared as well. The carriage jerked backward as the coachman struggled with the reins. Niccolo spun around.

And then, suddenly, Raoul was there. Just as Niccolo reached for Amelie, pulling her away from the horse, shielding her with his own body, Raoul caught Anastasia up into his arms. Lifting her, then whirling her away from the horse's hooves just as they came slashing down. The coachman gave the horses their heads, sending them flying around the courtyard, then back out onto the road. The dappled gray Niccolo had ridden snorted and pranced, but, at a sharp command from Raoul, it grew still and quiet once more.

"Your coachman is a wise man, lady," Raoul said, into the great silence that suddenly filled the courtyard. "He will let them run off their fear. It won't take long, not on these muddy roads."

Only then did he look down at the young woman he held

in his arms. "They will be back by the time your room is pre-pared, my fine young mistress. Though, if you were my daugh-ter, such foolish behavior would earn you a night in the barn."

For a moment, Anastasia stared up at him through wide and startled eyes. Then the color in her face flamed bright red.

"Put. Me. Down," she said through clenched teeth, spacing each word out slowly and carefully, as if Raoul might be too simple to understand them otherwise.

"Do you hear me? Put me down right now! I did not give you permission to touch me. You're nothing but a stable boy and you reek of horses. Now I shall need a bath as well, to get rid of the smell."

Raoul let one of his arms drop away so suddenly Anastasia gave a startled cry as her legs swung down. With a bone-jarring smack, her feet connected with the cobblestones. But I noticed that he kept his second arm around her back until he was cer-tain she was steady on her feet.

"In that case, you will have to reconsider your plan to avoid the kitchen," he said. "For that is where we heat the water for our baths at the end of the world."

He moved toward the gray, even as my stepmother began to hurry toward her daughters. "I will see to the horse," he said to Niccolo. "For something tells me you may be needed else-where."

Entirely without warning, he gave a wolfish grin, and Niccolo grinned back.

"Welcome home, Niccolo."

"My girls," Chantal de Saint-Andre said, as she held out her arms. "Are you both unharmed?"

"I am fine, Mother," Amelie replied. She did not move immediately to her mother's arms, I noticed, but stood her ground. "For which I must thank you, Niccolo."

She extended her hand. Niccolo took it, holding it by no more than the fingertips, and executed what I could only assume was a perfect court bow.

"It is my pleasure to serve you, Lady Amelie," he said as he slowly let her fingers go. "Though I hope you will not be insulted if I say I hope we never have to do that again."

"And I hope *you* will not be insulted when I say that I agree," Amelie answered with a smile.

"Well, I am far from fine," Anastasia remarked tartly, but I saw the way she went into her mother's arms and clung. "I am cold and tired, and now I smell like horses besides."

Chantal de Saint-Andre rested her chin atop her daughter's head. Just for a moment, she closed her eyes.

"I think," she said, as she opened them again, "that it is time for us all to go inside. And if you even think of arguing with me, my lovely Anastasia, you will smell like many more things than horses, for I will take that young man's advice and send you to sleep in the barn."

"You wouldn't!" Anastasia exclaimed.

"Oh, yes, I would," said her mother. "This long, cold day has gone on long enough. Let us see if a kitchen fire cannot begin to set us all to rights."

And so, with Old Mathilde leading the way, the mother and sisters I had wished for walked up the steps and into the great stone house.

Seven

"HOW MUCH LONGER ARE YOU GOING TO WAIT BEFORE YOU tell them?"

I gave a pillowcase a smart snap, then pinned it to the clothesline. Several weeks had gone by and we had reached the end of March. I was taking advantage of a rare sunny day to do an extra washing. With three new people, all of them fine ladies, the last few weeks had brought a number of changes to the great stone house.

The day after Chantal de Saint-Andre's arrival, and with her blessing, Old Mathilde had gone to the village at the foot of our cliff and hired extra help. Susanne and Charlotte now had more hands in the kitchen. Joseph and Robert, help with the grounds. Old Mathilde had two new girls to help handle the housework. Though we had never neglected it, in less than a month, the great stone house had once again begun to shine with life. I wondered if my father realized what he had done.

With so many other people to look after the house, caring for my stepmother and stepsisters had fallen to me. In the weeks since their arrival, I had acquired several new skills: I now knew how to dress a lady's hair, the best way to remove wrinkles from silk, how to starch and iron a fine linen collar. Chantal and Amelie had been calm and patient in their instructions. Anastasia had been a tyrant.

It was her sheets I was hanging on the line. Though they had been freshly changed just this morning, she had refused, point blank, to sleep upon them, insisting they smelled as damp and musty as the weather we had endured all month. My personal opinion was that she simply liked the fact that she could order me about. Giving other people orders made Anastasia feel important.

"And just when would you suggest I tell them?" I inquired of Raoul now. "Before or after I pin up their hair and fasten their gowns? Here, help me with this."

I tossed the end of one of Anastasia's sheets in Raoul's direction. Together, we pulled it along the length of the clothesline, then pegged it so it wouldn't blow away. Except for when he came to the kitchen for his meals, Raoul spent most of his time in the stable, or out of doors. His mood had been as glowering as the dark March weather, particularly once Niccolo had gone back to court after he made sure my stepmother and stepsisters were safely settled.

"How should I know when you should tell them?" Raoul asked now, his tone grumpy. "The way she treats you is wrong. I know that much." I didn't have to ask who *she* was. We both knew well enough.

"I don't particularly care for it myself," I answered, as we began to peg the second sheet onto the line. "But I can hardly just blurt out who I am at this point. I have to find a way to do it that doesn't make it seem as if I've played them false. If I simply announce who I am now, it's going to look as if we've all deliberately made fools of them."

"All right. I guess I can see that," Raoul said grudgingly. "What does Old Mathilde say?"

"Nothing."

Raoul paused, a clothespin in midair. "What do you mean, nothing?"

"I mean nothing," I answered, my voice grumpy now. "She hasn't mentioned it at all. Not even once."

Raoul made a face. "That doesn't sound like her."

"No," I said. "It doesn't. Which leads me to believe there's a lesson lurking just around the corner. I really am thinking about the situation, Raoul. Sometimes, it feels like all I think about. I didn't just wish for any old stepmother and stepsisters. I wished for some that I might love, some who might love me. But they can't do that if they don't know who I am, and they can't know who I am unless I tell them. The whole situation makes my head hurt, if you want to know the truth."

"Do you love me?" Raoul asked suddenly.

"Of course I do," I said. "What does that have to do with anything?"

"You don't know who I am. None of us do," Raoul answered quietly.

"That's not true," I replied, somewhat hotly. "You are Raoul. You're generous and grumpy, the best horseman in the county. You like peach pie better than apple, and Old Mathilde's ginger cookies best of all. I would trust you with my life. I may not know where you came from, but that's not the same as not knowing who you are."

"Some days, it feels that way to me," Raoul said. "And I like cherry pie best of all."

"Did I leave out deliberately contrary?" I said sweetly. "Incredibly annoying?"

"I don't really smell of horse, do I?"

I opened my mouth, then closed it again, as I felt my hand ball into a fist at my side. *Anastasia again,* I thought. *That foolish girl has a great deal to answer for.* It took a lot to get under Raoul's skin. She had done it the very first night, and now her cruel and thoughtless words were a part of him.

"The question isn't whether or not you smell of horses,"

I answered. "But whether or not horses smell. Specifically, whether or not they smell bad."

"Anastasia seems to think so," Raoul said. "She made that clear enough."

"Why do you care what she thinks?" I asked. "She may be as old as we are, but she's nothing more than a spoiled child. The way she treated you is just as bad as the way she treats me, Raoul. And if she thinks you smell bad after working with the horses, I suggest you pay her a visit after you've been mucking out the pig sty."

Raoul's lips gave a reluctant twitch. "You're trying to tell me I'm being an idiot," he said.

"No," I replied. "I'm trying to tell you Anastasia is one. The fact that she hurt your feelings doesn't make her right, you know."

"I do know that," Raoul said. "It's just—"

"It's just that even idiots sometimes have a way with words," I said. "And some words have sharp tongues. I know."

"I *am* being an idiot," Raoul said.

"Well, if you insist," I replied. I picked up the empty laundry basket, settled it onto one hip. "I should go back inside. Just this morning, Anastasia suddenly discovered half a dozen dresses in immediate need of mending. She'll pitch a fit if I don't at least get started on them."

Before I quite realized what he intended, Raoul leaned forward and kissed me on the cheek. I felt my face flame, put my hand to the spot, as if to hold the kiss in place.

"What was that for?"

"To thank you," Raoul replied, his own cheeks ruddy now. Displays of affection were rare between us, between Raoul and anyone. "You're a good friend to have, Rilla."

"As are you," I said. "And I'm going to remind you of those fine words the next time I annoy you."

A light I knew very well came into Raoul's eyes. "Maybe you should just start now."

I laughed suddenly, threw my arms around his neck, and kissed him back. "I'll see you at supper," I said. "Don't forget to wash up."

"Oh, I intend to," Raoul said. "But first, I think I'll just go and see how the pigs are doing."

He was whistling as he turned on his heel and sauntered across the courtyard.

"Oh, Cendrillon," Anastasia said as I entered her room in obedience to the bright *come in* that had answered my knock. "There you are. I was beginning to think this dreadful March wind had blown you out to sea, you were taking so long."

She was standing at the window, staring out toward the water, wearing a white dress with pale pink flowers embroidered all over it. It was the perfect foil for her dark beauty. All of a sudden, I felt a strange lump in my throat. Would I be beautiful, too, if I had a dress like this? If I had dozens of them? What might I look like, if I could dress like the nobleman's daughter that I was?

In the next second, I grew ashamed of myself. *Perhaps you shouldn't be so quick to think you know yourself or anyone else, Cendrillon,* I thought. Jealousy had never been a part of my nature, not until Anastasia had arrived.

She turned from the window. "I am waiting," she said, in a tone like cold, clear glass. I could almost feel the way it pressed against me, trying to find a way to cut.

I hesitated, sensing the trap, but unable to see how I could avoid stepping into it anyhow. I gave up the struggle and spoke.

"For what?"

"Not even you can possibly be so stupid," Anastasia snapped. "For my apology, of course."

"Your apology!" I exclaimed before I could help myself. Abruptly, I could feel my own temper start to rise. I was spending hours agonizing over how to tell Anastasia, her mother, and her sister the truth about who I was in a way that wouldn't hurt their feelings, and this vain and silly girl stood there in her finery demanding an apology for only she knew what.

"Why on earth should I apologize to you? I haven't done anything wrong."

"That is a matter of opinion," Anastasia huffed. "As servants do not have opinions, none that count anyway, the only opinion in this room is mine. And I say you owe me an apology for keeping me waiting. You are here to serve me, not to chat in the yard with foul-smelling stable boys."

"Raoul is not foul-smelling," I said hotly.

"Don't be absurd," Anastasia replied. She gave a sniff, as if to emphasize her words. "I can practically smell the stables from here. Girls like you can be dismissed for your kind of behavior, you know."

Abruptly, I felt my temper reach its boiling point.

"I *am* sorry," I said sweetly, and caught the satisfaction that flashed across Anastasia's face. "But then I'm just a plain country girl, unaccustomed to the ways of fine ladies. Explain to me how hanging out sheets that didn't need washing in the first place is cause to have me dismissed."

Two bright spots of color flared in my stepsister's cheeks. "How dare you?" she cried. "How dare you speak to me in such a way? I can have you dismissed for anything, any time I want to. And don't think I didn't see the way you touched each other, because I did. I saw it all."

"Then you are blind as well as ill-tempered and spoiled. Raoul and I have known each other since we were two weeks old. He put spiders in my hair, and I put garter snakes in both his boots. We are hardly likely to be flirting over a clothesline."

"If you think for one moment that I care what the two of you do together—," Anastasia began.

"I don't," I said, ruthlessly cutting her off. "The simple truth is, Raoul and I both try not to think about you at all."

A terrible silence filled the room. Anastasia's cheeks were pale as milk now. And I saw, to my absolute horror, that her eyes were filled with tears.

"Oh, Cendrillon," Amelie's voice slipped quietly into the room. "How fortunate. I was hoping you might help me with something, and here you are."

Anastasia turned away, moved to the window seat, and sat down upon it with such force that the cushions beneath her sighed. *Oh, Cendrillon,* I thought to myself. *What have you just done?*

"Of course I will help you," I said, as I turned to Amelie. "If you will just give me a moment to collect your sister's mending."

"Actually," Anastasia said in a brittle voice. "I find that I have changed my mind. Instead of mending just these few dresses, I think it will be necessary to attend to my entire wardrobe."

She turned away from the window to face me again, and, though her eyes were still too bright, I could see that they were dry. I felt my stomach give a funny little twist.

"I'm not going to be stuck out here in the country forever, you know," Anastasia went on. "And neither is Amelie. Etienne de Brabant is an important man at court, and daughters of marriageable age are an asset, whether he wants them or not. I intend to be ready when he sends for us." She tilted her head, and her eyes as they met mine were cold as snow. In them, I read dislike and a challenge.

"You understand what I require?"

"I do," I acknowledged. And it was nothing less than looking over every single item in her entire wardrobe. Every seam of every dress. Every stitch which fastened on a ribbon or a seed pearl. Every hem and button. Everything must be in perfect order. I had no doubt it was a task she could make stretch on for weeks.

"I am pleased to hear it," Anastasia replied in a sweet voice. "Naturally, I will need to supervise you closely, to make certain the job is done right." She tilted her head in the other direction. "A pity you will have no more time to flirt with stable boys."

She turned her back on me then, her gesture a clear sign of dismissal.

"Please help my sister with whatever she needs, then do me the pleasure of staying out of my sight for the rest of the day," she went on. "I'm sure you and I will both appreciate having one less thing to think about."

"As you wish," I said. And, to my surprise, Anastasia's head whipped back around.

"It shall be as I wish," she said fiercely, and now her eyes were hot and bright. "Do you hear me? I say it shall. Now get out of my room. I'm tired of looking at you. I'm tired of every single thing about this dreadful place."

She turned back to the window. For a moment, I thought that Amelie would go to her. Instead, she gave a little sigh.

"Come with me, Cendrillon, if you please," she said. She preceded me into the hall. I closed the door quietly behind us, then hurried to keep up as Amelie had already set off at a brisk pace down the corridor.

"I think this place is beautiful," she said after a moment. "Especially the house. I didn't think I would. I didn't think I'd like anything about this place when we first arrived."

"What made you change your mind?" I asked, then cursed myself for an idiot when Amelie stopped abruptly and turned around. I had spoken to her like an equal, as if I had the right to ask her what she felt and thought. As far as she was concerned, of course, I did not. I was no more than a servant in Amelie's eyes. The fact that she treated me better than her sister did didn't change things a bit.

"You have lived here a long time, I think," Amelie observed. "And you love this place."

"I have lived here all my life," I answered, deciding to focus on the first statement and let the second go. "I was born here, in fact. Old Mathilde delivered me."

Amelie's expression brightened. There was something about her that always reminded me of a sparrow, though she was neither drab nor plump. But she had a sparrow's bright, dark eyes. A bird's darting interest and intelligence.

"I did not know that," she said. She turned back around. If we had truly been equals, she might have inquired about the rest of my family, my mother and father, but she did not. Instead, she set off once more along the hall, her pace so brisk I had to almost trot along behind her to keep up.

"But it makes you the perfect person to answer my question," she went on.

"What question is that?" I asked, as Amelie finally came to a halt.

"I am hoping you can tell me," she said, "why this door is kept locked. None of the others are. I know. I've checked them myself."

I swallowed past a suddenly dry throat. I had been so busy worrying about giving myself away, I had failed to notice that Amelie was heading straight toward my mother's door. *Tell her. Tell her all of it, the truth about who you are,* I thought. There might never be a better time.

I opened my mouth, but the words I wished to say seemed to stick inside my throat. If I claimed Constanze d'Este as my mother, then I must also claim Etienne de Brabant as my father. Etienne de Brabant, who had sent his new wife and step-daughters to the great stone house without bothering to inform them of my existence, so great was his desire to deny I was even alive.

How would Amelie take the news if I told her? Would she be kind? Would she even believe me at all? But it was thinking of what Anastasia's reaction might be that finally made up my mind. Her scorn I could bear, but not her pity, and, in that moment, pity seemed the only possible outcome of the telling of a tale such as mine.

"This room belonged to Etienne de Brabant's first wife," I finally answered, deciding there was no point in telling a lie. All Amelie would have to do would be to ask someone else. "He locked the door and threw away the key when she died."

Amelie put her hands on her hips, pursing her lips and putting her head to one side. She studied the locked door as if it were a puzzle, just waiting to be solved.

"And has it never been opened since? Has no one even tried?"

"Never," I said. And it occurred to me suddenly that not even I had ever been through that door, not since I had gone out it on the day that I was born. I had no idea what my mother's room contained.

"What was her name, do you know?"

"Her name was Constanze d'Este," I said.

"Ah," Amelie answered, and her voice was like a sigh. She took her hands from her hips and, to my surprise, laid one palm very gently on the surface of my mother's door.

"I have heard of Constanze d'Este," Amelie went on softly. "Whispers of her name were everywhere when we were at court, particularly on the day my mother and Etienne de Brabant spoke their wedding vows. Constanze d'Este's beauty had no equal, I heard them say, and the loss of her tore a great hole in Etienne de Brabant's heart. One that has never been filled, and never will be."

She turned her head to look at me. "Does that mean his heart is empty, do you suppose?"

"I honestly don't know," I said.

Amelie let her hand drop. "Nor do I. And neither, I think, does Maman, not that it will make much difference, in either the long or the short run. There is no chance of love between them. Maman's heart is not whole, either. The king has seen to that by breaking his promise."

"I don't understand," I said. "I'm sorry."

Amelie stood for a moment, gazing at the locked door. She seemed to have completely forgotten the fact that I was a servant, so great was her need to confide in someone.

"My mother and the king grew up together," she said. "Both made marriages of state, though I think my parents' marriage was happier than the king's ever was. When my father was killed in a border war, the king made my mother a promise that, if she married again, it could be for love."

"Then why did he marry her to Etienne de Brabant?" I asked.

Amelie sighed. "That is a very good question," she said. "I think it is because he is the leader of the queen's faction at court. With the queen's brother on a throne of his own now, who can say what brother and sister might plot? But if Etienne de Brabant were married to someone loyal to the king, someone he trusts . . ."

She broke off and shook her head. "But my new stepfather is clever. As soon as the marriage festivities were over, he packed us up and sent us off. My mother can hardly keep an eye on him from this great distance."

"So the king has accomplished nothing," I said softly. "Save betraying your mother's trust."

"That's it exactly," Amelie replied. "She's stuck in a loveless marriage, and we're all stuck here, so very far from home."

"Spring is coming almost any day now," I said. It seemed paltry consolation, but surely it was better than none. "Things will get better then. I promise."

My stepsister gave me a trembling smile. "Thank you, Cendrillon," she said. "You are really very kind. But for obvious reasons, I think I would prefer it if we avoided making promises, at least for the time being."

Before I could answer, she drew in a deep breath, and stepped back from the door. "But what am I saying?" she said, as she turned away. "Of course things will be better when the spring truly comes. Spring works wonders everywhere, don't you think? And naturally you will not mention the conversation we have had today to anyone."

I opened my mouth to give an assurance, but Amelie had already set off down the hall. *I am back to being a servant*, I thought. At the landing at the head of the stairs, Amelie halted abruptly.

"Where is Constanze d'Este buried? Do you know?"

"In her garden," I answered. "On the far side of the house. I can take you there, if you like."

"I believe I would like that," Amelie said slowly. "But not today. Today I have discovered quite enough."

"In April, when the daffodils bloom," I suddenly blurted out.

Amelie's eyebrows rose. "That sounds lovely, thank you, Cendrillon. I am fond of daffodils. There are great fields of them where I grew up."

"Where is your home?"

A strange expression flashed into Amelie's eyes. There and gone so quickly I didn't quite have time to figure out what it was.

"This is my home, now, Cendrillon," she said.

Then she turned and was gone.

Eight

Spring came in a great and colorful rush. In April the daffodils bloomed. In May, the peonies. In June, the roses. The fruit trees in the orchard gave every sign that this would be a year when they would behave themselves and provide the kind of fruit they were supposed to.

As the weather grew warmer, both Amelie and Anastasia began to spend more time out of doors, often in my mother's garden. Amelie in particular seemed drawn to it, even beginning to go so far as to work in the garden herself. Since the day I had taken her to see Constanze d'Este's grave, the same day I finally finished the seemingly endless task of going through Anastasia's dresses, as it happened, it seemed to me that Amelie was working hard to make her peace with the circumstances that had brought her to the great stone house.

Even Anastasia seemed calmer now that the weather had improved. She would sit on a stone bench in the shade, her own sun hat firmly in place upon her head, chiding Amelie for the fact that hers had fallen off and that her hands and nails were filthy from working the soil. To which Amelie always replied that some young men found freckles attractive, and dirt could be washed off. But it was a gentle sort of teasing, as if the warmth of the weather had mellowed them both. Now that she was finished torturing me with the endless examination of her wardrobe, Anastasia seemed content to leave me alone. Neither of us mentioned Raoul again.

The only one who did not seem warmed by the change in the weather was my stepmother. She roamed the house and grounds like a phantom as if unable to settle, to find peace anywhere, her skin still as fine and pale as the winter's day upon which she had first crossed our threshold. More and more often, I was reminded of my first impression of her: that she was like a spring in full flood with its surface still encased in ice.

At first, I had believed that this was a sign of the strength of her own will, her refusal to give way to the turmoil and despair which filled her mind and heart. But, as the days and weeks went by, I began to wonder whether or not Chantal de Saint-Andre had made herself a prisoner of what she felt. If my father's heart was empty, then my stepmother's was too full. And

I wondered what would happen when the ice finally broke.

"Poor lady," Susanne sighed while preparing dinner one night. She was chopping vigorously, the knife thunking against the cutting board. Susanne had made getting my stepmother to eat her own personal crusade. To that end, she tried a different dish each night. Tonight's attempt involved chicken and vegetables cooked on top of the stove. The smell of it filled the whole house.

"Forced into a loveless marriage, then packed off like a piece of furniture that's gone out of style. She'll waste away to nothing, you mark my words, and then Etienne de Brabant will have what he wants."

"What do you mean?" I asked from the far end of the table, where I was preparing a great pile of green beans. I had kept the conversation I had shared with Amelie outside my mother's door strictly to myself. But there wasn't one person in all the great stone house who believed my father had married Chantal de Saint-Andre for love.

"What does he want?" I asked now.

"Why, to be rid of her, of course," Susanne snorted. "Why else would he send her to the ends of the earth and then leave her alone, without any kind of word, for five whole months? It would eat me alive with frustration and fury, I promise you that. If you ask me, unless something happens to change the way things are going, that man will be a widower before the year is out."

"Then it's fortunate nobody did ask," Old Mathilde's voice suddenly sliced through the room, sharper than any kitchen knife. Susanne dropped hers with a clatter and pressed a hand to her heart.

"Gracious, Mathilde," she exclaimed. "Don't you know better than to startle a body like that?"

"I know better than to indulge in idle gossip," Old Mathilde replied, and I saw the way she glanced at me out of the corner of my eye. "You may hold whatever opinions you like, Susanne, but in the future, I would appreciate it if you kept them to yourself. This house is troubled enough without your wild surmises.

"Our mistress would like a cup of tea," she went on in a more quiet voice. "Cendrillon, perhaps you would be so good as to make one and to take it to her."

"Of course I will," I said, as I finished the last of the beans, gathered them up, and dumped them into their cooking pot. I set it on the back of the stove and put the tea kettle on to boil. Susanne was chopping once again, the sound of the knife informing all who heard it and knew how to listen that her nose was out of joint.

"Susanne didn't mean anything, Mathilde," I felt obliged to say. "Nothing bad, anyhow. And she's right, you know. Chantal de Saint-Andre does not look well. Do you think she has an illness?"

Old Mathilde shook her head. "Not one that comes from

any outside cause. As for the inside one, well . . ." Her voice trailed off.

Steam began to rush from the spout of the kettle. I took it from the hob, poured a little water into the teapot to warm it. Then I emptied it out, added the tea, and poured the boiling water over all. I set it on a tray, then wrapped the pot in red flannel to help keep it warm. Once upon a time, I had been kept warm in much the same manner. The thought brought a sudden smile.

"Didn't you make seed cake this morning?" I asked Old Mathilde. She gave a nod. "Chantal likes that, doesn't she? Perhaps I'll take some of that along as well."

"That is very thoughtful of you," Old Mathilde said, as I found the loaf of cake and began to slice it. "She is in the sun room."

The sun room was small and filled with light, even in winter. Tucked into a far corner of the main floor of the house, it had windows on two sides. One looked straight out over the ocean, the other, toward the tops of the trees in the orchards. Chantal often spent time there. It was her favorite room in the house.

I cut two thick slices of seed cake and put them on my favorite plate, one with sunflowers painted on it. I fetched the cup and saucer to match, placed both upon the tray beside the teapot. Sugar in its bowl came next; milk in a sturdy little jug. I added a blue napkin, then hefted the tray.

"That's nicely done and no mistake," Susanne said, her tone

approving. "Lovely looking tray like that would cheer anybody up. Look sharp she doesn't eat too much and spoil her dinner, mind you."

"I will, Susanne," I promised.

I carried the tray upstairs, careful to hold it level, then made my way to the sun room. Chantal de Saint-Andre was sitting in a chair, a shawl around her shoulders, her legs tucked under her like a child. One of her elbows rested on the arm of the chair. She had her chin on one hand, and her eyes gazed straight out at nothing.

"I've brought your tea, ma'am," I said from the open doorway.

My stepmother turned toward me then. "Oh," she said. "It is you, Cendrillon. I was expecting Old Mathilde."

I hesitated, uncertain whether I should go back or forward. "I could fetch her, if you like."

Chantal de Saint-Andre seemed to give herself a little mental shake. "No," she said. "Of course not. You brought the tea, you said? Thank you. Tea will be most welcome. I know that it is spring, but I cannot seem to get warm."

I moved forward then, placing the tray on a low table near the chair. "I brought some of Old Mathilde's seed cake," I went on, as I began the ritual of pouring out. "But I fear we are both under strict instructions from Susanne. I am to make certain you don't eat too much cake and spoil your appetite for supper."

At this, my stepmother actually smiled. "I seem to recall giving my daughters similar instructions, once upon a time. Tell Susanne that I will be a good girl."

I lifted the cup and saucer and extended it toward her. Halfway in the act of reaching for it, Chantal de Saint-Andre's hand paused in midair.

"Oh," she said. "Sunflowers."

Not until then did I realize what I had done. I had prepared the tray for my stepmother precisely as I would have for myself. Choosing not the fanciest plate or cup and saucer, but the ones that made me feel cheerful, even on the gloomiest of days. I felt the way my hand wished to tremble, but held it steady.

"If you do not care for them," I said. "I can bring you something else."

"Sunflowers are my favorite flower in all the world," my stepmother said, almost as if she were speaking to herself. "In the summer, there are great fields of them along the roadsides on the lands where I raised my daughters, and where I, myself, grew up. The old folks say they have never been planted but, every year, there they are. I have seen many growing things since we came here, but not a single sunflower. I think it is too cold for them to grow."

As if to prove her point, she shivered, and drew her shawl a little more tightly around her shoulders.

"Where is it?" I asked, hardly daring to breathe. "The place where you grew up?"

"In the very center of the country," my stepmother replied.

"They say our very first king was born there, and so it is our country's heart. The land is flat, the fields are fertile, and the sun is warm."

For a moment, I thought she would say more. Instead she leaned forward, took the saucer between her thumb and fore-finger. I let go.

"Did you prepare this tray yourself?" she asked.

"Yes, ma'am," I answered.

"Then I thank you, Cendrillon." She took a sip of tea, clos-ing her eyes as she swallowed, as if the simple action gave her just a taste of the peace she so desperately sought. She opened her eyes, then set the cup and saucer on the wide arm of the chair.

"Was there something else?"

"It can be beautiful here, too," I heard myself blurt out. "You just have to know how to look, and . . ." My voice faltered but I forced it to go on. "I wish you could be happy here. All of you. I'm sorry that you're not."

My stepmother jerked, as if I'd poked her with a pin. I bit down, hard, on the tip of my tongue, my eyes suddenly fasci-nated by the hardwood floor. *Fool, idiot,* I thought. *She thinks you're a serving girl. What difference could it possibly make to you whether she and her daughters are happy here or not?*

"Look at me, please, Cendrillon," Chantal de Saint-Andre said in a firm, soft voice. I lifted my eyes. For several abso-lutely silent seconds, my stepmother and I gazed at each other. I watched her cheeks flush, then go absolutely bloodless.

"You pity me," she said. And in that moment, I realized that she had seen her own face, reflected in my eyes.

Before I could answer, she made a quick movement, as if to push what she had seen away. Her hand struck the saucer on the arm of the chair, sending it and the cup flying. Hot liquid arced through the air, then splashed to the floor. The cup and saucer hit the hardwood and were dashed to pieces. My stepmother gave a heartbroken cry.

Even as I knelt to pick up the shards, I heard the sound of fast-moving feet. Amelie and Anastasia burst into the sun room, one right after the other. But it was Anastasia who spoke first.

"You dreadful girl," she cried, as she moved quickly to her mother. "What have you done?"

"Nothing," I gasped out. "That is, I didn't mean . . ."

To call you here in the first place, I thought. Not at such a terrible cost.

I had made a wish and it had been answered. Didn't that make their misery all my fault? I felt a sudden sharp pain as one of the broken pieces of the saucer cut into my hand.

"How dare you?" Anastasia demanded. "How dare you lie? Look at her. You've made her cry, and she never does that. Not even on the day the king made her marry the queen's man. My mother is not a coward. She is brave and strong. You must have done something truly terrible to make her do this, and I want to know what it is right now."

"Oh, stop it, Anastasia," Amelie said. "Can't you see she's cut herself?"

"I don't care if she bleeds to death," Anastasia all but shouted.

"No one is going to bleed to death," Chantal de Saint-Andre said in a calm and terrible voice. With the backs of her hands, she wiped the tears from her pale cheeks with quick, angry gestures, as if as furious with herself as Anastasia was with me. "Please stop shouting, Anastasia. My head hurts enough as it is."

Anastasia took a stumbling step back, as if her mother's words had made her lose her balance.

"You are defending her," she whispered. "That horrible girl made you cry and now you are taking her side."

"Cendrillon is not a horrible girl," her mother answered, as she got up from the chair. "And there is no question of taking sides. I broke a cup and saucer, and that's all there is to that."

Before I realized what she intended, she knelt beside me. "Let me see your hand, Cendrillon."

"It's nothing," I protested, though I knew the cut was deep, a great slash across one palm. Blood flowed over its surface to trickle through my fingers. "If you will just let me go for Old Mathilde."

"I'll go," Amelie offered now. She picked up the tray.

"What are you doing?" Anastasia shrieked. "Put that down."

"Be quiet, Anastasia," Amelie said briskly. She walked quickly from the room, her shoes making sharp sounds against the hardwood floor.

94

"I'm sorry," I whispered, as I gazed at my hand, cradled between my stepmother's. "I didn't mean for any of this to happen. I'm so sorry."

"I think that's enough apologies for one afternoon," Chantal said, her tone the brisk match of Amelie's. "It is only a cup and saucer."

Oh, no. It is much, much more than that, I thought. And if she knew how much, one thing seemed certain: This woman I had wished for could never learn to love me.

"There is still the plate," I said.

Chantal sat back, still cradling my hand in hers. "I believe you are growing light-headed," she said. "What are you talking about?"

"The plate," I said once more. "With the seed cake on it. It has sunflowers, too. Not everything is broken."

"I see," my stepmother said, and for the second time that day, she looked into my eyes. This time, I was the one who saw my own reflection: an image of a girl just on the cusp of womanhood.

A girl with tears and secrets in her eyes.

Nine

THERE WERE NO MORE CHORES FOR ME THE REST OF THAT DAY,
nor for several more besides. The cut was both long and deep;
my hand was stiff and sore. At Old Mathilde's insistence, I slept
on a cot in a corner of the kitchen, much as I had done when
I was a child. She could keep a better eye on me that way, she
said, without having to climb up and down all the stairs to my
room at the very top of the house. Too many stairs were hard
on old bones, or so she claimed.

The days slid into August, and the weather stayed hot and
fine. Still the ice inside my stepmother did not quite thaw.
Anastasia stopped speaking to me altogether, not even to give me
orders. The day she discovered that Amelie had traded a fancy

dress to one of the village girls so that she might have a simple one to tramp around outside in, she all but stopped speaking to Amelie, as well. In her new dress, which she felt free to get as dirty as she liked, a sturdy pair of boots, and her sun hat, Amelie took to prowling the grounds. She was always popping up in unexpected places, poking into long-forgotten corners both inside and out. There were times, and many of them, too, when it seemed to me that she was searching for something.

Slowly, the wound on my hand healed. But I could not quite forget the wound I had seen in my stepmother's eyes. A wound I greatly feared I had helped to inflict myself.

"I just keep thinking it's all my fault," I said one day to Old Mathilde. It was midmorning, the heat of the day not yet upon us. Old Mathilde was standing at the stove stirring a great kettle of blackberry jam. My hand back to normal now, I was shucking ears of corn.

"If I hadn't wished for them, they wouldn't have come. And if they hadn't come, they wouldn't all be so unhappy."

"Tut, now," Old Mathilde said, as she added sugar to the pot. "Nothing is ever quite as simple as that and you should know it. You sound like your father when you speak so."

I yanked at a corn husk. It gave way with a shrieking sound. "There's no need to insult me," I said. "I'm just trying to figure out what to do to make things right."

Old Mathilde's spoon circled in the pot like a hawk after a mouse. "What makes you think that responsibility lies with you alone?" she asked. "You made a wish, that much is true, but you did not wish for anyone to be made unhappy. You made a wish for love. In my experience, such wishes have a way of coming true in the end, which is not the same as saying the journey isn't difficult and long."

I sat for a moment, pondering her words. The noise of Old Mathilde's spoon, swishing against the bottom of the cast-iron pot, was the only sound.

"Have I ever told you the story of how your parents met?" she inquired at last. If she had asked me if I realized I had suddenly grown two heads, I could not have been more surprised.

"Never," I said. "And you know that perfectly well."

"No one ever dreamed that they would love each other," Old Mathilde went on, as if I hadn't spoken at all. "Least of all Etienne and Constanze themselves. Their marriage was arranged to help secure an alliance, of course. But I think it's fair to say that your father loved your mother from the first moment that he saw her, and that for her to love him took no longer."

"Love at first sight," I said, my voice hushed, the ears of corn I should have been shucking entirely forgotten. "It really happens, then?"

"On occasion." Old Mathilde nodded. "I've heard it runs in families, if you must know. Your mother's love was much like her garden. Its roots went deep, though it wasn't always showy. But your father's love was like a diamond, hard and bright, so dazzling it hurt the eyes to look upon it. His love for your mother, hers for him, were the greatest astonishments, the greatest treasures, of his life."

"And I took them away," I said, as I felt a swift, hot pain spear straight through my heart.

"That is certainly what Etienne believes, or what he says he does," Old Mathilde answered. "Help me with this now."

She lifted the pot from the heat, and, together, we worked to ladle the steaming liquid into jars. Carefully, Old Mathilde spooned hot wax atop each one to seal the jam in, then set them in a neat row on the pantry shelf. They glowed like purple jewels.

"They are beautiful," I said. "Can we have pancakes for breakfast tomorrow morning?"

"I believe we might do that," Old Mathilde answered as she put an arm around my shoulders.

"I'll do the washing up," I said, as I leaned against her. "You should go sit down. You've been standing up most of the morning."

"I believe we might do that, too," Old Mathilde said with a smile. She sat down in the chair I had vacated. I filled a pitcher of water from the kitchen pump, then poured it into the jam kettle.

"Wait a few minutes," Mathilde instructed. "Let the water do its work while the pot cools down. Come and sit beside me for a moment. There is something more I wish to say."

I dried my hands on my apron and sat down across the table

from her. Old Mathilde reached across and took my hands in hers.

"Your mother loved your father, Cendrillon. To the end of her last breath, with all her heart. And she loved you just as much as she loved him. That kind of love does not simply pack its bags and depart, even when the heart that brought it into being ceases to beat. Love so joyfully and freely given can never be taken away. It is never truly gone."

"Then where is it?" I whispered. "Why does it seem so hard to find?"

"It is all around you," Old Mathilde said. "It lives in every beat of your own heart. This is what your mother knew your father would never understand, for she saw him truly, and she foresaw that his grief would dazzle just as his love did. It would blind him.

"To heal, we must do more than grieve. We must also find a way to mourn."

"I'm not so sure I understand the difference," I said.

Old Mathilde gave my hands a squeeze. "I am not surprised, for the difference is a fine one. But when you figure it out, you will know what to do about many things, I think.

"Remember that yours is not the only heart that may be wishing for love."

Late that night, I could not sleep. I might have convinced myself it was because my bedroom was too hot, for my room was right beneath the roof and the day had been warm. I might have convinced myself it was the light of the full moon, shining through my window, that was making me toss and turn so often.

I might have convinced myself of many things, if I had been willing to lie.

But because I was not, I threw back my rumpled sheet and got out of bed. I made my silent way down to the kitchen, slipped my shawl from its peg, and tucked my feet into my wooden garden clogs. I took the long, thin knife Susanne used for boning chickens from its slot in the wooden block and wrapped the blade in a towel. Then I let myself out the kitchen door, heading in the direction of the pumpkin patch. I had no need to take a lantern, for the face of the moon shone like a beacon in the clear night sky.

Though they were far from ripe, anyone with eyes could see that, unlike last year's wide variety, this year, each and every vine in the pumpkin patch was busy producing pumpkins of precisely the same kind. Ones just like those I had planted on my mother's grave, in spite of the fact that I had saved no seeds from them. They glowed a deep and mysterious green in the moonlight.

I took a deep breath, then knelt down among them. Before I would be able to sleep, there was something I must discover, a task I must perform.

Sliding the knife from the towel, I sliced neatly through

the stem of the pumpkin at my feet and set it upright in front of me. Then, without stopping to think and so lose my nerve, I plunged the knife through the pumpkin's skin and into the flesh beneath, slicing first through one side, and then the other. Setting the knife on the ground at my feet, I wiggled my fingers into the gap I had made in the top, then pried the pumpkin open. The two halves parted with a high, tearing sound. The pungent smell of pumpkin rose up sharply.

Not rotten inside, I thought. *Not rotten at all, but firm and pure and sound.* And in that moment, I had the answer to the question that had driven me here in the middle of the night in the first place. I began to weep in great choking sobs.

Please, I thought. *Let me find a way to make my father's pain, his grief, release their hold. Let me find a way to help love flourish. Let me understand what it means to mourn.*

I knelt in the pumpkin patch until all my tears were spent, then returned to my bed and slept a dreamless sleep till morning.

"*Cendrillon.*"

There were hands on my shoulders, shaking me awake.

"Cendrillon!"

Swimming up through layers of sleep, I opened startled eyes. Amelie's flushed face was hovering over mine.

"You have to get up. You have to come and see," she said.

"What is it?" I asked, as I struggled to sit up. "What's wrong?"

"Where is she? Is she coming?" hissed a voice outside my door. I sat bolt upright then.

"Is that Anastasia?"

"Get dressed and be quick about it," Amelie said. "We'll wait for you downstairs. Don't be long."

She dashed from my room. I tossed back the sheets and fumbled into my clothes. I pinned my braids up with trembling fingers, then raced downstairs.

"What is it?" I asked when I reached the great hall. Amelie and Anastasia were standing, hands clasped tightly together, just inside the front door. Without a single word, Amelie grabbed my hand and the two of them tugged me outside.

"Amelie, please, tell me what it is," I begged. "What's wrong?"

"Nothing's wrong," Anastasia snapped, and I actually felt a trickle of relief at her tone. At least she was sounding like her usual self. Hands still linked, we rounded the corner of the house. The early morning sun smiled down on the kitchen garden.

"We just don't understand what it means, that's all," she went on. "And we want to, before we go and fetch Maman."

"Understand what *what* means?" I asked.

"There," Amelie said, pointing. "In the pumpkin patch."

I skidded to a stop. Together the three of us stood and stared. The pumpkins were no longer green, still working to ripen for it was only August. Instead, they glowed like the sun as it sinks into the sea, a hot and vivid orange. And growing up between the rows, taller than a tall man's head, their brown and golden faces already turning toward the sun, was something I knew quite well had not been there the night before.

Sunflowers.

They grew an inch a day, till they were as tall as the back of our tallest horse, and then the saplings in our orchards. Bluebirds came from miles around to flutter around the sunflowers' brown and golden heads. Squirrels climbed up the stalks and sat upon them, turning them into stools and dinner plates all at the same time.

My stepmother brought great armfuls of flowers into the house every day, till the very stones themselves seemed suffused with a golden glow. Each time she cut a plant down, another sprang up overnight to take its place. For the first time since they had arrived, I heard Anastasia laugh, saw my stepmother smile not just with her face, but with her eyes. In my heart, I felt a strange new plant take root: hope.

My father had shed no tears, and on the grave of my mother not a plant would thrive. But I had wept, and with my tears I had brought something to life that had never been seen on the grounds of the great stone house before. I still could not quite see the way for it to happen, but, with the coming of the sunflowers, I began to believe that all might yet be well. Old Mathilde was right. Love was all around me. I simply had to find a way to make it thrive.

"Well, I am off," Amelie's voice suddenly broke into my thoughts as she appeared at the kitchen door. She came into the room, took a basket Old Mathilde had woven from willow branches down from its hook, and settled it into the crook of one arm.

"Where to today?" I inquired.

Ever since the appearance of the sunflowers, Amelie had given up her fancy dresses entirely. She could have been mistaken for a servant just as easily as I had been. In her plain homespun dress, her sun hat firmly upon her head at her mother's insistence, she had taken her explorations out of doors. With every layer of finery Amelie had shed, it seemed to me that a barrier between us had been shed as well. She did not quite treat me as an equal. We had not come so far as that. But she did not quite treat me like I wasn't, either.

"I am going to the beach," she said, giving the basket a little swing. "Raoul says there are stairs."

I made a face. "There are. Endless ones."

"No matter," Amelie said cheerfully. "As long as they go both up and down."

She moved to the door that led outside and stepped through it.

"Amelie," I said. "May I ask you something?" She turned back, the bright morning sun behind her shadowing her face but glancing off her hair like a halo.

"Of course you may, Cendrillon," she replied.

"What are you looking for?"

I sensed, rather than saw, the way she made a face. "You have to promise not to tell me it's impossible," she said.

"I'll tell you what Old Mathilde would say if she heard you say that," I replied. "She would say that nothing is truly impossible. It's all a matter of looking at things in just the right way."

"That's it!" Amelie cried. "Though I suppose I should say it's a matter of looking *for* things in just the right way.

"I am looking for the thing that cannot be found by searching for it," she said. "The thing Niccolo found, that made him wish to return. I am looking for a surprise."

Ten

THE WEATHER STAYED FINE ALL THROUGH AUGUST, AND THEN September arrived. And with it, though our days were no less pleasant, a certain sense of urgency took up residence in the great stone house. September is a changeable sort of month. One foot in summer and the other in autumn. And if autumn was coming, then winter would not be far behind. It didn't take a fortune-teller to figure out that my stepmother and stepsisters were not looking forward to a winter in a stone house over-looking a cold gray sea.

Anastasia didn't laugh anymore. Instead, she became more exacting than ever, as if determined to make up for lost time. *"Fetch me my slippers, Cendrillon. No not the yellow ones, you stupid girl."* (Though these were the ones that matched her dress.) *"The blue ones. Bring me my shawl. Can't you see that I am cold?"*

For days on end, she kept me running to do her bidding so often I began to fear the soles of my shoes would wear out. Then, one morning, the very same one on which Amelie announced she had at long last finished her explorations at the beach and would spend her day in the peach orchard instead, Anastasia declared her desire to go riding.

"Riding," Raoul exclaimed in disgust when I went to the stable to bring him the news. He was pitching fresh hay into the horses' stalls, spreading it with the tines of a pitchfork. "And my presence is requested, I suppose."

"Not by Anastasia," I answered. "But by her mother. It's not unreasonable, Raoul. No high-born lady would ride without a groom, and Anastasia doesn't know where she is going."

Raoul gave a snort. "That's true enough, in more ways than one." He spread a final forkful of hay. "Who does Chantal de Saint-Andre expect will do my work while I'm babysitting her daughter?"

"I don't imagine she thinks of it quite like that," I said.

This time, Raoul gave a sigh.

"Amelie is not so bad," he admitted, as he returned the pitchfork to its proper place. "If nothing else, she is comfortable with being quiet. But something tells me looking after Miss High-and-Mighty will be a different matter altogether."

"Don't think of it as looking after her, then," I suggested. "Think of it as looking after the horse."

Raoul laughed, then looped an arm around my shoulders. "An excellent suggestion," he admitted, as he brushed his knuckles across the top of my head. "I will do my best to follow it."

"Cendrillon!" Anastasia's imperious voice called. "Why can I never find you when I need you? Where are you? I'm ready to go."

Raoul rolled his eyes, but I could see the wariness that crept into their expression, the way his mouth thinned and tightened at the sound of Anastasia's voice.

"You could always try not saying much," I suggested in a low voice. "It drives her crazy when she can't get a rise out of me." I stepped out of his hold. "I'm in the stable, Anastasia," I called, lifting my voice.

"Where else would you be?" Raoul murmured, but he went to fetch and saddle the horses.

Anastasia was standing in the courtyard, her hands on her hips, wearing the riding habit I had spent most of the morning preparing to her satisfaction. Never, or so it seemed to me, had she looked more lovely. The fabric of the habit was a deep and lustrous blue. In her pale face, her blue eyes blazed like sapphires. She was tapping one booted foot upon the cobblestones with impatience.

"I am ready to go," she said again. "How long does it take that silly stable boy to saddle two horses?"

"If you think he's so silly, I wonder that you feel safe riding out with him," I couldn't quite resist saying, and saw the way she flushed.

"Thank you for your concern," she said tartly.

She continued to tap her foot as the minutes went by, the tempo accelerating the longer we stood in the courtyard. She caught her lower lip between her teeth, shooting anxious glances toward the stable.

She is nervous, I realized suddenly.

Before I had time to consider what that might mean, Raoul appeared, leading two horses. One, the tall black he preferred now that he'd given the dappled gray to Niccolo, and a mare the color of honey. Both were neatly saddled, their coats brushed to a glossy shine. He'd brushed his own hair, as well, I noticed.

Anastasia's color rose a little higher, but her voice stayed as sharp as always.

"There you are. It's about time."

For a fraction of a second, I thought Raoul would answer back. I could almost see him bite the inside of one cheek to hold in the smart reply. Then, in a move so unexpected both Anastasia and I blinked, he sketched a quick but perfectly acceptable bow.

"I am at your service, lady," he said, as he straightened up. And then he smiled. Anastasia caught her breath with an audible sound. She opened her mouth, then closed it again. "I'm ready to go whenever you are," Raoul went on sweetly. "But perhaps you've changed your mind."

I bit the inside of my own cheek now, for it seemed to me I understood. He was going to drive Anastasia mad with kindness. Be so attentive she couldn't possibly complain.

I saw her give a little shake, as if snapping herself out of a dream. "Of course I haven't changed my mind," she said. "Help me to mount."

Without a backward glance, she began to march smartly toward the riding block, the small raised platform a lady might use to mount her horse more easily. I expected Raoul to bring the mare to her. He stayed right where he was. When she realized he wasn't moving, Anastasia stopped and turned around. She put her hands on her hips and glared. His face expressionless, Raoul gazed back.

He is daring her to come to him, I realized.

At first it seemed she wouldn't do it. Then, with a lift of her chin, Anastasia took up the challenge. She closed the distance between them with brisk, rapid steps. Raoul bent at the waist, and linked his hands together to form a stirrup. Anastasia placed the toe of her soft leather riding boot between his hands, rested one of her own hands on Raoul's shoulder for balance.

In the next moment, Raoul straightened, and, graceful as a bird, Anastasia went flying upward. She landed in the saddle in a flurry of dark blue skirts. She hooked one knee over the pommel on her lady's riding saddle, gathered the reins into her gloved hands.

"Thank you," she said.

"You are more than welcome."

I stared, not sure which of them had astonished me more. It was the first time I had heard Anastasia say thank you for anything. Raoul sounded polite as a lord. Then, as if to make absolutely certain it was clear who was in charge, Anastasia rapped her heels smartly against the mare's sides, putting her in motion. Raoul had to step back quickly to avoid being stomped on.

"I don't like to be kept waiting," Anastasia announced, even as Raoul was vaulting into his own saddle. "Do try to keep up."

They were gone the whole afternoon, as the weather changed, turning thick and sultry and still, a ring of clouds creeping in from the edges of the sky.

"Thunderstorm weather," Susanne announced with a click of her tongue. "You mark my words, there'll be a storm before the night is out."

By late afternoon I was fractious and edgy, as if my clothes had suddenly grown too tight. Amelie came home from the peach orchard without her sun hat, her face flushed. Chantal lost her temper and gave her a scolding. Amelie went upstairs and did not come back down. After that, my stepmother took to pacing back and forth in the great hall, opening the front door as if she heard Anastasia returning, then closing it again on no one. I often swept the great hall at this time of day, and once a week I scrubbed the flagstones. But it was apparent I would get no work done on this particular afternoon.

"Raoul would never let anything happen to her," I finally volunteered, worn out by my stepmother's pacing as if I had been doing it right alongside her. "He's the best horseman in the county. And he knows every inch of de Brabant lands. He would never let Anastasia come to any harm."

Chantal de Saint-Andre started, as if she'd forgotten I was there.

"Gracious, Cendrillon," she said. "You startled me. And it isn't that I'm worried, it's just . . ." She broke off, raising a hand to her forehead, as if to brush away unwelcome thoughts.

"I am so edgy today. Everything about this place still feels so foreign and wild, and Anastasia can be so headstrong. She's always been that way, ever since she was a child. But since we came here, I . . ." She shook her head, as if to clear it. "All day long, I have felt afraid without quite knowing why. I know it's foolish but . . ."

She broke off as we both heard the clatter of hooves. My stepmother was at the door almost before I could blink, flinging it open wide. She dashed out onto the steps, with me close behind her, just as Anastasia swept into the courtyard.

Gone was the prim and proper maiden who had departed just that morning. In her place was a young woman with her emotions barely under control. Anastasia's long, dark hair had come unbound to stream across her shoulders and down her back like an inky waterfall. Her eyes were enormous. The color in her cheeks was high. It was clear that something had happened, and that it had affected her deeply. The question was, what?

She brought the mare to a quick and sudden stop just as Raoul cantered in behind her, his own face the match of the threatening thunderclouds overhead. He dismounted quickly, moved to where Anastasia sat, still as a marble statue on her horse.

"Not you," Anastasia said, her voice slightly breathless. "Go get someone else. I do not want you to touch me."

"My touch is no different than it was a few moments ago," Raoul answered, his voice cracking with temper and something that ran deeper, a thing I could not quite identify. "Besides, there isn't anyone else and you know it. Why must you always behave like a spoiled child?"

Anastasia's flushed cheeks paled. She pressed her lips together, looped her reins over the pommel, and leaned down. She braced herself on Raoul's shoulders as he reached up and swept her from the saddle so swiftly that her long dark hair tumbled forward over her shoulder to stream across his own, obscuring both their faces for the time it took Raoul to set her on her feet. Then Anastasia stepped back, brushing her hair from her face with a fierce gesture.

"Anastasia," said her mother, as she moved down the steps. "Thank goodness you are home."

"Oh, Maman," Anastasia said. She turned away from Raoul, but her long hair would not quite release its hold. It clung to his shirt, like a sweetheart not ready to be parted from him. Raoul turned away, lifting a hand to brush it aside.

"*Maman,*" Anastasia said once more, and I heard the way her voice broke.

"Heavens," her mother exclaimed, as she reached her. "What is it, my child?"

"Nothing. It is nothing," Anastasia said fiercely. "I stayed too long in the sun, that's all. And the weather today makes me feel so strange."

"It's because there's a storm coming," her mother said. "It makes us all feel that way." She put an arm around Anastasia's waist, then pressed a hand to her forehead. "Gracious, you are burning up. Come into the house. We'll get you out of these clothes."

"I want you to help me, Maman," Anastasia said, her voice suddenly small and pleading like a child's. "I don't want anyone else. I don't need anyone else. Not anyone."

"But of course I will help you," her mother said. Without another word, she led Anastasia into the house.

Raoul stood beside Anastasia's horse, his eyes gazing straightforward at nothing. I came down the steps till I stood at his side.

"Would you like me to help rub down the horses?" I asked.

Raoul gave a start. "What?"

"Would you like me to help with the horses?" I said once

more, even as I saw something hot and furious flash into Raoul's eyes. By way of answer, he took two steps, hauled me up against him, and pressed his lips to mine.

Raoul's lips felt just as his eyes looked, desperate, angry, wild. His arm around my waist felt like a band of solid iron. I felt the world do two entirely contradictory things at once. Explode wide open. Narrow down. I felt the way Raoul's heart thundered in his chest, heard the echo of its rhythm in my own. And suddenly I understood the sound that it was making.

No, my heart said, even as it pounded more furious than it ever had before. *Not this. Not him. Not this. No. No. No.*

I made a sound, and Raoul let me go.

We stood for a moment, staring at each other, while the wind explored the corners of the courtyard.

"Oh, damn," Raoul said suddenly. "I've made a mess of things, haven't I? I'm sorry, Cendrillon."

I made a second sound now. A strange combination of outrage and laughter.

"You're *sorry*?" I cried. "You kiss me out of the blue and then stand there and tell me that you're sorry? How can you possibly be such a dolt?"

Raoul's face clouded. Seizing the mare's reins, he began to turn her around. "Fine. You don't want an apology, I'll save my breath."

I planted myself in front of him. "You even think about taking another step," I said, "and I swear on my mother's grave I'll break your arm. I don't want an apology, Raoul. What I want is an explanation."

Raoul dropped the reins, put his hands on his hips. "I was trying," he said succinctly, "to avoid a broken heart."

I felt all my exasperation evaporate as suddenly as it had come upon me. "Oh," I said, and somehow, it didn't sound foolish at all. "Anastasia," I said. "It's Anastasia, isn't it?"

Love at first sight, I thought. I wondered why I hadn't recognized the signs for what they were before now.

They had been there in the tight silences between Raoul and Anastasia whenever they met, the compressed lips, the quick glances from the corners of their eyes. Not all love is joyful, particularly when it seems hopeless. She was a noble-born lady, and proud of it. Raoul was a country stable boy.

"What it is," Raoul declared now, as he picked up the reins once more and began to lead the horses into the barn, "is absolutely impossible."

"So it is Anastasia, then," I said. I followed Raoul into the barn. Together, we undid straps, pulled off saddles, began to rub the horses down, working in silence as we had so often before. But this silence was different, as if the memory of the kiss we'd shared still hovered in the air between us. The knowledge of all the things it had been, and the things that it had not.

I suppose every girl wonders who her true love will be. Will it be some handsome stranger, or the boy next door? I can't precisely claim I had dreamed of falling in love with Raoul, but

I would be a liar if I said the possibility had never crossed my mind.

I took the curry brush from its place and began to brush the coat of the mare Anastasia had ridden to a rich and glossy shine.

"How long have you known?"

Raoul remained silent just long enough that I thought he wasn't going to answer.

"Almost from the first moment," he finally replied. "And don't think I haven't tried to talk myself out of it, because I have, every single day since they all arrived." He shot a quick glance in my direction, as if gauging my reaction. "I'm not a complete idiot," he said. "Even if I am a dolt. Just because I can fall in love with Anastasia doesn't mean I believe we can have a future together."

"I'm sorry I called you names," I said. "I was a little . . ." I took a second to ponder the word I wanted. "Annoyed. For future reference, don't ever kiss a girl and then tell her you're sorry that you've done it." I handed him the brush.

"Thank you for the advice," he said. "It comes a little late, but I'll keep it in mind for the future."

"Don't tell me you kissed her, too!" I cried. "Wait a minute. Of course you did. That's why she looked and behaved the way she did when the two of you arrived."

"Yes, I kissed her," Raoul burst out. "She kissed me right back, if you must know. And it doesn't mean a thing. I am no one, and she is noble-born. She may have forgotten it for a moment or two, but she remembered soon enough. Life would have been a lot simpler if it could have been you."

"Oh, Raoul," I said. I stopped brushing the horse, turned, and put my arms around him even though his back was to me. Raoul rested his head against his horse's flank, then pivoted to return the embrace. I felt the warmth of his breath against my throat.

"I suppose you're quite sure that you don't love me?" he inquired after a while.

I thumped a fist against his back. "I love you with all my heart, as you very well know. It's just not the happily-ever-after kind of love. I apologize if I've ruined all your plans."

"*I've* ruined all my plans," Raoul replied. "But there's no help for it. I got myself into this mess. I'll just have to figure out a way to get myself back out of it."

"And just how do you intend to do that?" inquired a new voice. Raoul and I sprang apart. Anastasia was standing at the entrance to the stall.

"Anastasia," Raoul said hoarsely.

"Do not speak to me," she cut him off in a ragged voice. "I did not give you permission to use my name. I did not give you permission to tell me that you loved me. I believed you, fool that I was."

Her voice rose, the tone mimicking and shrill. *"I can't bear this any longer, Anastasia. No matter what I do, I can't get you out of my mind. I think of you when I should be attending to my duties. I dream of you at night."*

She stamped her foot, as if the action might drive Raoul's words away. "And I let what you said turn my head. It was so surprising, so eloquent for a stable boy. Now I see the reason you're so good at fine words. You've been practicing on Cendrillon."

Before either Raoul or I realized what she intended, Anastasia strode forward and seized me by the arm. "He's kissed you, hasn't he?" she demanded.

"No," I protested. "Not that way."

Anastasia gave my arm a little shake. "You're lying," she said. "I can see it in your eyes."

"He was just trying to prove he didn't love me," I said.

"I don't care if he does love you," Anastasia all but shouted.

With a quick, hard jerk, Anastasia began to tug me out of the stall and toward the stable door. "I don't care if he's always loved you. A stable boy and a kitchen maid. The two of you are perfect for each other. You can live happily ever after for all I care."

We were out in the courtyard now. I felt a sudden gust of wind and the first few drops of rain begin to fall.

"But I will not be made a fool of in my own house."

"It's not your house," Raoul said furiously as he charged after us. "It's Cendrillon's."

"Raoul," I said. "Stop."

"So she was born in this miserable place," Anastasia flashed out, as she continued to pull me across the courtyard. "What difference does that make? She's still just a servant. She can be dismissed like any other."

We reached the front steps. "Maman!" Anastasia suddenly called out. *"Maman!"*

The front door flew open and Chantal de Saint-Andre dashed out. "What in the world is happening?" she cried. "Anastasia, I thought you were in your room resting. What is wrong?"

"I want you to dismiss Cendrillon," Anastasia said, all but sobbing now. "I will not have her in the house one more moment. I want you to send her away. I demand that you send her away."

"You can't just pack her off like a piece of unwanted baggage," Raoul said hotly.

Anastasia's face went bone white. "Don't you tell me what I can and cannot do," she said. "You are no one. I am a daughter of the house."

Raoul turned to me, and I saw the fury and pain, both bright, in his eyes. "Tell her," he said urgently. "Tell them both right now. If you don't do it, then I will."

"Tell us what, if you please?" Chantal de Saint-Andre said in a firm yet quiet tone. She came partway down the steps. "Do not fear to speak, Cendrillon. I don't understand what is happening, but I do know you have the right to speak, to defend yourself."

"I don't need to be defended," I answered. "For I have done nothing wrong."

"Then speak because I ask you to," she said. "What is being hidden that should be told?"

I lifted my chin, and met my stepmother's eyes.

"I am not a servant, to be sent away on a whim," I said. "I am Etienne de Brabant's daughter."

Eleven

ABSOLUTE SILENCE FILLED THE COURTYARD. IT SEEMED TO ME that even the wind stopped blowing. The rain held off, as if uncertain where to fall. Only my stepmother's gaze remained steady, her eyes looking straight into mine.

Then, utterly without warning, Anastasia moved. She released my arm. But only so she could raise her hand to slap me smartly across the face.

"Liar!" she cried.

"Anastasia," her mother's voice cracked like a whip. "That is quite enough." She walked down the remaining steps that separated her from Anastasia, Raoul, and me. Over her shoulder, I saw Amelie skitter out onto the front porch.

"You must never strike another, not even in anger," Chantal de Saint-Andre went on. "Now, calm down, all of you, and tell me what this is all about."

"I caught them together in the stable, Maman," Anastasia hurried into speech. "They had their arms around each other. I won't have that kind of behavior. *I will not have it*. I want them both dismissed at once."

"You can't dismiss either of us," I said. "This is as much Raoul's house as it is mine. He is forbidden to leave de Brabant lands by my father's own order."

"How is it possible," Chantal de Saint-Andre said, "that Etienne de Brabant is your father and I know nothing about it? Is there anyone else who can vouch for the truth of what you say?"

"There is Old Mathilde," I replied. "She delivered me."

"And who was your mother?" Anastasia sneered. "Some local peasant girl, perhaps?"

"My mother was Constanze d'Este," I replied, and as I spoke the words, I felt a burden lift from my heart. My father might never claim me, but here, in this moment, I had finally claimed my mother for my own.

Anastasia's face went white to the lips, and her mother's dark eyes grew wide.

"I have heard that name," Chantal de Saint-Andre said softly. "There were whispers of it at court, the day Etienne and I took our vows. Constanze d'Este, whose beauty had no equal, who died young. But not one whisper that she died bringing a child into the world. Why did your father not tell me of you himself?"

"Because he wishes I had never been born. My father has never forgiven me for taking my mother out of the world by coming into it. He has never acknowledged me, not to anyone outside this house."

"I don't care what you say, I don't believe you," Anastasia declared. "It's a touching story, I must admit, but how do we know it's not a pack of lies?"

"Because Cendrillon looks just like her mother," Amelie said, speaking for the very first time. Her mother and sisters swung around.

"How can you know that?" Chantal demanded. "Constanze d'Este died before you were born."

"I have seen her portrait," Amelie answered simply. "It's in the room at the end of the hall, the one that's been locked ever since we arrived. I found the key just this morning, in the peach orchard."

"The peach orchard," my stepmother echoed in a dazed voice.

Amelie came down the steps, her dark eyes both thoughtful and excited as they met mine.

"I got hungry, so I picked a peach," she went on. "Instead of a pit, there was a key inside. I remembered what you had told me, Cendrillon. That Etienne de Brabant was so heartbroken after the death of his first wife that he locked the door to her room, and threw away the key."

"And you found it inside a peach?" Anastasia exclaimed, her tone scoffing. "That's not possible and you know it. You've been out in the sun too long."

"Sunflowers shouldn't have been possible, either," Amelie replied. "But you and Maman picked armloads of those. I searched for something, and I found it."

"Your surprise," I said. "You found your surprise."

Amelie nodded. "A greater one than even I knew to hope for. That day in the hall, why didn't you tell me you were Constanze d'Este and Etienne de Brabant's daughter?"

"I wanted to," I said. "But I didn't know how." I let my gaze take in Chantal and Anastasia. "I didn't know how to tell any of you. I'm sorry. I never meant to make things worse than they already are."

Amelie put a hand into the pocket of the apron she had taken to wearing. She pulled it out to reveal a key resting in the center of her palm.

"I would have let you be the first to open the door," she said, as she held it out toward me. "But I didn't know I should, Cendrillon. Not until I saw the portrait. After that, I came to find everyone. I was about halfway down the stairs when I heard Anastasia bellowing."

Anastasia sucked in a breath. But her mother spoke before she could reply. "I will see this portrait," she said. "And then we will decide what is to be done."

* * *

"I didn't like the thought of locking the room back up again," Amelie said when the four of us arrived outside my mother's door. My stepmother had dispatched Raoul to find Old Mathilde. "But it didn't seem right to just leave the door standing open, so I closed it again."

"Open it, please, Cendrillon," my stepmother said quietly.

I put my hand on the latch, squeezed to lift it upward. I heard the sharp *click* as the catch released. Slowly, as if the hinges couldn't quite remember what it was they were supposed to do, the door to my mother's room swung open.

Great ropes of cobwebs hung down from the ceiling, swaying gently in the sudden movement of the air. The path of Amelie's footprints was plain upon the dusty floor. Moving from the doorway to the far corner of the room, disappearing around a wall which formed an alcove. On the wall closest to us stood a great four-poster bed, its hangings gray with dust. A straight-backed chair sat before the window closest to the bed.

Old Mathilde's chair, I thought.

"Where is the portrait?" I asked, and my own voice sounded as dry as the dust.

"In the alcove," Amelie said.

I took a breath, and stepped across the threshold.

It was no more than fifteen paces from the doorway to the place where the portrait of my mother, Constanze d'Este, still hung upon the wall. Fifteen paces, one for every year that I had

CAMERON DOKEY

been alive. But, then as now, that walk across my mother's room seemed set apart from time. I may be walking across that room still, for all I know. Still making the journey from the doorway to my first glimpse of the face of the woman who had given up her life the night she gave me the gift of mine.

I reached the edge of the alcove, turned the corner, and suddenly I was face-to-face with a woman with hair the color of leaves in autumn, eyes the color of a fresh spring lawn. High cheekbones, pointed chin, a firm and determined mouth. But none of these were the things which brought the fierce and sudden rush of tears to my eyes. The thing that did that was a complete and utter surprise.

"Oh, come and see," I heard my own voice say. "Come and see what love looks like."

Quietly, their footsteps stirring up the dust, Chantal de Saint-Andre and her daughters came to stand at my side. I heard my stepmother catch her breath and, as she did, my tears began to fall.

For never had I seen an expression such as the one that gazed out at us from my mother's portrait. Never had I seen any face so filled with light, with such a pure and radiant joy. There could be only one reason for a look like that, just one cause: looking into the face of the person you loved best in all the world, and finding what you felt reflected back. For the thing that was in my mother's face, shining out from it like a torch in the night, was love.

"Oh, but it is wicked," I suddenly heard my stepmother say, and I barely recognized the sound of her voice. "So terribly wicked, to be given such a gift and throw it all away. So terribly, terribly wrong."

"Maman, what is it? What's the matter?" I heard Amelie exclaim. "Maman!"

I turned my head, then, to look at my stepmother, and found to my astonishment that Chantal de Saint-Andre was weeping also. Huge tears streamed down her face to stain the silk of her gown. The ice inside her was well and truly melted now.

"I have been such a fool!" she cried. "I should have had this door broken down the very day that I arrived. I have behaved no better than your father, Cendrillon. I was so certain I had been betrayed by the one I trusted most of all. So furious with the king for making me marry your father that I forgot the reason I'd given him my trust in the first place. I forgot about love."

She turned to face me then, and I saw that her tears were already beginning to dry. In her face was a light that I had never seen before.

"But here love is," Chantal de Saint-Andre said. "Shining out from your mother's face, locked up, hidden away for all this time. I look at it, and I feel ashamed, for your betrayal is much greater than mine has ever been, Cendrillon. Your father threw away the greatest gift your mother could bestow—the gift of

what their love created. I think that I have never heard of anything so wrongheaded, or so blind."

"I wished for you," I heard myself say. "A mother to love me,
a mother I might love. And two sisters in the bargain."

"Why two?" Anastasia asked at once.

"So that at least one of them might like me," I said.

Before I knew quite what she intended, Chantal stepped
forward. She slipped the kerchief from my head, unpinned my
braids so that they tumbled down. Then she untied the scraps of
fabric at the ends of my hair, and with her quick, gentle fingers,
combed out the braids until my hair lay thick and unbound
across my shoulders, flowing down my back till its ends tickled
the backs of my knees.

Then she turned me, her touch still gentle, to once again
face my mother's portrait.

"I cannot claim that I can be the mother she would have
been," Chantal de Saint-Andre said quietly. "In this moment,
I cannot even claim to love you, Cendrillon, for to truly love
takes seeing truly, and I am seeing you now for the very first
time.

"But I can promise you that I will try. Let there be no more
throwing away of love while I am mistress of this house."

"I don't know what to say to you," I said.

"It's simple enough," Anastasia said. "You say, 'Thank you,
Maman.'"

"Oh, there you are!" her mother said to her. "There is the

daughter that I know and love. I knew you could not have lost yourself forever." She turned me to face her now, gathering us both, and Amelie, too, into her arms. "Another daughter," she said. "What a wonderful gift."

"Thank you," I said. "Thank you, Maman."

Twelve

I SLEPT A DEEP AND DREAMLESS SLEEP THAT NIGHT, AND IN the morning awoke to yet another series of surprises. The first was that my stepmother and Old Mathilde had put their heads together and decided that I was to be treated like a servant no longer. Instead, I was to take my place as what I truly was: a daughter of the house. With that in mind, my stepmother escorted me into breakfast herself. Seated at the table was the second surprise.

"Niccolo!" I cried. "When did you arrive?"

He got to his feet at once, made me a perfect court bow, then swept me up into a hug.

"Late last night," he replied. "I didn't want to wake the

house, so I roused Raoul in the stable instead. Somehow, I knew that's where I'd find him."

And where he would remain as much as possible, I thought, as I returned Niccolo's embrace, then let him go. My status in the great stone house might have changed overnight, but Raoul's was still the same as always.

"I thought I brought important news," Niccolo went on as he pulled out a chair for me. I took it, feeling more than a little self-conscious. "But *your* news, little Cendrillon . . ."

"Why does everyone insist on calling me little?" I said. "I'm just as tall as Amelie."

Niccolo helped my stepmother to the chair at the head of the table, then took a place beside me. He and I were on one side of the table, Amelie and Anastasia on the other. Niccolo shot a quick glance in Amelie's direction, then cocked his head in a perfect imitation of her. I heard Chantal chuckle. She made a gesture, and the village girl waiting by the table began to serve the breakfast.

"He has captured you, Amelie," observed her mother.

Amelie lifted her chin, her eyes gazing straight into Niccolo's. I saw the way they sparkled. Then she cocked her head in the opposite direction of the one that he had chosen. I bit down on my tongue to keep from laughing, and even Anastasia smiled.

"Has he?" Amelie inquired. "I can't imagine why you would say such a thing."

"No?" Niccolo said, as he tilted his head to the other side. Slowly, her eyes still holding his, Amelie tilted her head in the opposite direction.

"No."

Niccolo laughed aloud. "You are too clever for me, lady Amelie," he said. "In the future, I will make certain to keep that in mind."

"Oh, I don't know," Amelie replied, her eyes on her own hands as she added some of Old Mathilde's blackberry jam to a piece of buttered toast. "I would have thought we were pretty well matched."

"*Amelie,*" Anastasia said, scandalized.

Amelie lifted her eyes. The expression in them was absolutely guileless. "What?" she asked. From the corner of my eye, I thought I saw her mother smile.

So that is the way of things, I realized. I flicked a glance in Niccolo's direction and found him industriously studying his napkin. *They will make a good pair,* I thought. Amelie's inquisitive nature and Niccolo's open one. And I had to admit, he did look well. His cheeks were tanned from whatever journeys he had undertaken in the summer months. He had a fine new suit of clothes. *He looks like what he is, now,* I thought suddenly. *A nobleman's son, even if a younger one.*

Anastasia cleared her throat. "You said you had news from court, Niccolo," she said. "Will you tell us?"

"But of course," Niccolo answered, and there was both

excitement and a note of something deeper in his eyes. "The news I come with is this: The prince has returned to the court."

"Prince Pascal? I have not seen him since he was a small boy," my stepmother said.

"Surely you have seen the prince, Niccolo." Anastasia said, her voice eager. "Tell us what he is like."

"Ah!" Niccolo said, and now his eyes were dancing with mischief. "Here, I fear I must disappoint you. It is true that I have seen the prince, but equally true that I can tell you almost nothing about him save what everybody knows."

"There is some story in this, I think," I said over my step-sisters' exclamations of dismay.

Niccolo nodded. "There is, and I will tell it if you will but give me a moment."

"Be quiet, Amelie," Anastasia said at once. I bit down hard on the tip of my tongue.

"The prince is much away from court," Niccolo explained by way of a beginning. "This has been so for many years, ever since the Prince Pascal was little more than a boy. His travels served as a way for him to learn all the corners of his land and the people he will rule someday."

"Not to mention keeping him outside his mother's influence," Amelie observed.

Niccolo gave a quick nod. "That is so," he acknowledged. "In this, the cleverness of the king is crystal clear, for, over the years the bond between the prince and the common people has grown strong. Though he is young, he is just, and loved wherever he goes."

"He sounds boring," Amelie remarked.

"Amelie!" Anastasia exclaimed. "He's a prince."

Amelie turned toward her sister. "Is there some rule that says a young man can't be a handsome prince and a terrible bore all at the same time?"

Anastasia began to sputter. "Pay no attention to them," I advised. "It's what I do. Go on, Niccolo."

"I don't know how things have been here," Niccolo continued, "but in the capital we have had as fine a summer as any could wish for. But the very day the prince was set to return from the journeys that have kept him away all summer long, we had an unexpected thunderstorm. The rain fell thick as blankets, and the raindrops themselves were as big as coins. Fields and roads that had been dry as dust were suddenly filled with nothing but mud."

"That sounds strangely familiar," Anastasia said.

Niccolo chuckled. "I wondered if it might. Not an hour after the rain ceased, the prince and his retainers rode into the palace courtyard. At once, a great hue and cry went up. The king and queen were sent for. Anyone who could, dashed to a window to look out.

"The prince and his household were so covered in mud there was only one face among them it was easy to recognize—that of Gaspard Turenne, who has been the prince's principal retainer for many years. The king first set him to serve the prince when Pascal was only a boy. Gaspard Turenne has shoulders as broad as an ox, and sports a great dark beard besides.

"After the grooms had taken the horses, Turenne thought to make himself a bit more presentable by cleaning the mud from his face in a nearby water trough. No sooner did he bend over it, than one of the others snuck up behind him and pushed him in. He came up with a great roar, reached up, and dragged the culprit in beside him."

"Don't tell me," I said. "It was Prince Pascal."

"It was," Niccolo replied with a broad smile, as if he could see the scene before him, even now. "By the time the king and queen finally arrived, there was a full-fledged water fight going on. Every single member of the prince's household was involved. The king laughed so hard tears ran down his face as he embraced both Turenne and his son.

"He put an arm around each, and led them both inside. The others followed, still laughing and joking. They looked for all the world like a pack of sorry, soggy dogs. But I heard a man standing near me say that every single man among them would step between the prince and death without a second thought."

"So he is not boring at all," I observed. "And he inspires devotion in those around him. He sounds as if he will make a fine king someday."

"I believe that he will," Niccolo said. "And it is clear his father does, as well. But that is all the glimpse I had of the prince, I'm sorry to say. He stayed in close conference with his father all that evening. The next morning, all the messengers were sent from court to carry the result of that conference throughout the land. We could not even stay to hear it officially proclaimed, but were ordered to set off at once."

"Hear what proclaimed, Niccolo?" my stepmother asked.

"By order of the king, Prince Pascal will marry," Niccolo answered. "That is what I have come to tell you. And there is more: The prince himself will select his bride. The mourning period for the queen's father will be up in three weeks' time. The day after it is ended, there will be a great ball held in the palace. Every eligible maiden in the kingdom is required to attend. From among them, the prince will choose a bride."

A startled silence filled the dining room. Then my stepmother began to laugh.

"Oh, that is well done. No foreign princess to complicate matters by creating yet another alliance. Instead, the prince will marry one of his own. The queen must be beside herself with fury. She will perceive it as a slight that her son should marry a subject, no matter how high-born."

"You are right about that, I think," Niccolo said. "Though of course she has made no protest in public."

"And Prince Pascal?" I asked. "What does he think about it?"

"Nobody knows for certain," Niccolo said. "To be perfectly honest, I don't think it would occur to anyone to ask. He is a prince. It is his duty to marry, and he'll have more choice in the matter than his father ever did."

"But don't you see what this means?" Anastasia broke in excitedly. "It means we can leave this place at last. We can go to court. Indeed, we must. Every eligible maiden is ordered to attend."

Impulsively, she leaned forward to grip Amelie by the hand. "That means us!"

"Indeed it does," Amelie said. "And Cendrillon, too, of course."

Anastasia's face went blank. "That is what I meant," she said. "Cendrillon, too, of course."

"There's no need for me to go," I said quickly. "I have no desire to see the court." Just the thought of it made a strange cold hole in the pit of my stomach. My father, the father I had never seen, who had never wished to see me, had spent his whole life at court.

"It is the king's command," my stepmother replied in a thoughtful voice. "The fact that you've been overlooked for all these years doesn't change the fact that you are noble-born." She drummed her fingertips upon the tabletop. "When is this ball to be, did you say?"

"In mid-October," Niccolo said. "Not quite three weeks' time."

My stepmother stood up abruptly. "In that case, we have no time to waste," she said smartly. "Come along, my girls. We have work to do." She strode toward the doorway, then turned back, a smile dancing at the edges of her mouth.

"I mean you, too, my little Cendrillon."

"No, no, take small steps, *small steps,*" Anastasia exclaimed in irritation several days later. "How many times must you be reminded? You are a young lady walking into a roomful of eager suitors, not a milkmaid striding into a barn."

"I'll bet the milkmaid's shoes are more comfortable," I said, as I finally managed to get across the room and flop down onto a couch. "These pinch."

"That's good," Anastasia said. "They're supposed to. It will remind you to slow down."

A week had passed since Niccolo's return. One solid week of torture. At my stepmother's instigation, and with Old Mathilde's full approval, a campaign was under way to make a proper young lady of me before we set out for court. Even Anastasia had embraced the plan with enthusiasm. Secretly, I believed it had to do with the fact that transforming me into a lady opened up whole new realms of possibilities when it came to ordering me around.

"Sit up straight, Cendrillon," Anastasia said now. "You're slumping. A young lady always keeps her back straight, and her feet tucked neatly underneath her skirts."

I glared at where she sat in a straight-backed chair across the room, effortlessly demonstrating the desired posture.

"Do you never get tired of giving orders?" I inquired. "Amelie must be around somewhere. Why not go pick on her for a change?"

"Because Amelie knows how to behave like a lady when she wants to," Anastasia replied serenely. "Whereas you do not."

"I know part of it involves being polite," I came right back. "Apparently, you missed that part."

Anastasia made a disparaging sound, but I thought I caught a glimpse of a smile at the corners of her mouth. The truth is, I think she was beginning to enjoy our sparring. Now that we were of equal rank, I made a more worthy and interesting opponent.

"Do you want to make a good impression on the prince or not?" she inquired.

"There are going to be hundreds of girls at the ball," I said. "I'm hardly likely to make any impression at all, among so many of them."

Anastasia cocked her head in a perfect imitation of Amelie, her eyes thoughtful now. "You are wrong about that, I think," she said in a voice that matched her eyes. "Much as I hate to admit it, you really are incredibly lovely, Cendrillon."

I sat up a little straighter, as if she'd poked me with a pin.

"That's it," Anastasia exclaimed in delight. "Keep your back just like that."

"You and Amelie are beautiful," I protested.

"I never said we weren't," Anastasia replied. "Cross your

ankles and keep your legs beneath your skirts." I complied. "Now clasp your hands loosely and place them in your lap." I did this, too, and actually won a smile.

"That's absolutely perfect," Anastasia said. She regarded me for a moment, as if trying to decide whether or not to go on. "There will be many dark-haired girls at court. Some will have blue eyes, and some brown. But if there's another one who looks like you among them, I'll eat my riding gloves."

I held my body still, trying to understand what sitting like a lady felt like. "Would you marry the prince, if he asked you to?"

Surprise flickered over Anastasia's features. "Of course."

"Even though you don't love him, nor he you?"

Anastasia lifted an eyebrow. "You think I am unlovable?"

"I didn't say that," I replied. *Raoul loves you,* I thought, but didn't quite dare to say aloud. "It's just—don't you want to marry for love?"

"Of course I do," Anastasia said simply. "Isn't that what every girl dreams of? But noble-born girls do not always have the luxury of having their wishes come true."

"You don't have to be noble-born to be disappointed," I said.

Anastasia nodded. "True enough."

We sat silently for a moment, my gaze on her, her gaze on nothing.

"About Raoul," I said, taking courage firmly between both loosely clasped ladylike hands.

"Oh, no," Anastasia said suddenly. "Please, don't."

"There is nothing between us," I said. "Nothing that could stand in the way of him loving someone else."

"Why are you being so nice to me?" Anastasia cried out suddenly. "I've done nothing but torment you since the day I arrived. And yet there you sit, as good as telling me that Raoul can be mine. He can't be, and we all know it. I am a nobleman's daughter, and he's a stable boy. That sort of arrangement may work out well in stories and in dreams. But not in real life."

"No one knows who Raoul really is," I said. "Not even Raoul himself. My father brought him here when he was just two weeks old. Did you not know this?"

"No," Anastasia whispered, her cheeks pale. "No, I did not. Why has no one spoken of this before?"

"Because the subject pains him," I said, and prayed Raoul would not think that I was betraying his confidence. "And there may be no sense in getting your hopes up. He may turn out to be nothing more than what you see right now. Or his origins may always remain a mystery, though I hope that they do not, for learning who he truly is has always been the first wish of his heart.

"I do know this much, though. If I were you, I'd go take a good look at my mother's portrait before I decided to throw away a chance at love."

Anastasia drew a shaky breath. "I do believe," she said, "that this is your attempt to order me around."

I laughed before I quite realized what I'd done. "Perhaps you're right," I acknowledged.

"I will think about what you've said," Anastasia promised. She clapped her hands together sharply. "Now. Let me see you walk across the room one more time. If you do it to my satisfaction, I'll let you put on those terrible gardening clogs."

"At least they don't pinch," I said, as I got to my feet. But before I could so much as take a step forward, Amelie came flying into the room.

"There's been a messenger from Etienne de Brabant," she said breathlessly. "You must both come at once."

Thirteen

THE MESSAGE WAS BRIEF AND TO THE POINT. ALTHOUGH THE king had ordered every eligible maiden in the kingdom to attend the ball in Prince Pascal's honor, Etienne de Brabant was ordering his wife and stepdaughters to stay home.

"He says he fears for your safety," Niccolo said as he scanned the thick sheet of paper. The messenger who'd brought it was being fed in the kitchen. Raoul was seeing to his horse. My stepmother, stepsisters, Niccolo, and I were in the sun room, the tiny space crowded with so many of us. Pale October sunlight came in through the windows. A fire was kindled in the hearth, for the day was chilly in spite of the light.

"The journey from this place to the court takes several days, and he has heard that there are bandits on all the main roads," Niccolo went on. "A high-born lady and her daughters traveling together would surely attract their attention. Therefore, for your safety and that of your daughters, he commands you to stay at home.

"In your stead, I . . ." Niccolo broke off, his startled eyes rising up from the paper to focus on mine. "In your stead, I am to bring Raoul."

Chantal de Saint-Andre extended a hand. "Thank you, Niccolo," she said. "Please let me see the note."

Niccolo placed it into her hand. As she read the words my father had written, Chantal de Saint-Andre tapped her foot rapidly, to what seemed to me must be the rhythm of her thoughts. Then, with a suddenness that left all of us gasping, she tore the note in two, and then in two once more. Taking three quick steps, she moved to the fireplace.

"What a pity those same bandits set upon my husband's messenger and delayed him," she said serenely, as she cast the scraps of paper upon the fire. "So that the command to keep us all at home did not arrive in time."

"But, Maman, the messenger," Amelie began.

"Will be well cared for and kept busy here till we are well on our way," her mother replied. "He looked as if he could use a little country air, don't you think?"

Her foot began to tap once more. Her dark eyes shone with determination. "I know there are decisions to be made, obstacles to overcome, but we are *not* staying home. It is by the king's command that we are summoned to the palace, and to the palace we shall go. Etienne de Brabant may believe he is my lord and master, but the king is his."

All of a sudden, she gave a grin. "The command of a king trumps that of a husband, every time."

"And Raoul?" I inquired.

Chantal de Saint-Andre's foot stilled.

"Deciding what to do about Raoul," she said, her smile fading away, "may be our very first obstacle. I know that you are close to him, Cendrillon, but I must tell you plainly that the wisest course of action might be to leave Raoul behind. Etienne has always been the queen's man for many years, and I fear some mischief is behind this sudden request. I do not trust this fine husband of mine."

I opened my mouth to protest such a course of action, but before I could speak, my stepmother lifted a hand.

"That is not what I am going to do, however. It would be cruel to leave Raoul at home. Instead, we will all go, including Old Mathilde."

She glanced at Niccolo, who was standing near the fireplace. "The second thing we must decide is what to do about you, Niccolo. If you help us, you will be acting against my husband's wishes, and, for all we know, the queen's as well. Perhaps it is you who should stay here."

Niccolo was silent for a moment. "Thank you, my lady," he

said at last. "Your words are just what I have come to expect, both kind and thoughtful." He looked up from his contemplation of the fire then, and met Amelie's eyes.

"But I think, perhaps, I have done all I can in your husband's service, and in the queen's, if the truth must be told. Since going to court I . . ." He broke off, as if he could not quite put what had happened into words.

He no longer supports the queen, I thought. *And he loves Amelie. He would not wish to do anything which might jeopardize her family.*

"It is time to choose a new allegiance, one more in keeping with the wishes of my own heart," Niccolo went on. He switched his attention back to Chantal. "I will serve you, if you will have me."

"With pleasure," my stepmother replied. "Now all we have to do is find some means of getting to the capital that does not run the risk of alerting my fine and clever husband that we're coming after all. That will mean we cannot take the coach."

"I know," I said suddenly, as the idea sprang, full-blown, into my mind. I could only hope Anastasia was feeling flexible. "Pumpkins."

By the end of the day, a plan had been agreed upon. We would travel as a country family, eager to catch a glimpse of the prince we had never seen, and the lovely young ladies from among whom he would select his bride. To this end, we would harvest our pumpkins, fill the largest wagon with them, and travel to the market in the capital.

"But where will we stay once we get there?" Amelie inquired. "We can hardly put up at an inn, nor can we go to Etienne de Brabant's rooms at court."

"I believe that I can provide a solution to that," Old Mathilde spoke up. We were sitting at the table in the dining room, all of us together, like the family we would soon be impersonating. "I lived in the city, long ago. My sister still lives in the house our parents owned. She will welcome us, and though it will be cozy, there should be room for all."

"You lived in the city?" I exclaimed in astonishment. I had never heard her speak of this before.

Old Mathilde simply smiled and said no more.

"It would seem that you are right, Niccolo," I huffed. "This house is full of surprises."

The journey to the city took three days, days so full of sights and sounds that, though the road we traveled ran straight enough, our path upon it never runs quite the same way twice when I call it to mind. It does not roll out smoothly, like a length of ribbon unfurling across a tabletop, but splinters into different pieces, tumbling all together, then coming together into a single episode, like the spin and halt of a kaleidoscope.

Give one turn and there is Old Mathilde, driving the wagon with Amelie beside her, while Niccolo, dressed like a country lad now, makes his horse prance alongside. He reaches down and, before Amelie quite realizes what he intends, he snatches her up and sets her before him. She throws her arms around his neck to keep from falling off, though even Niccolo knows that this is mostly for show. Amelie is as fine a horsewoman as her sister is. There's not much chance she's going to take a tumble. Niccolo's dark eyes are dancing with mischief. Amelie's cheeks have a rosy glow.

"That looks pretty settled to me," Old Mathilde says, at which my stepmother gives a laugh.

"So it does," she answers. "So it does."

The kaleidoscope gives another turn and I see my stepmother, in the back of the wagon, perched high atop a pile of pumpkins. The wagon hits an unexpected bump in the road. She struggles not to topple out, howling with unrestrained laughter the whole while.

A third twist and Anastasia and Raoul come into view, walking side by side. It is almost twilight, the hour when the day birds are busy finishing up what they have to say before the dark descends and they fall silent for the night. Raoul is teaching Anastasia how to tell which bird is which, for he knows them all by sound alone.

Without warning, the air around us falls silent, and then, into that silence, comes a single bird call. Anastasia stops walking so abruptly Raoul goes several steps beyond her before he even realizes she's no longer beside him.

"Chickadee!" Anastasia cries. "It says its own name when it sings."

Raoul's face splits into a smile. "That's exactly right."

At his words, the bird calls once more, and Anastasia claps her hands together like a small child. "I did it!" she says, spinning toward the wagon. "Did you hear? I did it, Maman!"

And then, at last, the kaleidoscope spins and settles, and we are at the nightfall which followed. One that had us passing through the city gates, our three-day journey almost over.

"My house is in the oldest part of the city," Old Mathilde explained as we began to wind our way through the narrow streets. Mathilde was driving the horse once more. Raoul walked at its head, the better to guide it and keep it calm. Personally, I think the horse was feeling just as nervous as I was, overwhelmed by the sheer size and complexity of this place to which we had come. Passing through the gate, traveling along the cobblestoned streets, was like entering another country. The narrow streets were bordered by still narrower sidewalks with tall buildings leaning out over all.

"The palace came first, on top of the hill, with the old town directly below it," Old Mathilde went on. "As more people arrived, the town grew down the slopes of the hill."

"It looks like a garden," I said, as we took a turn. "Terraced up the hillside."

Old Mathilde smiled. "That is a good description," she said.

"Well, I think it looks like a crown," Anastasia suddenly spoke up. "All the lights in the windows sparkle like jewels, don't you think?"

"You're just seeing crowns everywhere, now that you're about to meet the prince at last," Amelie teased.

"I am not!" Anastasia cried.

"Girls," their mother said. "It is late, and we are all tired. Let us see if we can make it to our destination without calling attention to ourselves by quarreling in the street, shall we?"

"The lights in the windows are placed there by order of the king," Niccolo supplied into the awkward silence. He had dismounted to lead his horse, as well. He followed along behind the cart. The street was too narrow for us to go abreast.

"Every household must keep a candle burning in each groundfloor window until midnight. After that, the watch patrols the streets, calling out if all is well."

The street took a tight turn, then opened up as we came to an intersection. Niccolo pointed. "Even the palace follows this law. There. You can see it now."

I turned my head, followed the reach of his arm with my eyes, and saw the palace for the very first time. A seemingly impossible collection of turrets, towers, and walls. A light shone from every window on the lower levels, with a smattering of lights twinkling from the floors above.

This is where my father has spent my entire life, I thought.

What would I feel like when I finally set foot inside it? When he finally set eyes upon me, what would be Etienne de Brabant's response?

In the safety of the great stone house, coming to the capital to attend the ball against my father's wishes had seemed the right thing to do, a fine act of rebellion and defiance. But now, gazing up at the palace, I was not so sure. What would it be like to enter the palace as the young noblewoman that I was, to come face-to-face with the father who had neglected me for all my life, with the eyes of countless strangers upon us?

I felt a hard fist of fear begin to form, solid as a snowball, in my gut. Then Old Mathilde clicked to the horse, and the wagon started forward.

"Not much farther now."

Two blocks later, Mathilde brought us to a halt before a house that had a sprig of rosemary and a mortar and pestle painted on a sign hanging over the door. Even in the street, it seemed to me that I could catch a quick aroma of earth, the scent of pungent leaves drying. An apothecary shop. I felt the fist of ice in my belly begin to thaw.

"Your sister is a healer too?" I asked.

Old Mathilde nodded. "As was our mother before us. This was her shop before it was ours. My sister has kept it for us both, while I had other things to do."

She got down from the wagon, handed the reins to Raoul,

then rapped smartly on the door. Only then did I realize we had sent no word of our coming. Before I could express my concern, the door opened. Warm light spilled out into the street, partially cut off as a figure stepped into the doorway.

"I see you are come home at last, Mathilde," a woman's voice said, the sound of it like music. "It's about time."

Old Mathilde's sister was named Justine, and she was a younger, plumper version of Mathilde herself. Her cheeks were pink, and her face as wrinkled as an apple doll's.

"I am afraid the young men must sleep in the stable with the horses," she said, as she made us welcome. The apothecary shop filled the entire downstairs. There were living quarters on the floors above.

"I don't think either of them will mind that," I said. "Raoul sleeps with the horses at home most nights, anyhow."

Justine gave a chuckle. "Then I will leave them to settle themselves," she said. "And after they have done so, they must come in to supper. You young ladies, follow me now."

She led the way upstairs, the rustling of her petticoats beneath her skirts reminding me of the herbs she dried.

"So you are the girl Mathilde has cared for all these years," she said, as she climbed the stairs.

"You know about me?" I asked, astonished. "But how?"

Justine chuckled. "Mathilde and I have our little ways," she said. With that, she threw open a door halfway down the upstairs corridor, then stepped inside. Before us stretched a dormer room that ran the length of the house. Down its center, at regularly spaced intervals, were four neatly made beds, precisely as if they were waiting for us.

"There should be room for all of you in here," Justine said. "The room on the other side gets better light, so we'll save that for the sewing." She turned to my stepmother. "I have taken the liberty of laying in a few things I thought you might find useful," she said. "I hope you don't mind."

"Mind?" my stepmother cried. "You are a lifesaver, Justine, just as your sister is. Part of me wants to ask how you know what to do, the other informs the rest that a gift is best accepted with thanks and not inquired after too closely. So I will simply say thank you, I think. With all my heart."

Justine smiled. "And with all mine, lady, you are most welcome. I will leave you to get settled in, then," she said. "Over supper, we can discuss what must be done."

The rest of that week was a blur of activity, a whirl of fabrics, ribbons, buttons, and pearls. For what seemed like endless hours, Amelie, Anastasia, and I took turns standing in place while Old Mathilde and Justine held up pieces of muslin and made mysterious markings on them. After this we were sent to the kitchen for a cup of tea, but even in that far away room of the house it seemed to me that I could hear the sound of scissors, swishing and snipping their way through the silks and satins my stepmother had chosen. I went to bed each night with visions of pins and needles dancing in my head, and any dreams I had were of thimbles and thread.

Tuesday came and went, then Wednesday, and Friday was the night of the ball.

"We won't be ready in time," Anastasia declared late Thursday afternoon. "I simply don't see how it can be done. We've only got so many hands and hours in a day."

"My hands are sewing as fast as they can," I said. I was working on Anastasia's dress, a fine blue silk that matched her eyes, stitching a smattering of seed pearls across the bodice. With it would go a circlet of pearls for her forehead, pearl-covered slippers for her feet. Justine was working on Amelie's dress, Chantal on her own, and Old Mathilde on mine. She would not let me see it. I didn't even know what color it was.

As the week progressed, Old Mathilde had come to find me from time to time. She would wrap some body part with a tape measure, make a note of what she'd learned, then go off again, muttering instructions to herself.

"That isn't what I meant," Anastasia said. "I do not mean to criticize. I genuinely do not understand how we can be ready in time."

"Perhaps it is not a matter for understanding," Amelie put in. She was weaving together a circlet of dried flowers for her hair, with a flutter of ribbons that would stream down her back. "Perhaps it is more along the lines of a wish we all hope may come true."

"If I were you," I advised, "I would wish and sew at the same time. Hand me that spool of thread, if you please."

But by bedtime, even I began to have my doubts. We worked through the entire length of a brand-new candle, then went to bed with the dresses still undone.

Late that night, I was suddenly awakened by a pair of hands upon my shoulders. Amelie was leaning over my bed, a pale shape in her white nightgown. Anastasia was kneeling at the head of the bed.

"Come into the sewing room," she said. "There is something you should see. But be quiet. We do not want to wake Maman."

I tossed back my covers and got out of bed, following my stepsisters on tiptoe across the hall. In the light of the waning moon, just inside the sewing-room door, two dress forms stood, side by side. One was wearing a dress of pale blue, the other, a pink as soft as inside of a seashell.

"Look," Amelie said. "There we are."

"Oh, but they are perfect," I exclaimed softly. "Perfect in every detail." On silent feet, I moved forward, then knelt to lift the hem of Amelie's dress. "Your hem is finished, Amelie."

She nodded. "And Anastasia's buttons. And look . . ." She gestured to the circlet of flowers she had been working on just that afternoon. Woven in among the blossoms were ropes of tiny seashells. Shell buckles adorned her shoes. In the moonlight, the pearls on Anastasia's dress made the dress glimmer like cool spring rain.

"You are going to be so beautiful," I said, as I stood up. "Both of you."

"Not as beautiful as you will be," Anastasia replied. "Come and see."

"No, wait," Amelie whispered. "Better yet, close your eyes. Don't worry," she went on when I hesitated. "I won't let Anastasia trip you."

"Oh, stop," Anastasia protested, but I caught the laughter in her quiet voice. "She's right, though. Close your eyes, Cendrillon. Please."

Pulling in a deep breath, I obeyed, and felt my stepsisters each clasp a hand. Slowly and carefully, they led me through what felt like the full length of the sewing room.

"Now," Amelie whispered, as she gave my hand a squeeze. "Open your eyes."

I discovered I couldn't quite manage both at once. Instead, I did it one at a time. First the left eye, and then the right. Before me, in a shaft of moonlight coming through the window in the farthest corner of the room, stood the third and final dress form. I blinked. I rubbed my eyes, then blinked again.

"Oh," I said. "Oh, my."

The dress before me was the loveliest that I had ever seen, yard upon yard of ivory-colored satin shot through with threads of gold. The smooth, tight-fitting bodice was embroidered all over with raised gold flowers, their centers brilliants that caught the light. More brilliants danced across the full, billowing skirt.

"It's the same color as the moonlight," Anastasia breathed. "And see—for your hair . . ." She caught up a length of lace as fine as spiderweb, tossed it up and over my head. More brilliants flashed, even in the pale moonlight.

"You will be more beautiful than just the moon," she said. "You will be the moon and the stars combined. We are going to have to resign ourselves to lives as ladies in waiting, Amelie. One look at Cendrillon, and the prince will fall in love at first sight."

"Look," Amelie said. She knelt before the dress form, then rose. "Your slippers are made of glass."

My heart had begun to beat so hard and fast, I feared it would explode. At the sight of the slippers, I put my hands to my mouth.

"What the prince is going to do is die laughing when I fall flat on my face in those. I'm just a country girl, no matter who my mother was. I don't belong in a palace. I can't wear a dress like that."

A dress so beautiful it made my throat ache, so exquisite it made me want to cry. I lifted the lace from my hair, laid it gently against the shoulder of the dress form.

"I'm afraid. I'm so afraid," I whispered.

"It's just for a few hours," Anastasia said softly. "Though remarkable things may happen in even that short amount of time. You surprised us. Perhaps it's time to surprise yourself."

"If I can keep from falling over when I curtsy to the prince,"

I said, "that may be remarkable enough. Now let's go back to bed. It won't matter how beautiful our dresses are if we all have bags under our eyes."

Carefully, Amelie returned my glass slippers to their place. "I still don't understand how all this got done in time," she said, as she rose. "Is it magic, do you suppose?"

"The strongest kind there is, I think," I said.

"And what is that?" Anastasia asked.

"Love."

Fourteen

THE DAY OF THE BALL DAWNED CLEAR AND FINE. WE AROSE TO eat a hearty breakfast, after which Old Mathilde herded us into the bath, one by one. Then she sent us to the sunniest room in the house to comb out our hair and let it dry. Niccolo and Raoul went out into the city to make the arrangements for the coach that would take us to the palace that night. They had been whispering and chuckling together ever since the day before. If Susanne had been with us, she'd have called them thick as thieves. It was clear that they were up to something.

Late in the afternoon, there came a sudden lull in our activities, like the calm before the storm. My stepsisters and

I were in our room, sitting in a circle with our backs to one another. I brushed Anastasia's hair, Anastasia Amelie's, and Amelie mine.

"What happens if they can't find a carriage?" Anastasia suddenly said. "We can't go in the wagon and we can't possibly walk. Those shoes are gorgeous, but they hurt my feet. Ouch, Cendrillon. You're pulling my hair!"

"I'm not," I replied. "Stop fussing, Anastasia. Raoul and Niccolo know what they're about."

As if summoned by our words, we heard a shout from the street below. I heard my stepmother begin to laugh.

"Oh, it is absolutely perfect," she cried. "I could not have done better if I'd chosen it myself."

Anastasia flew to the window, opening the casement so that she could lean out. A moment later, I heard her laugh too.

"Oh, do come look!" she cried.

Amelie and I crowded into the window so that we all three together gazed down into the street below. Raoul sat behind two fine new horses, hitched to a conveyance, the likes of which I had never seen before. It had tall, thin wheels with spokes of painted gold. The coachman's seat was perched so high it was a wonder Raoul didn't fall right off. But the carriage itself was the most astonishing sight of all. Great and round, with great round windows to match. Like the wheels, it was painted gold.

"How do you like it?" Raoul called up with a doff of his new hat. He looked like a fine gentleman in his recently acquired city clothes. He and Niccolo would drive us to the palace that night.

"Leave it to you," Anastasia said, "to find the only carriage in all the city that looks exactly like a pumpkin."

Anastasia, Amelie, and I dressed together, aided by Mathilde and Justine. Then Justine shooed my stepsisters across the hall to their mother, giving Old Mathilde and me a moment alone. Carefully, Mathilde arranged the lace upon my hair, securing it in place with two jeweled clips studded with stones the same green color as my eyes.

"These belonged to your mother," she said, as she slid them into place. "I have saved them for you until now."

She turned me to face the mirror, and it seemed to me that a stranger gazed back. I did not know this girl in her fine gown. As if she sensed my sudden uncertainty, Old Mathilde came to stand behind me, so that the mirror reflected us both.

"I have worked and waited many years for a day such as this one," she said softly. "To see the light of Constanze's love shine out into the world once more. You are like the plants in your mother's garden, my Cendrillon. A bulb long hidden under-ground. But the blossom is all the more beautiful for being unexpected."

Old Mathilde leaned forward then, and kissed me on the cheek. "Do not be afraid to grow."

"I am afraid," I whispered. "But I will not let my fear stop me. I will be my mother's child, and yours. I love you, Mathilde."

"As I love you, my little cinder-child. Hurry now; your family is waiting."

And so the child of cinders went to the ball.

"Remember to keep your back straight when you curtsy to the prince," Anastasia instructed as the carriage inched its way through the crowded streets. "Incline your head and keep your eyes down."

Inside my fine glass slippers, I wiggled my toes. The carriage turned a corner and the palace came into view. I felt a trickle of unease slide down my spine. During our frantic days of preparation, I had worked hard to push all thoughts of my father to the back of my mind. But soon, we would be at the palace. I would see my father for the very first time.

"Look, there is the palace! How beautiful it is," Amelie cried. Every window was ablaze with light so that the palace itself seemed to shine like the evening star. "Have you ever seen anything so beautiful, Maman?"

"Only my three daughters," Chantal de Saint-Andre replied.

"How is it you always know the right thing to say?" I asked, and earned a chuckle.

"I hardly think I do that," my stepmother replied. "If I did, I would have found a way to say, *no thank you, Your Majesty,* when it came to marrying your father. Though, if I had, I would never have had you for a daughter. All in all, I am satisfied with my share of the bargain."

"My father will be angry, won't he?" I asked.

My stepmother reached to give my hand a squeeze. "I imagine he will be," she acknowledged. "I also imagine he will not dare to show it. We are here by the king's command. When we obey him, we show we are his loyal subjects."

"Are you not afraid for yourself, then?" I asked.

"No, I am not," Chantal answered after a moment. "I believe it genuinely angered the king when Etienne sent me from court. My family has served His Majesty long and well. I will call on his protection, if I must."

"We're here!" Anastasia cried suddenly. Raoul brought the carriage to a halt before a broad staircase. At once, Niccolo leaped down from his place at the back to open the carriage door. One by one, we alighted behind my stepmother. Niccolo closed the door, stepped back.

"There will not be four more lovely ladies in all the ballroom," he declared. "Do you not think so, Raoul?"

Raoul looked down from his high perch. "I do think so. And I think you will turn all their heads if you stand there admiring them another moment. Come along, Niccolo."

"Send to the stables when you are ready for us," Niccolo said. He resumed his position, Raoul clucked to the horses and the carriage started off. With my stepmother in the lead, the four of us started up the steps to the palace.

* * *

The ballroom was a sea of faces, a dazzling blur of color and of light. Great ropes of flowers looped down from the ceiling. Mirrored sconces lined the walls. Courtiers in their best attire jostled for position at the edges of the room. In a whirl of skirts and fancy footwork, couples performed an elaborate dance in a far corner. Snaking through the center was a line of young women, looking like jewels in a necklace in their colorful, shimmering finery. Even as my stomach began to knot in apprehension, I felt a moment of compassion for Prince Pascal.

"I'll bet the prince is wishing his father's kingdom was smaller than it already is," I murmured as we inched our way forward, making our way to the front of the line. My stepmother first, then Anastasia. I came next, with Amelie last in line. I was grateful to be sandwiched between my stepsisters. If not for them, I might have been all too tempted to simply turn tail and run right out the door.

"I hear Gaspard Turenne will be standing beside the prince with a great leather-bound book," Anastasia whispered back. "The name of every eligible maiden will be recorded in it as we all parade by, one by one. If the prince so much as smiles, a special mark is made by that girl's name."

Amelie gave a snort. "Let us hope Monsieur Turenne changed out of his muddy clothes."

We moved a little farther along. I could see a tight knot of courtiers now, those privileged enough to attend the king and queen and prince. Chances were very good my father was one of them. *Don't think about that now,* I told myself. If I thought about my father, I'd never be able to keep on going.

"What happens if Prince Pascal wants to ask someone to dance?" I asked instead, keeping up the game Anastasia had started.

"Then she gets two marks beside her name," Amelie supplied in a low voice. "And a circle around it besides. After all, an invitation to dance is practically a proposal of marriage."

Anastasia gave a gurgle of suppressed laughter.

"Girls," murmured my stepmother. "Behave yourselves."

We took another few steps, and suddenly the space before us opened up. I had a glimpse of glittering garments, jewels gleaming in circlets of gold. And then Chantal was sinking into a deep and graceful curtsy, with Anastasia right behind her. Mindful of my stepsister's endless instructions, I was careful to keep my back straight and my eyes lowered as I, too, sank down.

"But how is this, Etienne?" I heard a woman's voice exclaim. "I thought we were to be denied the pleasure of seeing your wife and daughters tonight."

"I thought so, too, Your Highness," a man's deep voice replied. "I am delighted to be proved wrong." From the corner of my eye, I could see Chantal's skirts move as she began to rise. My heart was pounding so loudly I could hardly believe the whole room didn't echo with the sound.

That is my father's voice, I thought. Polished, with a fine-honed edge, just like a knife.

"Madam," Etienne de Brabant went on smoothly. "This is a most welcome surprise."

"I am happy to hear you say so, my lord," my stepmother answered, her own voice calm and even. I tried to hold its cadence in my mind. *She is so strong,* I thought. Precisely what I would need to be, what I wished to be. "We were delighted to receive His Majesty's summons. It is always our pleasure to obey the king in all things," she went on.

"Chantal," I heard a voice that could only be the king's say now. "You are most welcome back to court. No, no—stop bobbing up and down. And here are those lovely daughters of yours. I have been singing their praises to Pascal ever since he arrived."

"All of my daughters are here, Majesty," my stepmother answered. "Including one I think you do not know. Girls."

In front of me, Anastasia began to rise from her curtsy. I followed suit, though my body felt stiff and clumsy. A strange coldness seemed to grip all my limbs, put there by the sound of my father's voice. I hoped my legs would hold me.

"Your Majesties, may I present to you my stepdaughter?" Chantal went on. "She is named Constanze, after her mother, but those of us who love her call her Cendrillon."

"Oh, but she is lovely," I heard the queen's voice exclaim. "The very image of her mother, if I recall. Where have you kept her hidden all this time, Etienne?" She gave a laugh like a chime of silver bells on a winter's day, beautiful yet cold.

"Oh, dear," she went on, her tone playful. "We have made

her nervous with all this attention, I'm afraid. Stop blushing and look up, child."

I can't, I thought. Every single part of my body seemed frozen in its present position.

Then I felt Anastasia slip her arm through mine. At the exact same time, Amelie did the same, and in that moment, the strange cold which had seized me at the first sound of my father's voice abruptly loosed its hold. Warmth flooded through me.

My wish has finally come true, I thought. *I have a mother and sisters to love me, a mother and sisters whom I love.* We were all together, a family united. I lifted my head, and looked into my father's eyes for the very first time.

He was handsome. I could see that at once. Fair-haired and blue-eyed. But in his face, I could see no expression, nothing to inspire the look that gazed so lovingly from out of my mother's portrait. Etienne de Brabant's face was as closed as the door he had locked so long ago. There would be no love for me from him at this late date. As he had begun, so my father would carry on.

Ever so slowly, Etienne de Brabant extended his hand. I placed mine into it, even as I curtsied once more. He pressed his lips to my knuckles for a fraction of a second.

"My daughter," he said. "You are welcome to court."

"Thank you," I said. "My lord." For I discovered that my mouth would not, could not, shape the word "father." Not for this man.

"Come now," I heard the king say, and, at the sound of his

voice, I suddenly found the courage to look into his face. It was open and kind. It was easy to see why my stepmother would give her allegiance to such a man.

"You will have time for reunions later. We must not forget why we are here tonight. Pascal." He made a gesture and a young man dressed in soft gray velvet stepped to his side. On his brow was a circlet of silver set with moonstone. Beside me, I heard Anastasia stifle a sound.

And then my eyes were on the prince's face, a face I knew as well as I did my own. There was the hair, dark as a raven's wing, the stormcloud-colored eyes. They were staring into mine with a startled expression as if, in my own face, he was seeing things he had not known existed before.

"Oh," I said. "Oh, of course."

And only when I saw his expression change did I realize that I had spoken aloud. A great roaring seemed to fill my ears. But it was not until I felt myself jostled from behind that I realized it was coming from the crowd in the ballroom and not from the thousands of unanswered questions streaming through my own mind.

A figure pushed its way forward, fell to its knees before Prince Pascal. Even as it did, the guards surrounding the royal party surged forward, their swords singing in their sheaths as they were drawn. My own body moved as if of its own volition. I dropped to my knees, shielding the body of the figure on the floor with my own.

"No! You must not!" I cried out. "He means no harm."

"Stand away," I heard the prince's voice command.

"Your Highness," protested the captain of the guards. He had been the first to react, the tip of his sword no more than a hand's breadth away from my throat.

"Stand away," the prince said once more, his voice as bright and sharp as the swords drawn in his protection. "Step aside."

"Do as my son says," the king said in a firm, low voice.

Reluctantly, the guards fell back. At a gesture from the captain, several moved to push the crowd back, then stood behind my stepmother and sisters, so that we were all surrounded by a ring of unsheathed swords.

"Let me see your face," the prince said. "Do not be afraid, but look up."

Raoul lifted up his head, and all who saw his features gasped aloud. For a space of time impossible to measure, the two young men stared at each other.

"So," Raoul whispered. "My wish has come true at last."

Then he pitched forward, flat on his face, at the feet of his twin brother.

Fifteen

"I TRIED TO STOP HIM," NICCOLO SAID, HIS VOICE CRACKING with the strain of his distress. "I swear, I tried. The moment I saw the prince's face, I thought I understood why Etienne de Brabant finally ordered Raoul to court."

Several hours later, we were all still at the palace, still in our finery, for, as yet, we had no other clothes. At the king's command, my stepmother's household had been given a special suite of rooms, separate from those of my father. Raoul's sudden appearance had put an end to the evening's festivities.

"To bring about what actually happened," I spoke up, not quite sure I recognized the sound of my own voice.

How could it be safe to feel I recognized anyone anymore?

In the blink of an eye, my childhood companion had become a prince. And I was the daughter of the man who had known this, and concealed it, all along. Who had taken an innocent baby and left him to grow up ignorant of what he was, reducing him to nothing more than a political pawn.

"To disrupt the king's plans for Prince Pascal to marry by revealing the fact that there are two princes, not just one," I went on. I turned to Niccolo, who was standing beside Amelie. She had an arm around his waist, as if to show her support. Their love glowed as brightly as any candle in the room, the one bright and steady spot in an otherwise turbulent night.

"What was it you said the queen has always vowed?" I asked Niccolo.

"That she would never be satisfied until the first son of her heart and blood sits on her husband's throne," he replied.

"A vow which made no sense," I said, "when there was only Prince Pascal. But if there was another son, hidden away since birth, put into the care of the one person in all this land the queen trusts the most. And if that son . . ."

I swallowed against the sudden taste of bile at the back of my throat. "If that son were the first born . . ."

"Oh, but that is wicked!" Anastasia said suddenly, speaking for the first time. "To rob one son of his right, to deny the other all knowledge of who he is for so very long. How can any good come of this? The queen will break Raoul's heart."

"Not to mention the king's," my stepmother chimed in softly. "He loves Pascal very much."

"But how did you and Niccolo come to be in the ballroom in the first place?" Amelie asked. "I thought you were going to wait in the stables."

Niccolo nodded. "We did plan that," he acknowledged. "But Raoul was restless and edgy. He wanted to see what was happening at the ball. He wished to see all of you, I think."

He glanced at me, his expression hesitant, as if uncertain of how I would react to what he was about to reveal. I gave a nod.

"But most of all, he wished to see you, Cendrillon. He was excited for you, worried for you, proud of you, all at once. I tried to talk him out of it. He wouldn't budge. So . . ." Niccolo paused and took a breath.

"I snuck him into the palace, onto one of the balconies overlooking the ballroom. We saw you greet your father, Cendrillon. Then the king made a gesture, a young man who could only be the prince stepped forward, and it was as if both Raoul and I had been turned to stone. He was off and running as if the hounds of hell were at his heels almost before I knew he'd left my side. I could not catch up with him. I'm sorry."

"Don't be," I said quietly. "Even if you had managed to catch him, Raoul would have found some way to keep on going. His whole life, he's wanted to know who he is, wished for this one thing more than anything else. Once he had seen Prince Pascal's face, I don't think anything on earth could have stopped him."

And what of Prince Pascal himself? I wondered. How did he feel about the fact that he had a brother, an identical twin? My stepmother had worried about the king's heart, Anastasia and I worried about Raoul's. Was there no one to worry over Prince Pascal's heart?

My stepmother stood up. "One thing is for certain," she said. "We won't do anyone any good by staying up and worrying all night. A good night's sleep is in order, I think. Perhaps things will look less dire in the morning."

"What about Old Mathilde?" I asked. "Shouldn't we try and get word to her?"

"I have been thinking about that." Chantal nodded. "I think it is best to say nothing about the fact that she is in the city, for now. When we know more about what may happen, then we can decide what to do. But she should be told what has occurred tonight. It concerns her."

"I will take a message to her," Niccolo offered.

"I was hoping you would say that," my stepmother acknowledged. "But be careful of how you come and go, Niccolo. When you are with us, you are under the king's protection. But when you are on your own . . ."

"I will take care," he promised, and I saw the way that Amelie's arms tightened. She saw him to the door. When she turned back to face the room, her face was wet with tears.

"Maman," she began.

Her mother moved to her quickly, silencing her with an

arm around her shoulders. "I know, *ma petite,*" she said. "I know. I see what you feel for him, and he for you. Niccolo is clever and resourceful. He will stay out of danger. Take heart. All will yet be well."

"Then you do not disapprove?" Amelie asked.

"Of course not," her mother answered with a smile. "I like him very well. And he will be just the one to take you on all those adventures you've always dreamed about." She turned back to Anastasia and me. "Come," she said. "Let us all go to bed."

Anastasia moved at once to her mother's side.

"I will stay up for a few moments longer, if I may," I said. I didn't think I'd be able to sleep if my life depended on it.

"Of course," said my stepmother. "Try not to worry too much about Raoul. If nothing else, he is now too valuable to come to any harm." Together, the three of them vanished into the sleeping chambers.

I sat in a chair by the window, watching the play of candle-light upon the stone of the palace walls, so different from the stone of the walls at home. *So much has happened,* I thought. *And yet so little time has gone by.*

A thousand images seemed to crowd for space inside my head. Raoul as a boy, fuming over some imagined insult, laughing at some unexpected joy. Standing beside me at my mother's grave each and every year on the birthday that we shared, making the same wish, asking the same question, over and over: *Who am I?*

And now, that question had been answered and nothing would ever be the same. Not for Raoul. Not for any of us.

All of a sudden, large as it was, the room seemed too small, the air within it, stifling. The palace itself seemed to bear down upon me. No longer beautiful, but a trap that had snatched my oldest friend away and would send him back a stranger.

I want to get out of here, I thought. Without stopping to think, I leaped to my feet and ran to the door. Pulling it open, I dashed into the corridor. And then I was simply running, flying along the hallways of the palace on glass-slippered feet, not knowing, not caring where I was going. The journey, not the destination, was all that mattered. The sense of freedom, never mind that it was false, that always comes with motion.

Eventually, my headlong race carried me to the top of a wide and curving set of stairs and here, at last, my feet slowed and stopped. Below me stretched the ballroom I had been so nervous to enter, just a few short hours ago. The air was thick here, too, this time with the scent of flowers. The garlands of them were still in place, but they were drooping now. The candles guttered in their sconces. Only a few still flickered along the walls. I set my hands upon the balustrade, felt the cool of the stone through my palms.

"Cendrillon," I thought I heard a voice say, floating like a phantom on the air, and at the sound of it, I started.

"Who is it? Who is there?" I called.

In answer to my question, a figure below me stepped into a

patch of light. I had not noticed him before, for he was dressed in clothing almost the same shade as the shadows which surrounded him. He tilted his face up. At the sight of it, I caught my breath.

It was Prince Pascal.

Sixteen

"Your Highness," I said as I began to sink into a curtsy.

"Oh, don't," he said, bringing my motion to a halt. "Please. It's just us. I wonder—I would like to speak with you, if I might. Will you come down?"

I opened my mouth to say I couldn't, then changed my mind. There was something in the sound, the timbre of his voice, that I had heard before. Raoul had always sounded just like this, when he was asking for something he wished for very much, so much he was almost afraid to ask in case the answer would be *no*.

"Of course I will come down, if that is what you wish," I said.

"It is," the prince replied. Slowly, carefully, I descended the stairs, my skirts whispering around me as if telling secrets. I reached the bottom and the prince materialized at my side. He extended an arm, bent at the elbow. I placed my own upon it and stepped off the stair, onto the ballroom floor.

"Thank you," he said simply. Then, as if suddenly realizing he wasn't sure quite what to do now that he had convinced me to join him, he began to lead me around the ballroom, for all the world as if we were taking an afternoon stroll in the park.

"You knew me," Prince Pascal said after a moment. "You did not mistake me for . . ." His voice faltered for a fraction of a second before it went on. "My brother."

"Of course not," I said at once. "Surely no one who truly knew either of you could mistake one for the other."

"And you believe you know him truly?" the prince inquired.

"I believe I know him as well as anyone else does," I answered. We reached a junction of the ballroom walls. Pascal put a hand to my waist, and gently guided me out into the middle of the room. "I've known him since he was two weeks old."

"The age he was when your father brought him to your estate," the prince filled in, and now I heard the temper of steel in his voice. Young though he was, he would not be a good man to cross, I thought. And I remembered suddenly what Niccolo had said: That Pascal was loved wherever he traveled, that the people found him fair and just.

I nodded. "That is so."

"What of the future?" the prince asked.

I frowned. "I'm sorry," I said. "I don't understand what you are asking."

"You and Raoul," Pascal said. "What do you hope for now? You must be childhood sweethearts, with a story like that."

I gave a quick peal of laughter before I could stop myself. "Whatever gave you that idea?" I inquired. "Raoul is in love with my stepsister, Anastasia, to tell you the truth. A somewhat complicated and unhappy state of affairs until tonight's . . ." I paused, searching for the right word. "Surprise."

"I'm sorry if I've offended you," Prince Pascal said at once. "When you moved so quickly to protect him, I naturally thought . . ."

"I am not in the least offended," I answered. "I am also not the least bit in love with Raoul."

"I see," Pascal said. We walked in silence for a moment. "I saw you and your stepsisters whispering together as you approached the front of the line," he said. "You were the only girls all evening who showed any sort of real expression at all. Everyone else just looked incredibly hopeful or completely terrified.

"It made me wonder about you before I even knew who you were. It certainly made me wonder what you were talking about."

"Oh," I said, coming to a dead stop as I suddenly remembered what our topic of conversation had been. "Oh, dear. Oh, no. Please don't ask me to tell you."

CAMERON DOKEY

The prince laughed, the sound surprised, as if laughing was a thing he didn't do very often. "It can't be all that bad. I can command you to tell me, you know."

"That's what I call unfair," I said, at which he laughed once more.

"That's twice you've made me laugh," he said. "I'm afraid I'm going to have to insist."

I shook my head. "Oh, very well. Since you must know, I remarked that the line of eligible maidens seemed so long, I wondered if you were wishing your father ruled a smaller kingdom."

Prince Pascal's lips twitched. "Indeed, I did wish that," he said. "What else?"

"Then Anastasia claimed there was a special book in which the names of all the eligible maidens were being written down. A special mark would be placed by a girl's name if you so much as smiled. And Amelie claimed that, if you asked one to dance, it would be almost as good as a marriage proposal. That's when my stepmother told us to hush."

Prince Pascal stopped walking. "I wonder," he said, in a tone I could not quite interpret, "if you would care to dance with me now."

"Your Highness," I faltered, then wondered how I had managed to speak at all when my heart had leaped straight into my throat.

"I could insist again," he said. "But I think that I will not.

182

Instead, I will say please. Will you please do me the honor of dancing with me, Cendrillon? Will you do me the honor of saying my name? For I find that I would like you to do both, very much."

He stepped back and sketched a quick bow, his face tilted downward so that his expression was in shadow. Then he straightened up and held out a hand. I placed trembling fingers within it.

"It would be my pleasure to dance with you, Pascal," I said. And I stepped forward, into his arms.

Here, oh, here, I thought, as we began to move in small, then great, sweeping circles, my skirts flying out, the brilliants catching the moonlight as Pascal and I danced across the ballroom floor.

This was the feeling, the certainty, that I had not found in Raoul's arms—the deep and absolute belief that here, at last, was where I belonged. I was filled with the sudden knowledge that I had been searching my whole life for just this moment, just this feeling, and all without realizing I had been searching at all.

I saw Pascal's face change then, saw something kindle deep within his storm-tossed eyes. A thing so bright and pure it let me see my own gaze reflected in it, and instantly, I knew the truth: I was gazing into the face of joy. This was what my mother had seen within my father's face, the look that I had been able only to imagine until now. The sheer surprise, unbridled wonder, and exquisite joy of unexpected love. Love at first sight.

"Cendrillon," Pascal said. "I . . ."

My footsteps faltered then, as one of my glass slippers encountered something smooth and slick, spent flower petals that had fallen to the ballroom floor. I felt my ankle twist, my foot slip from the shoe, just as Pascal lifted me up, leaving the shoe behind. And then I stopped caring about shoes and feet, stopped thinking of anything at all. For Pascal's arms around me were both gentle and tight, and then his lips found mine.

Sweet, so very sweet, I thought. Sweet and firm and strong. I kissed him back, kissed him as I had dreamed of being kissed, but had never quite believed I might be. *It is all decided now,* I thought. I had wondered who would be the one to worry over what was in Prince Pascal's heart, and now I knew the truth: It was me.

Slowly, slowly, Pascal set me on my feet. But before either of us could say a word, there came another voice, one I thought I recognized.

"My apologies for interrupting you, Your Highness," said my father's voice, and once again, I was reminded of the blade of a knife. "But your lady mother is asking for you."

All trace of what he was feeling vanished from Pascal's face. It went completely blank, as if he had drawn a curtain across whatever might be inside. I felt a sudden pang of loneliness seize my heart. *I have only just found you,* I thought. *Don't go yet. Don't go.*

"Thank you for your care, my lord de Brabant," the prince said. "Please be so good as to inform my mother I will be with her in a moment."

"With your permission, I would be happy to escort my daughter back to her rooms," offered my father. "She is a stranger to the palace and might lose her way otherwise."

At this, finally, Pascal stepped back. "As always, your suggestions are most reasonable, my lord. Thank you for your care." He bowed over my hand, the faintest brush of his lips across the backs of my knuckles. "I will look forward to seeing you tomorrow, Cendrillon."

He turned and left without another word. My father stepped forward. For several humming moments, the two of us regarded each other.

"It would seem that you are to be congratulated," Etienne de Brabant said at last. "I doubt that the prince will so much as look at anyone else now."

"I don't know what you mean," I said.

My father made a curt, dismissive gesture. "Do not play the fool with me," he said, his voice not quite so smooth and polished now. "Surely you cannot be so naïve, even if you are country-bred. You have made a conquest, and you should be proud of it. But neither of you is sitting on a throne quite yet. If I were you, I wouldn't count on it."

He moved then, before I realized what he intended, giving me no time to step back. He caught me by the shoulders, leaning close to study my face, then released me and stepped back.

"You are not quite what I expected you might be," he pronounced at last. "And Pascal's attraction to you is certainly unexpected. Perhaps we may be of some use to each other yet before all this is done."

I stood perfectly still, staring at him. "Why should I wish to be of any use to you?" I inquired in a tone like ice. "I have seen my mother's face, seen the portrait in her room, and so I know how much she loved you. If she could look upon you now, I wonder if she would recognize the man you have become. If someone painted her face tonight, what expression would it show, I wonder?"

I brushed past him, moving up the stairs, doing my best to keep my back straight and my head held high. An affect that was almost spoiled by the fact that I was wearing only one shoe, a fact my father's presence had nearly driven from my mind. *I will not go back for it,* I thought. *I will not go back at all.*

"You may not speak so to me," Etienne de Brabant said as I reached the top of the stairs, and now his voice was fierce and hard, as if everything he had felt for the last sixteen years, all the things he had denied, were clenched tight as a fist inside him, and now the fist was pounding, demanding to be let out. "I am your father."

"And I am your daughter," I replied, as I turned back after all. "The one you never wanted. You have blamed me for an act not of my making, not of my desire, every single day of my life. Aside from courtesy, my lord, what is it that you think I owe you? I will not be made a pawn in your games. I will find my own way back. Good night."

I turned, and left him standing in the ballroom.

Seventeen

WHEN I GOT BACK TO MY ROOM, RAOUL WAS THERE, HOVERING like a ghost outside the door.

"Cendrillon," he said when he saw me, and I heard the way his voice broke, whether in joy or sorrow I could not tell.

"Raoul," I said, as I caught him to me. For a moment, we clung together. "How are you?" I asked at last. "Are you well?"

"Well enough," he said. He gave a shaky laugh as he let me go. "In fact, I—"

He broke off with a glance over his shoulder and only then did I realize that a guard such as the ones I had seen in the ballroom stood several paces down the hall.

"Come inside," I said. "You can do that, can't you?"

"I'm a prince now," Raoul said, though I could tell by his voice that he did not quite believe it, even now. "Within reason, I can do whatever I want."

"Then come in," I said. "Let's stop skulking in the hall."

I opened the door to our rooms, ushered him inside, then closed the door behind us. The large common room was empty, my stepmother and stepsisters having gone to bed. Candles still burned on several low tables, and in the window enclosure. Raoul moved restlessly around the room, finally coming to a halt before the window, gazing out at the city below.

"The lights are still burning in the windows of the town," he said. "How can so many things have happened and yet it isn't even midnight?"

"What has happened?" I asked, as I sat down upon a padded stool. "Tell me."

"I've been speaking with all of them," he said. "My father." His voice stumbled slightly on the word. "My mother and brother. Do you have any idea what it's like to look into someone else's face and see your own gazing back?"

"No," I answered quietly. "Everyone says I look like my mother, but it's not the same thing."

"I have been given my own suite of rooms," Raoul said. "Not far from Prince Pascal's. A guard to keep me safe."

"Safe," I said. "From what?"

Raoul turned to face me then, and I could see the strange and tortured expression in his eyes.

"I have just come from speaking with the queen," he said. "She wanted us to speak, privately. No one was present, except for your father. She says, the queen, my mother says . . ." Raoul's voice faltered, then steadied. "That I am the elder son. That is why your father took me, all those years ago. To keep me safe. It is I who should be king when my father dies and not Pascal."

So, I thought. *It is as my stepmother and Niccolo thought.* The queen would try to place Raoul upon the throne. Use him to perform a coup, now that her brother's armies had been destroyed.

What kind of a woman could do such a thing? I wondered. To achieve her own ambition, she had deprived one son of his childhood birthright. Now, she would pit him against the brother he had barely begun to know. If she broke the king's heart in the process, so much the better. And Etienne de Brabant had been her instrument. My father, who no longer seemed to have any heart at all.

She does not care about you, Raoul, I thought. *All she cares about is that we are all under her control.*

"You say you have just come from her?" I said. "She has just sent for Pascal. I wonder how she will tell him what she has told you."

"You have seen the prince?" Raoul asked, surprised. And I could not help but notice that, in spite of what he now believed he could claim for himself, he still spoke as if there was only one.

I nodded. "I came from him just now. We did not plan to meet. It just sort of . . . happened."

Before I understood what he intended, Raoul crossed the room and caught my face between his hands, tilting it toward the candlelight.

"You love him!" he exclaimed. "I can see it in your face. You met him for the first time tonight, and yet you love him already."

"It didn't take you much longer to fall in love with Anastasia," I remarked. "Let go, Raoul. You're pinching my chin. Besides, you know what I look like."

"No," he said, drawing out the syllable as he released me. "I don't think I do. Not altogether. Not quite." He stepped back, but his eyes stayed on my face. "Does it hurt, this newfound love?"

"I haven't decided yet," I admitted.

"Does he love you?"

"I think he does."

"You might be queen someday then," Raoul said. "If not for me."

"Oh, will you stop being so stupid?" I exclaimed crossly, as I stood up. "I don't care about that and you should know it. Neither will you, if you are smart. You have only the queen's word about the fact that you are firstborn, Raoul. If she's demonstrated anything, it's that she's someone it's not safe to trust.

"What will you do if Pascal and your father object to this

sudden rearranging of things? Will you fight them?"

"I don't know what I'll do!" Raoul cried out, his voice anguished. "How can I? For as long as I can remember, I've wished for just one thing, and you know it as well as I do. The same thing, year in, year out. Now, in the blink of an eye, my wish has been answered. I know who I am. I woke up a stable boy, but I'll go to bed a prince. Who is to say that I might not be king one day besides?"

"So you would fight," I said. "You would make war on your father and brother. The queen will have no more need for foreign mercenaries. She will get you to do her fighting for her."

"Rilla," Raoul said, and at the sound of my childhood nickname, my heart gave a pang. "Don't I have the right to claim what is mine?"

"Of course you do," I said. I went to him, my feet awkward with only one shoe, and laid a hand upon his arm. I felt the way his own trembled as he laid it over mine. "But surely not at any cost. That day we stood in the pumpkin patch and saw the ships, we made a wish together, the only time we've ever wished for the same thing in all our lives. We wished to find a way to make the fighting stop.

"The queen is just trying to use you, don't you see? She doesn't love you any more than my father loves me. She is the one who has deprived you of your birthright, not your father or brother. She sent you away, when she should have kept you close."

Raoul stood absolutely motionless, staring down at me with devastated eyes. "I thought you would be happy for me," he said. "I thought you would want what I want."

"Not if it means you're going to fight your own brother, Raoul," I said. "Not if it means starting a war and tearing the country apart."

"It's because you love him, isn't it?" he asked. He dropped his hand from my arm and stepped away. "It's because you love Pascal."

"It's because I love *you*," I said at once. "Of course I am happy that you have finally discovered who you really are. But I can hardly rejoice if you plan to fight the father and brother you've only just found. How can that be what you want for yourself? How can that be who you truly are?"

"I don't have to explain myself to you," Raoul said.

"No," I replied. "You don't. But no matter who you are, you are answerable to yourself."

"You'll go to him, won't you?" he suddenly challenged. "As soon as I leave this room, you'll go to Pascal. You'll find him and warn him."

"I honestly don't know what I'll do." I sighed. "You're my oldest and dearest friend, Raoul. I have loved you for almost as long as I have been alive. Don't ask me to choose between an old love and the new. That's no choice at all, and in your heart, you know it."

I watched the struggle come and go across his face. "I will think about what you have said," Raoul answered finally. "Please—I would like to ask you to do nothing tonight. Please wait, give me time to think, and let us speak again in the morning."

"Is it the new prince or my old friend who asks me this?" I said.

"It is both," Raoul replied. "I'm trying to find the way to make them both fit inside my skin. It's harder than I thought. I haven't learned how to be both yet. Please, Rilla. Give me some time."

"Very well," I said. "I will give you until tomorrow, as you ask."

"Thank you, Rilla," Raoul said. "You are a good friend."

"And you are good at getting your own way," I replied.

For a moment, I thought he would say something more, then I saw the way his eyes shifted to take in something over my shoulder.

"It must be midnight," he said. "The lights are going out."

I turned to face the city then, and saw that he was right. Through the window of our suite of rooms, I could see the lights in the town below us begin to go out, one by one. Then, as if a great wind had suddenly come up, the streets went dark, all at once. I felt a quick shiver slide straight down my back.

It looks like an omen, I thought. Of what, I wasn't sure I cared to guess.

I turned back toward Raoul, and heard the click of the closing door.

"He's gone, isn't he?" Anastasia's voice said.

"Yes," I said. "He's gone." I turned to face her, saw the tears upon her cheeks. "If you love him, go after him," I said. "Don't let him go."

"How can I?" she said in a low and tortured voice. "I made so much of the differences between us. What will he think if I go after him now?"

"You'll never know unless you do it," I said. "Help him, Anastasia. Don't throw away love."

"I'll never understand why you don't hate me," she said. "But I'll tell you this. I'm grateful that you don't."

She moved swiftly to the door and pulled it open. "Raoul," she called in a low voice.

The moment she stepped into the hall, I knew he had turned back. Anastasia darted forward, and I moved to stand in the open door. I saw the way she moved toward him swiftly, then faltered. And as she did, Raoul stepped forward in his turn, and pulled her into his arms. She put her head upon his shoulder. He, an arm around her waist. Entirely heedless of the guard who still stood several respectful paces off, they moved off together down the hall.

I'll never know what made me sense the danger. A change in the air, perhaps. A strange scent. An unexpected hint of sound. It didn't matter, as it turned out. Because I wasn't quick enough. Before I quite realized what was happening, something thick and dark and stifling was being thrown over my head. Strong arms banded around mine from behind. I felt myself being lifted, kicked out once, and felt my second shoe go flying. I heard the chime of broken glass as it crashed to the floor.

And then, nothing.

Eighteen

IT WAS ANASTASIA WHO FIRST TOLD ME THE STORY OF WHAT happened next, who helped me see what I could not. How, after settling things between them, pledging to love each other now and forever, no matter who they were or might become, she and Raoul had walked back to the rooms we shared and there discovered the heel of one glass shoe and a scatter of broken glass outside our door.

When a quick and frantic search failed to produce any additional sign of me, Raoul did not hesitate, but, accompanied by my stepmother and stepsisters, went directly to the king and Prince Pascal. He told them of the queen's treachery, of his fear that my father had seized me and carried me from the palace. The king sent for my father at once. When he did not answer the summons, when he, too, could not be found, Raoul knew his worst fears had been realized.

"Where would he take her?" Pascal asked, the fear in his eyes and in his voice telling anyone with eyes and ears of their own all they needed to know about what was in his heart. "He could be anywhere by now. Where would he go?"

"I think I know the answer to that," Raoul had said. "He will take her to the great stone house by the sea. He will take her home."

"Then we must go after her at once," Pascal said.

"If I may, Your Highness." Amelie had surprised them all by speaking up. At a gesture from Pascal to continue, she turned to Raoul. "You should take Niccolo. He will want to help. And he knows the road better than you do."

"That is a good thought," Raoul said at once. "And let us send for Old Mathilde." He turned back to Pascal. "She raised Cendrillon. No one knows her better or loves her more."

"I will trust your judgment in this," Pascal said.

And so Niccolo and Mathilde were sent for. As soon as they arrived, the party set off, the two princes and Niccolo taking swift horses and riding ahead, my stepmother, stepsisters, and Old Mathilde following in a carriage. Only the king stayed behind. His first act once the others had departed was to see that the queen was close confined. Save for the members of her immediate household, all carefully selected by the king, she was never seen in public again.

The story I told in return goes like this: That I awakened to find myself slung across the back of my father's horse like an unwanted parcel. All that night, and all the day that followed, Etienne de Brabant spurred his horse along the road. His only concession to my presence was to allow me to sit up behind him once he knew I was awake.

Just before nightfall at the end of the second day, we came to the great stone house. The journey had taken a full day less than the one which had brought me to the palace in the first place, so great was my father's desire to reach his destination. Etienne de Brabant dismounted, pulled me from the horse, carried me up the steps. With one booted foot, he kicked open the front door, all but scaring the wits out of Susanne, who had come to see what all the commotion was about, and had gotten no farther than the great hall.

At a sharp command, she scurried to get out of the way. My father set me down. Then, with a yank that had my head rocking on my shoulders, he set off across the great hall and up the stairs that led to the second story. Down the corridor to the very end we went, until at last we stood outside my mother's door.

"Open it," he commanded.

But I heard what was in his voice. I had been frightened when my father first seized me, and for many moments on our long, wild ride. But I was not afraid of anything within the great stone house, not even him, and it was fear that I heard inside my father's voice. Fear of what he had tried, without success, to lock away from the world, and from himself. And so I lifted my chin and stepped back.

"I am not the one who is afraid of what lies beyond that door," I said. "Open it yourself."

He started then, staring at me as if seeing me for the very first time. Not as what he had imagined for nearly sixteen long years, but as what I truly was: Constanze d'Este's daughter, his own true child. For the time it took my heart to beat six times, he did not move. Then, slowly, my father reached out, seized the latch, lifted it up, and opened my mother's bedroom door.

Gone were the cobwebs, the dust that had greeted me on my first glimpse of this room. Old Mathilde and I had taken down the bedhangings and the curtains to launder and iron them. We had scrubbed the floors and washed the windows till they shone. In the glow of twilight, the room looked warm and welcoming, as if its occupant had stepped out of it just minutes before. Slowly, his feet making absolutely no sound, my father crossed the room until he reached the alcove. I knew the second he saw my mother's face. He faltered back a step, then stood as still as stone.

"She loved you," I said from where I stood within the open door. "You can see it in her eyes. Old Mathilde told me once that a love that strong and pure never really dies. It lives on in all who live and remember, teaching them how to discover such a love for themselves. I try to imagine how I would feel if I had known a love like that, then had it snatched away. All my life, I've tried to understand how you could love her, and not love me.

"But when I look into her face, I cannot do it. I do not understand it at all. Constanze d'Este loved you, and all you might create together. You thought you loved her, but you loved yourself more."

I pointed to the window behind him, and, as if my gesture was a summons, my father slowly turned around.

"From that window, you can see my mother's grave, the only piece of earth on all your lands where not a single living thing will thrive. But it is not my mother's heart that is buried there. Instead, I think that it is yours."

With a cry my father whirled back, strode across the room to seize me by the arms. He pulled me to the window, turning me so that I, too, looked down.

"I have carried the image of your mother's grave with me for sixteen years," he said fiercely. "Nothing I have ever done has been able to drive it from my mind. Don't think you can stand there and lecture me. You can never understand what I have lost."

"You did not lose!" I cried, as I struck his hands away. For the first time, I thought I tasted his bitterness in my own mouth. "You gave it away of your own free will. You gave *me* away. You gave away love."

And because of it, he had wasted the span of my entire life, I thought. What might my father and I have learned together, shared together, if he had not been so swift to give up on love? Regret shot through me then, swift and sudden as the plunge of a knife straight through my heart. I staggered, and put my hand upon the windowsill. Felt my father reach to hold me up.

Oh, Mathilde, I thought. *I see what you were trying to tell me now, that day in the kitchen so long ago.*

Grief and sorrow are one and the same. But until you feel regret for what is now forever out of reach, you do not truly mourn.

Finally, I felt my anger for my father turn to ashes. I saw the desolation in his face now. Saw the way it ran bone-deep.

"I know what you wished for me," I said softly. "The one and only time you ever saw me until now. You wished that you might never see me again unless the sight of me could give you back the peace I stole. But I am not the true thief, father. You have robbed yourself. You have no peace because you cling to sorrow and to anger.

"You have no peace because you do not mourn."

"No," Etienne de Brabant answered, with a shuddering breath. "No. That cannot be right; it cannot be so."

"Go to my mother's grave," I said. "Kneel down beside it. Feel the dead grass with your hand. Place your palm on the dead trunk of the tree Constanze d'Este planted as your bride. Then tell me you have no regrets. That you do not see all the things that you have stolen from us both, but from yourself most of all.

"Then do what, in my heart, I think my mother would have wished. Make a new wish for yourself."

He released me then, his movement so unexpected that, had I not caught the back of the chair, I might have tumbled to the floor. Without a backward glance my father ran from the bedroom, down the corridor. I heard the clatter of his boots as he hastened down the great hall stairs, the sound of the front door as it opened, then slammed closed.

Slowly, I sank down in the chair, the one in which Old Mathilde had sat the night I had been born. Gazing out the window, by the light of the moon, I saw my father stagger to my mother's graveside. He fell down upon his knees, lifted his face up to the heavens as he had so many years ago. Perhaps it was some trick of the light, but I swear that, even from the second-story window, I saw the tracks of tears upon his cheeks. After almost sixteen years, my father wept beside my mother's grave, while I wept to see him, looking down.

I will make a wish for you, Father, I thought. The fourth most powerful kind of wish there is. One you make when you discover that, against all odds and appearances to the contrary, you have not quite given up hope after all.

I wish that the tears you shed may make what you wished for sixteen years ago come true. I wish you peace, at last.

Nineteen

LATE THAT NIGHT, I HEARD THE SOUND OF HORSES IN THE
courtyard. Long before then, I had moved through every room
on the ground floor in the great stone house, placing a lighted
candle in every single window, as if to guide travellers home.
Outside the moon was gold and full, its light bright enough to
read a book by.

I changed out of my bedraggled ballroom finery into one
of the dresses my stepmother and I had made over for me. With
my hair braided and pinned on top of my head, a pair of sturdy
and practical shoes on my feet, I felt like myself, once more.

"Cendrillon!" I heard Raoul's voice cry out above the sound
of the horse's hooves. "Cendrillon!"

I flung open the front door, flew down the steps. He leaped from his horse to swing me around in a great circle, my legs flying.

"I knew you would know what to do," I said. "I knew you would come."

Raoul set me on my feet. "You lighted candles just like they do in the city," he said. "It's beautiful. I didn't come alone."

It was only at that moment that I realized there were two other horses in the courtyard. Niccolo sat upon one. This, I might have expected. What I did not expect was that the third rider should be Prince Pascal. I felt my heart perform a long, slow somersault inside my chest.

"You came together," I said. "Oh, Raoul." I threw my arms around him once more.

"I may be an idiot on occasion," Raoul whispered in my ear. "But at least I can admit when I've been wrong. Besides, you are more important than any crown. Now stop hugging me. Your prince will get the wrong idea about us."

He stepped back. "Is Susanne still up?" he asked aloud.

"She is in the kitchen waiting for you," I said. "If I know her, she started frying rashers of bacon the second she heard horses' hooves in the courtyard. She took a cherry pie out of the oven not half an hour ago."

Raoul gave a shout of laughter and sprinted for the kitchen door. Niccolo tossed a leg over the saddle and slid lightly to the ground. He came to me and caught me by the hands.

"You don't look any worse for wear," he said. "It gives me joy to see that you are well."

"Thank you, Niccolo," I said. "And I hope I will be calling you brother before too long."

He leaned forward and kissed me on the cheek. "I hope so too," he replied. "Your mother and sisters send their love. They should be here sometime tomorrow. Old Mathilde is with them."

He moved past me into the house. Now, it was just Pascal and me in the courtyard. In the moonlight, I could see every plane and angle of his face, but I could not read what his expression held.

"You have just had a long, hard ride," I said at last. "Don't you at least want to get down?"

Without a word, Pascal swung down from the saddle and came toward me.

"Raoul said you would be here," he said. "That your father would bring you home."

"I don't imagine that he thought of it that way," I answered. "But Raoul was right. My mother is buried in this place. She died the night that I was born. All my life, my father has blamed me for this. He had to bring me here, I think, before he could truly decide what to do with me, or what not to do."

"Where is he?" asked Pascal.

"He is gone. He sat beside my mother's grave until the moon came up, then got on his horse and rode out the gate. I do not think any of us will ever see him again."

"So you are quite safe," Pascal said. "You've been safe for hours. You didn't really need rescuing at all."

"Maybe not," I said. "But I'm glad that you have come."

"Are you?" he asked. "Why?"

"Will you walk with me?" I said, by way of an answer. "There is something I would like to show you."

Giving me an answer of his own, Pascal offered me his arm. I took it and together we walked around the side of the house, along its length, until we reached the gate in the stone wall that was just higher than a tall man's head and led to my mother's garden. I opened the latch, pushed the gate open wide. Then I led Pascal across the soft green lawn until we reached my mother's grave.

It was covered with pumpkin vines. Pansies with brave faces. Bee balm. Every single thing that I had ever tried to grow upon my mother's grave had come to life, watered by my father's tears. Only the tree my mother had planted herself remained unchanged.

"This is the place my mother is buried," I said. "Every year, on my birthday, I have made a wish here for as long as I can recall. And what I wished for was this: that what I planted here might grow and thrive. Tomorrow is my birthday. My wish has finally come true."

"It's beautiful," Pascal said.

"It wasn't," I answered. "Not until tonight. Tonight my

father mourned my mother truly for the very first time. Old Mathilde, who raised me, said my parents loved each other from the moment they met, love at first sight. She says such a talent runs in families, and I think that she is right. For I believe that my heart knew you from the moment you first held me in your arms.

"I wish to be my mother's daughter," I said. "I will make many mistakes, have many regrets, take many risks, but I will not do what my father did. I will not turn my back on love."

"Are you saying that you love me?" Pascal said, and I felt the way his arm trembled beneath my fingers.

"Yes," I replied. "I know it's traditional for the man to speak first, especially when he's a prince, and I know that it is sudden."

"I think," Pascal said carefully, "that I would like to ask you something."

"Anything," I said.

"Will you please sit down?"

"Sit down?" I echoed, altogether stunned.

"Yes," Prince Pascal said. "Here, on this pumpkin."

"Of course I will," I said, but my heart had begun to beat with a sound like thunder. I had just told the handsome prince I'd known for less than three days that I loved him, and he had asked me to sit down upon a pumpkin. At least I knew it would be sturdy enough to hold me.

Remember what you promised yourself, Cendrillon, I thought fiercely. *Never regret love.*

"I went back," Pascal said, as he settled me upon the pumpkin. "To the ballroom. After Etienne had called me away, I got halfway to my mother's rooms and thought . . ."

All of a sudden, he began to pace, just outside the reach of the pumpkin vines. I felt my heartbeats begin to steady. He was not quite as composed as I had thought.

"I thought to myself, *You are an idiot, Pascal!*" he went on. "You've just held the girl you love, the one you know you want to marry in your arms. And what did you do? You let some smooth-talking courtier take you away, never mind the fact that he's her father. So I turned around and went back, but by then you were gone."

He stopped pacing and reached inside his coat. From an inside pocket, he removed an object wrapped in cloth. Carefully, as if what he held was infinitely precious, he pulled the cloth aside and let it flutter to the ground.

"I found this in the ballroom. You had gone, but you left this behind. And so I wonder . . ." With a graceful movement, he knelt at my feet. "I wonder if I might persuade you to try on this shoe, so that I can be certain that it fits you, and you alone. Please show me I haven't dreamed this whole thing from start to finish."

Slowly, Prince Pascal reached out. I put my right foot into his hand. He untied the laces of my sturdy, sensible shoe, then eased it off and set it gently on the ground. In its place, he slid on the slipper made of glass.

"Marry me," he said. "Please say that you will marry me, Cendrillon. Love me. Let me love you."

"Yes," I said. "Yes to all of it."

He leaned forward then, and kissed me for the second time. And as he did, I felt a band around my heart, one I had grown so accustomed to holding it in place that I no longer noticed its presence, open up, loosen its hold. And as it did, my heart flew free.

Behind us, at the head of my mother's grave, the dead tree gave a moan. Catching me to him, Pascal sprang up. With a great crack, the blackened bark split open. A great trembling seized the tree's every limb, and then the bark peeled back like the skin of an onion. Revealing strong new bark beneath, glimmering pale and fresh in the moonlight.

The whole tree seemed to give itself a shake, its limbs reaching upward as if stretching after a dream of standing motionless for far too long. And then, in a rush so full and joyous it almost made a sound, every single branch burst into bloom. Our eyes were filled with the sight of blossoms of pure silver, our noses with a scent as sweet as honey.

"This is why they say love stories end 'happily ever after,'" I whispered. For surely, if this was anything, it was the power of true love. The power to bring life and hope where none had been before.

Hand in hand, Pascal and I left my mother's garden and walked back to the front of the house. As we approached, the candles I had placed in all the downstairs windows flickered, and then went out.

And that is how I knew the truth. My story had been given the start of its happy ending at the very same time in which it had first begun: just before midnight.

The tree above my mother's grave grew and bloomed as the love Pascal and I shared together did, every single day for the rest of our lives. It is blooming there still, for all I know. For Old Mathilde had the right of things. True love never dies.

A FUNNY THING HAPPENED ON THE WAY TO THE BALL.

When my editor and I first discussed the possibility of having me add the story of Cinderella to the Once upon a Time series, I decided it would be interesting to refresh my memory about the early versions of this incredibly famous tale. So I marched to the bookshelf in search of my copy of *The Complete Tales of the Brothers Grimm*. Sure enough, "Cinderella" was there. I thought I knew, in a general sort of way, what to expect. Boy, did I get a surprise. Because almost the first thing their rendition does is to mention the fact that Cinderella's father is still alive.

Intrigued, I turned to an even earlier version, that of the French author Charles Perrault (1628–1703), generally considered the father of the modern fairy tale. Like the Grimm boys who came after him (late seventeen hundreds to mid eighteen hundreds), Perrault draws heavily on older, oral folktale traditions for his stories. Would Cinderella's father show up here as well? The answer was yes.

Okay, I thought. *Wait just a minute here.*

Both renditions do make similar points, that the father falls so under the control of his second wife that he will do whatever she wants. He then pretty much vanishes from the tale completely, leaving Cinderella's stepmother in control. But the fact that he was there at all simply proved too intriguing a notion for me to pass up.

If Cinderella's father is still alive, but takes no action to save or protect her, what might this say about both him and the woman to whom we are all accustomed to assigning the role of the bad guy? What would happen if I put a father back into the mix? With that, my own version of the story was off and running. I decided to add my own tribute to Perrault by giving my heroine the French version of her name: Cendrillon.

GOLDEN

For the staff of Magnolia's Bookstore.
This one never would have happened without you.
And for Lissa. Even when the world seems dark,
I see the way your heart shines, golden.

Prologue

IT BEGAN WITH A THEFT AND ENDED WITH A GIFT. AND IF I were truly as impossible as it once pleased Rue to claim, I'd demonstrate it now. Stop right there, I'd tell you. That's really all you need to know about the story of my life. Thank you very much for coming, but you might as well go home now.

Except there is this problem:

A beginning and an ending, though satisfying in their own individual ways, are simply that. A start and a conclusion, nothing more. It's what comes in between that does the work, that builds the life and tells the story. Believing you can see the second while still busy with the first can be a dangerous mistake, a fact of life sometimes difficult for the young to grasp. When you are young, you think your eyesight is perfect, even as it fails you and you fail to notice. It's easy to get distracted, caught up in dilemmas and questions that eventually turn out to be less important than you originally thought.

For instance, here is a puzzle that many minds have pondered: If a tree falls in the forest, and there is no one there to hear it, does it still make a sound?

When, really, much more challenging puzzles sound a good deal simpler:

How do you recognize the face of love?

Can love happen in an instant, or can it only grow slowly, bolstered by the course of time? Is it possible that love might be both? A thing that takes forever to reach its true conclusion, made possible by what occurs in no more than the blink of an eye?

Yes, I think I know the answers, for myself, at least. But then, I am no longer young. I am old now. My life has been a long and happy one, but even the longest, happiest life will, one day, draw down to its close. Fold itself up and be put away, like a favorite sweater into a cedar chest, a garment that has served well for many, many years, but now has just plain too many holes to be worn.

Don't bother to suggest that I will be immortal because my tale will continue to be told. That sort of sentiment just makes me impatient and annoyed. In the first place, because the tale you know is hardly the whole story. And in the second, because it is the tale itself that will live on, not I. I will come to an end, as all living creatures must. And when I do, what I know will perish with me.

Perhaps that is why I have the urge to speak of it now.

More and more these days, I find myself thinking back to the beginning, particularly when I am sitting in the garden. This is not surprising, I suppose. For it was in a garden that my tale began. It makes no difference that I hadn't been born yet at the time. I listen to the sound the first bees make in spring, so loud it always takes me by surprise. I sit on the bench my husband made me as a wedding gift, surrounded by the daffodils I planted with my own hands, so very long ago now. Their scent hangs around me like a curtain of silk.

I close my eyes, and I am young once more.

One

H ERE ARE THE THINGS I THINK YOU THINK YOU KNOW ABOUT
my story, for these are the ones that have often been told.

The girl I would become was the only child of a poor man
and his wife who had waited many years for any child at all to
be born. During her pregnancy, my mother developed a craving
for a particular herb, a kind of parsley. In the country in which
my parents were then living, this herb was called "rapunzel."

As luck would have it, the house next door to my parents'
home possessed a beautiful and wondrous garden. In it grew
the most delicious-looking rapunzel my mother had ever seen.
So wonderful, in fact, she decided that she could not live without it. Day after day, hour after hour, she begged my father to

procure her some. She must have that rapunzel and no other, my mother swore, or she would simply die.

There was a catch, of course. A rather large one. The garden was the property of a powerful sorceress.

This discouraged my father from simply walking up the house next door's front steps, ringing the bell, and asking politely if the garden's owner would share some of her delicious herb, which is precisely what he should have done. The front doorbell even possessed a unique talent, or so the sorceress herself later informed me. When it rang, the person who caused it to sound heard whatever tune he or she liked best.

Not that it made any difference, for no one ever rang the bell. To approach a sorceress by the front way was apparently deemed too risky. So my father did what everyone before him had done: He went in through the back. He climbed over the wall that divided the sorceress's garden from his own and stole the rapunzel.

He even got away with it—the first time around. But, though he had picked all the herb that he could carry, it was not enough for my mother. She devoured it in great greedy handfuls, then begged for more. My father took a satchel, to carry even more rapunzel, and returned to the sorceress's garden. But this time, though the herb was still plentiful, my father's luck ran out. The sorceress caught him with his hands full of rapunzel and his legs halfway up the garden wall.

"Foolish man!" she scolded. "Come down here at once!

Don't you know it's just plain stupid to climb over a sorceress's back wall and steal from her garden, particularly when she has a perfectly good front doorbell?"

At this, my father fell from the wall and to his knees.

"Forgive me," he cried. "I am not normally an ungracious thief. In fact, I'm not normally either one."

The sorceress pursed her lips. "I suppose this means you think you have a good reason for your actions," she snorted.

"I do," my father replied. "Will it please you to hear it?"

"I sincerely doubt it," the sorceress said. "But get up and tell it to me anyhow."

My father now explained about my mother's craving. How she had claimed she must have rapunzel, this rapunzel and no other, or she would simply die. And how, out of love for her and fear for the life of the child she carried, he had done what he must to obtain the herb, even though he knew that stealing it was wrong.

After he had finished, the sorceress stood silent, looking at him for what must have seemed like a very long time.

"There is no such thing as an act without consequence," she said softly, at last. "No act stands alone. It is always connected to at least one other, even if it cannot be seen yet, even if it is still approaching, over the horizon line. If you had asked me for the rapunzel, I would have given it freely, but as it is—"

"I understand," my father said, before he quite realized that he was interrupting. "You are speaking of payment. I am a poor man, but I will do my best to discharge this debt."

The sorceress was silent for an even longer time.

"I will see this wife of yours," she finally pronounced. "Then I will know what must be done."

Here are the things I know you do *not* know about my story, for, until now, they have never been told:

The woman who gave birth to me was very beautiful. Her skin was as white and smooth as cream. Her eyes, the color of bluebells in the spring. Her lips, like damask roses.

This is nothing so special in and of itself, of course.

Many women are beautiful, including those who don't resemble my mother in the slightest. But her beauty was my mother's greatest treasure, more important to her than anything else. And the feature she prized above all others was her hair, as luxuriant and flowing as a river in spring. As golden as a polished florin.

When my father brought the sorceress into the house, my mother was sitting up in bed, giving her hair its morning-time one hundred strokes with her ivory-handled brush. Even in their most extreme poverty, she had refused to part with this item.

"My dear," my father began.

"Quiet!" my mother said at once. "I haven't finished yet, and you know how I dislike being interrupted."

My father and the sorceress stood in the doorway while my mother finished counting off her strokes.

"Ninety-six, ninety-seven, ninety-eight . . ." The white-backed brush flashed through the golden hair. "Ninety-nine, one hundred. There now!"

She set down the brush and regarded her husband and the stranger with a frown. "Who is this person that you have brought me instead of the rapunzel that you promised?"

"This is the sorceress who lives next door," my father replied. "It's her rapunzel."

"Oh," said my mother.

"Oh, indeed," the sorceress at last spoke up. She walked into the room, stopping only when she reached my mother's bedside, and gazed upon her much as she had earlier gazed upon my father.

"Madam," she said after many moments. "I will make you the following bargain. Until your child is born, you may have as much rapunzel as you like from my garden. But on the day your child arrives, if it is a girl, and I very much think it will be, you must swear to love her just as she is, for that will mean you will love whatever she becomes. If you cannot, then I will claim her in payment for the rapunzel.

"Do we have a deal?"

"Yes," my mother immediately said, in spite of the fact that my father said "No!" at precisely the same moment.

The sorceress then turned away from my mother and walked to my father, laying a hand upon his arm.

"Good man," she said, "I know the cost seems high. But

have no fear. I mean your child no harm. Instead, if she comes to me, I swear to you that I will love her and raise her as my own. It may even be that you will see her again some day. My eyes are good, but even they cannot see that far, for that is a thing that will depend on your heart rather than mine."

My father swallowed once or twice, as if his throat had suddenly gone dry.

"If," he finally said.

"Just so," the sorceress replied.

And she left my parents' house and did not return until the day that I was born.

On that day my mother labored mightily to bring me into the world. After many hours, I arrived. The midwife took me and gave me my very first bath. Exhausted from her labors, my mother closed her eyes. She opened them again when I was put into her arms. At my mother's first sight of me, a thick silence filled the room. The sound of my father's boots dashing wildly up the stairs could be heard through the open bedroom door. But before he could reach his baby daughter, his wife cried out, "She is hideous! Take her away! I can never love this child!"

My father gave a great cry of anguish.

"A bargain is a bargain," the sorceress said, for she had come up the stairs right behind my father. "Come now, little one. Let us see what all the ruckus is about."

And she strode to the bedside, plucked me from my mother's arms, and lifted me up into the light. Now the whole world, if it had cared to look, could have seen what had so horrified my unfortunate maternal parent.

I had no hair at all. Absolutely none.

There was not even the faintest suggestion of hair, the soft down of fuzz that many infants possess at birth, visible only when someone does just what the sorceress was doing, holding me up to the light of the sun. I did have cheeks like shiny red apples, and eyes as dark and bright as two jet buttons. None of this made one bit of difference to my mother. She could see only that I lacked her greatest treasure: I had no hair of gold. No hair of any kind. My head was as smooth as a hard-boiled egg. It was impossible for my mother to imagine that I might grow up to be beautiful, yet not like her. She had no room for this possibility in her heart.

This lack of space was her undoing, as a mother anyway, for it separated us on the very day that I was born. And it did more. It fixed her lack so firmly upon my head that I could never shake it off. For the rest of my days, mine would be a head upon which no hair would grow.

But the sorceress simply pulled a dark brown kerchief from her own head and wrapped it around mine. At that point, I imagine I must have looked remarkably like a tiny walnut, for my swaddling was of brown homespun. Then, for a moment or two only, the sorceress turned to my father and placed me in his arms.

"Remember your words to me," my father said, when he

could speak for the tears that closed his throat. "Remember them all."

"Good man, I will," the sorceress replied. "For they are written in my heart, as they are in yours." Then she took me back and, gazing down into my face, said: "Well, little Rapunzel, let us go out into the world and discover whether or not you are the one I have been waiting for."

That is the true beginning of this, my life's true story.

Two

And so I grew up in the home of the sorceress.

Though not, it hardly need be said, in the house next door to the one in which I had been born. When I was still an infant, too young to remember such a thing, the sorceress and I moved to a place where gently rolling hills gradually grew steeper and more rocky until they became a great mountain range that divided the land from side to side.

There, in a fold of two such hills, the sorceress and I had a small, one-room house for ourselves, and a large, one-room barn for the livestock. Our house had a roof of thatch, and the barn a roof of sloping boards. We had an orchard of fruit trees climbing up one hill, with a rushing stream at its base. And, of course, we had a beautiful and prosperous herb and vegetable garden. Above all else, the sorceress dearly loved to help things grow. I suppose it could be said that I was one of them.

I learned much in the sorceress's home. She taught me to spin and sew. To sweep the floor of our small dwelling without raising up a single cloud of dust. To gather eggs, to separate them and make the yolks into a custard, and then to beat the whites so long and hard that I could bake a cake as white as snow, and as tall as our oven door.

Together, we helped the cows give birth, carded wool from our own sheep to create cloth. It was from the sorceress that I learned to climb the apple trees in our orchard. I even bested her when it came to baking apple pies. I learned to help rehatch the roof, a task I dearly loved, and to whitewash our walls, which I did not. Best of all, I learned to read and write, great gifts, not often bestowed upon girls at that time.

I also learned never to ask a question unless I truly wished to hear the answer, for the sorceress always replied honestly. I learned not to call her "mother." She would not allow it. Instead, as the sorceress called me by my name, so I called her by hers. It was my first word, in fact, and it was this: Melisande.

But of all I learned in the sorceress's home, sorcery was not a part. This is not as odd as you might suppose. Think of your own life for a moment. Are there truly no questions you con- sider asking, then reconsider, deciding you'd rather not hear the answers after all? Or perhaps the questions never even occur to you in the first place. We all grow accustomed to our lives just the way they are. For me it was a combination, I think. I'd reached the fairly advanced age of eight or nine, in fact, before I even discovered that Melisande was a sorceress at all.

It happened in this way: On a market day in late September, the sorceress hitched up our wagon and announced that we were going to the closest town. She did not like to do so, she said. Towns were filled with people, more unpredictable than spring weather. But the last of our needles had snapped in two the night before and, without replacements, we could make no winter clothes.

"Tie your kerchief tightly around your head, Rapunzel," she said. "I will do the same."

No woman or girl went with her head uncovered in those days. It simply wasn't proper. To make sure that I had tied my own kerchief to her satisfaction, Melisande reached down and gave the knot a tug. I opened my mouth to ask why our kerchiefs needed particular attention on this particular day, then closed it again, having said nothing at all. As an interesting side benefit of learning which questions to ask and which to keep to myself, I had developed the ability to answer many on my own.

It has to do with the fact that my head is different, I thought. I would learn much more about what this meant before the day was done. In the meantime, however, I was excited, for, though

Melisande had sometimes spoken of such places, I had never seen a town before.

The day was fine. By the time we reached the market square, I had a crick in my neck from trying to turn it in every direction all at the same time. I had never seen so many people assembled in one place, nor imagined how many buildings it might take to house them all. Our horse's shoes made an unfamiliar sound on the cobblestone streets.

In the center of the town stood a great open square, completely filled with stalls selling goods of every imaginable kind. Through them, I could just catch a glimpse of green grass in the very center, and the tall brick sides of a well. Water was at the heart of every town, Melisande had explained as we'd ridden along. Without water, there could be no life.

She found a place to stable the horse and cart, and we set off for the stalls.

"Stay close to me, Rapunzel," Melisande said. "The town is a big place. It would be easy for you to lose yourself."

"I won't get lost," I replied. Which, as I'm sure you've already noticed for yourself, was not quite the same as giving a promise.

For a while, though, the point was moot. I was content to stay at the sorceress's side. Wonderful and exotic goods filled the market stalls, or so it seemed to me at the time. Only the fruit and vegetable stalls failed to tempt me. They didn't hold a candle to what we grew at home. Eventually, however, Melisande fell to haggling over the price of needles, and I grew bored. I took one step from her side, and then another. By the time I had taken half a dozen, I had broken the invisible tether that tied me to her and been swallowed up by the crowd.

Even then, I had no fear of getting lost. I knew right where I was going: to that patch of green at the very center. I wanted to see what the heart of a town truly looked like. I can't say quite what I was expecting, though I can say it wasn't what I found. On the lush green grass in the center of the square, a group of town children were playing a game that involved running and kicking a ball. It was just a blown-up pig's bladder, no more special than balls I had played with myself, but it was tied with a strip of cloth more blue than any sky.

At this sight, my heart gave a great leap. I was a fast runner and knew well how to kick a ball. I had dreamed many dreams in my small warm bed at night, and wished upon many a star. The wish I had breathed most often had been for playmates. So when the ball tied with that bright cloth abruptly sailed my way, I did not hesitate, but kicked it straight to the player my eyes had gone to first and lingered on the longest: a tall lad several years older than I. Right on the cusp of being a young man. If it hadn't been a market day, he probably wouldn't have been playing at such games at all.

Instantly, my action caused a great hue and cry; of joy on the part of the lad and his team, and outrage on the part of his opponents. For, until the moment I had intervened, the ball had been in their possession, and they'd looked fair to win the day.

"Oh, well done!" the lad cried. "Now let's show 'em! Come on!"

I joined the game, running for all I was worth, which turned out to be a great deal, for I was small. Like a minnow in a stream, I slipped in and out of places larger fish could not go. The catastrophe occurred in just this way, as I attempted to dive with the ball through the legs of the captain of the opposing team. He pulled his legs together, trapping me between them, then reached down to capture the ball.

This, he missed, for I managed to give it a great push and send it flying. His fingers found my kerchief instead. With one hard yank, he pulled it off. The fact that I had tied the knots so carefully and tightly that morning made not one bit of difference.

My head was exposed.

The boy gave a great yelp and leaped back. Instantly the game stopped. So profound a silence fell over each and every child that the adults in the closest stalls noticed, stopped their work, and came to see what had caused the lack of commotion. Before I could so much as reach for my kerchief, I found myself completely surrounded by curious, hostile eyes.

Eight years had changed some things about the top of my head. It was no longer white, but brown, from spending time in the sun. Its most significant feature, however, hadn't changed a bit: It was still completely smooth, and I completely bald.

I could feel a horrible flush spread up my neck and over my

face, one that had absolutely nothing to do with the fact that I'd just been running hard. I sat as still as I possibly could, praying that the earth would miraculously open up and swallow me whole.

It didn't, as I hardly need tell you. Instead, somebody stepped forward: the lad who had first encouraged me to join the game. He didn't look so enthusiastic now. His eyes, which I suddenly noticed were the same color blue as the cloth around the ball, had gone wide. The expression on his face was flat and blank, as if he was trying to give away nothing of what he might be feeling, particularly if that thing was fear. This I instantly understood, for I knew that to show fear was to give your opponent an advantage you frequently could not afford.

"Why do you look that way?" he asked. "What did you do wrong?"

"Nothing," I answered swiftly, responding to the second question and ignoring the first entirely.

"You must have done something," he countered at once. "You must have. You don't look right."

"No one knows that better than I do," I answered tartly. "I'm bald, not stupid or blind."

"Perhaps she is a changeling," another voice suddenly spoke up, a grown-up's this time. At these words, the entire crowd sucked in a single breath, after which many voices began to cry out, all at once.

"Stay away from her!"

"Don't touch her!"

"Pick her up and throw her in the well! That'll show us what she's made of. That's the test for witches."

"Enough!"

At the sound of this final voice, all others fell silent. I saw the crowd ripple, the way the rows of corn in our garden do when the wind strikes them. Then the crowd parted and through it stepped Melisande.

The expression on her face was one I'd never seen before: grief and fury and regret so mixed together it was almost impossible to tell them apart. Without a word, she walked to my side and helped me to my feet. Then she stooped and retrieved my kerchief from the ground.

"It seems those knots weren't quite as tight as we supposed," she said, for my ears alone, as she worked them free and wrapped the kerchief around my head once more. Her face was set as she tied a new set of knots herself, but her fingers were as gentle as always.

"I'm sorry," I said. "I didn't mean for it to happen."

"Of course you didn't," she replied. "There's no need for you to be sorry. You're not the one who should apologize."

At this, she turned back to face the crowd.

It's hard to describe precisely what happened then. Later I realized that I had been given my first real glimpse of sorcery. As Melisande gazed upon them, many in the crowd cried out. Some fell to their knees and covered their faces with their hands, while others stood perfectly still, as if they had been turned to stone. In the end, though, they were all the same in one thing: Each and every one of them looked down. No person there assembled could hold the sorceress's eyes with their own.

Then she glanced down at me, and it seemed to me as if my heart would rise straight up out of my chest. All my fears were laid bare, and my hopes also. A voice in the back of my mind instructed me to look away or I would have no secrets left, but I did not. What had I to conceal? This was not some stranger, who saw only my own strangeness. This was the woman who had raised me since my birth. The only one I knew and trusted. This was Melisande.

And so I held her eyes and did not look away. After a moment, she smiled. I smiled back, and at this, my heart resumed its proper place and all was right once more.

"I thought so," she said, as she turned back to the crowd. "This girl has more courage than any of you. Have no fear. We will not come amongst you again. But I think there will be many of you who will now come to seek me out."

Then she reached down for my hand, I reached up to place mine within hers, and, together, we made our way back through the crowd. It wasn't until we were almost through it that any-one made a sound at all. And even then, it was just a single word muttered under the breath.

"Sorceress."

I stumbled, my feet abruptly growing clumsy, but Melisande's footsteps never faltered at all, though she did stop walking.

"Fearmonger," she replied. "Coward, I see what is in your heart. Be careful what you sow there, for it may prove to be your only harvest, and a bitter one at that."

She did not speak again until we reached our own door. But though I stayed as silent as she, that single word, *sorceress*, rang in my head all the way home.

Three

In the years that followed, some things changed.

Others did not.

The hair on Melisande's head got a little longer and began to turn gray. I turned first nine, then ten, and finally, in their proper times and places, eleven, twelve, and thirteen, and all the while the top of my head stayed as bald as any egg I could find in our henhouse.

I did blister it badly with sunburn the year I was ten, having refused to wear a kerchief or hat in a fit of pique over something I cannot now recall. But aside from that, it didn't change a bit. Mine remained a head upon which no hair would grow.

My eyes, however, functioned just fine, and I began to

keep them peeled for additional signs of sorcery, watching Melisande when I was sure she didn't notice (though of course she did—not because she was a sorceress but because she was a grown-up).

She kept her eyes on me; I wasn't quite sure why. But I finally figured out that she undoubtedly saw me watching her, because I began to notice that *she* was watching *me*. Her face would take on a sort of considering expression from time to time, as if she were weighing the image of me her eyes presented with one she was holding in her mind. Each and every time, at the precise moment I decided she had finally made up her mind to speak of whatever was in it, she looked away and said nothing at all.

But the biggest change of all, I suppose, was that after that day in the town, we were no longer quite as alone as we had been before.

Melisande had been quite right when she predicted that the fact that people knew there was a sorceress in their general vicinity would draw them to her, even if they were not always quite convinced that it was altogether safe for them to come. Word of her presence and her power spread, and, as it did, more and more visitors began to appear at our door.

At our back door, to be precise, which always made me smile. It made no difference that a perfectly good road came right up to our front gate. Every single person who traveled to see us for the purposes of sorcery preferred to present themselves at the back door. Some knocked loudly, boldly demanding entry. Others merely scratched, as if, even as they asked for admittance, they were second-guessing themselves and wishing they were on their way back home.

How does sorcery work, where you come from?

For I have learned, since that day in the village green when I first discovered its presence in the world at all, that the workings of sorcery are not universal. They have to do with the individual who performs them. Sometimes her powers exist to fill a great need in the land in which she lives. Other times they exist to fill a need within the sorceress herself. More often than not, of course, it's likely to be both. For sorcery is no simple thing, though simpletons often think it so.

The gift of sorcery that Melisande possessed was this: to see into the hearts of others even when they themselves could not, and to show them what she saw.

That was what she had done that day on the village green, what had caused every single person present to drop his or her eyes. She had looked into their hearts and seen their fear of me, of what I looked like, and their desire to cast me out because of it. And she had done more. For she had both seen and revealed the villagers' deepest, most secret fear of all: that my presence among them might prove infectious, bringing down upon their own heads the fate they wished for me, regardless of whether the heads in question had hair on them or not.

Some were horrified to discover their hearts could hold such feelings and fears. Others knew they were there full well and were horrified at having been found out. In the end, though, it made no difference: Not one was able to meet the message of her or his heart as seen within the sorceress's gaze. Each and every person dropped their eyes.

After such an inauspicious beginning, you might think no one would want to come to see us. But this was far from true. There were many, or so it seemed, who were willing to brave the sorceress's gaze to catch a glimpse of the innermost workings of their own hearts, never mind that it might be said they should have been figuring out a way to do this for themselves.

"Why do they come?" I finally asked one day, after a particularly disastrous departure.

A young woman, one of the loveliest I had ever seen, her beautiful features streaked with tears, had come barreling out the back door just as I had been on the point of coming in with a basket of apples from the orchard. I stepped back quickly to avoid her and lost my footing, which sent me to the ground and the basket and its contents flying.

Well, I guess I'll be making applesauce instead of pies tonight, I thought.

"What did you show her, the end of her beauty?" I asked crossly as Melisande appeared in the doorway. Together we watched the young woman hurry away, the sound of her sobs drifting back over her shoulder. "I recognize that look. It's disappointed hopes. A few more years of that and no one will remember she was beautiful in the first place. What on earth do they expect you to do for them, anyhow?"

"That is a very good question, my Rapunzel," answered Melisande. She knelt beside me and began to help me retrieve the apples, the bruises already showing on their skins. "And one I wish these fools would ask themselves before they come."

Her words startled me, I must admit. She rarely spoke of those who sought her help, never passed judgement on them. I stayed quiet, gathering up the apples. I'd asked more questions than usual, but I knew that, sooner or later, she would answer them all, and answer them honestly. That was the way things worked around our house.

"They come," the sorceress said at last, "because they confuse seeing a thing with understanding it, and they believe that my true power lies in the bestowing of this shortcut."

"Then they are idiots, as well as lazy," I snorted. "For the first lies within your power, it is true, but the second may or may not. And either way, it makes no difference. A shortcut may be fine if you're walking through a field, but it hardly seems in order when you're dealing with the heart."

"Well spoken on all counts," Melisande said, and at this she smiled. "I had not thought to have you follow in my footsteps, but perhaps I should reconsider. With thinking like that, you have all the makings of a first-class sorceress."

"No, thank you," I said. "I think I'm odd enough." A quick

silence fell. *Oh, excellent, Rapunzel,* I thought. *That was nicely done.* "Not that I think you're odd," I added.

"Don't be ridiculous," Melisande said. "Of course I am. I'm a sorceress, aren't I?"

"I have heard that," I said. "Though I haven't felt the need to test it for myself."

I saw the considering expression come into her face then. *Aha!* I thought. *Perhaps now I will know.*

But the sorceress simply picked up the basket, got to her feet, and said: "I'll peel the apples. The peelings will make a nice treat for the pigs. Perhaps there will be enough for pies tomorrow."

And so I learned no more on that day, and the very next, Mr. Jones came into our lives.

I have told you that I learned many things from Melisande, the exception being sorcery itself. But here I must confess one failure. No matter how hard or how often Melisande tried to teach me, I could never learn to tell one plant in the garden from another, let alone what they were called.

I was not entirely hopeless, of course. I could do the large and obvious things. I could tell an apple from a raspberry; cauliflower from corn. But when it came to knowing things by the shapes of their leaves, by what they smelled like when you plucked them and rubbed them between your palms, even whether a plant was a weed or whether it was not, these things I simply could not keep straight in my mind.

On the day that Mr. Jones came into our lives, I was working among the rows of vegetables where, insteading of ridding the carrots of weeds as I should have, I rid the weeds of carrots by pulling up every single seedling, carefully and methodically, one by one. When I realized my mistake, I sat back on my heels with a sharp cry of dismay, which caused Melisande to appear at the back door. It was open, for the day was warm and fine.

"What is it?" she called. She didn't actually say, "this time," but then she didn't need to. I could hear it in her voice like the chime of a bell.

"Carrots," I admitted, and saw her wince, for carrots were a highly useful vegetable, good in summer, autumn, and winter alike.

"All of them?" she inquired.

"All of them," I nodded.

Even at the distance from the garden to the back door, I heard her sigh. She came over to hunker down beside me, surveying the damage.

"Perhaps it is to be expected," she murmured after a while. More to herself than to me, really. I think this may have been what finally broke open a place inside me. A place I had always suspected, but been not quite certain I wished to acknowledge, for it was a place of anger and confusion.

"You mean because I'm named for a plant in the garden?" I asked tartly. "In that case, why didn't you encourage my mother to name me for something inanimate and impossible to kill, like a cutting board or a set of fireplace tongs?"

"You'd only have dropped them on your foot, or had some other accident," Melisande replied. Her voice sounded calm, but I could see the surprise flicker across her face. "And it was not your mother who named you Rapunzel," she continued. "It was I."

Just for a moment, I felt the world tilt. This is what happens when something truly takes you by surprise. Not that I hadn't been asking about my parents, because of course, I had been. The sorceress and I had carefully avoided the topic until now, which was as much my doing as hers. For, if I asked, I knew that she would answer, and answer honestly. This fact of life had made me very careful about what I asked, and what I did not.

"Why did you name me Rapunzel?" I inquired, after what felt like a very long moment.

Melisande was silent herself, for a moment that felt even longer than mine.

"Because it seemed the proper choice at the time," she finally replied. "Your mother ate large quantities of it before you were born. I first met your father, in fact, when I caught him stealing great handfuls of rapunzel from my garden."

"So my name is a punishment then," I said.

"Don't be silly," Melisande said. "Of course not."

I stared down the row of carrots, their tiny green tops already wilting now that they were no longer in the ground.

"Why do I live with you? Are my parents dead? Didn't they want me?"

There. I had done it. Asked the three most important and difficult questions, the ones I'd hidden away within that space I hadn't even been certain was there inside me. And I'd asked them all at once. If I could survive the answers to these, I had to figure I could survive almost anything.

"You live with me because I love you," Melisande said. "And your parents are still living, as far as I know."

"You left one out," I said, when she stopped speaking. "They didn't want me, did they? That's the real reason you took me in."

"Ah, my Rapunzel," Melisande said on a sigh. She looked up for a moment, her eyes on mine. "When you are a little older, you will realize that not all questions have such simple answers."

"That doesn't mean I won't ask them anyway," I said, at which she smiled.

"No. I'm quite certain it does not. Nor am I saying you should, just so you know. You'll soon learn for yourself that even the simplest question can be complicated, and the answer to it even more so. But very well, since you have asked, I will tell you what I know. Your mother was a very beautiful woman, but her heart was less lovely than her face, for it had room for only one."

"My father," I guessed at once.

"No," Melisande answered in a quiet voice. "Your mother's heart had room in it for herself alone. When I saw this, I did the only thing I could. I made room for you inside my own heart. There you have stayed from that day to this. That is why you live in my house: because you lived first within my heart."

I felt my own heart start to thump at this. Her words had brought me pain and joy. In all fairness, I had asked for both.

"It's because I'm bald, isn't it?" I asked. "That's the reason she didn't want me."

"Yes," Melisande said. I felt a great roaring start to fill my head. "And no," the sorceress went on, at which the roaring stopped. "When your mother looked at you, what she wished to see was a version of her own beauty. She could not see who you might become. It was this emptiness in her that caused her to turn you away. Your bare head is the true reflection of your mother's heart."

"Well, that's not fair at all," I said.

"No," Melisande answered. "It is not. But you are not the first example of the faults of the parents being visited upon the children, nor will you be the last."

"That's comforting," I said. "Thank you very much. What about my father?" I asked after a moment. "Where was he when all this was going on?"

"Your father loves you as much as anything in the world," Melisande replied. "But he could not interfere. He had done a thing that he should not have, and a bargain is a bargain."

"Where are my parents? Will I ever see them again?"

"Those are questions to which I do not know the answers. I am sorry, my Rapunzel."

Well, that's that, I thought. I'd asked, and she had answered. Now I knew, and life would go on.

"That's all right," I said at last. "Perhaps I will go to look for them myself, for my father at least, when I am old enough. In the meantime, I think I will be content to remain what I have always been."

"And what is that?" Melisande asked.

"Just what you have said I am. Your Rapunzel," I replied.

"My Rapunzel," Melisande said. And, for the first time that I could remember, I saw that she had tears in her eyes.

"What on earth is that?" I suddenly said.

"What?"

"That," I said. "That sound."

The sorceress cocked her head. The air was filled with it now. A noise that sounded like a set of pots and pans, doing their best to impersonate a set of wind chimes.

"I haven't the faintest idea," Melisande said. "Why don't you go and find out?"

"At least we know one thing," I said, as I got to my feet.

"And what is that?"

"Whoever it is, they haven't come for sorcery. They're at the front door."

The sound of Melisande's laughter followed me all the way around the side of the house.

Four

THERE WAS A WAGON IN OUR FRONT YARD, THE LIKES OF WHICH I had never seen before. Behind the driver's seat was what looked for all the world like a house made of canvas. It had a pitched canvas roof and four sturdy canvas sides. One of them actually seemed to have a window cut out of it. Lashing ropes held the sides in place, but I thought I could see how they could be raised as well, causing the house to disappear entirely when the weather stayed fine.

Along each of the sides dangled the strangest assortment of items I had ever seen. On the side nearest to me was a set of pots and pans, with a set of wind chimes right beside them. *Well, that explains the sound*, I thought. Though why a wagon such as this should have arrived at our front door, I could not possibly imagine.

"If you're looking for the town, you're on the wrong road," I said, then bit down hard on the tip of my tongue. There's a reason you're not supposed to say the very first thing that comes into your head. If you don't take the time to think through your words, you end up being rude just as often as not.

But the man in the wagon simply pushed the hat back on his head and looked me up and down. He had a round face with a pleasant expression, for all that it was deeply lined by the sun. A set of ginger whiskers just beginning to go gray sprouted from his chin. Hair the same color peeked out from under the brim of his hat. Beneath ginger eyebrows were eyes as black and lustrous as mine.

At the moment they were blinking, rapidly, the way you do when you are trying not to cry, or you step outside on a summer's day, then step right back again because the light out there was brighter than you thought.

"I am not looking for the town," the stranger finally replied, and I found that I liked the sound of his voice. It was low and warm, a good voice for storytelling, or so I suddenly thought. "But if I were, I would know where to find it," he went on. "I am good at knowing how to get where I am going. You could say it's a necessary part of my job."

"And what is that, exactly?" I inquired.

At this, the expression on his face, which had seemed highly changeable at first, settled down and became one I recognized: surprise.

"Have you never seen a tinker before?"

"Why would I be asking if I had?" I said, then flushed, for that was twice in a row I had been rude now. But the tinker did not seem to take offense. Instead he simply tilted his head to one side, as if he were a bird and I a worm he was trying to figure out the best way to tug from the ground.

"What is your name, young one?" he inquired.

"Rapunzel," I replied. "And I'm thirteen, just so you know." And it was only as I felt my name in my own mouth that I realized that I had never had to answer this question before, for no one had ever inquired of me who I was.

To my surprise, the tinker's face changed once again, this time growing as flushed as mine. His hands tightened upon the reins still resting in his lap, so that the horse that pulled the wagon whinnied and tried to back up into the wagon itself. At this, the tinker dropped the reins, got down from his place, and moved to the horse's side. He soothed her with gentle voice and hands and produced a carrot from deep within some hidden pocket.

"You are skilled in plant lore, then?" he asked at last. His face had resumed its former color, though he did not look at me again. Instead, his eyes intent upon his task, he offered the carrot to the horse on one flat palm.

I gave a snort.

"Far from it. As a matter of fact, I'm completely hopeless. I've just spent the morning yanking up every single carrot in the garden. Not on purpose, though," I added quickly.

At this, the tinker's face began a war with itself. I realized what the battle was about when he lost it and began to smile.

"Perhaps I might interest you in a packet of seeds, then," he suggested, as the horse finished up its treat and began to nuzzle at the tinker's legs for more. "To help you recover from your losses of this morning. To have no carrots is a terrible thing. What will you do for stew in the wintertime?"

"That's a very good question," I said. "And one I'm sure Melisande has been pondering."

"Melisande," the tinker echoed. "That is your mother?"

"No," I answered honestly. "But I love her as if she were, which makes her much the same thing, I suppose. If you will step around the back of the house, I will take you to her, and draw you a dipper of water from our well. You must be thirsty, and your horse as well. If you've come down our road, you have come a long way, even if you weren't trying to end up in the town."

"Well said," Melisande's voice suddenly floated across the yard. "I'm pleased to see you finally remembered your manners."

At the sound of her voice, the tinker looked up and found the place where Melisande stood. I held my breath. The tinker held the sorceress's eyes. And it seemed to me, in the moments that followed, that I caught my second glimpse of sorcery.

The very air around us seemed to change, solidifying and becoming thick and glossy. It reminded me of the pieces of glass that Melisande and I had swept up last winter, when a limb from one of the apple trees had come loose and been blown all the way across the orchard, only to come crashing down against the windowpanes of our greenhouse. The broken pieces were just the way the air was now. Thick and clear enough to see right through, but also sharp enough to cut you.

"Good day to you, sorceress," the tinker said finally.

"And to you, traveler," Melisande responded. "You have come a long way, I think."

"I have," the tinker acknowledged. "But I do not mind the miles, for I think that, in this place, they will now be well rewarded."

The air began to waver, then. Rippling like water.

"As to that, I cannot say," Melisande answered softly. "But I will say this: I hope it may be so. In the meantime, however, I can say this much more: Wherever we dwell, you will be welcome."

And, just like that, the air returned to normal. It was, in fact, so completely like itself that I found myself wondering if I had imagined the entire episode. The air does not change its substance, as a general rule. Unless you count things like rain or snow.

"Your words are both kind and honest," the tinker said. "A

difficult combination to manage, I think. I thank you for them."

You didn't imagine anything, Rapunzel, I thought. For, even though my young ears were young, they could still detect that there was much more being said here than what was being spoken.

"I will see to your horse, if you like," I offered.

"Thank you," the tinker said with a nod.

But as I went to free the horse from its tracings, a commotion occurred within the wagon, a great caterwauling of sound. A moment later, a small orange kitten burst out the front, as if fired from a gun. It took two great leaps, landing first upon the horse's back, and then upon my shoulder.

Once there, it turned swiftly, hissing and spitting, just in time to face a long-nosed terrier that thrust its head out from between the fabric at the wagon's entrance and began to bark in its best imitation of a larger, more ferocious dog.

"I don't suppose you'd care to have a cat?" the tinker inquired over the sound.

As the kitten's claws dug into my neck, I winced and met Melisande's eyes. Our old mouser, Timothy, had died over the winter, and I missed him sorely, though the mice did not.

"Rapunzel," Melisande said.

"Thank you," I said, on a great rush of delight. "We'd love one." Precisely as if the kitten had understood my words, it removed its claws from my neck, turned around twice more, then sat down upon my shoulder, as if ending up right there had been its intention all along, and began to lick one ginger paw.

"Excellent. That's settled, then," the tinker replied. He moved to silence the terrier, who was well on its way to yapping itself hoarse.

"Rapunzel," Melisande said. "Perhaps you should introduce the cat to the barn."

"What will you name him?" the tinker called after me. The terrier, feeling it had won the day, retired back inside the wagon and order was restored.

I turned and regarded the tinker's ginger whiskers for a moment. I had never been offered the opportunity to name a living thing before. It was a big responsibility, and I wanted to make the right choice.

"How are you called?" I finally asked, as an idea took shape in my mind.

"Mr. Jones."

"Then that's what I'll call him, too," I said. "So that I may always remember you for this gift. Also, your hair is the same color."

At this the tinker gave a laugh, Melisande smiled, and I knew I had done well. And that is how I acquired two new friends in the very same day, and both of them named Mr. Jones.

Late that night I came suddenly awake, my body sitting straight up in the darkness before my mind had the chance to understand why. I stayed still for a moment, listening hard with both my ears. I had not been prone to nightmares, even when I was small. So it never once occurred to me that I might have been roused by some phantom. If I had awakened, it was for a good cause.

I listened to Melisande's quiet breathing, coming from across the room. The tinker, Mr. Jones, had shared our supper and was now asleep in his own wagon, which still stood in our front yard. I heard the wind moving through the trees in the orchard, the faint clank it raised from the items on the tinker's wagon. *Not these*, I thought. For these had helped lull me to sleep in the first place. And that was when I heard it: the stamp and blow of the horses in the barn.

In a flash I had thrown back the covers and leaped out of bed, causing the kitten, Mr. Jones, to send up a protesting meow. I snatched up the clogs that always sat by the side of my bed when my feet weren't in them, and moved swiftly to the front door. There I slipped the clogs on, pulled my shawl from its peg, and tossed it over my head and shoulders. Then I opened the door as quietly as I could and eased out into the yard.

The tinker's wagon was a great lumpen shape in the moon-light. I could hear the horses more clearly now. I had put the tinker's horse in with our own, so that they might be company for one another. I might be a total loss when it came to the garden, but I was good with animals of all kinds. And so I knew the cause of the sounds as clearly as if the horses had spoken and told me what was happening themselves.

There was an intruder in the barn.

You will wonder, I suppose, why I didn't take the time to summon Melisande or Mr. Jones. But the simple truth is that, in the heat of the moment, it never even occurred to me. I was the one who had heard the horses. It was up to me to settle the situation on my own. If I had been older, I might have recognized my own danger and taken an indirect approach. But I was young, and the shortest distance between two points was still a straight line. And so I marched straight over to the barn and slid its great door open as far as I could. For if there is one thing upon which a thief relies, it is stealth.

"You'd better get away from those horses," I said in a loud, strong voice. "Or I'll make you. I can do that, you know. I'm a powerful sorceress."

"You are not."

I'm not sure which one of us jumped the higher, me or the boy. For that's who it was inside the barn. A lad, a year or so older than I was by the look I got of him in the moonlight. Chin lifted in defiance, though I noticed he was not quite as close to the horses as I thought he'd been when I first opened the barn door. Even the threat of sorcery will do that to a person.

"Am too," I said. "I'll prove it if you don't watch out."

"You're not the sorceress," he insisted. "The other one is. Be quiet, will you? Just come in and close the door. I'm not stealing anything, I promise."

"Only because I caught you before you could," I said right back. But I did step in and slid the door partly closed behind me. To this day, I can't quite say why. There was something in his expression that I recognized, I think. Some sort of longing, mixed in with all that defiance.

"Well?" I said. "I'm waiting for an explanation."

He put his hands on hips at this. "And you can keep on waiting. Just who do you think you are?"

"I could ask you the same question," I remarked. "In fact, I think I have the right. You're the one standing in my barn."

"I'm Harry," he said, after a moment's consideration. "And I'm running away."

"In that case, I'm Rapunzel," I said. "And not with our horse, you're not."

"I'll take the tinker's horse, then," the lad named Harry offered. "He'll never miss it. He has lots of other things."

"He most certainly will miss her," I said, for the horse was a mare, and in the course of the afternoon I had grown fond of her. "Particularly when he has to pull the cart himself." I took a step closer, studying Harry's features. "Why should you wish to steal from the tinker? He seems nice enough."

"He took me away from my parents," he said, after a slight hesitation.

"What?"

"It's true. He did," Harry blustered.

"No," I said. "That can't be right. Or even if it is, there must be more. If he was as evil as that, Melisande would have seen it in his heart. She never would have let him into our house or fed him our food."

And I remembered, suddenly, the way Mr. Jones had made Melisande smile by patting his belly at the end of the meal and remarking mournfully that the food was so good he hated to leave any behind. She'd fixed him a plate to take out to the wagon. I had a feeling I knew now who it had really been for. But to think of the tinker keeping this lad a prisoner inside the wagon just didn't make sense.

"Tell me the whole truth right now," I demanded. "Or I'll scream very loudly. Then you'll have even more explaining to do."

"They were dead," Harry said quickly, whether to prevent me from making good on my threat or because it was the only way he could get the information out, I couldn't quite tell. "Of the sweating sickness. No one else would take me, for fear that I had it as well. I did, in fact."

"So the tinker did you a great service," I said, not bothering to hide the outrage in my voice. "He saved your life. And to repay him for this kindness, you wish to steal his horse and run off."

"I do not want to be a tinker's boy!" Harry suddenly burst out. "I want to go back to the way things were! I—"

Without warning, his face seemed to crumple, for all that he was older than I was.

"I want a home," he whispered. "And they make fun of me

in the towns. The other boys laugh and call me names. If I stay with the tinker, I'll never have any friends. I'd be better off on my own."

"You wouldn't, you know," I said quietly. "If you are different, it's better to have someone who cares for you, who looks out for you. It's better not to be alone."

"What would you know about it?" Harry said.

In answer, I let the shawl fall back from my head. Absolute stillness filled the barn. Not even the animals moved, or the dust motes in the shafts of moonlight.

"Did she do that to you?" Harry asked at last. "The sorceress?"

"Don't be ridiculous," I said. "She loves me. I don't know how it happened, as a matter of fact. It's just the way things are."

He took a step closer then, studying me as I'd studied him earlier. "How do you know?"

"How do I know what?"

"That she loves you," Harry replied.

"Because I asked her and she told me so," I answered. "And she always tells the truth. She has to, I think. It's related to her sorcery."

"Where are your parents?" Harry asked.

I shook my head. "I don't know. Melisande said my mother's heart had no room in it for me, and so she did the only thing she could: She made room inside her own. Perhaps it is the same with the tinker, did you stop to think of that? Maybe he's made room for you inside his heart. He might be sad if you went off and left him, and took his horse into the bargain."

"I doubt it," Harry said with a snort. "I'm not the easiest person to get along with."

"No, really?" I asked. And suddenly he smiled. He sat down on the floor and put his back against the door of the stall where I'd put the tinker's mare. She leaned over and lipped the top of his head.

"So we are both orphans, then, after a fashion," he said, as he reached up to stroke her long nose.

"I suppose we are," I acknowledged. I stood where I was for several more minutes, watching Harry with the horse, then went to sit on a bale of hay nearby.

"Does the tinker come this way often?" he asked, when I was seated.

"I have no idea," I said. "I never saw him until today, but we're hardly on the main road."

He kept his face angled downward, making it difficult to read his expression. "But if he did come back this way, he might stop, and you might be here?"

"We've lived here for as long as I can remember," I said. "We have no plans to leave, as far as I know."

"That might be all right, then," Harry said.

"It might be," I acknowledged. I stood up after a moment. "There's plenty of hay in the loft," I said. "Though I could get you a blanket, if you like."

"No, but I thank you," Harry said. "I'm sure hay will be enough."

"Good night, then, Harry," I said.

"Good night to you, Rapunzel. That means something, doesn't it?"

"It's a kind of parsley," I confessed. "To tell you the truth, it tastes pretty awful, but that's just my opinion."

He waited until I was all the way across the barn before he spoke again.

"What makes you so sure I won't steal the horse after you're gone?"

"Because you love her," I said. "And I have seen how much she loves the tinker. You can figure out the rest for yourself."

It wasn't until I was all the way back to the house that I realized my head was still bare, and I hadn't thought about it once.

Five

Harry stayed with the tinker, of course. In the years that followed—three of them, to be precise, until I turned sixteen and Harry a year or so older than that—as often as their ramblings permitted, the tinker and the young man stopped at our door. Mr. Jones liked to say he was calling upon his namesake, who had grown up sleek and fat and as copper as a penny and was the terror of every rodent for miles around.

The tinker himself grew slightly less ginger and somewhat more gray, while Harry shot up like a great weed that even I would have been able to recognize for what it was. For I had often heard Melisande say that it was the weeds that grew the strongest, the fastest, and the tallest, and Harry grew up both strong and tall.

His eyes, which I hadn't been able to see all that well in the barn that night, turned out to be a startling green, the same color as the leaves the apple trees put out in the springtime. His hair was the color of rich river mud. I never tired of reminding him of this second fact, just as he never tired of remarking in return that surely it was better to be blessed with even mud-colored hair than to be cursed with none.

We stared at each other, the first time he and the tinker returned. To tell you the truth, I don't think either of us truly expected to see the other again, for all the words that we had spoken. I'd thought of him often enough, though, and I wondered if he had thought of me. The two orphans.

"So, you are still here, Parsley."

As it happened, we were standing in the garden. After the great carrot disaster, Melisande had tried a new technique. Each row was clearly labeled with a little drawing of what the plant should look like, with its name written beneath. So far it seemed to be working. I was better both at their names and at pulling out what I was supposed to rather than what I was not.

"That was never much in doubt," I answered as tartly as I could. For the truth was, I was pleased to see him, but I knew it would never do to let him know this right off. "You were the one who was planning to steal a horse and run away, as I recall. And my name is Rapunzel."

"That's right. I remember now," he said. And then he flashed me a smile.

Oh ho, so that is the way of the world, I thought. For it seemed to me that, just beneath the skin of that smile, I could see the man that he would one day become. He was going to be a heartbreaker, at the rate he was going. I would have to make sure he didn't break mine.

"You came back," I said. "I wasn't all that certain that you would."

"Neither was I," he answered honestly. "But I kept remembering the things you'd said. Besides, I was curious." He shrugged.

"About what?"

"I thought maybe you'd grow some hair in my absence."

"I hate to disappoint you," I said, as I plucked off my garden hat to reveal the head underneath. "But I did not."

"I'm not disappointed," Harry said. "I brought something for you."

And it was only at that moment that I realized he'd been holding one hand behind his back.

"You brought me something?" I asked, astonished. So astonished that I forgot to put the hat back on my head.

"There's no need to get carried away," Harry said quickly, as if my reaction was cause for alarm. "It's just a piece of cloth. That's all."

He held it out, and I moved forward to take it from him.

He was right. It was, indeed, just a piece of cloth. But the cloth was the finest muslin I had ever seen, embroidered all over with gold-petaled flowers. They stood stiffly out from dark centers the exact same color as my eyes. The stitches were so fine and close, I could hardly see the muslin underneath.

"I know what these are," I said, and I couldn't have kept the delight from my voice if I'd tried. "These are black-eyed Susans. They're my favorite flowers. How did you know?"

"What makes you think I did?" Harry asked. He began to stand first on one foot, and then the other, shifting his weight from side to side. "Maybe I just guessed and got it right, or chose it on a whim."

I looked up then, confused by his tone. He was sounding awfully surly and aggressive for someone offering a gift.

"It wouldn't matter if you had," I answered carefully but honestly. "I don't get gifts all that often."

He stood stock-still at this. "What's that supposed to mean?" he asked.

"Nothing," I said, beginning to get irritated in my turn. "It's just—there's only me and Melisande. She gives me a present on my birthday, of course, but until Mr. Jones gave me Mr. Jones . . ."

I let my voice run out. I was pretty sure I sounded ridiculous, and feared I might sound pathetic, which would have been much worse.

"I thought you might, you know, on your head," Harry said. "Even from here, I can hardly see the muslin. All you see is the gold, really, like—"

"Golden hair," I said. My chest felt tight and funny. I had never told anyone why I loved these particular flowers so much, not even Melisande. Their petals were the exact color I'd always dreamed my hair might be, assuming my head ever decided to cooperate and actually grow some.

"Thank you, Harry. It's lovely," I said.

He opened his mouth to make a smart remark, I was all but certain. He shut it with a snap, then tried a second time.

"You're welcome, Parsley," he said. "Don't you want to put it on?"

"Hold this," I said, and I handed him my gardening hat, then tied the kerchief on. It was soft and smooth against my head. "How does it look?"

He began to shift his weight again in fits and starts, as if his shoes were too tight. I gazed down at them, suddenly afraid to meet his eyes.

"How should I know? It looks all right."

"There's roast chicken and new potatoes for supper," I said. "With peas and mint, I think."

"Is there a pie?"

"A cherry pie," I said, looking back up. "I baked it just this morning."

Something came into his face then, a look that made me want to smile and weep all at the same time.

"My mother used to make cherry pies," he said. "They were my father's favorites."

"And yours?" I asked.

He nodded. "And mine."

"So we'd be even then," I said.

"We might be," he acknowledged. "Can I sleep in the hay-loft? Mr. Jones snores."

"So does the cat," I said. And had the pleasure of hearing his quick laugh ring out.

"I can carry that," he said, extending a hand for the basket in which I'd carefully been placing lettuce leaves. I'd forgotten that I still had it over my arm. I held it back. I didn't need some boy carrying my things.

"So can I."

"I can do it better, though. I'm bigger and stronger. And I've seen more of the world than you have."

"What does that have to do with anything?"

"Parsley."

"Tinker's boy."

"Ah, so the two of you are making friends," a new voice said.

I turned to see Mr. Jones standing at the back door.

"Actually, we're already friends," I said, and was rewarded by the sound of Harry sucking in his breath. "We met once before."

"Is that so?" the tinker asked. His face stayed perfectly straight, but I could see the twinkle in the back of his eyes. *He's known all along about that first meeting,* I thought. And the only wonder was that Harry hadn't realized this long ago.

"Melisande says if you're quite finished, she would be pleased to have the lettuce you're supposed to be fetching in for supper."

"Here it is," Harry said. And, before I could prevent him, he snatched the basket right off my arm, then made a dash for the back door. With a laugh, Mr. Jones scooted over quickly to avoid being flattened. That was when I saw it. Perhaps Melisande was right, and I had a gift for sorcery after all. For I'm sure that what I saw then was a quick and sudden glimpse into the tinker's heart.

I could see Harry, green eyes alight with mischief. And I thought I saw a girl as well. But she seemed far away, as if her place in Mr. Jones's heart was older than Harry's was. No less present, just not in front. For some reason I could neither see nor understand, she had been relegated to the background. I could not see her features clearly, but around her face, I thought I caught a glimpse of summer gold.

Not me, then, I thought.

And at the unexpected pang my own heart felt, my vision faltered, and Mr. Jones was just a man with graying ginger whiskers standing in an open door.

"Come in to dinner, Rapunzel," he said.

And so I did, and did not speak of what I had seen. For he had not asked me to look, and that which lies in another's heart, even if glimpsed out of turn, should never be told out of turn, if it can be helped.

Six

I THOUGHT ABOUT IT, THOUGH, FROM TIME TO TIME. WHO was the girl Mr. Jones kept at the back of his heart? Just as I wondered about the identity of the person Melisande kept hidden inside hers but never spoke of. *I made room for you inside my heart,* she'd told me on the day we first met Mr. Jones. But who had she asked to scoot over so that I might have a place?

I did not ask either of these questions, though.

There are some subjects that, no matter how much your brain may tell you it would like an explanation, your heart and tongue refuse to touch. And so the question of who shared the sorceress's heart with me remained unanswered, because I could not bring myself to ask it.

And then it was forgotten, at least for a while.

For something changed the year I turned sixteen. A thing that at first seemed to have nothing to do with either Melisande or me, though it turned out to have a great deal to do with both of us.

It started out simply, with the weather. That summer was the hottest I could remember, the hottest I had ever known. For many weeks, too many, in fact, there had been no rain at all. Each day, early in the morning before the sun rose too high, Melisande and I labored together in the garden, carrying water from the stream that ran at the base of the apple orchard. Even then, our plants drooped and languished, as if they couldn't quite make up their minds to expend the energy required to stay alive.

It was the only time I ever saw the garden look anything other than rich and abundant. And if even Melisande's garden struggled as it did, I didn't want to think too long and hard about what might be happening to the gardens, and the people, in the town.

Some mornings, after our work was finished, I climbed to the top of the tallest apple tree, the one that grew at the very crest of the hill and so provided the best view of the surrounding countryside. This had been a favorite place for as long as I could remember. A place to sit and dream, to imagine where the roads I saw might go, or whether or not I might grow hair, and to watch for the arrival of Harry and Mr. Jones.

And so I was the first to notice the exodus from the city. One day the land was mostly empty, the next there were people, sometimes singly, sometimes in groups, moving in weary fits and starts down the thin brown snake of dusty road. Some toward the mountains, but most in the opposite direction, as if they wanted to put as great a distance between themselves and their misery as they could, in as short a time as possible.

Every once in a while, a single traveler would cut across country and end up outside our back door. From them we heard tales of sickness in the city. Of a stillness of the air that was stifling the simplest breath and begetting a fever like none experienced before. Fear had come to live in the city, the travelers said, taking up more than its fair share of space and driving people from their homes. There were murmurs of some great evil magic at work in the land, the need to find its source and drive it out. Only then did I realize that most of those who came to us had known the way because they had been here before.

And so I came to understand their words for what they truly were: a warning.

The hot weather went on.

Several times I caught Melisande looking at me with that considering expression on her face, or standing perfectly still with her head cocked to one side, as if gauging the approach of something. The first time I saw this I felt my blood run as cold as our stream did all winter. *She is listening for the mob,* I thought.

But gradually I came to realize that it was something else. Which was not quite the same as saying we did not fear the mob would come. As the days passed and we still remained in our small house in the valley, I came to understand that Melisande was listening for the approach of Mr. Jones. It had to do with that very first conversation between them, I think, and of all that had not been spoken when the sorceress had told the tinker he would be welcome wherever we might dwell. We would wait for him now, or so it seemed, even with the risk of danger growing closer by the minute while, as far as I could hear, Mr. Jones did not.

One day, the day the radishes, the beans, and the spinach all expired at the exact same instant, I came to a decision of my own. I waited until the sorceress was busy in the house at the hottest part of the day, then I put my favorite kerchief on my head, the one that Harry had given me, with the black-eyed Susans embroidered upon it, and set off for the apple orchard. Not to climb my favorite tree, but to go beyond the orchard itself to the nearest farm.

The man who farmed the property closest to ours had always been a good neighbor, unconcerned and unafraid of sorcery. Once, several years ago now, he had come to Melisande in the middle of the night. His wife had gone into labor before her time. It was going badly, and he feared to leave her to make the journey to the town to fetch the midwife. And so, though she was no more skilled in childbirth than any other woman might be, Melisande had returned with him and done her best; by morning, the children had been born.

A boy and a girl, whom the farmer and his wife named William and Eleanor. They were small, for they had been born early, but they grew strong quickly. And they grew to be great squabblers, though they loved each other well, a fact of life that always made their father smile. It was the reason they had been born too soon, he said. They'd shared their mother's womb no more peaceably than they did their father's farmhouse.

The young boy, William, had a fondness for our apples. I often spied him in the orchard when the fruit was ripe. That time had not come yet, but I was hoping to catch a glimpse of William anyway, for I knew he liked to climb trees as much as I did. I found him in the second tallest tree in the orchard. My tree was the tallest, and that tree he never climbed.

"Come down, William," I said. "I want you to do an errand for me, if you will. Please go and fetch your father. I need to speak with him."

"What will you give me if I do?" the boy asked. In addition to squabbling, he also drove a hard bargain.

"I will give you this orchard for your very own," I replied. "Would you like that?"

"You can't," he said at once, but he did slide down out of the tree to stand beside me. "It doesn't belong to you. It belongs to the sorceress."

"What makes you think I would make such an offer without

her permission?" I inquired, though in fact, I had not yet spoken to Melisande. The boy stood for a moment, staring at me with wide eyes. "Go fetch your father, William," I said again. "It's important."

Without another word, he turned and ran for home.

Before too many minutes had passed, I saw the farmer climbing swiftly up the hill. He was alone.

"Good day to you, Rapunzel," he said.

"Good day to you, Farmer Harris," I replied.

"My son has been telling me wild tales," the farmer said.

"Sooner or later, Melisande and I must leave this place," I said, seeing no reason not to come straight to the point. "You know what they have been saying in the town."

"I do," he nodded. He hesitated for a moment, as if uncertain whether to say any more. "I had thought, perhaps, to see you and the sorceress go before now."

I shook my head. "We will go when Melisande decides the time is right and not before. But I would not . . ." To my dismay, my voice faltered. Now that I had come to speak of it, the truth of what I was about to say struck hard. Very soon now, we would have to leave the only home that I had ever known.

"There's the livestock," I said. "And what's left of the crops. If the mob comes . . ."

"I know," the farmer said at once, and his face grew sober. "I know, Rapunzel."

"Would it not be a fine thing," I asked, "if both these farms were yours? One could be William's when he grows up. The other could be a dowry for your daughter."

"It might be a very fine thing," Farmer Harris said slowly. "It would be hard work until my son is grown, though."

"I cannot help with that," I said. "But perhaps, if the livestock were already in your own barn? They could be more easily cared for that way, I think. Except for the horse. We might need her for the journey."

"My wife's brother is young and strong," the farmer said, as if thinking it over. "He might come."

"That would be a great help," I said, at which he gave a quick smile.

"You have it all worked out, then?" he asked.

"No," I said. "Of course not. It's just—they'll drive us away," I burst out suddenly. "You know they will. I don't want everything we've cared for so well and for so long to belong to those who wish us ill. Not if I can help it."

"If they arrive before you are ready, come to me," the farmer said, and now his voice was strong and resolved. "My barn can hold more than extra livestock. On behalf of my son and daughter, I thank you for this kindness."

"I'll start bringing the animals tomorrow," I said.

And so we left one another.

I got home to find the sorceress standing at our back door.

"I've told Farmer Harris he can have the place when we leave it," I said. "I'll start taking over the first of the livestock tomorrow. If he already has them, it will be harder for others to take them away."

"That's good thinking," Melisande said quietly. "Thank you, Rapunzel." She made a gesture, the first I'd ever seen from her that looked anything like helplessness. "I meant to speak of this before now, but—"

"It doesn't matter," I interrupted swiftly. "As long as we both agree now."

"We agree," the sorceress said.

"So that's all right, then," I answered. "Now, what else needs to be done?"

Melisande's expression changed then, though I would be hard put to explain just how. It was as if I had answered a question for her, rather than asked one of her. And the answer had settled things, once and for all.

"We should decide what we want to take with us," she said. "And have it ready, for we may have to go at a moment's notice."

"That is easily done," I replied. "For there's not much I want, save for you and the cat, and this kerchief, but I usually have it on."

"Life is very simple, then," Melisande agreed. "For as long as you are with me, I am satisfied."

"A little food and water might be a good idea, though," I said, amazed to feel myself starting to smile. I might share her heart, but for the moment it seemed that I alone was all that she required.

"Oh, indeed," the sorceress replied.

In the days that followed, we set about doing what needed to be done. By the end of that week, all our livestock—the goats, the cow, the sheep and the pigs—had been walked across the fields to the Harris farm. The belongings Melisande and I planned to take with us were tied in two large shawls, which sat in readiness by the front door. Melisande's sewing basket, which had a hinged lid, stood ready to carry the cat. I spent many moments explaining this future indignity to him, promising that it was absolutely necessary and would be as short-lived as possible.

And still the weather stayed hot, and the tinker and his boy did not come.

Seven

EVENTUALLY, OF COURSE, THE MATTER WAS TAKEN OUT OF OUR hands, for that is the way of things, more often than not. Returning from the orchard late one day, where I had been battling wasps for apples that the heat had brought down before their time, I saw a great cloud of dust. From the hill on which the orchard stood, I could trace the cloud's path with my eyes: from the main road, off onto the several branching ones that, eventually, led to our front door.

No! I thought. It would be bad enough for the mob to catch us at all, but for them to find Melisande alone . . .

Without another thought in my head, I sprinted for home. Halfway there, my brain kicked in, reminding me that if I simply burst in upon whatever I might find, not only would I be unable to aid the sorceress, I'd hand myself over to our enemies as well. So I stopped, set the basket of apples down, and took a breath. Then, leaving the basket where it was, I continued more slowly.

There was no one in the garden. The back door was shut, and I could hear no sound from inside the house. In the whole yard, there seemed to be not a single breath of air. The back of my neck prickled with tension. I crept around to the front and found a horse standing in our yard. Its flanks were covered with sweat. White foam flecked its mouth. I stood for a moment, while my own sweat dampened the back of my dress, trying to decide what should be done. Unless cared for, a horse ridden as hard as this one could sicken.

I suppose there's nothing for it, I thought, as I took a single step forward. If its master had evil intentions, the horse would suffer quite enough without my adding to its misery.

"Don't you touch him. Stay away," a shrill voice called.

Instantly I took the same step back, cursing myself. I'd let my love for animals get in the way of my good sense. Again.

"I only want to wipe him down," I said. "He shouldn't be left to stand. He's been ridden too hard."

"I said stay away," the voice said again, and now I could see to whom it belonged. In the lane right outside our gate sat a serving boy on a horse of his own. The lad was big and strapping, for all that his voice had been shrill. He had ears like pitchers. Great, doughy hands clutched hard at the reins so that the horse's feet were never still. It tossed its head and showed the whites of its eyes.

He is infected by his rider's fear, I thought.

"I only want to wipe him down," I said again. "And I can bring you a drink of water, if you like."

"You'll do no such thing," the boy replied. "How do I know what you might put in it? You serve the evil sorceress."

"I do not," I answered smartly, probably more smartly than I should have done. But that word, evil, was pounding in my head, driving out caution. "I'm nobody's servant, and if you think that Melisande would harm anyone, you're just plain wrong. Maybe you should consider keeping your mouth shut. Your ignorance is showing, and it's not a pretty sight."

"What would you know about pretty?" the boy shot back. "I've heard about you. They say that you are cursed and have no hair at all."

"That's ridiculous," I said, though I was responding to the first part of his words, of course. My voice was loud and brave, but by now my heart had begun to knock against my ribs. What was I doing, standing here arguing in the yard?

"Show me your head and prove it, then," the boy challenged, for of course I had a kerchief on, as always, and my favorite one besides.

"I don't have to prove anything to you," I said. At which he laughed, and it was not a joyful sound.

"You're afraid of me," he said. "You ought to be."

All of a sudden, I understood the urge to strike the first blow, to harm those you think mean to injure you before they get the chance. For his words made me angry, and my fingers itched to find a rock and throw it. But before I could do anything so rash— before, in fact, I could do anything else at all—the front door of the house slammed back and a man stalked out into the yard. I spun toward him. He stopped short. We stared at one another.

He was a few years older than I was, or so I judged, dressed in the fine clothes of a wealthy man from the town. A merchant, perhaps. They always dressed well.

"So," he said at last. "You have grown up tall. I wondered if you might, your legs were so strong."

I did my best to hide my confusion, but I must not have been very successful.

"You don't remember me, do you?" he inquired.

I opened my mouth to say that of course I didn't, when I looked into his eyes. They were a color I had seen just once before, a blue more blue than any sky. In that moment, a memory I had forgotten I possessed returned to me, and I discovered that I knew him after all.

"You are the boy," I said. "The tall boy who kicked the ball so well."

He smiled then, and it was like the sun appearing on a cloudy day, just when you have given up any hope that such a moment might come.

"And you are the girl who was faster than any of us," he said. He made a gesture, as if both calling attention to and dismissing the rich garments that he wore. "As you can see, we have both grown up."

"You have done well," I said.

He shrugged. "My father died young and I am his only son. But I . . ." He paused and took a breath. "I have never forgotten the day we met."

The things you saw in your own heart, I thought. But I did not say so aloud. For this I did remember clearly: Not even he had been able to hold Melisande's eyes.

"And so I came to offer you and the sorceress this warning: Leave this place with all possible speed, or you will answer with your lives."

I exhaled a breath I hadn't realized I'd been holding in.

"You came to warn us," I said. "Not to drive us off."

"The first will accomplish the second, so I'm not sure it makes much difference," he said. "But no, I did not come to drive you off. I failed to defend you once. I would prefer not to make the same mistake a second time. Consider this the payment of a debt."

He moved then, striding across the yard to mount his horse. Then, for one moment only, he looked down.

"I do not think that we will meet again. Go quickly, and fare you well."

Then he spurred his horse back into the lane and vanished

down it in the same cloud of dust with which he had arrived. But the serving boy, freed from his master's presence and his fear alike, was not quite done. With a great cry, he aimed his horse through the gate, straight at me, acting so quickly I had no time to step aside. With one fierce gesture, he yanked the kerchief from my head.

"I knew it! I knew it! You *are* cursed!" he cried.

With a final flourish, he tossed the fabric high into the air, then sped after his master, the horse's legs eating up the road. And it was only then that I turned and saw Harry, standing at the corner of the house. In one white-knuckled fist, he clutched the tallest of our pitchforks.

Slowly I crossed the yard, retrieved my kerchief, shook it out, and put it back on. I did my best to keep my spine straight, like the stems of the black-eyed Susans that I so loved. Only then did I realize what strength it took to stand up so tall and straight and unafraid, no matter what comes.

"I'm sorry, Rapunzel," Harry said.

"You didn't do anything," I said. "You don't have anything to be sorry for."

"Don't I?" Harry asked. "Thank you for reminding me." And he came forward then, taking several steps and driving the pitchfork, hard, into the parched ground.

"What are you talking about?" I asked. Every bone in my body seemed to ache, all of a sudden. Even my brain ached, for it felt worn out and tired.

"How can you ask me that?" Harry cried. "I just stood there. I stood there while he hurt you and did nothing. It was over before I knew what should be done."

"He didn't hurt me," I said.

"Of course he did. Why else are you crying?"

And it was only as he said this that I realized it was the truth. My dusty cheeks were wet with tears.

"I'm crying because I'm angry, not hurt," I said as I dashed them aside. "The wound he wanted to inflict was over and done with long ago. We've done nothing to them. Nothing! But still they'll come to drive us from our home. All because we're different, and they are fearful fools who require a scapegoat. Where's Melisande?"

"Here," I heard the sorceress call.

She stepped out into the yard. On her back she had tied her own bundle. She set mine down at her feet. Her sewing basket rested in the crook of one arm.

"The cat and I have been coming to an arrangement," she said. "He agrees not to scratch or cry out, if we agree to keep him in this basket for as short a time as possible."

"I'm glad you had better luck convincing him than I did," I said. I moved to her side and shouldered my own bundle. She handed over the basket containing Mr. Jones, then went back inside for the one in which we'd packed our food supplies. Then she came all the way out and shut the door behind her.

"Harry," she said, precisely as if she had expected to see him there on this afternoon and no other. "There you are."

"The tinker is at the next farm over," Harry said. "He said that you would know the one. And he said you should go quickly to join him. There isn't much time."

"I know," said Melisande.

"What are you going to do?" I asked him. For there had been a note in his voice, one I wasn't certain that I liked.

"I've been thinking about that," Harry said. "I'm taking the horse."

"Oh, no, you're not," I said. "He's coming with us."

"No," Harry said at once, and his eyes went to Melisande's as if seeking support. "Surely you can see that isn't wise. It's well enough known that the tinker stops at your door. If he's seen on the road with your horse . . ."

"But . . . ," I said.

"Harry is right," Melisande spoke up. "If we are to ride with the tinker, we cannot afford to give anyone cause to search the wagon."

"If anyone asks, I can always say that I stole it," Harry went on. "I can travel fast and light, and meet up with you later."

"In that case," I said tartly, "I sincerely hope one of us knows where we're going."

"Across the mountains," Melisande said. "Three days' journey through the passes, two days across the plains beyond. On the morning of the sixth day, look for a tower rising straight up out of the plain. That is where we are going."

"Why?" I asked.

But the sorceress shook her head. "Not now. There will be time enough for that when we are safely away from this place." She turned to go, then paused, her eyes on Harry. "Say your good-byes quickly. I'll wait for you at the top of the hill, Rapunzel."

With that, she turned on one heel and disappeared around the side of the house, leaving Harry and me standing in the yard.

"Six days," Harry said. "That's not so bad. Surely even you can stay out of trouble for that long, Parsley."

"I am never any trouble," I retorted. "That falls to horse-stealing tinker's boys."

But I moved to him and reached for his hand before I quite knew what I had done.

"Be careful," I said. "I want you to promise."

"You're the one they're hunting, not me," he said.

"Harry."

"Oh, all right. I promise, Parsley."

"Why must you always do that?" I asked, horrified that I could once more feel the prick of tears at the back of my eyes, and I knew that anger hadn't brought them on this time. I stamped my foot, to drive them away. "I have a proper name. You might learn to say it."

"Rapunzel," Harry said. And again, "Rapunzel."

And then he did the very last thing I expected. He caught

my face between his hands and pressed his lips to mine. I forgot
the heat of the day, forgot my own danger. All I could feel was
the touch of his mouth. All I could hear was the sound my own
heart made.

Home, it said. *Home.*

Then, quickly as it had arrived, the moment was over. He let
me go, stepped back, and spun me around.

"Now, run, Parsley. If I find out you've let them catch you,
I'll hunt you down and tar and feather you myself."

I did run then, all the way to the crest of the hill, where the
sorceress was waiting beneath my favorite apple tree. Then, just
once and only for a moment, I stopped and turned around.

The house sat just where it always had, and beyond it the
barn. But of our horse, with the tinker's boy upon its back, I
could see no sign. Melisande reached out and put a hand on
my arm.

"I know," I said. "I know."

And so, together, we turned away and hurried down the far
side of the hill.

But to the end of my days, my heart retained this picture:
an image of the black-eyed Susans standing tall and straight and
true in the ruins of our abandoned garden.

Eight

OUR JOURNEY WENT JUST AS THE SORCERESS HAD SAID IT would. Three days through the mountain passes, two days across the plains beyond. We stayed inside the wagon all the first three days, until we reached a place where the mountains ended suddenly, as if cut off with a knife, and a wide, flat plain stretched out in every direction, eventually becoming the horizon line.

It was hot and stuffy in the wagon. All four sides were down, lashed tight, in spite of the fact that it was summer and the weather was warm. My body ached from the inactivity. I had never been so restricted before, never even thought about what it might be like to be unable to do something as simple as taking a few steps. To be unable to feel the wind or see the sky. I would rouse from sudden stupors to find my hands had clenched themselves into fists, as if I had dreamed fierce dreams while I dozed.

None of us spoke very much.

At night the tinker sat beside his fire and conversed with those who stopped to share its light. But they were few, though the road held travelers other than ourselves. It was as if all were infected by the sickness that had struck the town. Not the fever, but the sickness of suspicion. Fear walked that road, planting its feet as solidly as those of Mr. Jones's horse.

And so the first three days passed slowly, until, at last, we left the mountains behind.

Free of the mountains, the land opened up like a child suddenly freed of a heavy winter coat, gleefully spreading its arms. The road we traveled upon opened up also, becoming wide and broad. There was a flash of light off to the west. Somewhere in the distance, a river flowed. It was cooler on the far side of the mountains, as if the heat that had held us in so tight a grip had hands but no legs and so had been unable to make the climb. About mid-morning on the fourth day, Mr. Jones brought the horse and wagon to a sudden halt. A moment later he poked his head through the opening at his back.

"I have seen no other people for a good two hours," he said. "I think it's safe for you to come out now."

"You go first, Rapunzel," Melisande said. "Perhaps it will still be better if we don't both suddenly appear at once."

I wish I could tell you that at this moment I was overcome by a fit of thoughtfulness. That I turned to the woman who had raised me and said, "Oh, no, Melisande. You go first. You've been just as cramped and miserable as I."

I didn't, though.

Instead, I scrambled for the front of the wagon without another word, almost tumbling over the seat and onto the horse's back in my eagerness to reach the outside.

"Take it easy," Mr. Jones said. "The world's not going anywhere, you know."

"I don't know that, as a matter of fact," I said.

And then I did what I had started to do three days ago and hadn't finished yet. I began to run.

I ran until my legs ached just as much with exertion as they had with inertia. Until the breath scorched going down my parched throat and burned inside my lungs. Until the kerchief I wore was plastered to my head with sweat, and then the sweat dripped down into my eyes. I ran until my hands hung limply, too worn out to make fists at my sides. And then I stopped and caught my breath, and sat down to wait by the side of the road.

By the time the wagon pulled up beside me, Melisande was sitting next to Mr. Jones.

"You ran a long way," she said. "Was it far enough?"

"I'm not sure I know."

"You'll appreciate a drink of water, in any case," the tinker said.

"I would," I acknowledged. "And a change of headgear, I think."

"Fortunately for you, I believe I can assist with both." He handed over the waterskin, then climbed down from the seat of the wagon and began to rummage in the wagon itself. The sides had been rolled up, I noticed. Our hiding place was now completely gone.

"Harry found this, our last trip together," the tinker said, and he handed me what my fingers told me was yet another piece of cloth, even as my eyes watched it flash in the sun. "He intended to give it to you himself, of course."

After that first gift of cloth for a kerchief, Harry had continued to bring me such presents from time to time. Each more elaborate and fanciful than the next, till even Melisande looked forward to seeing what would arrive. Some were shot through with threads of gold and silver. Others were woven of every color I could imagine, and even some that I could not. The most recent had been stitched to resemble a peacock's tail, with actual feathers fluttering along its edges. We'd put that one on the head of the scarecrow in the cornfield, where it had successfully intimidated the crows.

I held the fabric by one corner and let the rest flutter out in the breeze.

"For heaven's sake, I can't wear this!" I exclaimed. "I'll blind the horse."

"You might at that," Mr. Jones agreed. For, rather than being covered only with embroidery, this cloth was decorated with tiny mirrors held in place with elaborate stitches in red and silver. "It's very beautiful, though. I can see why Harry thought you might like it."

"Harry," I said, and tried not to hear the way my voice threatened to turn those two syllables into a sob.

"He'll be all right, Rapunzel," the tinker said. "He's young and strong, and he knows the roads."

"Of course he'll be all right," I said, as if I could hide my fears by the crossness in my voice. "It's just so like him to be late."

"He's not late yet," said Melisande. Then, to my surprise, she hopped down from the wagon seat. "Here," she said. "You ride and I'll run for a while. By nightfall we will come to a place where the river turns to run beside the road. There is a small stand of trees where the river bends that makes a fine campsite. There I will answer all the questions you've been so careful not to ask. For which I am most grateful, by the way."

"Can I have a bath?" I inquired.

"Yes," the sorceress answered, and she smiled. "That question I can answer now."

"I heard what he said to you," Melisande said, late that night. "The boy, that last day, in our yard. He said that you were cursed. Not only is this cruel and unfair, it's also untrue. For it is not you who is cursed, my Rapunzel. It is I."

We had come to the bend in the river, just as the sorceress had declared we would. Made camp, eaten our dinner, and washed from our bodies the stains that fear makes, and the dust from the road. Now the three of us sat around a small, bright campfire, while Mr. Jones's horse grazed nearby.

The tinker had brought out a pipe, and its bowl illuminated his face, then darkened it again, as he puffed. Its fragrant smoke mingled with the smoke of the fire. The water beside us made a cheerful sound. I was grateful for this, for I had found to my surprise that the land made me nervous in the darkness. It was so great and open and wide. In it, Melisande's words seemed to fly out in every direction, gone almost before I could understand what she had said.

"How can that be?" I asked. "Who has the power to curse a sorceress?"

"The answer to that is simple," the sorceress herself replied. "One whose power is greater than mine. In this case, it was a wizard, and for this reason: He had witnessed me doing a thing that I should not have done. Once, a very long time ago now, I committed an act of unkindness."

"But," I said, then stopped short. Who was I to question the actions of a wizard, after all? But Melisande seemed to understand what my objection might have been, had I decided to say it aloud.

"True enough," she acknowledged. "Acts of unkindness happen every day, some intentional, others not. Mine was of the second variety, not that it made any difference in the long run."

"I'm not sure I understand," I said.

"That is not surprising," Melisande answered. "For it has taken many years for me to understand it myself."

She fell silent for a moment, gazing into the fire, then lifted her eyes to mine. When she did, I got a jolt. For it seemed to me that, just as I had done with the tinker on that day so long ago now, I caught a glimpse into the sorceress's heart. In it I thought I recognized myself. But behind me, moving closer even as I watched, was the person Melisande had asked to step aside. Though for many years we had not discussed how I had first come to live with her, I had never forgotten her words: *I made room for you inside my heart.*

It is another girl, I realized. Just as I thought she might come close enough for me to see her features, Melisande spoke again, and the vision vanished.

"I have wanted to tell you this story many times, Rapunzel," she said. "Even more, I have known that I must. But every time I wondered if the time was right, my heart counseled me to wait, and I listened to its voice. For that is supposed to be my gift, is it not? To see what is in the heart?"

"In another's heart, yes," I answered without thinking, for my head was still full of what I believed I had seen, trying to figure it out. Mr. Jones shifted position suddenly, as if he would have answered differently if the question had been put to him. But the sorceress simply nodded.

"That is a just response. To see into another's heart is one thing. To see into one's own heart may require a different power entirely. I'm still not entirely certain it's one that I possess."

And so the sorceress told us her story.

Nine

"MANY YEARS AGO," MELISANDE SAID, "LONG BEFORE YOU were born, Rapunzel, the world was less afraid of magic than it is now. As a result, magic itself was more powerful. In this, I suppose it could be said that it was like a radish in our garden."

"Better that than a carrot," I said, and heard both the tinker and the sorceress chuckle. And with that, I felt the tension around our fire ease, as if, now that the story had at last commenced, we all understood we would stick with it till the close. What might happen then was anyone's guess, but for now, we would all be united in the telling and hearing of it.

"Though it could be any plant," I went on, "assuming that I've grasped your point. If you give a plant room, it will grow and flourish. But if you crowd it, you may choke it out."

"That is indeed my point," Melisande agreed. "Not that magic has died out entirely in these days. But fear is strong. Fear of what is different, of what cannot easily be explained, particularly explained away. We've had proof enough of that recently, I think, you and I."

"But this is not a story of these days," I said.

"No," Melisande agreed. "Or at least, the start of it is not, for this story is still ongoing. It has not yet come to its conclusion, though I hope that the day for that is not far off. It is a cautionary tale, one that shows how, even when used with the best intentions, the strongest magic can still go wrong.

"Like many such tales, it began innocently enough. One fine market day, a sorceress and her daughter, who was just the age that you are now, Rapunzel, left their home and went to the nearest town."

"Wait a minute. Stop right there," I said. I felt a shock, as if I had suddenly been plunged into cold, deep water. "You have a daughter. A daughter of your own blood."

"I do," answered Melisande. "Her father and I were childhood sweethearts. He died long ago. My daughter was once all that I had in the world."

I opened my mouth, then closed it, then opened it again, and still no sound came out. The numbness of shock was being replaced by a strange sensation, tingling in all my limbs as if my entire being was undergoing some great rearrangement of its very essence. All these years the sorceress had had a child, a daughter who was all she had in the world, yet not once had she ever spoken of her.

"What is her name?" the tinker asked quietly.

"I do not speak the name I gave her at her birth," Melisande answered, matching his tone. "She lost it the same day as the events I am about to tell. For many years now, she has been called Rue. She dwells in the tower we will reach in another day's time."

Rue, I thought. Another plant in the garden. A name even more bitter than mine. Rue for sorrow. Rue for regret.

"What a terrible thing to be called," I said aloud, before I quite realized I had done so.

"I understand this must be difficult for you," Melisande began.

"Oh, do you?" I burst out. "I don't think you understand anything at all. I know I don't."

How could you? I wanted to cry. *How can you say you love me and hold something like this back?*

It did no good for my mind to insist that the sorceress had always told me the truth. She had not told me of her own, her other, child. An omission so large and strange that, in that moment, it felt no different than the telling of a lie.

"Let her finish, Rapunzel," Mr. Jones said, his own voice calm. "There can be time for pain and outrage later, if that is still what you feel. But we'll never get anywhere if you indulge in them now."

Almost, I did it. Stood up and left the fire. Almost, I walked off into that great, vast darkness that surrounded us. Walked off and kept on going. For it didn't seem like such a foreign country now. In the moments since the sorceress had revealed that she had a daughter, vast and dark and empty had become familiar territory. It was just the same as the inside of my heart.

I didn't move, though. Instead I took hold of my pain and throttled it down. *Mr. Jones is right,* I thought. There would be time for pain and outrage later. Later I could scream and weep to my certainly confused and maybe even broken heart's content. For the moment, however, only by being silent could I learn what I needed to know.

"I'm sorry," I said. "Please, go on."

"I'm sorry too," answered Melisande. "More sorry than you know. And so I will begin with two unkindnesses, it seems. One, tonight. The first, long ago."

"Upon a market day, you said," I prompted, suddenly eager to get the telling of this tale over and done with. "You took *me* to town upon a market day also, as I recall."

"I did," said Melisande. "And though what happened brought you pain, it also showed me that your heart was strong. Stronger than you knew then. Perhaps it is still stronger than you know."

"So it was a test, then?" I asked, as the pain and confusion I was trying to master grew too strong and slipped their hold. Was my childhood nothing but a series of hidden checks and balances, not really what I thought I had experienced at all?

"How fortunate for us that I passed it," I went on, unable to keep the bitterness from my voice. "How many more are there to be, or don't I get to know until they're all over?"

"Enough, Rapunzel," Mr. Jones said. I shut my mouth with a snap and pressed the tip of my tongue against the back of my teeth. "Let the sorceress tell what must be told."

"Upon a market day, as I have said," Melisande resumed her tale, "my daughter and I went to town. There she saw a bright ribbon for her hair. She had eyes for nothing else. I had eyes for no one but my child. On that day, I, whose gift it is to see into the hearts of others, failed to see that my daughter's heart was not the only one filled with desire. She had that ribbon for her hair, while another woman's child had none."

"Oh, but surely—" I began to protest, then stopped. We were never going to get anywhere if I kept interrupting every other sentence. Not only that, I was contradicting myself. A moment ago I had been ready to use my words to lash out. Now here I was, jumping to Melisande's defense.

"You are exactly right," she said at once, precisely as if she understood the objection I had planned to make.

"The act was simple and unintentional, not deliberately cruel, but merely thoughtless. I thought only of myself and what I loved. Everyday people do this all the time, though I suppose it could be said the world might be a better place if they did not. But I am not an everyday sort of person. I possess a gift, the gift to see what lies inside another's heart.

"On that day, I did not look. I let myself be blind. It was this fact more than any other that weighed against me in the end. That made the wizard who saw my actions decide I needed to be taught a lesson in the uses of power."

"But *why*?" I cried.

"My gift is not simply a skill I *may* use, it is a skill I *must* use," Melisande replied. "Not that I am required to act on what my eyes discover. My gift, my responsibility, is to see and nothing more. I am free to choose my own actions. Indeed, like everyone else, I must be so. A good act that is compelled is not goodness at all, but merely force.

"It might even have been better if I had been deliberately unkind. A will to be unkind is like a sickness. It can be healed or driven out. But to be unkind because you are thoughtless is the worst kind of blindness: difficult to cure, because you cannot see the fault even as you commit it."

"And that's why the wizard put a curse on you?" I asked.

"It is," Melisande replied. "Because I failed to look for what another held in her heart, I would be unable to see what I held in mine, for a time. It would not wither. It would not fade away. But neither would it grow. It would remain just as it was, as if in a dream of life, until I found the means to awaken it and set it free."

"What is it about wizards?" Mr. Jones remarked. "They expend so much effort to say so little."

"I couldn't agree more," Melisande replied, with a slight smile. "If the wizard had been less fond of the sound of his own voice, he might have realized he was making a mistake of his own. Power was what he held most closely in his own heart, so he assumed it was the same for mine. He therefore hoped to teach me a lesson in the uses of power by depriving me of it. Instead he deprived me of a thing I loved much more."

"Your daughter," I said suddenly, and felt my pain and anger begin to drain away and be replaced by something else, though I wasn't sure quite what.

"My daughter," Melisande echoed quietly. "The wizard did not mean his curse to touch my child, any more than I meant to be unkind to the child of another. But, like my own thoughtless action, once the wizard's curse was uttered, it could not be undone. And so I kept sight of my power, but lost sight of the thing I valued most: my child.

"The wizard took her and placed her in a tower he used his magic to build in two nights and the day that fell between them. It is made of smooth, gray stone. Windows made of starlight ring the top. Its door may be seen and opened only by the power of a love other than my own. There my child has stayed from that day to this, waiting for me to bring the key, the means of awakening and freeing her heart."

"You think it's me," I said. By now I felt so many different things, I was well on my way to deciding it might be preferable to feel nothing. "That's the real reason you took me in and raised me. You need me to free your daughter. You don't love me at all."

"That's not true," Melisande said at once. "I took you in and raised you for the same reason I have always said: Because I loved you from the moment I first saw you, Rapunzel. But I will admit that there is more. When I gazed into your mother's heart and found no room for you within it, I heard a sound, like the opening of a door. It seemed to me that her inability to look with the eyes of love could not be coincidence. At long last, perhaps I was being offered the chance to redeem the daughter I had lost.

"But only if I could take you in and love you truly, if I could teach you all the things my heart had learned in the days since Rue had been taken and locked away. And so I did what the woman who gave birth to you could not. I looked with the eyes of love, claimed you, and raised you as my own."

"And never mentioned your daughter once," I added, finishing the list. "Until tonight, when I'm supposed to meet her tomorrow. Is this my final test? What happens if we can't stand the sight of one another?"

"I don't know," Melisande said, her own voice rising for the very first time. "I can't see the future. That is not my gift. I don't know what is to come. I've done what I thought was right, what I thought I must. That's all I can tell you."

"What about what I want to do?" I asked. "Suppose all I want to do is turn around and go back home? Does what I want even matter? Do I have a choice?"

"Of course you have a choice," Mr. Jones said, his first words for what seemed like a very long time. "The sorceress has said what she has done, but she cannot say what you will do. That, only you can decide."

"Thank you," I said. "I'm glad to see somebody's on my side."

Mr. Jones knocked his pipe out on a stone without looking up. "It is not a matter of taking sides. It is what it has always been: a matter of the heart. You may think you are listening, but you're hearing only what you want to hear, Rapunzel. What is in the heart cannot be forced. This, the sorceress has already acknowledged. If the heart bends, it must be of its own free will, or not at all.

"Personally, I think she's right. Your heart is stronger than you know. But you may never learn how strong unless you put it to the test."

"I'm tired of being tested," I replied.

"Now that," the tinker said briskly, as he got to his feet, "is a feeling I understand very well. I'm sorry to tell you that it may not make much difference in the long run, though." He came over and kissed me on the cheek, an action he had never performed before. "I suggest we all go to sleep. I don't know about anyone else, but I am tired. I'd put an extra blanket on if I were you, Rapunzel. Even summer nights on the plain are cold."

With that, he moved to the wagon, pulled his own bedroll from it, and went to bed down close to the horse. I went to lie in my usual position, wrapping myself in an extra blanket as the tinker had suggested, my arms around my knees as if to make myself as small as possible. For the first and only time that I could remember, Melisande and I did not say good night.

All through that night, the sorceress stayed beside the fire. What her thoughts were, as the fire died down to nothing more than cold gray ash, I cannot say. To the best of my knowledge, she never told another living soul.

Ten

I DID NOT GO BACK HOME IN THE END, OF COURSE.

You've heard the saying, better the devil you know than the one you do not? What a load of poppycock. In fact, if I had to make a guess, it would be that whoever came up with that particular phrase was never called upon to face any sort of devil in his or her life.

What did I have to go back for, after all? I'd only be going right back into danger, the very same danger I'd just gone to such great lengths to avoid. It was hardly as if there would be anyone at the end of the road, or even anywhere along it, waiting to welcome me with open arms.

It wasn't all that likely there would be open arms if I went forward, either, but at least I would be going into the unknown. And here is a fact of life that those who are quick to speak of devils never mention: As long as a thing is unknown, it belongs to us in a way that well-known things do not. For we have the opportunity to fill the empty, unknown spaces for ourselves, and in them there is room for imagination and for hope.

If I went forward, I might imagine that I could somehow pass this impossible test. Maybe my heart *was* stronger than I knew, and all would yet be well. So, on the morning of the fifth day, going forward was precisely what I did. On the morning of the sixth day, I saw Rue's tower for the very first time.

I might have guessed there was some magic at work in its construction, even if I had not been told this ahead of time. Surely any sort of structure should have been visible for miles away in that flat land. Instead, you could see the tower clearly only when you had actually arrived. It rose up out of the ground like a great tree trunk of hard, gray stone, its roots indistinguishable from the very bones of the earth itself.

The tower the wizard had created to house the innocent victim of his curse was perfectly cylindrical, perfectly smooth. I could neither see nor feel one seam or chink to show that the stone had ever been cut. At what I thought of as the tower's back, though this was merely my own fancy as a circle has no such thing, was the river. A dense forest held it in a great, green embrace on its other three sides. All around, just as wide as two carts abreast, ran a close-cropped greensward.

If I leaned back and shaded my eyes, I could see a wrought-iron railing, intricately carved, running around the tower's very top. Just behind it, a circle of windows caught the light. But no matter how many times I walked around it, three to be precise, I could find no sign of any door. At the end of my third circuit I stopped beside the sorceress and said, "How do we get up? I assume that's what you have in mind."

Conversation between us was still stilted, at best. Among all of us, if it came to that. Even Mr. Jones had kept silent during the last day of our journey, as if wrapped in his own thoughts. Not that there was much use in talking. It would be deeds, not words, that would end the story and decide its outcome.

While I walked around the tower and Melisande stood perfectly still, Mr. Jones unhitched the horse and let her wade into the river, which here was broad and shallow. As if he had no other care in the world, the tinker washed clothes at the river's edge, then spread them out to dry. I knew what he was doing, of course. He was letting the sorceress and me sort things out on our own. Mr. Jones was hidden now by the bulk of the tower, for Melisande and I stood with our backs to the forest, and the river was on the other side, out of sight.

"More wizardry," Melisande replied now. "There's a password of sorts. Rapunzel, I—"

"I really wish you wouldn't," I interrupted swiftly, suddenly afraid that I might cry. I was trying to do what Melisande herself had done—what I thought was right, what I thought I must. But I was still hurt and uncertain, and more than a little afraid. If we stood around talking about it for very much longer, chances were good I'd lose my nerve entirely.

"By my own free will, I shall go up," I said. "But I cannot promise I'll be willing to stay, not from down here, anyhow. Your daughter and I must decide that together, I think."

"Fair enough," said Melisande.

I pulled in what felt too much like my last breath of free air. "Okay," I said. "I'm ready whenever you are."

Melisande took a deep breath of her own, as if steeling herself. Then, in a loud, firm voice, she pronounced the following words:

"One so fair, let down your hair. Let me go from here to there."

What on earth? I thought.

For many moments nothing seemed to happen, unless you count the fact that my heart suddenly began to pound. Then, with a start, I realized that the tower was changing before my eyes. No longer did the stone look dull and gray. Instead it seemed to flush. Veins of color suddenly appeared, spreading upward, branching out as blood runs through a body. They shimmered as they caught the light.

It looks alive, I thought. As if the tower had been sleeping as bears do in the winter, and Melisande's words were the harbingers of spring, the wake-up call.

Together, the sorceress and I watched the flush of color rise all the way to the tower's top. Then, with a sound like a flock of birds all launching themselves into the air at once, a single pane of glass flew back, and a thick woven rope came flying out. It wrapped itself twice around the iron railing, as if it wished to anchor itself more firmly, then plummeted straight over the side to land at our feet with a soft *plunk*.

It was the most beautiful golden color that I had ever seen. Braided tightly together, almost too thick for my hands to close around. At its end was tied a ribbon of so dark a red it was almost black. *Heart's blood,* I thought. And in that moment, I thought I understood, and could have sworn I felt my own heart stop.

This wizardry is a terrible thing, I thought.

Then Melisande reached for the golden braid, and I saw that her hand trembled for the one and only time in all the years that I had known her. At this, my heart gave a great jolt of pity within my breast, then began to beat in its normal way once more. But before Melisande could take hold of the braid, a streak of copper caught my eye. Running as hard as he could, Mr. Jones, the cat, streaked around the side of the tower, gave a great leap with all four legs outstretched, landed upon the golden braid, and began to scramble upward. Halfway up the tower he stopped and seemed to glance back at us over one furry shoulder.

What are you waiting for? his expression inquired. Clearly, this was the most exciting adventure in the world, and only a fool would decline to be a part of it.

"After you," I said. Melisande's fingers wrapped around the golden braid. We began to climb upward in single file.

It was hard work. Much harder than it looked, particularly if one judged by the cat. The braid was thick and soft, difficult to hold. More than once I had the feeling that, if I loosened my grip for even a second, the braid would slip right through my hands and I'd tumble to the ground. Several times I wished for Mr. Jones's claws. Not only that, the braid wouldn't stay still. No kind of rope ladder ever does, I suppose. Melisande's exertions pulled it one way, while mine pulled it another. Slowly, we made our precarious and strenuous way up the side of the tower.

Eventually I felt the braid give a great jerk. I looked up, startled, just in time to see Melisande throw one foot over the iron railing. In the next moment, she had disappeared over its side. Then her head reappeared, and she reached down and helped to pull me up after her. I tumbled over the railing in a great ungainly heap, then lay flat on my back, on a wide shelf of stone at the tower's top. After a few moments, Mr. Jones came over and sat upon my chest, gazing down at me with pleased and excited eyes.

"Show-off," I muttered. "It's considered impolite to gloat, you know."

He licked one paw, then sprang from my chest so abruptly that what little air I had in them shot from my lungs. As I sat up, I caught a glimpse of the golden braid uncoiling from around the railing, then whisking out of sight inside the tower.

Still more wizardry, I thought. Did that great shining mass actually possess a life of its own?

Melisande reached down and helped me to my feet.

"Don't be afraid," she said. "Nothing here will harm you."

If you say so, I thought.

Melisande took a step forward, toward the open pane of glass. Almost before I realized what I was doing, I stopped her, clutching tightly at her arm. Suddenly I was dizzy standing at the top of that tower, made of the bones of the earth and topped by the light of only-a-wizard-knew-how-many stars. The air blew cold against my skin, and it seemed to me that it was a very, very long way down to the ground. A very long way from anything I knew or understood.

"What happens if I cannot help?" I panted. "If I try and fail? What happens to your daughter then?"

What happens to me? Will you still love me? I thought.

"Nothing but what happens to us all," Melisande replied after a moment. "My daughter will grow old and die. During the years she has been imprisoned in this place, time has not moved in the same way for Rue as it has for you and me. Her days have been a waking dream, peaceful and quiet. At the turning of each year, she has aged a single day, no more. With our coming, time has resumed its normal course. Whether you leave or stay, whether you succeed or fail, from this day forward, Rue will move through time as the rest of us."

"Merciful heavens," I whispered, appalled at the ramifications of Melisande's words. Rue had been safe, in a way, while she'd been left alone. But our very coming had set in motion a sequence of events that could not be stopped. Now the sorceress's daughter would no longer be spared the passage of time. Instead, she would be free to count every single moment of her captivity. This would be the only freedom I would give her, if I failed to find the way to awaken her heart.

"What have we done?" I whispered.

And Melisande answered simply, "What we must."

I looked at her then, standing still as the cold wind at the top of the tower blew against us both. It came to me, in that moment, that Melisande was old. For more years than I had been alive she had carried the wizard's curse within her heart. She could have let it turn her hard and bitter, but she had not. Instead she had found room inside her heart for me. She had kept her hopes for her daughter alive.

How strong her heart must be, I thought. Could mine learn to be as strong?

That was the moment I thought I understood. I could let two days of pain and confusion wipe away all the love that had come before. I could make that the full measure of my heart. If I did, I would fail us all, but myself the most.

No, I thought. *I will not repay love with selfishness. I will not bring down such a curse upon myself.*

Yes, I was afraid, clear through to the marrow of my bones. But I could not afford to take the easy way out. I would not let my fear be stronger than my hope. I would take this test, of my own free will.

"We might as well go in, then," I said. And prayed that, when I discovered my heart's true strength, it would be strong enough.

It could have been no more than fifteen paces from the tower railing to those great and shimmering panes of glass, one of which stood open to allow us inside. But moving across that short distance seemed to take as many years as I had been alive.

Now that I was close upon them, I could see that the panes were curiously made, curved even as the tower itself was. Their surfaces were as shiny as mirrors. I could not see through them to the tower's inside. I could see only my reflection and Melisande's as we stood together. I had my favorite kerchief on, the one with the black-eyed Susans embroidered on it that Harry had given me long ago.

At the thought of Harry, I stopped dead. *So much for promising to stay out of trouble,* I thought.

"Rapunzel?" said Melisande.

"Coming," I said. I walked the last two paces, trying very hard not to think about Harry, and stepped inside.

It was beautiful. I swear to you that this was my very first thought, as every other fled in wonder from my mind.

The room at the tower's top was high-ceilinged, soaring upward on great wings of stone. Far from being the cold gray it had seemed at first, the stone now seemed to give off its own light, glowing warm and golden. In the room's center, protected by an elaborate wrought-iron railing much like the one outside, a great staircase curved down. Beyond that, I could see a loom strung with all the colors of the rainbow. Its shape contained the only straight lines I had yet seen in this place.

But it was the young woman standing beside the loom who drew and held my eyes.

She was about my age, just as Melisande had said she would be, though that was the wizardry at work, of course. Slim and straight and taller than I was, with skin so fair I could see the blue veins running underneath, see the throb of the pulse at her temple and throat. Without thinking, I counted the beats and so discovered that they precisely matched my own. Her eyes were a color I had seen only in the garden. Dark, like the faces of pansies.

Beautiful, I thought once more.

But frozen, like a plant that had bloomed too soon and been caught by a sudden frost. The sorceress's daughter still possessed her outward form. But inside, it seemed to me that everything was brittle, holding its breath, as if waiting to discover if the next thing to come along would be the frost that would kill it, or the thaw that would bring it back to life.

I will be that force of nature, I thought. By my actions, I would determine both Rue's future and my own.

She moved, then, almost as if she'd heard me, as if I had spoken my troublesome thought aloud. No more than a tilt of her head, a shift of her shoulders, but it was enough. Enough to show me that my eyes had deceived me in one thing: It wasn't the stone giving off the golden light. It wasn't the stone at all.

Flowing over the young woman's shoulders, running the length of her body to curve in great shining coils at her feet, was the braid that Melisande and I had used to scale the tower. It was this that caused the room to glow as if alive, burning with its own inner fire. I had a feeling it would shine, just like this, even in the dead of night.

Hair, I thought.

Hair such as I had imagined only in my dreams. Hair as bright and shining as the sun. As golden as the petals of the flowers I had been forced to leave behind in our back garden.

If I could have wept then, I would have done it. But beneath Rue's violet gaze, my eyes were as dry as the stone walls that suddenly seemed to close in all around. *No wonder her mother heard the sound of a door opening,* I thought. At that moment, I could almost hear it myself. I could see the way that Rue and I might fit together. Two halves of the same circle. The lock and the key.

Then her gaze shifted, and Rue looked at Melisande. As their eyes met, a strange ripple of movement seemed to pass through them both, and I saw the sorceress press a hand to her heart. But whether it was because she felt a sudden stab of pain or joy, I could not tell.

Rue's lips parted, and she drew in a breath. "Mama," she said, her voice sounding musical and rusty all at once. Like a fine instrument that has gone unused for many years but has not yet forgotten how to sound a tone.

"Mama?" she said once more, a question this time, her voice stronger and more urgent.

"Rue. My child," said Melisande.

I did weep then, as I watched the sorceress and her daughter slowly move together until each had stepped into the other's outstretched arms.

Eleven

It was the cat who decided things, in the end. A turn of events I don't think any of us, not even Melisande, could have foretold. Not that I made the final decision to stay and help lightly. It was merely that Mr. Jones enabled me to catch a glimpse of something I might not have been able to see on my own. And this turned out to be what tipped the scales and changed the balance, weighing it down on Rue's side.

Prior to that particular moment, however, in spite of all my noble intentions, it was pretty touch and go. It's one thing to think you understand what the right thing to do is. Actually doing it isn't always as straightforward, or as noble, as it sounds.

"Rapunzel, this is my daughter, Rue," Melisande said, once

we had all shed tears for our own reasons and things had settled down. "Rue, this is Rapunzel, who is our hope."

She looked at me then with those violet eyes. In them I could read absolutely nothing at all. When Rue looked at her mother, her eyes seemed vivid and alive. But when she looked at me, they were flat and dull. I recognized the look; it seemed I was not the only one who was afraid and unwilling to show it.

"Why?" she asked simply.

Well, that's getting right to the point, I thought.

"Because I love her as I have loved no one else but you," Melisande answered, as honestly as always. "I hope this love may help her break the curse that binds you."

"She's supposed to find the way to free me?" Rue asked, and all of us could hear the disbelief in her voice. "But why can't you do it? I thought it would be you. You were the one who—"

I pulled in an audible breath and Rue broke off.

"I thought so too, for a time," Melisande answered after a moment. "But when I saw Rapunzel, I began to see another way, and so I made room for her inside my heart, took her in, and raised her as my own."

Rue's eyes flickered to me, and then away. They definitely held emotion now.

"All this time," she said. "She's been with you the whole time we've been kept apart?"

"Not all of it," Melisande answered, and I thought I could hear the effort she was making to keep her voice steady and calm. This meeting was hard on all of us. "Just the last sixteen years or so."

"I've been trapped in this tower, waiting," Rue continued, as if her mother hadn't spoken. "And you've been trying to replace me. You've been loving someone else."

"That's not altogether true," I said quietly. "Your mother loves me and I love her. That much is true enough. But she's never tried to replace you. She's never even let me call her mother. I think her heart is big enough to hold the both of us."

"What do you know about it?" Rue flashed out. "I never asked for your opinion, in case you didn't notice."

"Well, if I didn't," I came right back, "it's probably because I was distracted by the sight of you feeling sorry for yourself."

"I have a right to be unhappy," Rue began.

"Of course you do," I said. "But so do I. A week ago I had my very own bed, and apple trees to climb. My life wasn't perfect, but at least I had the illusion that it was mine. As of today, I've been dragged halfway across the country only to be informed that the reason your mother raised me in the first place was to help break the curse that keeps you in this tower.

"I learned about you yesterday, I'm meeting you for the first time today, and I have yet to decide whether or not I like you. What makes you think I'm any happier about all this than you are?"

"Well, don't expect me to ask you to stay," Rue said. "As far as I'm concerned, you can go whenever you want."

"Fine," I said. "Nice meeting you." I turned to her mother. "I'd like to go back down now."

"Rapunzel," said Melisande.

"No," I said. "I'm sorry, but no. 'Of my own free will,' you said. But she has to ask, some part of her has to want me to stay, or there's no point in this at all. I'm right and you know it."

"But I don't want you," Rue said. "I want—"

"I know, I know," I said. "You want a knight in shining armor."

"What's wrong with that?" Rue demanded.

"Not a thing," I responded. "But I'm not making any promises."

"You'll never get anything accomplished with an attitude like that."

"No, *we'll* never get anything accomplished unless you ask me to stay in the first place," I all but shouted.

We eyed each other for a moment, both of us breathing just a little too hard.

That was the moment the cat intervened. Bounding up the spiral staircase to pounce upon the ribbon at the end of Rue's hair. I hadn't thought about Mr. Jones since our arrival. But now here he was, a great fat copper penny wrestling with all that gold.

"Oh," Rue breathed. "A cat. Whose cat is it? Is it yours?"

At the tone of her daughter's voice, Melisande went very still. Together, we watched as Rue knelt and ran her fingers over

Mr. Jones's fur. A moment later, his rich purr filled the room.

"Does it have a name?"

"Of course it has a name," I said. "It is a he and his name is Mr. Jones."

Rue was sitting on the floor now, sitting on her own hair, though I don't think she noticed. If you can let people climb up your hair, sitting on it yourself probably counts as nothing.

"That's a silly name for a cat," she said, at which he crawled up into her lap as if he'd known her all his life, turned around three times, then curled up with his tail tucked beneath him, just the way he always did in my lap.

I felt a pang in my heart. *So that's the way things are going to be,* I thought.

"He's named for the person who gave him to me," I explained. "A tinker, called Mr. Jones. He has ginger whiskers. It was meant to be a compliment to all concerned, and it seemed a good idea at the time."

"Can we keep him?" Rue suddenly inquired. She looked up. Not at her mother, but straight at me, and now I could see the way those violet eyes could shine. Almost as brightly and beautifully as all that golden hair. "If you were to stay, could he stay too?"

"I hope so," I said simply. "For I love him."

Her expression changed then, and Melisande became even more still than before, so still she could have been one of the stones of the tower.

"Would you, could I—"

Rue exhaled a frustrated breath and began again, though I noticed she no longer met my eyes, but kept hers fixed on Mr. Jones.

"If you stayed, would you be willing to share him with me? Could I learn to love him as well?"

I took one very deep breath of my own, held it for a count of six, then let it out.

"I would be willing to share him," I said. "But whether or not you can learn to love him, only your heart can decide."

At this, Rue looked back up, her eyes wide. "You love him, but you would be willing to share," she said, as if she didn't quite trust that she'd heard me right the first time. "You wouldn't try to keep him all to yourself."

"Yes, I would share," I said. "Or at least I would try. That's the best thing to do with love, so I've always been told. If you can make room in your heart for the cat, I can make room in mine for the fact that you love him."

Her face changed then, her features slowly transforming themselves into an expression that I recognized: hope. Unexpected hope, at that, which is often the strongest kind.

"How would it work?" she asked, turning to her mother. "If I ask her to stay. How long?"

"Her name is Rapunzel," Melisande said. "You'll probably want to learn to say it. Together, the two of you must find the way to free you in the time it took to imprison you in the first place: two nights, the day that falls between, and the blink of an eye."

"Oh, for crying out loud!" I exclaimed. "Make it challenging, why don't you?"

"It isn't me . . . ," Melisande began.

"It's the wizard," I interrupted, "I know. You don't have to tell me. I'm beginning to think this world would have been a much better place if he'd simply learned to keep his mouth shut."

At this, Rue turned her head to look at me and did the very last thing I expected: She smiled. Before I quite knew what I was doing, I smiled back. Mr. Jones opened his mouth and gave a great, teeth-gnashing yawn. Rue's smile got a little bigger, and I felt my own hope suddenly kindle.

We can do this, I thought.

"Go ahead," I said. "It's not so difficult, once you put your mind to it. Just ask."

Rue gave a sigh, almost as if she'd hoped the fact that she already loved my cat meant I was going to let her off the hook.

"Will you stay with me, Rapunzel? Even though the outcome is uncertain?"

"Though the outcome is uncertain, I will stay with you, Rue," I said. "I will do my best to free us both."

And so the promise was made, and a bargain struck.

Twelve

I CANNOT TELL YOU WHAT WAS SAID AT THE SECOND PARTING between the sorceress and her daughter. It hardly seemed right for me to overhear it, so I went back out of that great golden room the same way I'd come, then walked around the tower's top until I could see the river and the tinker Mr. Jones, both far below me. I stood for a moment with my hands on the railing, as he looked up, and I looked down.

"You are going to stay, then," he said, his voice reaching me easily.

"I am," I said. "Though not for long, assuming all goes well. I'm to free the sorceress's daughter in the same time it took to make her a prisoner: two nights, the day that falls between, and the blink of an eye. How did you know? That I would stay, I mean."

"I didn't," the tinker answered. "I only thought you might."

"It's that heart thing again, isn't it?" I said, and, to my relief, we both smiled.

"Something like that," the tinker agreed. "Have you thought about what you'll tell Harry? He's going to want some sort of explanation, you know."

I felt the tower sway beneath my feet then, though my head knew it hadn't moved at all. Harry. I'd forgotten all about Harry. Again.

"No, I can see that you haven't," said Mr. Jones.

"I didn't mean . . . I never thought . . . ," I said.

"Take a deep breath," Mr. Jones said. "Stay calm. I'm sure you'll think of something when the time comes. You seem to have done all right so far."

"Where will you go? What will you do?" I asked. For, now that my brain was thinking beyond the tower, it seemed to me unlikely that the tinker and the sorceress would simply sit at its base and gaze upward for seventy-two hours, no matter how much Melisande might want to.

"I have traveled in this land a little," Mr. Jones said. "There is a town about a day's journey through the forest, the seat of the king who rules these parts. That's as good a place to go as any."

"What of Melisande?"

"You'd better ask her that yourself," the tinker said. At this,

I turned to discover the sorceress standing by my side.

"Ask me what?" said Melisande.

"I was wondering whether or not you'd go with him," I said. "He's going to the closest town. I think I'd feel better knowing the two of you were together."

"Are you asking me to do this?" Melisande said, and I thought I could see the barest hint of a twinkle at the back of her eyes.

One good question deserves another, I thought.

"Yes, I am asking you to do this," I said. "For my sake, will you please stay with Mr. Jones?"

"Gladly," Melisande replied. "For your sake, as well as my own."

With that, before I quite realized what she intended, she reached out and enfolded me in her arms. A thousand memories seemed to rush through me, as if summoned of their own accord.

The sorceress and I sitting before the fire on a winter's night as she patiently taught my fumbling fingers to knit. Standing in the kitchen on a hot summer's day, laughing as we realized that every single one of our mutual twenty fingers was stained the exact same color from picking blueberries the whole morning long. I remembered lying in my bed at night when I was supposed to be asleep, gazing instead at where Melisande sat brushing out her hair. Wondering if I would ever have hair of my own, knowing she would love me just the same even if I never did.

She loves me, I thought. Against all odds, and in the face of her own pain, she had made room for me inside her heart. Now the time had come for me to return the favor for her daughter, if I could.

"Thank you," she whispered, and she stepped back and let me go.

"Don't thank me yet," I answered. "I haven't done very much."

She raised her eyebrows at this. "You think not?"

"I'll do what I can," I said.

"That's all that can be asked of anyone," she replied.

With that, almost as if she was moving quickly before either of us could change our minds, the sorceress spoke the password once more.

"One so fair, let down your hair. Let me go from here to there."

No sooner had she spoken than the pane of glass behind us flew open and Rue's great golden braid came flying out. Once, twice it wrapped itself around the railing, just as it had before, then plummeted down to land beside the tinker with a *plunk.* Melisande gave me a final kiss, then, without another word, climbed down. As soon as her feet touched the greensward, the braid ascended, *whoosh*ing out of sight, and the pane of glass closed silently behind it.

"We'll see you in a couple of days," Mr. Jones called up. "When Harry finally gets here, tell him we've gone on to the town. He can follow if he wants to. He can't get lost. All he has to do is keep to the main road."

"I'll do that," I said. "Assuming he speaks to me at all."

"Oh, he'll speak to you," the tinker answered. "I have a feeling you can count on that."

Then he helped Melisande into the wagon and clucked once to the horse. I stood at the railing, waving until they were out of sight and then some. Finally I turned around. The great bank of windows at the tower's top showed me nothing but my own reflection, with the sky at my back.

Was Rue on the other side of the closest one? I wondered. Had she watched me say farewell to her mother?

Stop it, Rapunzel, I chastised myself. *If you start off thinking of this as a competition, the whole exercise will be nothing but a waste of time.*

Time, the one thing I could not afford to waste. Holding that fact firmly in my mind, I crossed the stone balcony, whose width was fifteen paces but felt like a hundred, and went back inside.

Rue had remained sitting right where I'd left her, at the top of the steps with Mr. Jones in her lap. She was teasing the cat with the end of that long, long braid.

"Does it hurt?" I asked suddenly. "When people go up and down?"

"No," she answered, with a quick shake of her head. "I don't feel it at all. I don't think I feel much of anything, to tell you the truth."

I was silent for a moment, taking this in. "Maybe it's just a side effect of all this wizardry," I suggested. "Something that will wear off."

"I'm not so sure I want it to," Rue answered, with an honesty that would have made her mother proud. "It's safer not to feel anything, don't you think? Besides, I'm used to it by now."

I thought of the life to which I'd been accustomed, just one short week ago. Having it all yanked away so abruptly had definitely been painful. In spite of the fact that I felt I could almost see time racing by me, I decided to go slowly now.

"It may have to wear off, sooner or later," I suggested gently. "The curse does say something about awakening your heart."

"Oh, so now you're the expert?" she asked, her tone ever so slightly sarcastic. "What makes you think you know anything about it? You're not the one who's been stuck up here for time out of mind."

Okay, I thought. *So much for going slow.* If this was the way things were going to be, might as well throw myself off the tower right this second and be done with it. Better yet, I'd throw her off.

"For someone who claims she doesn't feel anything, you're awfully quick to pick a fight," I remarked.

"Am not."

"Are too."

Rue gave a sudden snort and looked up then, her violet eyes laughing. "I suppose you think you're pretty smart."

"No, I don't," I said. "If I was smart, we'd both be out of here by now."

I could have kicked myself as I saw the laughter drain away as if I'd poked a hole in a bucket full of water.

"I wouldn't worry about it very much if I were you," she said. "We both know I'm never getting out of here anyhow."

"We do not know that," I answered, stung. "Why is there nothing to sit on in this stupid place?"

At this, the smile returned, though it wasn't a very cheerful one. "There's a stool at the loom," she said. "You could try that."

I fetched it and placed it where I could sit facing her.

"We are going to do this," I said firmly. "We're going to figure out the way to get you out. Putting you here was wrong and cruel. It should never have happened in the first place."

I could feel her resistance start to waver, even as I watched her shore it up. I was familiar with the sensation.

"If you say so," she replied.

"There you are, doing it again," I cried. I got to my feet, in spite of the fact that I'd just finished sitting down. "Acting as if you're the only one who's ever had to face a problem. I've got news for you: You're not. What's the matter? Are you so afraid you'll fail that you'd prefer not to try at all?"

Oh, right, Rapunzel, I thought, even as I heard myself speak. *As if the thought hadn't crossed your mind.*

"Of course not," Rue answered, her cheeks coloring. "It's just . . ." She swallowed then, a convulsive motion of her throat, and I realized how close she was to tears. "I've been in this tower for as long as I can remember. I'm afraid to ask *how* long. What if I can't remember how to live like other people? What if I'm broken and can't be fixed? What if I . . . you know."

"I don't," I said, which was the absolute truth.

"Love," she said loudly, causing Mr. Jones to give a startled and indignant meow. "What if I can't fall in love?"

"Of course you can fall in love," I said.

"You don't know that," she countered.

"Okay," I said, as I sank slowly back down upon the stool. "All right. Officially, maybe I don't. But you said you wanted to learn to love Mr. Jones. I'd say that's a good sign."

"It doesn't matter," Rue said quickly. "Nobody's ever going to want me anyhow."

"What are you talking about?" I asked.

"Look at me," she cried out. "Look. *Look.* Use your eyes!"

"Let me tell you what I see," I said. "You have skin as fine as any angel cake I ever baked. Your eyes are a color poets dream of writing about, and your hair is as golden and bountiful as a dragon's hoard. You may see these things as posing a problem, but believe me, you'll be the only one who does."

"You think *this* is beautiful?" Rue said. She shot to her own feet now, seizing her long, golden braid with both hands and shaking it as if it were a snake that she would like to choke the life right out of. Mr. Jones leaped from her lap in alarm and disappeared out of sight down the great curved staircase.

"You try living with it for a while. I trip over it when I walk. Get tangled up in it when I sleep. I can't cut it—the wizard took care of that. My own mother has to climb my hair just to come and visit. If this doesn't make me a freak, I don't know what does."

"At least you have some," I said.

"Have what?"

"Hair," I replied.

At this, all the fight seemed to drain right out of her. She rubbed a hand across her brow.

"I don't understand a word you're saying," she said.

I reached up for my kerchief, pulled it off.

"Oh," Rue said, and her mouth made the exact same shape in surprise. Slowly she sank back down to the floor. "Oh, my."

"That's one way of putting it," I said. In that moment, I realized how tired I was. "How about this," I proposed. "Let's both avoid the word 'freak,' shall we?"

"Good. That sounds good," Rue nodded. She fell silent for a moment as we gazed at one another. "I suppose I can see now why Mama thought this might work," she finally remarked. "There is a certain symmetry involved. Does it hurt?" she asked, her question the exact same as my own just minutes ago.

"No," I said. "Not unless I get clumsy and run it into something hard and unyielding." *Sort of like you,* I thought. I put the kerchief back on.

"This really might work," Rue said cautiously after another moment. "Given the actual circumstances, I mean."

"I suppose," I said. "It might."

"Not that it means we always have to get along."

"Thanks goodness for that," I said.

She gave a snort. "Naturally you would agree with that."

"Perhaps I haven't any sense," I said. "Maybe it goes along with not having any hair."

"Oh, I know you haven't any sense," Rue replied. "If you had, you'd have climbed down all this unnecessary hair at the first available opportunity."

"I couldn't do that," I said. "I made a promise."

"To my mother, you mean."

"No," I said. "To myself."

We were both silent once more, while this thought slowly circled inside the tower, then came back to rest between us.

"Can you really make an angel cake?" Rue asked.

I nodded. "As tall as the oven door. I'll bake one for you on your wedding day. How would that be?"

She smiled then, a neither-here-nor-there sort of smile. Not quite joyful, but not sad, either. A smile that left the future open.

"I think that I would like that. Thank you, Rapunzel."

Before either of us could say another word, a new voice floated up the length of the tower.

"Parsley," it shouted. "What in heaven's name have you done?"

Thirteen

"Oh, dear," I said as I shot to my feet. "I was afraid of this."

"Who on earth is that?" Rue asked as she, too, stood up. "And why is he calling you Parsley?"

"Because he's a wretched tinker's boy with no manners whatsoever," I said. "His name is Harry." *And the last time I saw him, he kissed me in my own front yard.*

"I know you're in there, Parsley," Harry's voice shouted once more. "I met the sorceress and Mr. Jones along the road. If you're not out where I can see you by the time I count to ten, I'm coming up to get you myself."

"He can't do that," Rue said.

"I know that and you know that," I said. "Even Harry may know. It's not going to make a single bit of difference. Harry is the reason somebody somewhere invented the word 'stubborn.'"

"One," his voice floated up from the bottom of the tower.

"I'm going to have to go out there," I said. "He'll only do something foolish and hurt himself."

"I'm not stopping you, am I?" Rue asked.

"Two. Threefourfive," Harry's voice said.

"Gee," I said. "Thanks for your support. It means the world to me.

"All right, Harry," I called back, lifting my voice so it would carry. "You've proven you can count. I'm coming."

With that, I simply moved to the pane of glass that seemed closest to the sound of his voice and pushed it open. Fifteen steps took me to the edge of the balcony. They only felt like about fifty this time around. When I got to the edge, I could see him standing far below. Our horse cropped the grass at his side. I was so relieved to see that he was safe, I almost forgot to be annoyed.

"So there you are, Parsley," he said. "It's about time."

"That's a fine thing for you to say," I came right back. "You're the one who's late, tinker's boy."

"I thought you were going to stay out of trouble," he said.

"I'm not in trouble. I'm in a tower," I replied.

"Oh, ha-ha," he said. "Very funny. You promised, or don't you recall?"

"Of course I do," I said. *I remember everything about the day we said good-bye.* "I'm not in trouble, Harry. Honestly, I'm not. I'm doing something for Melisande."

"Staying with her daughter," he nodded. "I know. I told you. I met them on the road. That's why I was late. I had to make a detour around a band of soldiers. Some unrest is brewing in this land. I'm not so sure it's any safer than the one we left behind."

"You'd better catch up with them, then," I said. "It might not be safe for you to be on your own."

Harry shook his head, and even from high above I recognized the stubborn set of his jaw.

"Not until I know that you're all right," he said.

"Harry," I said, doing my best to sound patient even when I didn't particularly feel that way. "I'm fine. This tower is protected by a wizard's magic. No one can get up here unless they know how to ask properly."

"The sorceress said there was a password," he admitted. He kicked irritably at the perfect swath of grass that surrounded the tower. "She wouldn't tell me what it was."

"That's as it should be," I said. "Now go away and come back with Mr. Jones and Melisande."

"Stop doing that," he suddenly said, and he used the foot that had been kicking grass to get in a good old-fashioned stomp. "Stop treating me as if you were all grown up and important and I'm no more than an irritating child. I haven't seen you for six days. I worried about you, dammit."

"I worried about you, too," I said.

"You might have waited for me, you know."

"I'm sorry, Harry," I said. "I didn't think I could."

He gave the grass one last stab with his toe.

"So, what's she like?"

"Who?" I said.

"Don't be stupid, Parsley," Harry said. "The sorceress's daughter, of course."

"As beautiful as an angel," I said.

"Fine. Don't tell me."

"I'm telling you the truth," I protested. And then a thought occurred to me. "Stay here. I'll be right back."

"Rapunzel, wait," Harry called. But by then, I'd already turned and marched back inside the tower. Rue was standing beside the window I'd left open, staring out as if she could see Harry far below.

"I need you to come outside," I said.

Rue backed up a step, her eyes growing wide. "What are you talking about?" she asked, as her already pale cheeks turned the even paler color of chalk. "I can't go outside. You know that."

"Not *outside* outside," I said. "Just out onto the balcony. I want Harry to see you, so he knows I'm all right."

Rue shook her head, the light dancing across her hair the same way it did upon water.

"I can't go out," she said again.

"Can't, or won't?" I asked. I put my hands on my hips as a

sudden suspicion occurred. "I'll bet you've never even tried."

She opened her mouth, seemed to think better of whatever she'd been about to say, and closed it with a snap.

"You're right," she admitted after a moment. "I've never even tried. There were times when I thought I wanted to. But then I thought, I feared, that if I tried and failed, it must surely break my heart."

Because her words made perfect sense, I moved to her and put a hand on her arm. She flinched, ever so slightly, though I don't think she minded the gesture. It was that, compared with the chill of her skin, mine felt so warm. My first impression had been right, I thought. The sorceress's daughter was like a plant held in thrall by a sudden frost. I would have to find the way to thaw her out. In this moment, I thought I saw how to make at least a start.

"What if you tried and succeeded?" I asked. "What might that do to your heart?"

"I haven't the faintest idea," she said. "But . . ." She took a breath and looked me straight in the eye. "If you ask me to go, I'll do my best."

I gave a quick laugh almost before I knew what I had done.

"That does seem only fair," I said. "Not to mention very sneaky of you. But very well: Will you please accompany me out onto the balcony, Rue?"

"Are you coming with me?" she asked.

"Absolutely," I answered.

"In that case, I think I would like to try."

"No changing your mind at the very last minute," I said. "If you do, I'm just going to drag you out anyhow. By all that hair, most likely."

"Thanks for your support. It means the world to me," she said, parroting my own words. But I could see the fear, rising like a tide in those lovely violet eyes.

"It's just a few steps, Rue," I said, as I linked my arm through hers. "You can do this."

"Okay," she said. "If you say so."

It was all of about six steps from where we stood to the pane of glass that let out onto the balcony. I solemnly swear they were the longest steps I'd ever taken in my life. Longer even than the time it had taken me to get from the balcony to the tower. How long the distance felt to Rue, I cannot tell.

"Just one more step," I finally said. And then, at last, we were standing outside. Rue raised a hand to shield her eyes.

"It's so bright," she said. "Okay, I did it. I think I'd like to go back in now."

"You have *not* done it," I said firmly, as I kept ahold of her arm. "We have to go all the way to the railing, so Harry can see you."

"Rapunzel," his voice floated up at precisely that moment. "What's happening up there? What's going on?"

"Just another minute, Harry," I called. "There's someone I'd like you to meet." I turned back to Rue. "It's only fifteen paces more. We can even count them out, if you think that will help."

"There's no need to treat me like a child," Rue snapped.

"Fine," I answered. "Then stop acting like one."

There's a reason that daring people to accept a challenge almost always works. Put fear and pride head to head, and pride will win almost every single time. At my words Rue lifted her chin, even as her eyes continued to squint against the outdoor sunlight, and yanked her arm from mine.

"I'm not a child," she said. "I'm not." Then, gathering up as much of that fat golden braid as her arms would carry, she marched the fifteen paces to the railing and looked down.

"You must be Harry," she said. "My name is Rue, and I'm very pleased to meet you." She let her hair drop down onto the balcony with a *thunk*.

There was a pause. In it I could hear the wind moving through the trees of the forest. The water of the river moving over stones. The croak of frogs at the water's edge. Birdsong.

Then Harry said, "Thank you. That's right. Harry. Yes. Harry. Thank you very much."

At that, I made it to the railing in record time. Fifteen paces that actually felt like less. Because, as Harry had spoken, I'd felt my heart give a sudden clutch. I gripped the railing, staring downward at him. He had lifted a hand as if he were dazzled, as if he were staring straight into the sun, when, in fact, it was behind him. Then he dropped it, and I could see the expression on his face.

Merciful heavens, I thought. *What have I done?*

It was Rue, of course. Even inside, she'd seemed to give off her own light. But in the true light of day, she was all but blinding. Her hair caught the sunlight and sent it back so that it gleamed like an enormous heap of newly minted coins. Even her dress, which I had thought as plain and simple as my own, I suddenly discovered to be shot through with golden thread, so that it glinted with every breath she took. Her face, so fearful and uncertain just moments before, was now filled with an intrigued delight.

I could almost hear the crack of the ice that had contained her, could almost see it be swept away, even as I saw Rue herself begin to come to life.

Beautiful, I thought, just as I had when I had seen her for the very first time. The most beautiful thing I'd seen in my entire life. And all of that beauty, all that awakening light, was streaming straight down at the young man I loved.

I turned away then and sank slowly down to the stone of the balcony, my back pressed against the railing. For I was afraid that, if I stood up straight for one moment longer, I would fall. That's what my heart was doing, a long slow tumble through space on its way to I wasn't quite sure what destination. Uncertain outcome.

When had it happened? I wondered. When had my heart decided that what it felt for the tinker's boy was love?

Had it been the day he'd given me the kerchief? The kiss,

so unexpected and so sweet, that last day in the yard? Could it even have been that very first night we'd met, when I had seen the way his fingers had reached up to gently stroke the nose of the horse he'd convinced himself he wanted to steal but knew in his own heart of hearts that he would not?

Or maybe, I thought, as my heart finally caught up with my body and seemed to come to rest, though not particularly comfortably, it was only now. Now, when I realized that it all might be for nothing. The moment I saw what it would mean if he didn't love me back, when I had seen him blinded by Rue's shining, golden light. This was the moment I knew that what I felt for the tinker's boy was love.

"Heavens, Rapunzel," her voice suddenly said, from what sounded like a very long way above my head. "Are you all right?"

"Fine," I said. "I just got a little dizzy, that's all. It's a long way down." *A long way to fall.*

"But it's so beautiful out here," she said. "You were right, to urge me to come."

"I'm glad, Rue," I said. "Honestly, I am."

She bent over me then, a frown snaking down between her eyebrows. I bit down on my tongue to hold back the bubble of hysterical laughter that threatened to explode right out of my chest. *Even her eyebrows are golden,* I thought.

"You're sure you're all right?" she said once more.

"No. Yes. Of course I am," I said.

"What is it?" I heard Harry's voice call. "What's going on?"

"Something seems to be the matter with Rapunzel," Rue called back.

"Rapunzel?" Harry echoed. And at that, so great a dizziness swept over me that I actually put my head down between my knees. He sounded as if he didn't even know who I was.

"Yes, Rapunzel," I said, as I forced myself to my feet. The world seemed to sway as I looked down. "You remember me, don't you?"

"What are you talking about? Of course I remember you," Harry said. He put his hands on his hips. "I'm not so sure I think you should stay up there. I think that tower may be affecting your mind."

Not my mind, I thought. *It's not my mind at all.*

"She does act strangely sometimes, doesn't she?" Rue suddenly asked, her voice as delighted as I'd ever heard it.

"You have no idea," Harry replied.

"Okay, that's it," I said. "Rue, I think it's time to go back in now."

"But I just came out," she protested. "I like it out here. You were right."

"You could get a sunburn," I said. "It hurts a lot. I should know. I really think you should come back in right this minute." I took her by the arm and began to tug her away from the railing, back toward the tower's inside.

"Stop it!" she snapped. "You're hurting my arm." She tugged

against my grip. "Good-bye, Harry," she called. "I hope you'll come back and visit us tomorrow. Maybe Rapunzel"—she gave her arm a hard enough jerk to free it—"will have recovered her senses by then.

"Though personally," she whispered for my ears alone, "I doubt it."

"Of course I'll come back," Harry said. "In fact, I'm thinking it might be a good idea if I stuck around. There are still those armed men to consider."

"What are you talking about?" I asked.

"I told you," Harry said. "It's the reason I was late in the first place. I spotted a band of armed men I decided it would be better to avoid. They could still be roaming around."

"So you're going to sit around here and wait for them to show up?" I inquired. "What good will that do? They can't come up here any more than we can come down."

"Well, I think it would be lovely if Harry stayed," Rue put in. "It will give me somebody to talk to."

"What's the matter?" I asked. "Don't I count?"

"Not at the moment, you don't," Rue replied.

"I'll see you tomorrow, then," Harry said. "I hope you feel better, Parsley."

"My name," I said through clenched teeth, "is Rapunzel."

Then I turned and marched back inside the tower.

Fourteen

"I DON'T UNDERSTAND WHAT'S THE MATTER WITH YOU," RUE said, as she came in right behind me. "I did what you asked. I met your friend. He seems nice."

"He certainly seemed to like you," I answered shortly.

"What's that supposed to mean?" she said. "I thought . . . ," she stopped, and, to my horror, I watched as her eyes filled with tears. "Don't you *want* him to like me?"

"Of course I do," I said. I'd thought I'd already experienced the most miserable day of my life, followed shortly by the most painful and confusing. Now I knew that I'd been wrong. Today was much worse than either one of those, for it combined all those elements into one.

I can't blame Rue, I thought. That would be taking the coward's way out. How could I blame her for failing to notice what I hadn't noticed myself until now? The fact that the only way I realized I was in love with Harry was by watching him fall for her like a ton of bricks could hardly be considered Rue's fault.

"Don't pay any attention to me. I'm sorry."

Rue stared at me for one long moment. "I've come to the conclusion that you are impossible," she declared.

"I know that," I said. "I know it."

"The most impossible brat it's ever been my misfortune to know. Stop doing that, by the way. And stop interrupting."

"Stop doing what?" I asked.

"Agreeing with me at exactly the moment you're not supposed to."

I could feel my lips start to twitch into a smile, even as my heart wanted to weep. She was waking up by leaps and bounds now.

"I solemnly swear never to agree with you again," I said. "Not only that, I apologize."

"Impossible. Definitely," Rue said. We stood, face-to-face, and regarded each other for a while. "Something just happened, didn't it?" she said. "Something important. I'm just not sure I know what it was."

"You went outside," I said. "You proved you don't have to be a prisoner anymore. Now all we have to do is to figure out how to find that stupid door."

"And how to open it. Don't forget that part."

"I'm not likely to," I responded.

Find the door. Open it so Rue could be free. Free to walk out of the tower and straight into Harry's waiting arms.

That night I could not sleep. Not surprising, I suppose. In the first place, there was the undeniable fact that I felt I ought to be doing something other than sleeping. I only had tonight, tomorrow, and the night that followed, after all. But, though I racked my brains, I couldn't think of a single, solitary act I should, or could, be performing.

I'd walked the tower from the top to the bottom, climbing up and down that great curving stair until my legs ached, and seen no sign of any door. Rue had sat at her loom, passing the shuttle back and forth, and hadn't said a word. Not long after, the sun had gone down in a great blaze of red, and I had given up entirely. After a while, Rue had gathered Mr. Jones up in her arms and gone to sleep. But my eyes stayed wide open.

How can I help her? I thought. How could I find the way to free Rue's heart, when I could no longer find my own?

For it seemed to me that my heart was lost. It roamed through some vast, uncharted wilderness, like the forest I could see when I looked out from the tower's top. It was dark where my heart roamed. The territory was so unfamiliar that, merely by setting foot within it, my heart had lost its way. It might wander in this dark place forever and never be found.

What if it's never even missed? I thought. At this my fear grew so great that my body could no longer remain still. I got up, and, on feet as silent as I could make them, I moved to the closest pane of glass, pushed it open, and stepped outside. The bright, clear day had been followed by an all but moonless night. The sky above me was a great and single sweep of dark. In it the stars sparkled like water drops. I found the closest one. Or maybe it was simply the biggest, pulsing now blue, now white.

"I don't even know what to wish for," I said, altogether failing to notice that I had spoken aloud. I often did this, particularly when I was troubled and trying to sort things out.

"I don't seem to know much of anything at all. How can I find the key to awaken someone else's heart, when I can't even keep track of my own?"

"Take mine."

I was glad I was nowhere near the railing, because the sound of a second voice so startled me that, if I'd been at the tower's edge, chances were good I'd have tumbled right off it in surprise.

"That isn't funny, Harry," I said.

"I wasn't joking," the voice replied. "I'm not Harry, either."

"What do you mean you're not Harry?" I said, though now that I knew to listen I had to acknowledge that the voice didn't sound quite right. "Who are you?"

"My name is Alexander," my unknown visitor replied. "Though most people simply say, 'Your Highness.'"

"Why would they do that?" I asked.

"Because I'm a prince," Alexander answered simply. "And you are?"

"Rapunzel."

"Pleased to make your acquaintance, Rapunzel," the voice claiming to be a prince named Alexander replied. "I don't suppose I could convince you to come out where I could get a better look at you?"

"It's too dark," I said at once. I was curious, I had to admit. Maybe I'd just had one too many surprises for one day, but I decided to stay right where I was. "There's no moon. It wouldn't make a difference anyhow."

"I suppose you're right," he said on what sounded suspiciously like a sigh. "Any chance I could convince you anyhow? I could say something princely and poetic. Something along the lines of love lending my eyes extra sight."

"You could," I acknowledged, as amusement began to take the place of shock. "But I wouldn't believe you, so you might as well save your breath. Are all princes this handy with words?"

"I think so," Alexander said. "All the ones I know are. It sort of goes along with the territory, I think. You know—diplomacy."

"So statescraft is only lies dressed up?"

"Of course not," he replied at once. "Though princes are taught early how to woo. It's how wars are averted, more often than not. Is your father worried about his neighbor? Fearful that he covets territory not his own? The solution is simple. Have your son marry the neighbor's daughter, never mind the fact that he hasn't set eyes upon her since she was six years old. Not that she's to know this is the cause, of course. Your number one duty, before anything else, is to convince her that your sudden devotion is nothing less than true love."

So that's the way it is, I thought. Now that my ears were learning how to listen, I could detect the strain of bitterness running through Prince Alexander's voice.

"I'm not a princess. You needn't practice your fine words on me."

"How can you not be a princess? You're in a tower."

"Good point," I said, beginning to be charmed in spite of myself. "Though it is an obvious one that changes nothing. I am still just plain Rapunzel." An idea was beginning to form in the back of my mind. So far it was just an outline. "Do princes see only what is right in front of them?" I asked.

"Some do, some don't," Alexander answered solemnly. "The best ones, the ones who grow up to be wise kings, know how to see what is there as well as what is not. That's what my father always says, anyhow."

"And will you master this skill, do you think?" I asked.

"I hope so," Alexander said. "For I am my father's only son."

"Oh, so you are on a quest, then," I said. "To help you gain wisdom and enlightenment."

"Not exactly," the prince answered with a snort. "I wasn't

joking about the king of the neighboring kingdom. He really is thinking of invading, and his army is much larger than ours. My father and his council are seriously considering marrying me to the king's daughter as a means of negotiating a way out. I've tried to reconcile myself, but . . ."

His voice trailed off.

"I'm sorry," I said, and meant it. At least when it came to helping Rue, I'd had a genuine choice. It sounded very much like Prince Alexander had none.

"You're sure you're not a princess?" he asked, his tone wistful. "It would solve so much."

"Quite sure," I said. "Though I am held in this place by enchantment. Might that help?"

"Absolutely," Alexander said at once, his voice picking up. "Damsels in enchanted distress trump neighboring princesses every single time. Nothing could be better than you being enchanted, in fact, for the princess's father is terrified by magic of any kind. I shall rescue you. We'll get married and live happily ever after. Meanwhile the king and his soldiers slink home in disgrace. How does that sound?"

"Like a fine plan," I said. "Always assuming it can be accomplished."

"But that's where you come in," Alexander pronounced. "If you'll just give me even one clue about the best way to free you, it would be a great help. Enchanted maidens often do this, you know."

"Where I come from, we call that cheating," I said.

"No," he countered swiftly. "Not if it's done in the cause of true love. If it's in the cause of true love, then we're in this together, striving against impossible odds."

"The only impossible thing around here is you," I said, though I did suddenly remember the way Rue had called me impossible only several hours before. At once, the idea that had been forming and re-forming in the back of my mind took a definite shape.

Rue, I thought. Rue, who feared she could never fall in love yet dreamed of being set free by a knight in shining armor. Not quite a description of Alexander, it was true, but pretty close.

"Why are you here?" I asked. "Why aren't you stargazing from the battlements of home? Tell me the truth. You have to, if you're going to attempt to free me in the cause of true love."

"The truth is that I ran away," he said, after a moment's pause. "And after that, I got lost. I encountered a band of our neighbor's soldiers in the woods. I think they were a scouting party. By the time I'd successfully avoided them, I realized I didn't have the faintest idea where I was. Then I saw the tower, and then I heard your voice."

"You could be in danger if you stay here, then," I said, suddenly alarmed.

"They were going in the opposite direction," Alexander

said. "Please don't tell me I'd be better off at home. I might be safer, for a little while anyway, but not better off. The only way I'll go is if you come with me."

"I've already told you," I said. "This tower is enchanted. I can't just come down."

"Then I'll stay until I find the way to free you," Alexander said stubbornly. "A real prince never abandons his true love."

"I am not your true love," I said. "You just met me not five minutes ago."

"Haven't you ever heard of love at first sight?"

"Love at first sight, yes," I said. "Not love at first sound. You've never even seen me. You've only heard my voice."

He gave a quick, unexpected laugh, and, just as unexpectedly, I felt my heart leap at the sound. *Oh, he is perfect,* I thought.

"I think you're splitting hairs, Rapunzel," he said.

Not I, I thought. *Not I.* But though I could not see him, I thought I could see my way now. So much would depend upon Rue, which was only fair, as it was her heart I was trying to free anyhow.

"What makes you think I'd be any easier to live with than the neighbor king's daughter?" I inquired.

"Just one important thing," Alexander answered. "I can choose you for myself."

Perfect, indeed, I thought. Now all I had to do was find the way to bring Rue and this prince together.

"Do you really want to help me?" I asked.

"I do," he said at once.

"Then come back again, tomorrow night. Promise me you'll stay hidden during the day, so the soldiers won't find you."

"I promise," he vowed.

"I mean it, Alexander," I said. "If you show up in broad day-light, I won't come out at all, even if you call my name until you're hoarse. I'll refuse to speak to you ever again. You'll have to go home and marry the princess next door after all."

"I promise, Rapunzel," Prince Alexander said again. "If you will promise something as well."

"What?" I asked.

"Promise that, sometimes, you will call me Alex."

"You want me to call you Alex?" I asked. "That's all?"

Even from the top of the tower, I thought I heard him sigh. As if many things he'd held inside for far too long had finally been let go.

"Just once more?"

"Alex," I said.

"Thank you, Rapunzel."

"You're welcome. I'll see you tomorrow night." No more than a figure of speech, of course. "And remember your promise."

"I will," Alexander said. "Good night, my Rapunzel."

I opened my mouth to say I wasn't his Rapunzel at all, then closed it before I made a sound.

"Good night, Alex," I said instead.

"So!" he said. "Three times, and the third time works the charm."

I thought I heard him move off then, for there came a rustle from far below. Then, without warning, I heard a sharp cry. I flew to the tower railing, my heart in my throat.

"It's never going to work, you know," a voice I knew quite well said.

"Harry," I hissed. "What have you done?"

Fifteen

"I DIDN'T DO A THING," HARRY SAID AT ONCE. "I DIDN'T NEED to. Your brave and handsome prince put his foot straight down a gopher hole, pitched forward into the trunk of the nearest tree, and knocked himself out. It's a miracle the soldiers didn't catch him earlier."

"You have to help him," I said. "Is he all right?"

"He'll be fine, Parsley," Harry said, and I shivered, for his voice seemed cold. "His head will probably be sore for a day or so. I'd thought better of you, I must admit."

"What are you talking about?" I demanded crossly. "And keep your voice down. I don't want to wake up Rue."

"Now why could that be, I wonder?" Harry inquired. "It

couldn't have anything to do with the fact that you're planning to sneak off and leave her with nothing, I suppose?"

"Of course I'm not planning to do that," I said. "What are you talking about?"

"Come back tomorrow night, Alex," Harry said, in a not particularly flattering imitation of my voice. *"Stay hidden during the day, so I'll know that you'll be safe."*

"You think I'd do that," I said, a statement, not a question. "You think I'd turn my back on Melisande and her daughter while the promises I made them both are still warm in my mouth. Are you sure you're not judging me by yourself, Harry? You were the one who once planned to steal a horse belonging to a man who'd saved you from death itself, as I recall."

"Don't think you can make yourself look better by throwing my past in my face," Harry said. "I heard what I heard."

"So you did," I said. "And now you can hear this as well: Good night."

I turned to go.

"Don't walk away. Don't you dare walk away from me, Rapunzel," Harry cried. "You owe me an explanation."

"I don't owe you a thing," I said, and wondered that I could speak at all for the way the words scalded my throat. This was what he thought of me, then. That I had so little spine, so little honor, that I would leave Rue to an unhappy fate and break my own word in less than a night.

"My debt is to the sorceress and her daughter. I mean to pay it in whatever way I can. Don't think that you can judge me, tinker's boy."

"Why must you always do that?" he demanded.

"Do what?"

"Call me by the one name you know I dislike the very most."

"I suppose that would be why," I said. "Just as that's why you call me Parsley."

"Your name is Parsley," he said.

"My name *means* parsley," I replied. "It's not the same thing at all. Go to bed, Harry. It's been a long day. But first, make sure Alexander is all right."

"He's really that important to you," Harry said.

"Yes," I replied. "He's really that important."

Not just to me, but to all of us, I thought.

I know what some of you are thinking: Why didn't I just come right out and tell him? Why didn't I explain what I had in mind? Here is the only answer I can give you: If you have to ask, you've never been in love. More than that, you've never had your feelings hurt by the one you want to trust and cherish you most of all.

So I did not explain why Prince Alexander was so important to me. I would let that be a lesson the tinker's boy learned for himself.

In time. If all went well.

"There's a woodcutter's cottage, not far within the trees,"

GOLDEN

Harry said. "It's old, but still well made and snug. I suppose there could be room for more than one. But don't expect me to wait on him or do his bidding. I wouldn't get your hopes up too high. He'll probably give up and wander off."

"Thank you, Harry," I said.

"I don't want your thanks," he answered shortly. "I'm not doing it for you. I'm doing it for Mr. Jones, and for Melisande. You're not the only one who knows how to discharge a debt."

"Thank you anyway," I said.

But my words were met with silence. Though I stayed on the balcony for many moments, listening with all my might, I heard only the sound of my own heart, and, high above my head, the wind, whispering secrets to the cold, unheeding stars.

"No!" Rue said. "Absolutely not!"

It was early evening on the second day. I had put off telling Rue what had happened for as long as I felt I could, a choice that had given me new sympathy for Melisande. There's something about knowing you have to tell someone something you know equally well they won't want to hear that definitely encourages you to hold your tongue.

I had to tell Rue sooner or later, though. The sun was about to go down.

"But it's the perfect solution. Don't you see?" I asked. "He already fancies himself half in love."

"With *you*," Rue said. "Half in love with *you*. I'm not a charity case, thank you very much. Besides, what's he going to do, call me Rapunzel?"

"What does it matter what he calls you?" I asked. "What's important is that he thinks it's love."

"But it would be a lie," Rue said. "A lie from the very beginning. How can a lie grow into true love?"

It was a good question, I had to admit, and one I had spent most of the day grappling with myself. I wasn't stupid. I could see the potential flaws in the plan I'd dreamed up so suddenly the night before, but I still thought it was worth a try.

Handsome princes lost in forests, and ones desperate to escape marrying the neighboring king's daughter to boot, weren't likely to come along very often. Personally, I saw no reason not to take advantage of the one we had, though I had to admit that the phrase "take advantage of" had a somewhat unfortunate ring, given what I was so eagerly proposing.

"The wizard who put you here turned love into a prison," I said. "That's not right either."

"So now two wrongs really do make a right? Is that what you're saying?" Rue asked crossly.

She was sitting at her loom, her fingers moving the shuttle back and forth in quick, irritated motions. Mr. Jones watched at her feet, his tail switching back and forth, waiting for the opportunity to pounce.

"Of course not," I confessed. "I'm just trying to point out that it's not always possible to see the end of something at its start."

"Very poetic," Rue said. She gave the shuttle another shove. Mr. Jones's head followed the movement of the shuttle. "But poetry is just words."

"You see, that's just what I mean!" I cried. "That's just the sort of thing I said to Alex, to Prince Alexander, last night. All you have to do is talk to him the same way you talk to me, and he'll never know the difference between us.

"Just go out and meet him," I urged. "Please, Rue. We're running out of time. I know this plan isn't beautiful and noble, but it's the only one we've got."

She was silent, frowning at the loom, but I noticed her fingers moved the shuttle more smoothly now.

"You realize this means you'd owe me a favor," she said. "This is twice you've asked for something now. I've only asked you for one thing. You'd be in my debt."

"I don't think that's quite the way it's supposed to work between friends," I said.

"Friends," she echoed, and she turned her head and looked at me with those violet eyes. "Friends," she said again. "Is that what we are?"

"Maybe not yet," I acknowledged. "But isn't that what we're working toward?"

"I honestly don't know," she said. "I guess so." She stopped weaving altogether. The second she stopped moving, Mr. Jones jumped. For a moment I feared he was aiming for the loom.

But instead he landed on Rue's lap, turning around three times, then settling in right where he was. I watched as her fingers absently stroked his fur.

"Waking up is hard work," she admitted after a moment. "Harder than I thought it would be. I was picturing—oh, I don't know—something more glamorous and a whole lot easier, I suppose."

"Sort of like a knight in shining armor?" I supplied.

She smiled at that, a smile that matched her name. A rueful smile. "It's just a dream," she said.

"Maybe," I answered. "Maybe not. Maybe all young men who love us become knights in shining armor when we love them back. Even if they don't, Prince Alexander comes pretty close all on his own."

"But he thinks he loves you," she protested.

"Of course he thinks he loves me," I said. "He thinks that I'm a damsel in distress, trapped by enchantment in this tower. I'm not, and we both know it. I'm the one who stayed here of her own free will. You're the one who's trapped. So which one of us does he think he's in love with now?"

"You're giving me a headache, Rapunzel," Rue said.

"It's one of my best talents," I said. "And that was a yes, wasn't it?"

She bent over then and buried her face in Mr. Jones's copper-colored fur. "Yes, that's a yes," she said after a moment. "I will meet this prince of yours."

"Of yours," I said firmly, as I got to my feet. "And remember, he likes to be called Alex."

She didn't speak again, not right away, but as we watched the sun go down in a blaze of orange in the river, I could swear I heard her practicing.

"Alex," she whispered. "Alex. Alex. Alex."

Sixteen

"I thought you weren't coming."

Of course I was coming, I opened my mouth to say. I was standing on the tower balcony, halfway between the windows and the railing, close enough to hear Alexander's voice but still be out of sight.

I've been looking forward to seeing you all day. Besides, it's not as if I have much else to do. I'm trapped up here, if you recall.

But instead, I bit down on the tip of my tongue and said nothing. For now it was Rue's turn to speak, to put in motion a sequence of events that would awaken her heart, win her a prince's love, and gain back her freedom, all at the same time. All she had to do was open her mouth and speak to Alex.

As opposed to what she was doing right this very moment, which was standing in one of the balcony's big casement windows, neither quite inside nor out, behaving precisely as if she'd just come down with a terminal case of laryngitis.

"Don't just stand there," I hissed over my shoulder. "Come out where he can see you. Say something."

"In a minute," she hissed back. "I'm working up to it. Don't rush me."

"I know you're there," Alexander called up. "Look, I brought a torch. Now we'll be able to see each other."

And the soldiers, if they're still around, will be able to spot you, I thought. *I'll bet Harry had a hand in this.*

"Just walk forward, as slowly as you like, until you reach the railing," I whispered to Rue. "Go see what he looks like. Trust me, the moment he sees you, matters will start to take care of themselves."

"You don't know that," Rue whispered back.

Oh, yes I do, I thought. "If you don't come out on your own two feet, I'm going to drag you out by your hair," I said.

"You wouldn't," Rue breathed. "My hair weighs more than you do. You're not strong enough."

"Look," I said, grasping my patience firmly with both hands instead of Rue's hair. "Just pretend you're taking medicine. Do it quickly and get it over with. I'm going to count to three."

"All right. All right," Rue said. "I'm coming. There's no need to—"

"Treat you like a child. I know," I said.

She stepped all the way onto the balcony and began to make her way toward the railing, Mr. Jones trailing along behind. As she passed me, I reached out to clasp her hand, then scooped up Mr. Jones. Five steps. Now eight. Now twelve. Then, at last, she stopped, and I saw her hands come up to grip the railing and hold it tightly. Perhaps it was simply the starlight reflecting off of all that golden hair, but it seemed to me that she glimmered like the last glow of twilight.

For fifteen beats of my heart, the same number of steps it had taken Rue to cross the balcony, she looked down, and the prince looked up.

"You are beautiful," Alexander said. "Even more beautiful than I spent all day imagining, my Rapunzel."

No, no! I thought. For, though highly poetical and romantic, it was altogether the wrong thing to say. It accomplished exactly what the sight of Alex had managed to make Rue forget: She was not Rapunzel. She turned abruptly from the railing and took two staggering steps away.

"Where are you going?" Alexander cried, and I could hear the pain and confusion in his voice. "I've waited all day, just as you asked. Now you won't even speak to me. What have I done?"

Without warning, Mr. Jones dug his claws into my unprotected neck. Stifling a cry, I let him go. He bounded across the balcony toward Rue. At the sight of him, her footsteps faltered.

She went to one knee and gathered him up into her arms.

"What is it, Rapunzel?" Alexander asked. "Are you unwell?"

Rue lifted her head then, and her dark eyes looked straight into mine. *You are a cruel and selfish creature, Rapunzel,* I thought. For Rue's eyes shimmered with unshed tears. Her heart was well and truly awake now. I had forced it out into the open before it was ready, then left it, defenseless, to fend for itself. All it had taken to wound it had been the sounding of my name.

So I did the only thing I could. The only thing my eyes and heart could see to do, in that dark night.

"I'm fine," I spoke. "It's just—"

"I know I look a little funny," Alex interrupted, the relief plain in his voice. "I'm sorry. I meant to say something, to warn you, but when I saw you, every single thought seemed to go right out of my head."

"There you go, sounding like a prince again," I scolded. "I thought we agreed we didn't need so many pretty words. What really happened?"

"I'm not sure I want to tell you," Alexander said. "It's too embarrassing. Let's just say I'll never make a good forester and leave it at that."

"Very well," I said. "If you say so."

"You're sure you're all right?" he asked again.

"I'm fine, Alex."

"Then come back out where I can see you."

At this, Rue made a distressed sound and shook her head.

CAMERON DOKEY

"I'm sorry. I can't do that," I said. "At least not for a few moments."

"I don't understand you tonight at all," Alexander said. "You seem so different. Don't you want to see me?"

"Of course I do," I said. "But this isn't some courtly game, Alex. You are free to walk away whenever you want, but I am trapped. It will take more than pretty words to set me free."

"I'm sorry," he said. "I didn't mean to sound false. What would you like me to say?"

"Tell me how you spent your day," I said.

"I made a friend," he replied at once, then laughed. Rue's head tilted toward the sound. "Listen to me," he said. "I sound like a five-year-old."

"A friend. That sounds promising. I'm happy to think you're not alone."

"His name is Harry," Alexander said. "I'm not so sure he thinks very much of me. He spent most of the day mumbling about useless princelings who can't see what's right in front of them. It has to do with what happened to my face. I think he was trying to be insulting."

Rue had turned her head to one side now, as if the better to hear Alexander's voice.

This can still work, I told myself. *Just keep talking.*

"Yet you call him a friend," I commented.

"I do," Alex said, and he laughed once more. "He may not think much of me, but I like him. He's certainly a change from

374

fawning courtiers and mealy-mouthed ambassadors. He has said that I may stay with him in the woodcutter's cottage, but not if I expect to be waited on. I wanted him to come with me tonight, so that I could introduce him. But he claims it's unnecessary, for you've already met."

"I have met Harry," I said.

"How long have you been in this place?" Alex suddenly asked, and I saw Rue wince.

"I'm not sure I know," I answered. "I don't think time has always moved in the same way for me as it has for everyone else."

"Have you no companions?" Alex asked.

"I have a cat named Mr. Jones," I said.

There was a beat of silence.

"I think," Alexander said at last, "that life in your tower must be very lonely. I meant what I said. I would like to find the way to free you."

"Because you feel sorry for me," I said.

"Because I love you," he answered.

I heard Rue pull in one shaking breath.

"How can you love me?" I asked. "We just met. Do you think love is a first impression and nothing more?"

"Of course not," Alexander said. "I have seen love. I can hardly claim to be an expert, but I think I know the real thing when I see it."

"Where have you seen love?" I asked. For it came to me, in

that moment, that I had never seen it for myself. Not the kind of love I wished for Rue, anyway. Nor the kind I wished for myself.

"There is a tale in my country," Alex said, by way of answer. "It is told to old people when they fall ill. Young ones hear it as they fall asleep at night. It tells of the days when a blight hung over our land. Nothing prospered. Nothing flourished. Not even zucchini would grow."

"It must have been a terrible blight indeed, if that were true," I said without thinking. Alex laughed, and it was a joyful sound.

"To tell you the truth," he confided, "I've never liked zucchini very much. But it does grow just about anywhere, so you have some sense of how bad things were."

"I do," I said. "I'm sorry for interrupting. Please, go on."

"The king of that time decided there was only one remedy," Alex continued. "He must marry his son to the wealthiest princess he could find, and hope that her dowry would help provide the means to bring the country back to life. This king's son was much more dutiful than I am. He met the girl his father had chosen on one day, married her on the second, and on the third, he brought her home to his castle, which was not much more than a pile of drafty stone. The princess took one look at it and said, 'I am now your wife. I have promised to honor and to cherish you, though I never promised to obey, for I have a mind of my own. Most of all, I have promised that I will find the way to love you truly. This, though I hardly even know you, for our acquaintance is no more than three days old. For these promises that I have made, and the ones you made in return, all on behalf of others, I would like to ask you to grant me one wish for myself alone.'

"'You have but to name it,' the newly wedded prince replied. Which was the gallant thing to say, if not the cautious one.

"'I wish you to build me a room,' his wife said. 'One single room where I will be warm in winter, and cool in summer. A room that will ring with my laughter, but where I will not be afraid to rage and cry. A room so well made I can trust that it will shelter me when all others fail, in which our children may be conceived and born. You must do this with your own two hands, for it is not a task that may be entrusted to any other. Will you grant me this wish?'

"The prince was understandably startled at this request. He had been taught to do many things, but building a room of any sort had hardly been among them. The truth was that he did not know how. But as he stood pondering how to answer, he discovered that he did know one thing: He knew how much he wanted to try. For the wish that had been growing in his heart all the while his wife had spoken was that he might prove worthy of whatever she might ask. And so he said, 'Madam, I am not certain I know how to grant this wish, but I am certain that I will try.'

"'That answer will suffice for now,' his bride said. And so, together, they went into the castle, and on their way in, the prince reached down and picked up a single stone.

"For many years the prince worked on the room his wife had wished for. Years that saw him become king, that saw his own sons and daughters born into the world to be princes and princesses. Years that saw his hair turn gray even as his kindom prospered. For the people of the land, inspired by their monarch's dedication, set about following his example. All they did, they strove to do well.

"There were many days when the king could do no work on the room at all. On those days, he would wrap his fingers tightly around the stone he had picked up on the day his wife had made her wish, as if, simply by touching this small piece of rock, he could make the room she had wished for grow. And, when, at long last, the day came when the king prepared to leave this life, on that day he turned to his wife with tears in his eyes.

"'I have loved you above all else,' he said. 'But still I have failed you, for the only thing you ever asked of me, a single room, remains undone.'

"'Great, foolish heart,' the queen replied. 'How can one so wise still be so blind? You have worked to build me what I asked for all the days of our lives. Even when the task seemed impossible, even when it would have been easier to give it up, you did not, but kept on going. You have kept me warm in winter, and cool in summer. You have laughed with me, and you have cried. You have given me the children who are almost, but not quite, my greatest joy.

"'For the greatest joy of all is the way you held my wish in the center of your heart through all the days of our lives. That is where the room that you have built for me lies. Just as the room I built for you lies within mine. And in this way have all our wishes been granted. Together, we have made ourselves a home.'

"Not long after this, the king died. Within the space of a year, his queen had followed, and the people mourned. But the tale of the young prince who set out to grant his new bride's single wish is still told to this day, and it inspires all who hear it.

"Do I think that love is no more than a first impression? No, I do not," Alexander said. "But I think that all love must start somewhere, and that place may be no more than the blink of an eye."

Oh, yes, I thought. For I was all but certain that I could see it for myself now. The way to free Rue. The way to free myself. The way to free love.

"Who were they?" I asked. "The king and queen in your story."

"My great-grandparents," Alexander said. "Their portraits hang behind my parents' thrones."

"And you're sure you don't want to marry that neighboring princess?" I asked. "Perhaps your father is only hoping that lightning will strike twice."

"Quite sure, thank you," Alexander replied. "Besides, it's too late. Lightning may indeed strike twice, but I fear it has already struck. I will have no bride but you, Rapunzel. That much my eyes, and my heart, have told me tonight."

There! I thought. Now all I had to do was prove to Rue that I was right.

"Did you hear that?" I whispered to Rue, who had been listening, her face bowed down over Mr. Jones's copper-colored fur, all this while.

"I heard," she murmured. "I heard him call me by your name. He calls me Rapunzel."

"Of course he calls you Rapunzel," I said. "It's the only name he knows. But he loves you."

At this, her head came up. "You don't know that," she whispered fiercely. "You don't *know*."

"Yes, I do," I said. "And I think I know the way to show you."

Grateful that I'd had the presence of mind to wrap myself in a dark cloak, I dropped to my knees and began to crawl forward. Illuminated by the light of the torch below, Alex should be easy to see. But I should blend into the night sky, for I had no golden hair to reflect the starlight.

"Rapunzel," Rue hissed, and she reached out and gripped me by the arm.

"Do you want to know, or don't you?" I asked. "This is it. There's only tonight. Let me do this. If I'm wrong, you can say 'I told you so' for the rest of our lives. I'm not even certain this is going to work, if that makes you feel any better."

"It doesn't," she said, but she let go of my arm. I scooted

forward another few inches. I was almost to the railing now.

"You don't answer," Alexander said, and I could hear both pain and wonder in his voice. "Is it that you don't believe me, or that you don't want my love?"

"Answer the question," I hissed over my shoulder, and saw the quick gleam of her hair as Rue whipped her head around.

"What?" she cried, then clapped a hand across her mouth. But by then it was too late, for she'd spoken aloud.

"It was hardly a trick question," Alex said. "I've said I want to marry you, and I mean it truly. You don't answer. Either you don't believe me, or you don't want my love."

"Just do it, Rue," I whispered. "Talk to him. You're going to have to do it sometime. Don't think. Just say what's in your heart."

"What if there's nothing there?" she asked.

"Of course something's there," I answered. "If there wasn't, why on earth would this be so hard? Don't make me count to three again."

"I hate you," she whispered.

"I know you do," I whispered back. Then I turned around and continued to crawl toward the railing.

"You think life is as simple as that?" I suddenly heard her voice lift. "The answers to important questions must be either yes or no?"

Oh, bravo, Rue, I thought. For surely it was better to meet anything—even love, or its loss—head on.

"Of course I don't," Alex protested. "It's just . . . I said I want to marry you. Doesn't that mean anything?"

"It does," Rue replied at once. "But first you have to get me out of here. And second . . ."

"What?"

That was the moment I finally reached my destination. I got to the railing and peered down. At the base of the tower, a torch blazed brightly. Beside it stood a young man, head thrown back, his hands on his hips and his face tilted upward. I could see a great bruise running down one cheek, precisely as if he'd done the thing I knew he had, run it straight into a tree trunk. His eyes sparkled as they caught the torchlight, and his hair shone like a polished copper kettle.

Like Mr. Jones, I thought, and made no attempt to hold back the smile. And then I had no time for any thoughts at all, for he looked up, and I discovered that I could do what I'd hoped: I could see into Prince Alexander's heart.

I almost looked away, for what I saw was blinding. A light golden and pure, without beginning or end, like looking straight into the sun. I blinked and it seemed to me that I saw a face. It was no more than an ivory oval, outlined by all that gold, but I thought I knew to whom it belonged. Never static, never still. Not the face of a beloved, set in stone, but set in light. A light that held the dreams of the future, the limitless possibilities.

That was what Alexander had seen when he looked into Rue's face. The seed of love, planted in the blink of an eye.

Yet from this no-more-than-an-instant beginning could grow a thing that would last the course of a lifetime. Nourished and tended like a plant in a garden. Built like the room for which his great-grandmother had wished, one stone at a time.

That is what love is, I thought. A possibility that becomes a choice. A choice you keep making, over and over. Day after day. Year after year. Time after time. And in that moment, I knew what I was seeing. Not simply Rue's face, though that was where it all began, but the very face of love itself.

And so, my eyes full of what I had found within Alexander's heart, I turned my head and looked into Rue's eyes.

I heard her catch her breath, then release it on one long, slow sigh. As if all her questions were being answered. And so I blinked again, and looked into her heart.

Rue's heart was a great confusion, and all of it caged and desperate to be let out. I heard a sound inside my head like the beat of frantic bird wings. The sound of footsteps going first down a great spiral staircase of stone, then back up again. Down and up. Down and up. Round and round. Round and round. I heard the sound her shuttle made as she pushed it back and forth.

But in the very center of her heart, no sound at all, only a single candle flame of light. A light I thought that I had seen, just once before. The light that had convinced me to stay with her in the first place. Rue's own hope, which—in spite of all the years she had spent relegated to the background of the only heart that knew of her existence—had still found the way to shine.

It was not as bright as the light in Alexander's heart. Not yet, but that didn't make it any less strong. For it had weathered storms his heart could never imagine and not gone out. In the very center of her heart, against all odds and misguided magic, Rue had kept alive the hope of love.

I closed my eyes then, and my visions vanished. I was just a girl in a dark cloak crouched at the top of an enchanted tower, and the wind blew all around.

"What's the second thing?" I heard Alexander ask. "Just tell me, and I'll try to accomplish it, whatever it is."

I opened my eyes and looked at Rue. She looked back, straight into my eyes. For a moment, the whole world seemed to fall away, leaving just the two of us at the top of the tower.

"There is a question that I have asked myself all my life," I said softly. "Though I have always known that I would never have an answer for it. I've wondered what it might be like to have hair. Shining, golden hair. Hair just like yours, though even I never imagined quite so much of it. You can give me the next best thing, if you will."

"How?" she whispered. "I don't see how."

"Don't leave this place as Rue," I said. "Leave it as Rapunzel. Rue was never your true name, but only the name of your mother's regret, and your own sorrow. Is that how you want to begin a new life?"

"No," Rue said. "No, it's not. But who will you be, if I am Rapunzel?"

"The same person I have always been," I said. "Only now my name can be one that I have chosen. From this day forward, if you are willing, when people speak of the longest, most beautiful golden hair in all the world, the name they speak will be Rapunzel. You would be giving me a very great gift. But only if that is what you wish to choose."

"Let me think," Rue said, and I could have sworn I saw a smile play at the corners of her mouth. "I can have my freedom and someone to love if I will take your name in the bargain?"

"Something like that," I acknowledged. "So what do you say? Is it a deal?"

"Oh, yes," Rue said. "I think so."

"Then tell your impatient prince the second thing that he must do," I said. "And so accomplish the first one in the bargain."

"All I wish," she said, raising her voice so that Alexander might hear, "is to be asked, rather than told."

"Is that all?" Alexander said.

"That is all," she replied.

"In that case, will you please marry me, Rapunzel?" Prince Alexander asked.

And the girl who would now carry my name for all the ages, the girl with the shining golden hair, answered.

"Yes."

Seventeen

"YOU COULD HAVE TOLD ME," HARRY SAID SEVERAL DAYS later as we walked beside the river. "I can keep a secret, you know."

"I see," I said. "That wouldn't be anything like the way you can trust me, would it?" I watched as a dull flush slowly made its way across his cheekbones.

"I've said I was sorry about that. More than once. How many more times would you like me to say it?"

"I don't know," I answered. "I'm still working that out. You hurt me, you know."

"I do know that," he said. "As I've said until I'm almost blue in the face, I'm sorry, Parsley. I never meant . . . Oh, for pity's sake," he suddenly exclaimed. "This is completely ridiculous. I don't even know what to call you."

"I've been working on that," I said, with a smile. "And I think I've come up with something."

"Just so long as it isn't Fenugreek," Harry said.

I laughed and slipped a hand into the crook of his arm.

It had been almost a week now since I had ceased to be Rapunzel. Days full of wonder that had seemed to fly by. No sooner had Rue accepted Alex's proposal than she and I were freed in a great burst of magic that lasted, as you can probably guess, no longer than the blink of an eye. Though it could have taken longer, I suppose. For the truth is that the experience was so overwhelming I kept my own eyes closed through most of it.

The tower first began to tremble, and then to shake, and then, with a sound like a thousand birds in flight, the whole edifice had come tumbling down. I had the sensation of falling head over heels, then landing lightly on my feet, through absolutely no effort I made myself. By the time I could bring myself to open my eyes again, I was standing on the greensward, which was now the size of a small meadow. At my back was the river, and where the tower had stood there was now a snug stone cottage with a slate roof and a bright red door.

Into each side was set a cunning curve of windows, which sparkled like stars. Later I learned that they had retained at least one of their former characteristics. From inside, it seemed that you could see the whole world, if you knew how to look. But from the outside, only your own reflection. The world could come in only if you invited it. Harry was standing in front of the cottage door, blinking rapidly, as if trying to figure out the impossible, which would be how he'd gotten there in the first place. He was holding the cat in his arms.

In the center of the meadow, a great ring of torches set fire to the night. And in the center of that stood Rue—Rapunzel now, of course—and Alex. Beside them was a very startled company of men on horseback. Soldiers, by the looks of them, each and every one with Harry's bemused and slightly alarmed expression on his face, and armed to the teeth besides.

The largest and tallest of them was just getting out of the saddle when I opened my eyes. He took several steps and threw his arms around Alex, lifting him in a hug so fierce he picked him clean up off the ground.

He set him down again and there were several moments of earnest conversation I wasn't quite close enough to hear. I was pretty certain I heard the words "battle" and "neighboring kingdom," and finally the word "magic," at which the king, for surely this could be no other than Alex's own father, gave a great laugh, took two more steps, and lifted Rapunzel off her feet too. And I remembered what Alexander had said, that the neighboring king feared magic of all kinds.

Then Alexander's father turned to his soldiers and, in a voice I was pretty sure was loud enough to be heard back at his own palace, a full day's ride away, said, "I give you Rapunzel, who has saved us from destruction and is to marry my son in three weeks' time."

At this, several more things happened all at once. The soldiers began to cheer. Harry dropped the cat, and I heard a sound like a set of pots and pans doing their best to impersonate a set of wind chimes. Into the meadow came the tinker's cart, with Mr. Jones sitting behind the horse and the sorceress at his side.

While Melisande was busy being reunited with her daughter, not to mention meeting her future son-in-law, the tinker had come to stand at my side.

"You were successful, then," he said.

"So it would seem," I replied.

He put his arm around my shoulders and gave them a squeeze. "I never doubted you would be, you know. I have always believed in the strength of your heart."

"You had more faith in it than I did," I answered.

"No," he said quietly. "I don't think that can be so. For if it were, none of what I see now would be happening. I gather you have given up your name."

I shrugged. "I never really liked it, to tell you the truth."

"What will you be called?"

"I don't quite know. I have something in mind, but I want to think it over a little more first. May I ask you a question?"

"Of course you may," the tinker said.

"Who is the girl that you hold in your heart? I didn't mean to look without permission, honestly I didn't. But I caught a glimpse once, years ago, and I—"

He put both hands on my shoulders, giving me a shake to stop the flow of words.

"Look now," he said. "See if you can answer that question for yourself."

And so, on that night when I thought I had already seen all that love might have to offer, I looked into the tinker's eyes. There was Harry, just as I expected, only now the girl I had seen before was almost at his side. She had but to take one step for them to stand shoulder to shoulder. To reach out to place her hand in his. And I understood that, in the tinker's heart at least, at Harry's side was where the girl belonged. Once more I saw the glint of gold that framed her face, and thought my own heart would crack with grief.

Then she shifted, ever so slightly, and I saw that the gold came from a kerchief with gold-petaled flowers embroidered on it. Flowers with centers as dark as the girl's eyes. And in those eyes, I saw the babe she had once been. I saw the tinker as a young man bow his head over hers as he held her in his arms. I saw him let her go, and what that letting go had cost.

I bowed my own head then, and closed my eyes. The visions wavered and were gone. When I looked back up, the tinker stood before me, only now I saw him truly. Saw what he had been all along.

"If my heart is strong, I inherited it from you," I said. "Father."

"My child," he said.

And then I walked straight into his arms.

The leave-takings began not long after that. For Alexander was understandably eager to introduce his bride-to-be to his mother, and the king wished to get back to the palace before rumors of his strange disappearance grew too dire and his wife too alarmed. Melisande would accompany her daughter to the palace. The tinker, Harry, and I would follow in two weeks' time.

"You are sure?" the girl who carried the name that I had possessed since I first drew breath inquired, as we prepared to part.

"I am sure," I said. "There was never any doubt in my mind."

"You really are impossible," she said.

I reached out and took a strand of that golden hair between my fingers. It was softer and finer than the finest embroidery silk. Not only that, it was the perfect length now. Flowing down her back to swing just above her heels, not quite as long as she was tall.

"Your hair is beautiful, Rapunzel," I said. "I thank you for it with all my heart."

At this, her eyes filled with tears. "I don't know how to thank you," she said. "I don't even know what to call you now."

"I'll tell you at the wedding," I said. "I owe you a cake, as I recall."

"An angel cake as tall as the oven door," she answered with a smile. Then she glanced over my shoulder, to where Harry stood talking with the tinker. "I'd like to say good-bye to Harry, unless you mind."

"Why should I mind?" I asked. At which her smile got a little wider.

"I'm sure I can't imagine," she said.

"Who's being impossible now?"

"Rapunzel tells me you have been a good friend to her," I heard a voice say as she moved away. I turned around and there was Alex.

Oh, you are a fine young prince, I thought. Even with that great bruise darkening one cheek, he was as fine and handsome a prince as any girl trapped in an enchanted tower could want. And he didn't stir my heart. Not one little bit.

"I have done my best," I replied.

He cocked his head then, as if listening to a tune he'd once heard, but whose name he couldn't quite recall.

"Have we met before?"

"You have never seen me before this moment," I answered, choosing my words with care, for I wanted to be honest. "But I will look forward to seeing you again, at your wedding."

He smiled. I watched the way his eyes sought out Rapunzel and stayed there. "She's beautiful, isn't she?" he asked.

"I have never seen anyone more beautiful," I answered, honestly once more.

"You would say this?" he asked, as his eyes flicked back to me. "I thought women were supposed to be jealous of one another."

"That is a tale that men tell to make themselves more important," I said, at which he laughed. "Besides, what's the point of being jealous of love?"

"I see that Rapunzel is right. You are a good friend, for you speak the truth," Alexander answered with a smile.

At that she came to him and took him by the arm. He gave me a bow, the first I had ever received from a prince, and together the two of them moved off.

Finally, the time came to say farewell to the sorceress.

"I don't know what to say to you," she said. "Though there is the obvious, of course."

"The obvious is the obvious because it works just fine," I said.

"I love you," she said simply. "Thank you for freeing my child."

"She did that herself," I said. "I just figured out how."

"She tells me you have inherited my gift," Melisande said. "I'm pleased."

I gave a snort. "It's a little uncomfortable, to tell you the truth. I'm sorry if I was unfair before."

But Melisande shook her head.

"I would like you to know this: I never let you call me Mother because I feared that if you did, when the time came, as

I knew it would, I would never have the strength to let you go. But I have loved you no less than the daughter I nurtured with my blood. You have lived inside my heart from the moment my eyes first beheld you. You have been mine from the first time I held you in my arms."

"I know that," I said. "I know it. Mr. Jones tells me that the woman who bore me died not long after I was born. Her heart simply could not find the way to beat, the doctors said. Perhaps the hole she had made in it was too wide."

"I hope you will call me Mother from this day forward," Melisande said.

"Thank you," I answered. "I will do so with much joy."

"Mother!" another voice called out. Melisande and I shared a smile.

"Your daughter Rapunzel is calling you," I said.

"So it would seem," the sorceress replied. "I'll see you at the wedding. I'll even help you beat the egg whites, if you like."

"I'll hold you to that promise," I said.

Then I watched as they rode away into the dawn.

Eighteen

It began with a theft and ended with a gift. And in between came an illusion, a sleight of hand, a choice that became the chance for love. For that is all we can see in just one blink of an eye. Love's possibility; its outline. After that, it's best to pick up a stone and put it in your pocket, to remind you of what you're trying to accomplish, what you're trying to build: a home inside your heart, a love that lasts a lifetime.

For Alex, it was a girl with shining golden hair, never mind what that girl was called. For me, it was a tinker's boy named Harry. And for Harry—I should tell you how we ended up, shouldn't I?

We lived happily ever after, of course. As did Rapunzel and

Alexander—and to the end of his days, she called him Alex.

What did Harry call me?

I'll tell you that as well.

After we had walked beside the river on that long-ago day, after all the others save the two Mr. Joneses had departed, we came to a place where a great rock sat in the center of the slow-moving current. I hitched up my skirts and waded out to it.

"What are you doing?" Harry asked. "Where are you going?"

"I'm going to sit on this rock," I said. "And, if you come too, I will both ask and tell you something. If you stay right where you are, you can just forget about it."

He gave a great sigh and waded out with much stomping and sloshing. But I knew him well enough by this time. I let him have his say with his legs and feet, and said nothing until he'd plopped down beside me. Then I took off my kerchief, the first that he had given me and still my favorite, the one with the black-eyed Susans embroidered on it. I held it in my lap, leaned out over the water to gaze at my reflection, and said, "This is what I look like."

"What are you talking about?" he said, his voice as cross as his legs had been. "Of course that's what you look like. That's what you've always looked like, more or less."

"I am not ever going to grow hair," I said. "In particular, I am not ever going to grow lovely, long, and flowing golden hair such as adorns the head of the girl who will now go through life being called Rapunzel."

"I still don't understand why you let her do that," Harry said.

"I didn't let her do it. I asked her to do it."

"What?"

"How would you rather be remembered?" I asked. "As the girl with the golden hair, or the girl who was bald as an egg?"

"Neither, if you want to know."

I gave him a push that would have sent him straight into the water if he hadn't known me well enough to brace himself first.

"You know perfectly well what I mean," I said.

"I don't care about your hair. Your lack of hair." He made an exasperated sound and dragged a hand through his own. "I've never cared about it. Is that what you're trying to ask?"

"Sort of," I said.

He leaned over and took me by the shoulders, turning me to face him. "I am only going to say this once, Parsley, so I hope you're paying attention. When I look at you, I don't see hair or no hair. I just see you."

"You kissed me. Why did you kiss me?" I asked.

"Not even you can be that stupid," he said. "Why do you think?"

And then he did it again.

His lips were impatient and just a little cool as they moved on mine, for the day was chilly, though it was fine. But the hands that held me close were gentle, and, beneath them, I felt my body start to warm. Just like the first time, my heart spoke one word and that was all.

Home, it said. *Home.*

Not very romantic, some of you may be thinking. To which I can only reply that you are the ones who haven't been paying attention. The kiss ended and I rested my face against Harry's chest.

"You make me crazy," he murmured, his lips playing against my smooth head. "You've always made me crazy. Do you know that?"

"I do it on purpose," I said. And felt what it sounded like when he laughed.

"What am I going to do with you?"

"You could marry me," I said. "We could make a home in that stone cottage."

"I could marry who?" Harry asked.

I lifted my head. In my lap I still held the kerchief. I looked down at it and said, "These are my favorite flowers."

"You told me that when I gave it to you. I know that," Harry said.

"Stop interrupting." I poked him in the stomach with one finger, and he sucked in a breath. "They're called black-eyed Susans."

"So?" Harry asked, but I thought I could see the beginnings of a smile play around the corners of his mouth. He was quick. He'd always been so quick. Quick and stubborn, with hair the color of mud and eyes like the promise of spring.

"Now who's making who crazy on purpose?" I asked.

"Susan," he said. "You want to be called Susan, am I getting this right?"

"I do," I said. "It's a good name. A straightforward name. A no-nonsense name with backbone."

"And it's not some nasty-tasting herb," Harry put in.

"It's not any kind of herb at all," I said. "So what do you think?"

"I think I love you whatever you're called, but I will call you Susan if that's what you wish."

"And you'll never call me Parsley again, right?"

"Oh, no. No promises about that," Harry said.

"Now wait just a minute, Harry," I began.

He reached over and gave me a push. I wasn't quite as quick as he had been. I hadn't braced myself, but I did grab him on the way down. We tumbled into the river together. Fortunately, it was shallow.

"So," I suddenly heard Mr. Jones call. "You've decided to live happily ever after."

"Looks that way, doesn't it?" Harry called back. He grinned down at me, and, in spite of the fact that I was soaking wet with small, sharp stones digging into my back, I felt my heart give a great roll inside my chest.

"Her name is Susan, in case you've been wondering," Harry said.

"Of course it is," Mr. Jones said. "Now come inside. It's time for supper."

"In a minute," Harry said.

He kissed me again, of course, until I could no longer tell whether the sound in my ears was the rushing of the water or my own blood.

"Marry me," he whispered. "Marry me soon."

"Yes," I whispered back. "Yes."

He let me up then. He pulled me to my feet and kept my hand in his as we waded back to shore. Just before we got there, he bent and picked up two stones, holding them out in the flat of his palm.

"You sneak!" I exclaimed. "I knew you were listening."

"Pick one," he said.

So I chose one, and Harry kept the other. And, though no one ever tells the tale of a girl named Susan and a boy named Harry, we have been living happily ever after, building the room that is our love, our home, inside our hearts from that day to this.

We build it, still, for as long as we draw breath.

Author's Note

WHY ON EARTH WOULD ANYONE DECIDE TO WRITE A VERSION of "Rapunzel" and take away her best-known feature? I can explain, honestly.

Several members of my family suffer from alopecia areata, an autoimmune skin disease, which can result in the loss of hair on the scalp and elsewhere on the body. It can occur in both women and men of all races. While not life-threatening, it is most certainly life-altering!

A couple of years ago, while home on a family visit, I happened to fall into conversation with one of my brothers-in-law. Both he and his daughter are affected by alopecia. I was mulling aloud over the fact that my editor was interested in a retelling of "Rapunzel." At which point my brother-in-law turned to me and said, "Could you do a version of 'Rapunzel' where she doesn't have any hair?" That was pretty much all it took to get me going.

I suppose you could say that, in addition to the official dedication at the front of the book, this story is also for those affected by alopecia areata. As I hope you found my characters discovered for themselves, beauty isn't merely in the eyes of the beholder. It's also in the heart.

WILD ORCHID

For Suzanne, Rosa, Anne, Sara, and Michel,
the gang at Cameron Catering without whose support
Mulan's adventures would not have been possible

One

WHEN THE WILD WOOD ORCHIDS BLOOM IN THE SPRING, pushing their brave faces from beneath the fallen leaves of winter, that is when mothers like to take their daughters on their knees and sing to them "The Ballad of Mulan," the story of the girl who saved all of China. For if you listen closely to the syllables of that name, this is what you'll hear there: *mu*—"wood"; *lan*—"orchid."

Listening is a good habit to learn for its own sake, as is the art of looking closely. All of us show many faces to the world. No one shows her true face all the time. To do that would be dangerous, for what is seen can also be known. And what is known can be outmaneuvered, outguessed. Lifted up, or hunted down. Uncovering that which is hidden is a fine and delicate skill, as great a weapon for a warrior to possess as a bow or a sword.

I sound very wise and knowledgeable for someone not yet twenty, don't I?

I certainly didn't sound that way at the beginning of my adventure. And there are plenty of times even now when wise and knowledgeable is not the way I sound, or feel. So what do I feel? A reasonable question, which deserves an honest answer.

I feel . . . fortunate.

I have not led an ordinary life, nor a life that would suit everyone. I took great risks, but because I did, I also earned great rewards. I found the way to show my true face freely, without fear. Because of this, I found true love.

Oh, yes. And I did save China.

But I am getting very far ahead of myself.

I was born in the year of the monkey, and I showed the monkey's quick and agile mind from the start, or so Min Xian, my nanny, always told me. I shared the monkey's delight in solving puzzles, its ability to improvise. Generally this took the form of escaping from places where I was supposed to stay put, and getting into places I wasn't supposed to go. My growing up was definitely a series of adventures, followed by bumps, bruises, and many scoldings.

There was the time I climbed the largest plum tree on our grounds, for instance. When the plum trees were in bloom, you could smell their sweetness from a distance so great I never could figure out quite how far it was. One year, the year I turned seven, I set myself a goal: to watch the highest bud on the tallest tree become a blossom. The tallest tree was my favorite. Ancient and gnarled, it stood with its feet in a stream that marked the boundary between my family's property and that of my closet friend—my only friend, in fact—a boy named Li Po.

Seven is considered an important age in China. In our seventh year, childhood comes to an end. Girls begin the lessons that will one day make them proper young women, and boys begin the lessons that will make them proper young men.

Li Po was several months older than me. He had already begun the first of his lessons, learning to read and write. My own would be much less interesting—as far as I was concerned, anyway. I would be taught to weave, to sew, and to embroider. Worst of all was the fact that all these lessons would occur in the very last place I wanted to be: indoors.

So in a gesture of defiance, on the morning of my seventh birthday, I woke up early, determined to climb the ancient plum tree and not come down until the bud I had my eye on blossomed. You can probably guess what happened next. I climbed higher than I should have, into branches that would not hold my weight, and, as a result, I fell. Old Lao, who looked after any part of the Hua family compound that Min Xian did not, claimed it was a wonder I didn't break any bones. I had plummeted from the top of the tree to the bottom, with only the freshly turned earth of the orchard to break my fall. The second wonder was that I hit the ground at all, and did not fall into the stream, which was shallow and full of stones.

Broken bones I may have been spared, but I still hit the earth with enough force to knock even the *thought* of breath right out of my lungs. For many moments all I could do was lie on my back, waiting for my breath to return, and gaze up through the dark branches of the tree at the blue spring sky beyond. And in this way I saw the first bud unfurl. So I suppose you could say that I accomplished what I'd set out to, after all.

Another child might have decided it was better, or at least just as good, to keep her feet firmly on the ground from then on. Had I not accomplished what I'd wanted? Could I not have done so standing beneath the tree and gazing upward, thereby saving myself the pain and trouble of a fall?

I, of course, derived another lesson entirely: I should practice climbing more.

This I did, escaping from my endless lessons whenever I could to climb any vertical surface I could get my unladylike hands on. I learned to climb, and to cling like a monkey, living up to the first promise of my horoscope, and I never fell again, save once. The exception is a story in and of itself, which I will tell you in its own good time.

But in my determination not to let gravity defeat me I revealed more than just a monkey's heart. For it is not only the animal of the year of our births that helps to shape who we are.

There are also the months and the hours of our births to consider. These contribute animals, and attributes, to our personalities as well. It's important to pay attention to these creatures because, if you watch them closely, you will discover that they are the ones who best reveal who we truly are.

I was born in the month of the dog.

From the dog I derive these qualities: I am a seeker of justice, honest and loyal. But I am also persistent, willing to perform a task over and over until I get it right. I am, in other words, *dogged*. Once I've set my heart on something, there's no use trying to convince me to give it up—and certainly not without a fight.

But there is still one animal more. The creature I am in my innermost heart of hearts, the one who claimed me for its own in the hour in which I was born. This is my secret animal, the most important one of all.

If the traits I acquired in the year of my birth are the flesh, and the month of my birth are the sinews of who I am, then the traits that became mine at the hour of my birth are my spine, my backbone. More difficult to see but forming the structure on which all the rest depends.

And in my spine, at the very core of me, I am a tiger. Passionate and daring, impetuous, longing to rebel. Unpredictable and quick-tempered. But also determined and as obstinate as a solid wall of *shidan*—stone.

Min Xian, who even in her old age possessed the best eyesight of anyone I ever knew, claims she knew and understood these things about me from the first moment she saw me, from the first time she heard me cry. Never had she heard a baby shriek so loudly, or so she claimed, particularly not a girl.

It was as if I were announcing that I was going to be different right from the start. This was only fitting, Min Xian said, for different is precisely what I was. Different from even before I drew that first breath; different from the moment I had been conceived. Different in my very blood, a direct bequest from both my parents. It was this that made my uniqueness so strong.

I had to take Min Xian's word for all of this, for I did not know my parents when I was growing up. My father was the great soldier Hua Wei. Throughout my childhood, and for many years before that, my father fought bravely in China's cause. Though it would be many years before I saw him face-to-face, I heard tales of my father's courage, discipline, and bravery from the moment my ears first were taught to listen.

My mother's name I never heard at all, just as I never saw her face nor heard her voice, for she died the day that I was born.

But the tale of how my parents came to marry I did hear. It was famous, repeated not just in our household but throughout all China. In a time when marriages were carefully arranged for the sake of family honor and social standing, when a bride and groom might meet in the morning and be married that same afternoon, my parents had done the unthinkable.

They had married for love.

It was all the emperor's doing, of course. Without the blessing of the Son of Heaven, my parents' union would never have been possible. My father, Hua Wei, was a soldier, as I have said. He had fought and won many battles for China's cause. In the years before I was born and for many years thereafter, our northern borders were often under attack by a fierce, proud people whom we called the Huns. There were many in our land who also called them barbarians. My father was not among them.

"You must never call your enemy by a name you choose for him, Mulan," he told me when we finally met, when I was all but grown. "Instead you must call him by the name he calls himself. What he chooses will reflect his pride; it will reveal his desires. But what you choose to call him will reveal your fears, which should be kept to yourself, lest your enemy find the way to exploit them."

There was a reason he had been so successful against the Huns, according to my father. Actually, there was more than one: My father never underestimated them, and he recognized that, as foreign as they seemed, they were also men, just as he was a man. Capable of coveting what other men possessed. Willing to fight to claim it for themselves. And what the Huns desired most, or so it seemed, was China.

To this end, one day more than a year before I was born, the Son of Heaven's best-loved son was snatched away by a Hun raiding party. My father rescued him and returned him to the safety of his father's arms. In gratitude the Son of Heaven promoted Hua Wei to general. But he did not stop there. He also granted my father an astonishing reward.

"You have given me back the child who holds the first place in my heart," the emperor told my father. "In return, I will grant the first wish your heart holds."

My father was already on his knees, but at the Son of Heaven's words he bowed even lower, and pressed his forehead to the ground. Not only was this the fitting way to show his thanks, it was also the perfect way for my father to cover his astonishment and give himself time to think. The boy that he had rescued, Prince Jian, was not yet ten years old and was not the emperor's only son. There were two older boys who might, as time went on, grow to become jealous of the fact that their younger brother held the greatest share of the Son of Heaven's heart.

At this prince's birth the soothsayers had proclaimed many omens, none of them understood in their entirety, for that is the way of such prophecies. One thing, however, seemed as clear as glass: It was Prince Jian's destiny to help determine the fate of China.

"My heart has what it desires, Majesty," my father finally said. "For it wants nothing more than to serve you."

It was a safe and diplomatic answer, at which it is said that the Son of Heaven smiled.

"You are doing that already," he replied. "And I hope you will continue to do so for many years to come. But listen to me closely: I command you now to choose one thing more. Do so quickly or you will make me angry. And do not speak with a courtier's tongue. I would have your heart speak—it is strong, and you have shown me that it can be trusted."

"As the Son of Heaven commands, so I shall obey," my father promised.

"Excellent," the emperor said. "Now let me see your face."

And so, though he remained on his knees, my father looked into the Son of Heaven's face when he spoke the first wish of his heart.

"It is long past time for me to marry," Hua Wei said. "If it pleases you, I ask that I be allowed to choose my own bride. Long has my heart known the lady it desires, for we grew up together. I have given the strength of my mind and body to your service gladly, but now let my heart serve itself. Let it choose love."

The Son of Heaven was greatly moved by my father's words, as were all who stood within earshot. The emperor agreed to my father's request at once. He gave him permission to return to his home in the countryside. My parents were married before the week was out. They then spent several happy months together, far away from the bustle of the court and the city, in the house where my father had grown up. But all the time the threat of war hung over their happiness. In the autumn my father was called back to the emperor's service to fight the Huns once more.

My father knew a baby was on the way when he departed. Of course, both my parents hoped that I would be a boy. I cannot fault them for this. Their thinking on the subject was no different from anyone else's. It is a son who carries on the family name, who cares for his parents when they grow old. Girls are gifts to be given in marriage to other families, to provide *them* with sons.

My young mother went into labor while her beloved husband was far away from home. If he had stayed by her side, might she have lived? Might she have proved strong enough to bring me into the world and still survive? There's not much point in asking such questions. I know this, but even so . . . I cannot help but wonder, sometimes, what my life would have been like if my mother had lived. Would I have learned to be more like other girls, or would the parts of me that made me so different still have made their presence felt?

If my mother had lived, might my father have come home sooner? Did he delay his return, not wishing to see the child who had taken away his only love, the first wish of his innermost heart?

When word reached him of my mother's death, it is said my father's strong heart cracked clean in two, and that the sound could be heard for miles around, even over the noise of war. For the one and only time in his life, the great general Hua Wei wept. And from that moment forward he forbade anyone to speak my mother's name aloud. The very syllables of her name were like fresh wounds, further scarring his already maimed and broken heart.

My mother had loved the tiny orchids that grow in the woods near our home. Those flowers are the true definition of "wild"—not just unwilling but *unable* to be tamed. A tidy garden bed, careful tending and watering—these things do not suit them at all. They cannot be transplanted. They must be as they are, or not at all.

With tears streaming down his cheeks my father named me for those wild plants—those *yesheng zhiwu*, wild wood orchids. In so doing he helped to set my feet upon a path unlike that of any other girl in China.

Even in his grief my father named me well, for the name he gave me was *Mulan*.

Two

My father might have left the "wild" out of my name, but it made no difference. It was still there inside me, running with the very blood in my veins, the blood that made me different from any other girl in China.

Min Xian did her best to tame me. Or, failing that, to render me not so wild as to bring the family dishonor. She had raised my mother before me, so she knew her business, and my father was bound to return someday, after all.

"You don't know that," I said crossly one night after a particularly stern scolding. Many years had passed since my fall out of the plum tree. I had just celebrated my thirteenth birthday. I was almost a young woman now. I would soon be old enough to become a bride. Whether I was wiser was a point Min Xian was always more than happy to debate, and I have to admit that the events of this particular day only served to prove her point.

I was covered from head to toe with bruises. As his birthday gift my best friend, Li Po, had offered to teach me how to use a sword.

The march toward adulthood had done nothing to diminish our friendship. If anything, it had only made us closer. Teaching me swordplay was just the latest in a long line of lessons Li Po had provided, which included learning to read and write, to shoot a bow and arrow, and to ride a horse.

The sword he'd offered to teach me with that day was only made of wood. We could not have truly injured each other. But a wooden sword can raise as fine and painful a welt as you are likely to see or feel, let me tell you.

I might have kept my sword lessons, and my bruises, a secret were it not for the fact that Min Xian still insisted on giving me my baths from time to time. In vain had I protested that at thirteen I was old enough and competent enough to bathe myself.

"I cared for your mother until the day she died," Min Xian declared stoutly. She made a flapping motion with her arms, as if shooing geese, to encourage me to move on along to the bathhouse. "What was good enough for her will be good enough for you, my fine young lady."

I opened my mouth to protest but then closed it again. Her voice might have sounded stern, but I knew from experience that Min Xian called me "young lady" only when she was upset about something. It didn't take much to figure out what it was.

Though she obeyed my father's orders, it had always bothered Min Xian that she could not speak my mother's name aloud to me, my mother's only child. In particular it pained her because she knew that learning my mother's name was the first of the three great wishes of my heart.

The other two things I wished for were that my father would discover that he loved me after all and that he would then come home. Neither of these last wishes was within Min Xian's power to grant, of course. This sometimes made her grouchy, around my birthday in particular. The day of one's birth is a time for the granting of wishes, not withholding them. And so I let her herd me toward the bathhouse, saving my voice for the explanations I knew I would soon be making.

When Min Xian saw my bruises, she hissed in sympathy and outrage combined.

"What on earth did you do to acquire those?" she asked, and then raised a bony hand. "On second thought, don't tell me. I want to be able to answer with a clean heart when Li Po's mother shows up, demanding if I know what you've been up to with her son."

"She isn't going to do that, and you know it," I answered. I sank into the fragrant bathwater, hissing myself as the hot water found my bruises one by one.

Li Po's mother fancied herself a great lady, and she did not care for my friendship with her son. The only thing that kept her from forbidding it altogether was the Hua family name, older and more respected than her own.

In particular Li Po's mother feared Li Po and I might follow in my parents' footsteps and fall in love. If Li Po asked for my hand and my father consented to the match, then his mother would have to accept me as her daughter-in-law whether she liked it or not. Ours was the older, more respected family. Marrying me would be a step up in the world for Li Po.

The fact that neither Li Po nor I had ever expressed the slightest wish to marry made no difference to his mother. Her son was young and handsome. The two of us had grown up together. Why should the day not come when we would fall in love? But Li Po's mother believed, as most people did, that love before marriage was not to be desired. It was unnatural; it complicated more things than it solved.

I wondered how Li Po's family would feel if they knew about the lessons he gave me, which were every bit as radical as marrying for love.

I'd never been able to figure out quite how Li Po managed to sneak away to give me the lessons he did, but I think it was because his family was more traditional than mine. Where I had only Min Xian and Old Lao, Li Po was surrounded by family, by aunts, uncles, and cousins, all forming one great and complex web where every member of the family knew precisely who they were in relation to everyone else.

It was both binding and liberating because with so many people around, it was easy for Li Po to slip away from time to time. By the time knowledge of his absence made its way through the family channels, Li Po was back where he belonged. This was the way most families operated. It was mine that fell outside the norm.

Yet another aspect of my parents' relationship that made them unusual was that each had been an only child. I had no cousins to run with, no aunties to help raise me, no uncles to help manage my father's estate while he was away fighting the Huns. I had only servants. The fact that I loved them as family made no difference. We were not true family, not related by blood. Save for my father, I had no one.

"Li Po's teaching me how to use a sword," I told Min Xian.

"Stop! Enough!" she cried as she began to scrub my back vigorously enough to bring tears to my eyes. "I told you, I do not wish to know."

"You do too," I countered, though my teeth threatened to rattle with the scrubbing. "Otherwise, how will you fuss?"

Quick as lightning, Min Xian gave me a dunk. I came up sputtering, wiping water from my eyes.

"First reading and writing, then archery and riding, and now this," she went on before I could so much as take a breath to protest, or get a word in edgewise. "What your father will say when he comes home I cannot imagine."

"You don't have to," I gasped out, as I finally managed to

wriggle free and scoot out of the reach of Min Xian's strong arm. I dunked my own head this time, tossing my hair back as I surfaced.

"We both know he'll say nothing at all. My father hasn't come home once, not in thirteen years. What makes you think he'll ever come home? If he wanted to see me, he'd have come back long ago."

Min Xian gazed at me, her lips pursed, as if she tasted something bitter that she longed to spit out.

"Your father serves the emperor," she said finally. "He has a place, a duty to perform." She frowned at me, just in case I was missing the point of her words, which, for the record, I was not.

"As do we all," she finished up.

"He'd have come home if I were a boy," I said sullenly. "Or sent word for me to go to him."

He'd have found a way to love me in spite of his sorrow over my mother's death, if I had been a son.

"You can't know what someone else will do ahead of time," Min Xian pronounced.

"That's not what Li Po says," I countered. "He says his tutor tells him that a man's actions can be predicted. That you can know what he *will* do by what he has, and has not, already done."

"That sounds like a lot of scholarly nonsense, if you ask me," Min Xian snorted. "You can never know everything about a person, for we each carry at least one secret."

"And what secret is that?" I inquired, intrigued now, in spite of myself.

"What we hold deep inside our hearts," Min Xian replied. "Until we release it, no mind can fathom what we will do. Sometimes not even our own."

She made an impatient gesture, as if to show she had had enough philosophizing. "The water's turning cold," she said. "Rinse the rest of that soap out of your hair. Then come sit by the fire so it can dry."

For once I did as Min Xian wished without argument, as she was right. The water did feel cold. But more than that, I obeyed her because she'd also given me something to think about.

Was there a secret hiding in my father's broken heart? If so, what was it? Maybe if I could discover what it was, I could finally find the way to make him love me.

Three

Sitting on a low stool before the fire, I thought all evening about what Min Xian had said, my hair fanned out across my shoulders and back as I waited for it to dry. Usually drying my hair drives me crazy. I have to sit still for far too long. My hair is long and thick. It flows down my back like a river of ink. Waiting for it to dry seems to take forever. That night, however, I was content to sit still and think.

What secrets did the hearts around me hold? What secrets did mine hold? Now that I was taking the time to stop and consider, I could see that it was not Li Po's clever young tutor who understood people best. It was old Min Xian.

All of us hold something unexpected deep within ourselves.

Something even we may not suspect or recognize. While our heart's rhythm may seem steady, so steady that we take it for granted, this does not mean the heart is not also full of wonders and surprises. That it beats in the first place may be the most surprisingly wonderful thing of all.

Without warning I felt my lips curve into a smile as one of the great surprises of my life popped into my mind, the day Li Po had first offered to share his lessons with me.

"I know you're up there, so you might as well come down," he'd called.

It was several weeks after that fateful seventh birthday. I was back in the plum tree, of course. Though I was trying my best to master my new assignments, wishing to make my father proud of me even from afar, the bald truth was that I found them boring.

If I had lived in the city, in Chang'an, my family's high status would have meant that I might at least be taught to read and write. But I did not live in the capital. I lived in the country, and neither Min Xian nor Old Lao could teach me such skills, for they did not know how. My father might have arranged a tutor for me, to remedy the situation, but he did not. On this as on every other aspect of my upbringing he remained silent. I tried to tell myself I did not mind this neglect.

I have never been very good at lying, not even to myself.

And so I was left to learning the tasks that Min Xian thought appropriate and could teach me. Of my three main assignments—

sewing, weaving, and embroidery—I disliked embroidery the most. I simply could not see the purpose of learning all those fine stitches, particularly as I wore plain clothes.

Most days I wore a long, straight tunic over a countrywoman's pants, and sturdy shoes that were good for being outdoors. My closet contained no embroidered slippers with curled toes, no brightly colored silk dresses with long, flowing sleeves and plunging necklines. Nor did I wear hairstyles so elaborate they could only be held in place by jeweled or enameled combs—hairstyles bearing names such as *yunji,* "resembling clouds," or *hudie ji,* "resembling the wings of a butterfly."

Instead I wore my hair in a long braid that fell straight down the center of my back. Most of the time I looked like a simple country girl, except for the days when I tucked my braid down the back of my tunic to keep it from getting caught on whatever tree I was climbing. On those days I looked like a boy. At no time did I look like the child of one of the greatest generals in all of China.

So when the day came that my embroidery needle would not cooperate no matter how carefully I tried to ply it—and the needle thrust deeply into one of my fingers, drawing bright drops of blood—I threw both the fabric on which I was working and the needle to the floor in disgust. What difference did it make that I was trying hard to learn my lessons? Trying to make my absent father proud? He was never going to see a single one of my accomplishments, even if I mastered them to perfection.

He was never going to see me, because I was just a girl, and my father, the great general Hua Wei, was never coming home.

Leaving my embroidery in a heap on the floor, I left the house. As always I headed for the ancient plum tree. It was where I always went when my emotions ran high, both in good times and in bad. And it was there that Li Po found me, for he knew just where to look.

"I can see you, you know. So you might as well come down."

"You can't either. I'm invisible," I said. "Now go away and leave me alone."

Another person might have taken me at my word, but Li Po did not. Instead he took a seat beneath the tree on a broad, flat rock that rested beside the stream. This was a favorite place, as well. Peering down through the branches, I could see Li Po had a long stick in one hand. He leaned over and began to make markings in the soft, damp earth beside the rock.

"I can stay here if I want to," he finally replied. "I'm on my family's side of the stream."

This was true enough, a fact that made me only more annoyed. I was in a mood to argue, not to be reasonable, and certainly not to give in. And my finger hurt, besides.

"Tell me what you're doing, then," I called down.

"Why should I?" asked Li Po. He continued moving the stick. "You're invisible, and a grouch."

"Try spending your day embroidering birds and flowers and see how you like it," I said.

Li Po stopped what he was doing and looked up.

"Embroidery again? I'm sorry, Mulan."

"Yes, well, you should be," I said, though even as I made my pronouncement, I knew Li Po was trying to make me feel better. The fact that he got to learn to read and write while I had to learn embroidery stitches was not his fault. And suddenly I knew what he'd been doing with the stick.

"You're writing—drawing characters—aren't you?" I asked. "Will you show me how?"

"I will if you come down," Li Po replied. "You'll give me a crick in the neck otherwise, trying to look up at you."

I climbed down. As I'd been practicing this a lot, it didn't take me very long. Soon I had crossed the stream and was kneeling on the rock beside Li Po, gazing down at the images he'd etched in the mud. I pointed to the closest one.

"That looks like a man," I said.

"It does, doesn't it?" Li Po nodded. "What do you think it represents?"

I narrowed my eyes, as if this might help me decipher the character's meaning. It couldn't simply be "*man*." That was too obvious.

"Is it a particular kind of man?" I asked. "A soldier?"

"No," Li Po said. "But you're thinking along the right lines.

Think of something a soldier must have. Not something extra, like a shield or sword, but . . ." He paused, as if searching for the right term. "An attribute. Something inside himself. Something you can figure out just by looking at the character."

Totally engrossed now, I gazed down at what Li Po had created. It really *did* look like a soldier, a helmet on his head, one arm extending out in front, as if to protect his body from a blow. The other hand rested on his hip, as if on the hilt of his sword. Just below it the back leg seemed bent, as if to carry all the weight. The front leg was fully extended, giving the whole figure an air of alertness, ready to pounce at a moment's notice.

But try as I might I couldn't quite make the connection between the form and what it represented.

"Determination?" I hazarded a guess.

"Close," Li Po said. He gave me a sidelong glance, as if to judge my temper. "Do you want me to tell you, or do you want to keep on guessing?"

"Tell me," I said at once. I wanted to understand more than I wanted to say I'd figured it out myself.

"Courage," Li Po declared, at which I clapped my hands.

"Of course!" I cried. "He's not certain what is coming next, so he holds one arm in front to protect himself, but he's also ready to attack if he needs to. Uncertain but prepared. Courageous."

I gazed at the character, as new possibilities seemed to explode inside my head.

"Does it always make you feel like this?" I asked.

"Like what?"

By way of an answer I captured Li Po's hand, pressing his fingers against the inside of my wrist. You could feel my heart beat there, hard and fast, as if I'd just run a race.

Li Po gave a sudden grin, understanding at once. "Yes," he said. "Every time I grasp a new meaning, it feels just like that."

"Can you show me how to draw the character?"

Li Po placed the stick in my hand and then closed his fingers over mine. "You begin this way," he said.

Together we made the stroke that ran straight up and down. That seemed to me to be the soldier's backbone. The rest followed from there. Within a few moments we had reproduced the character together. Li Po took his hand away.

"Now you try it on your own."

It was harder than it looked. I performed the motions half a dozen more times before re-creating the character to both Li Po's satisfaction and my own. I sat back on my heels, the stick still clutched in my fist, gazing at the row of tiny soldiers marching across the earth in front of me.

"It's beautiful," I said. "Much more beautiful than embroidery."

"It wouldn't look as nice on a dress," Li Po commented.

I laughed, too pleased and exhilarated to let his teasing make a dent in my joy.

"I don't care," I said. "I don't own any fancy dresses anyhow."

I poked the tip of the stick into the wet earth, a frown snaking down between my brows.

"What?" Li Po asked.

I jabbed a little harder. "Nothing," I said, which was a big, fat lie. But I wasn't sure how to ask for what I wanted. *Courage, Mulan,* I suddenly thought.

"Willyouteachme?" I asked, the words coming out so quickly it sounded as if they were one. I took a breath and then tried again. "The characters you're learning, will you teach me more of them? I know my father hasn't said I may, but I want to study them so much and I . . ."

All of a sudden I felt light-headed, and so I drew in a breath. "I think it's what my mother would have wanted."

Li Po was silent for a moment. "It must be awful," he finally said. "Not even knowing what she was called."

Without warning Li Po sat up straight, as if he'd been the one poked with my embroidery needle. "I know," he exclaimed. "We could make up a name, a secret name, one we'd never tell anyone. That way you'd have something to call her. You'd be able to talk to her, if you wanted to."

He squirmed a little on the hard rock seat, as if he'd grown uncomfortable. But I knew that wasn't it at all. Li Po was excited, just as I was.

"If I choose, will you show me how to write it?"

"I will," Li Po promised. "Pretend you're about to make a wish. Close your eyes. Then open them and tell me what you want your mother's name to be."

I inhaled deeply, closing my eyes. I listened to the water in the stream. I felt the warmth of the late afternoon sun beating down. And the name popped into my head, almost as if it had been waiting there all along.

"*Zao Xing,*" I said as I opened my eyes. "Morning Star."

"That's beautiful," Li Po said. "And look, the characters that form it look almost the same." Quickly he drew them, side by side.

"Thank you," I breathed when he was finished. Never had I been given a more wonderful gift. "Thank you, Li Po."

He smiled. "You're welcome, Little Orchid."

I made a rude sound. "I'm big enough to dump you in the stream," I threatened.

"Yes, but if you do that, I won't teach you how to read and write," Li Po replied.

I threw my arms around him. "You'll teach me? Honestly? You'll teach me everything you learn yourself?"

"Everything I learn myself," Li Po promised. "Now and forever. You're my best friend. I love you, Mulan."

"And I love you," I said. I kept my arms around him tight. "Let's make a pact," I said fiercely. "No matter what happens, let's promise to be friends for life."

"Friends for life," Li Po echoed as he returned my hug. "But we'll have to be careful, Mulan. You have to work hard at your own lessons too. If my family finds out what we're doing, they'll split us up for good."

"I know. I'll be careful, and I'll work hard. Honestly I will," I vowed. "It's just . . . being a girl is so hard sometimes. It always seems to be about pleasing somebody else."

"Then you must master your lessons as best you can so that you can find the way to please yourself."

I released him and sat back, my hands on my hips. "What makes you so wise, all of a sudden?"

"I'm going to be a great scholar someday. Haven't you heard? Everybody says so."

"Everybody being your mother, you mean," I said. But I stood up and made a bow. "I am honored to become the first student of the great master Li Po."

"I'm going to remember that, to make sure you pay me the proper respect," Li Po said. And then he grinned. "Now sit back down. There's one more character I want to show you."

I settled back in beside him. Li Po leaned forward and drew a character comprised of just four lines.

The first was a downward swipe, slanting right to left. This was followed by a quick stroke across it to form a *T,* moving left to right.

Then on the right side of the down stroke, just beneath the place where the two lines crossed, Li Po made a line that started boldly toward the right. Before it went far, though, it abruptly changed direction, sweeping back to the left and down so that it looked like a man's leg bent at the knee.

Li Po lifted the stick and then put the tip to the earth and made one last stroke, left to right, angling down just beneath the bent leg.

Finally he lifted the stick and sat back, his eyes on me.

I studied the character. I was almost certain I knew what it meant, but I didn't want to rush into anything. I wanted to take my time making up my mind.

"Give me your hand," I said.

Li Po reached out and placed his palm on top of mine. We clasped hands, squeezing them together tightly, and I knew that I was right.

Just below that sudden bending of the knee was a space, a triangle. And it was in this space that the character's meaning resided. For this was its center, its true heart.

It's just four lines, I thought. But placed so cleverly together that they represent two entities, joining in such a way as to create something else. That secret triangle, as if formed by two hands clasped.

"It's *friend,* isn't it?" I said.

"That's it precisely," Li Po answered with a smile.

There was no more discussion after that. No more lessons, no more talk. Instead my only friend and I sat together, hands clasped tightly, until the light left the sky and we headed home.

Four

In the years that followed there were many lessons, and the pact of friendship Li Po and I had forged that day continued to grow strong. Every time Li Po learned something new from his tutors, he taught me to master it as well. It wasn't long before I had added riding and archery to my list of unladylike skills. And so over the years a curious event transpired, though I don't think either Li Po or I realized it at the time.

I stopped being quite so wild, at least on the inside.

While the new skills I was mastering were considered very masculine, they also took hard work, dedication, and time. In other words they took discipline, and not even I could be disciplined and wild all at the same time.

Acting with discipline requires you to know your true nature and, having come to know it, to bring it under control. On the surface I might have appeared unruly and unladylike, preferring boys' tasks to my own. But I kept the promise I had made the day of my first writing lesson. I learned my own tasks as well as the ones Li Po set for me. There wasn't a girl in all China who had my unusual combination of skills, no matter that I looked like a simple country girl on the outside.

I still struggled at certain tasks, as if my hands were clumsy and unwilling to perform those skills that did not also fire my imagination or touch my heart. But Li Po had no such problem. It sometimes seemed to me that there was magic in Li Po's fingers, so deftly could he master anything he put his mind to.

Nowhere was this more apparent than when we practiced archery. I loved these lessons above all others, with the possible exception of horseback riding. When I rode, I could imagine I was free, imagine I was someplace where I didn't need to hide my own unusual accomplishments. A place that didn't require me to hide my own true face, but let me show it bravely and proudly. A place where I could be whomever I wanted.

In the absence of such a place, however, I practiced my archery.

I loved the feel of the bowstring against my fingers, pressing into my flesh, the stretch and burn of the muscles across my shoulders and back as I pulled the string back and held it taut. I loved the sensation in my legs as I planted them solidly against the earth, rooting me to it, making us one. It is not the air that gives the arrow its ability to fly. The air is full of currents, quick and mischievous, ready to send the arrow's flight off course. The thing that makes the arrow fly true is the ground. The ground calls to the arrow, making the arrow long to find its target and then return to earth, bringing its prize home.

I never lost my joy in setting the arrow free. Always it was as wonderful as it had been the very first time. I loved to watch it streaking toward the target, my heart not far behind it. On its way to the destination I intended and nowhere else.

On a good day, anyhow.

If I could have spent all my days shooting and retrieving arrows, I would have. But as good as I became, I could not match Li Po's skill. There were times when it seemed to me that he and the arrow shared some secret language, whispering together as Li Po held the feathers against his cheek, waiting patiently, watching his target, before letting the arrow fly. I could hit eight out of any ten targets we chose, but Li Po could hit anything at which he aimed, no matter how far away it was.

"Let me see you hit that," I challenged him late one summer afternoon. It was the time of day when we most often managed to snatch a few hours together. We were in our favorite place alongside the stream that separated his family's lands from mine. We often practiced shooting here, for there were many aspects to take into account—the steepness of the banks and the breath of the wind—and, of course, there were plenty of plums to use for targets.

The particular plum I had suggested as today's target was small, hanging on a branch toward the back of the tree. In order to pierce the target, Li Po would have to send his arrow through the heart of the tree, through many other branches filled with leaves and fruit.

I paced the bank opposite the tree. We were standing on Li Po's family's side of the stream.

"Shoot from here," I finally instructed. The place I selected was higher than the tree branch. Li Po would have to angle his shot down. This is always more difficult, because it's harder to judge the distance.

Li Po moved to stand beside me, eyeing both the branch and the location I had chosen, and then he gave a grunt. I stepped aside. Quickly Li Po took an arrow from the quiver on his back and set it to the bow. Then he set his feet in precisely the way that he had taught me, feeling the ground with his toes. Only when he was satisfied with his footing did he raise the bow and pull the arrow back, keeping his body relaxed even as the bowstring stretched taut.

For several seconds he stood just so. The wind moved the branches of the tree. I saw it ruffle the hair on Li Po's brow so that the hair threatened to tickle his eyes. He never even blinked. Then, for a moment, the wind fell away, and the instant that it ceased to breathe, Li Po let the arrow fly.

Straight across the stream it flew, passing amid the branches of the plum tree as if they weren't there at all. The arrow pierced the plum that was the target and then carried it to earth. I laughed and clapped my hands in appreciation as Li Po flashed a smile. Then, before I realized what he intended, Li Po bounded down the slope of the bank, splashed across the stream, and clambered up the opposite side to retrieve both his arrow and the plum.

He wiped the tip of the arrow on the grass and then thrust it back into his quiver. Returning to the stream, he bent to hold the plum in the cool water, washing the dirt from its pierced skin before straightening up and popping the small fruit into his mouth. He chewed vigorously, purple juice running down his chin. Then he spat the pit into the water and wiped a hand across his face. The grin he was wearing still remained, I noticed.

"I'll race you to the top of the tree," he challenged.

"No fair!" I cried. He had only to turn and take half a dozen steps to reach the tree's thick trunk. I was standing on the opposite bank. I still had the stream to cross.

I acted without thinking, just as Min Xian was always scolding me for doing. Taking several steps back to gather momentum before abruptly sprinting forward, I streaked toward the stream, my legs pumping as hard as they could go. As I ran, I gave what I fondly imagined was a fierce warrior's yell. I just had time to see Li Po's startled expression before I jumped.

Li Po's cry of warning came as I flew through the air, my arms stretched out in front. *Oh great dragon of the water,* I prayed as I flew across the stream. *Carry me safely above you. Help me reach my goal in safety. Or, if you cannot and I must fall, please don't let me break too many bones.*

No sooner had I finished my silent prayer than I sailed into the branches of the plum tree, hands and legs scrabbling for purchase but finding none. I slithered downward, leaves and plums showering around me, thin branches snapping against my face. Then, with a bone-jarring impact, my body finally found a branch that would hold it.

I wrapped my arms and legs around it, clinging like a monkey. I stayed that way for several moments, sucking air, feeling my heart knock against my ribs at my close call. When I had my breath back, I decided it was time to find a less precarious hold.

Carefully I levered myself onto the branch and then into a sitting position, clinging to another branch just above me for additional support. By the time Li Po clambered up to sit beside me, my heart was just beginning to settle.

"You're out of your mind. You know that, don't you?"

"You ought to know better than to issue a challenge," I reminded. However, I'd come close enough to disaster to admit, at least to myself, that Li Po was absolutely right.

Thank you, mighty dragon, I thought. Surely it had heard my prayer and helped to carry me across the stream. But I'd succeeded by no more than the reach of my fingers. Maybe I would think before I jumped next time around. There's a first time for everything, or so they say.

"Nice shot," I said, now that I had my breath back.

"Thank you," Li Po replied.

"You'll be a famous archer someday. You mark my words," I went on. "The pride of the Son of Heaven's army."

Li Po gave a snort. "Not if I can help it. Besides, you're the one who's always pining for adventure, not me. If you had your way, you'd ride off into the sunset and never look back."

I plucked a handful of leaves from a nearby branch and then released them, watching as they fluttered downward. They settled onto the surface of the water and were swiftly carried away.

"There's not much chance of that happening," I said. "I haven't got a horse of my own."

Li Po chuckled, but his eyes were not smiling. He was like this sometimes, in two places at once. It was one of the things I liked best about him. For Li Po the world was not always a simple place. It was filled with hills and valleys, with shadows and nuances.

"Where would you go?" he inquired.

"I don't know," I answered with a shrug. "I'm not even sure *where* is the point. I'd just like to be able to go. Girls don't get out much, or go very far when they do, just in case you hadn't noticed."

Li Po fell silent, gazing down into the water. "They go to their husband's homes," he said after a moment.

"Don't remind me," I said glumly. "Though I'm never going to get married. Didn't you hear? Min Xian said your mother told her so just the other morning. According to her there's not a family in all China who'd have me, in spite of the Hua family name. I'm far too unmanageable and wild. She said that's the real reason my father hasn't come home once since the day I was born."

"The great general Hua Wei is afraid of his own daughter? That doesn't seem very likely," Li Po remarked.

"Not out of fear—out of embarrassment," I replied. I yanked the closest plum from its hold and hurled it down into the water with all my might. "Your mother told Min Xian that she prays daily to her ancestors that you won't fall in love with me."

Li Po frowned, and I knew it meant he'd heard his mother say so too. "I've heard her tell my father she wishes they could send me to Chang'an," he said. "To the home of my father's older brother."

"But I thought they *were* sending you," I said. "When you turn fifteen."

Going to the capital would help complete Li Po's education and help turn him into the scholar his family desired. If all went well, he would pass one of the grueling tests that would make him eligible for a government position. Then both he and his family would be set for life.

"That was the plan," Li Po agreed. "But now she wants to hurry things along."

"It's because of me, isn't it?" I said. Girls married at fifteen, but most boys waited until they were older. Twenty was considered the proper age for a young man to take a wife.

"What does she think will happen? That I'll suddenly become an endless temptation? That I'll distract you from your studies?"

My chest ached with the effort I was making not to shout. The thought of me as an endless temptation, to Li Po or anyone else, was so ridiculous it should have made me laugh. So why on earth did I feel like crying?

It's because Li Po's mother is right, and you know it, Mulan, I thought. *No one is going to want you, in spite of the name of Hua. The only thing that will make it possible for you to marry is if you meet your bridegroom on your wedding day, so he doesn't have the chance to get to know you ahead of time.*

No one would want an unruly girl like me. Unlike my parents, I would not be offered the chance to marry for love.

All of a sudden I realized I was gripping the tree branch so tightly the knuckles on both hands had turned stark white.

"You can't really blame them for wanting what's best for me," Li Po said. "I'm their only son. I have to pass my examinations and marry well. It's expected, and I owe it to them, for raising me."

"In that case they're not making any sense," I snapped, completely overlooking the fact that I wasn't making much myself. "They'll have to look long and hard before they find a girl with a better family name than Hua."

"That is true," Li Po replied. "If the family name were all there was to think about. But marriage is not as simple as that, and you know it, Mulan. For example, do you really want my mother for your *popo*, your mother-in-law?"

"Of course not," I said at once. "No more than she wants me for a daughter-in-law. Or than I want you for a husband or you want me for a wife." All of a sudden a terrible doubt occurred. I twisted my head to look at Li Po more closely.

"You aren't thinking of asking me to marry you, are you?"

For the first time in our friendship I could not read Li Po's expression. Until that moment I would have said I knew any emotion he might show. Then he exhaled one long, slow breath, and I knew what his answer would be.

"Seriously?" he said. "I suppose not, no. But I'd be lying if I said I don't think about it sometimes. It would solve both our problems, Mulan. I'd have a wife who wouldn't pester me to be ambitious, to become something other than what I wanted. You'd have a husband who'd do the same for you. That wouldn't be so bad, would it?"

"No, it wouldn't," I replied.

Li Po and I had talked about many things during the course of our friendship, but we'd never really talked about the future. It had simply been there, looming in the distance, as dark and threatening as a storm cloud. Had we been hoping to make it go away by ignoring it? Or had we hoped to outrun it?

"What do you want to be?" I asked quietly, somewhat chagrined that the question had never occurred to me before now. I'd been so busy identifying the boundaries that contained me that I hadn't taken the time to see the ones that bound Li Po.

He gave a slightly self-conscious laugh. "I'm not sure I know. That's the problem. And I'm not so sure it would make any difference even if I did. Boys aren't allowed to make choices any more than girls are. I know you don't think this is so, but it's the truth, Mulan. If I go against the wishes of my family, if I bring them dishonor, everyone will suffer."

"But I thought you wanted to be a poet or a scholar," I said. "Isn't that what your family wants too?"

"It is what they want," Li Po agreed. "But how can I know if it's what I want when I've never been allowed to consider any other options? Just once I'd like to be free to listen to the voice inside my own head, to discover something all on my own.

"That's part of why I like being with you. You may be bossy . . ." He slid me a quick laughing glance to take in my reaction. "But you never boss me around. So, yes, I do wonder what it would be like to be married to you, sometimes. You'd let me be myself, and I'd do the same for you."

"And your mother?" I asked. "How would we convince her to leave us both alone?"

Li Po gave a sigh. "I don't have the faintest idea," he admitted.

"It sounds as if we should ride off into the sunset together," I said. "Very quietly, and on your horse."

"It does sound pretty silly when you put it that way, doesn't it?" Li Po said.

"Not silly," I answered. "Just impossible."

We sat quietly. The branches of the old plum tree swayed and whispered softly, almost as if they wished to console us.

"It's getting late," Li Po said finally. "I should probably be getting home. The last thing we want is for my mother to send out a search party."

"Shh!" I said suddenly, clamping a hand around his wrist to silence him. "Listen! I think someone's coming."

Above the voice of the stream, I heard a new sound—the sound of horses. Now that I'd acknowledged it was there, I realized I'd been hearing it for quite some time. But I'd been so wrapped up in my conversation with Li Po that I hadn't recognized all the other things my ears were trying to tell me.

I could identify the creak of leather, the faintest jingle of harness. And most of all, I could hear the sharp sound of horses picking their way carefully over stones.

They are coming up the streambed! I thought. *And there is more than one.* They were close. In another moment the horses would pass beneath the boughs of the plum tree that extended out over the water.

"Li Po, your legs," I whispered suddenly, for they were dangling down.

Li Po gave a frown. His head was cocked in my direction, though his eyes stayed fixed on the scene below.

"What?"

"Pull up your legs," I said, urgently now. "Whoever is coming will be able to see them. They're longer than mine."

To this day I'm not quite sure how it happened. As a general rule Li Po was no more clumsy than I. Perhaps it was the fear of being caught, the astonishment that whoever was coming had chosen to ride up the streambed rather than the road. But in his haste to get his feet up out of the way, Li Po lost his balance. He reached for a branch to steady himself. Unfortunately, he found me instead.

One moment I was sitting in the tree. The next, I was hurtling down. And that is how I came to fall from the same tree twice.

Five

I'D LIKE TO TELL YOU THAT I FELL IN BRAVE AND STOIC SILENCE, but the truth is that I shrieked like an outraged cat the whole way down. I landed in the stream this time around. The impact was painful. The water wasn't deep enough to truly cushion my fall, and the streambed was full of stones.

I had no time to consider my cuts and bruises, however, because I landed squarely in the path of the lead horse. Its cry of alarm and outrage echoed my own. I scrambled to get my legs back under me, scurrying backward like a crab. I tossed my drenched braid over my back and looked up just in time to see a pair of hooves pawing the air above me.

Every instinct screamed at me to *move*, to get out of the

way. But here my mind won out. I put my arms up to shield my head and stayed right where I was. To move now would only startle the horse further. And I had no idea just where those pawing hooves might fall. If I moved, I could put myself squarely beneath them. Terrifying as it was, I had to stay still and pray that the rider would soon get the frightened animal under control.

Above the high-pitched neighing of the horse, I heard a deep voice speaking sternly yet with great calm. The voice found its way to my racing heart, steadying its beats, though they still came fast and hard.

With a final cry of outrage the horse brought his front legs down, hooves *clacking* sharply as they struck the stones of the streambed less than a hand's breadth from where I knelt. The horse snorted and danced backward a few steps before finally agreeing to stand still, the stern, soothing voice of its rider congratulating it now.

I wished the earth would open up and swallow me whole. That way I wouldn't be required to provide explanations for my behavior, nor patiently accept the punishments that would no doubt be the result. I would simply disappear, my transgressions vanishing with me as if we had never existed at all.

But since I already knew all about wishes that never came true, I did the only thing I could: I lowered my arms from shielding my face and looked up.

The horse's legs were the first thing I saw.

They were pure white, as if he'd borrowed foam from the water, and they rose up to join a glossy dark coat the color of chestnuts. He had a broad chest and bright, intelligent eyes. Though, I could see from his still-quick breathing that only the will of his rider kept him in place.

The rider, I thought.

"*Yuanliang wo,*" I said, remembering my manners at long last. "Forgive me, elder."

Still kneeling in the stream, I bent over until my face was almost touching the water. I did not know who the stranger on this horse might be, but I knew enough to recognize that he had to be someone of rank—a court official, maybe even a nobleman. No ordinary man rode a horse such as this.

"I did not mean to startle your horse."

The horse blew out a great breath, as if to encourage its rider to speak. To my astonishment, it worked.

"But you did mean to fall from the tree," suggested a deep voice.

I straightened up in protest before I could help myself.

"No!" I cried. "I am a good climber. I've only fallen once before, and that was when I was much younger. This was all—"

Appalled with myself, I broke off, bowing low once more. Li Po had not fallen when I had. If I did not mention him, there was every reason to think I could keep him out of trouble.

"It's all my fault, elder," I heard Li Po say. Out of the corner of my eye I saw him march down the bank and make the proper obeisance. He'd climbed down from the tree while I was doing my best to avoid being trampled by the horse.

Oh, Li Po, you should have stayed put, I thought.

"And how is it your fault?" the stern voice asked. "I don't see you in the water."

"No, but you should," Li Po replied in a steady voice that I greatly admired. "I was also in the tree. I was the first to lose my balance."

"What were you doing up there in the first place?" a second voice inquired. It was not as deep and powerful as the first, but it was still a voice that commanded attention.

The second rider, I thought.

"Nothing in particular," Li Po said, but his voice was less certain now.

This was not an outright lie. We hadn't been doing anything in particular. Just talking. But even this was going to be difficult to explain. Girls and boys did not usually climb trees together— especially not when they'd reached our age.

"A tree is an unusual place for doing 'nothing in particular,'" the first rider observed. His horse shifted its weight once more. "You, in the stream, stand up," he barked suddenly. "I want to get a better look at you."

This was the moment I'd been dreading. *Be brave, Mulan,* I thought. *Don't let him know that you're afraid. Remember you are a soldier's daughter.*

I stood up, trying to ignore the way water dripped from

virtually every part of me. I stuck my chin out and squared my shoulders, actions I sincerely hoped would make me appear larger and braver than I actually felt. I was careful not to look into the nobleman's face. Asking to look at me was not the same as giving me permission to return the gaze. Instead I kept my eyes fixed at a spot just over the man's left shoulder.

A strange silence seemed to settle over all of us. In it I could hear the voice of the wind and the song of the stream. I could hear the nobleman's horse breathing through its great nose. I could hear my own heart pounding deep inside my chest. And I could hear my own blood rushing through my veins as if to reach some destination not even it had chosen yet. The blood that made me different, that set me apart from everyone else.

Say something! Why doesn't he say something? I thought. But it was the second rider who spoke up first.

"What is your name, child?" he inquired.

"I am called Mulan, sir," I replied.

"And your family name?" the first rider barked. His voice was strained and harsh.

"Of the family of Hua," I replied. "My father is the great general Hua Wei. He serves the emperor. And . . ." My voice trailed off, but I put my hands on my hips, planting my soaking feet more firmly in the stream. It was either this or start crying.

"You'd better watch out," I said stoutly. "If you hurt me, my father will track you down. Not that you'll be able to. I'll hurt you first, for I am not afraid of anyone!"

"Nor should you be," the second rider observed. "Not with the brave blood that flows through your veins." My ears searched for but failed to find any hint of laughter in his voice.

"Tell me something, Hua Mulan," he went on. "What does your father look like?"

"That is easy enough to answer," I replied with a snort. I was no longer cold. Instead I was warm with a false bravado that made me reckless.

"He looks just as a great general should," I went on. "He is broad-shouldered and strong, and his eyes are as keen as a hawk's. He has served the Son of Heaven well for many years. He has killed many Huns."

"Those last two are true enough, anyway," the second rider said, and as abruptly as it had swelled, my heart faltered.

He knows my father! I thought.

The second rider spurred his mount forward until the two horses stood side by side. He reached over and clapped his riding companion on the back.

"You should have come home sooner, my friend," he said. "It would seem your daughter has grown into a son."

"Huh," the first man said. It was a single syllable that could have meant anything, or nothing, but I was glad he said no more. I could hardly hear anything over the roar inside my head. "I have come home now," he said. "That must be enough."

He guided his horse forward to where I stood frozen with astonishment, and then he extended one arm. I stared at his outstretched hand as if I had never seen such an appendage.

"Get up behind me and I will take you home."

I did as he instructed. And in this way I met my father, the great general Hua Wei, for the very first time.

The ride home was anything but comfortable. But if my father hoped to test my mettle, I passed with flying colors. Though I clung to his back so tightly I could feel the weave of his leather armor beneath his shirt, and though my legs gripped the great stallion's flanks so firmly and with such determination that they were sore for days afterward, I did not complain.

And I did not fall off.

My father was silent the whole way home. I imagined his disapproval of me growing stronger with every step of the horse. He had sent Li Po off with barely a word, save for extracting his name and promising to visit his family as soon as possible.

Images of the punishments Li Po might incur for trying to stand up for me tormented me until I thought my head would spin right off my shoulders. It also made me bold in a way I might not have been if I'd felt the need to defend only myself.

"You must not blame Li Po," I said as soon as we arrived at the Hua family compound. Tall as my father's horse was, I slid down from his back without assistance, firming up my knees to keep my legs steady beneath me. I could not show weakness now.

"What happened today was not his fault. It was mine."

A look that might have been surprise flickered across my father's stern features, but whether it was in reaction to my words or my actions, I could not tell.

"We will not," he said succinctly as he swung down from the horse's back himself, "have this discussion, and we will most certainly not have it here and now. I am your father. It is not your place to tell me what to do."

His right leg moved stiffly, as if it did not wish to bend.

"But I have to," I protested. "You don't know Li Po as I do. He is smart and kind. And he . . ." I felt the hitch of tears at the back of my throat. "He's my only friend. He loves me more than you do, and I won't have you hurt him."

"Mulan!" I heard Min Xian's scandalized tone. She and Old Lao had come out into the courtyard at the sound of the horses.

"You must forgive her, master," she said as she went to her knees before my father. "She doesn't know what she's saying. It's just . . . the surprise . . ."

"Of course I know what I'm saying," I snapped.

What difference did it matter what I said at this point?

The reunion I'd waited for my whole life had happened at last. I'd finally met my father, face-to-face, and he hadn't so much as batted an eye. He hadn't shown by any word or gesture that he had missed me, that he was pleased to see me, or that he wished to claim me as his own. Instead he'd made it perfectly clear that our relationship was to be one of duty and of obedience and nothing more. His coldness, his indifference, pierced me, wounding just as deeply as any sword.

"My father does not love me," I said. I went to Min Xian and knelt down beside her. "You know this, and I know it, Min Xian. In my life there have been only three people who cared for me at all. You, Old Lao, and Li Po."

I raised Min Xian to her feet, keeping an arm firmly around her waist as I lifted my eyes to my father's. To this day I cannot tell you what made me feel so strong. It was as if, having encountered my worst fears, I had nothing left to lose.

I saw the truth now. The thing I wanted most had been lost long ago, lost on the day I was born. There would be no chance to win my father's love at this late date.

"Punish me as you like," I said now. "That is your right, for I am your child. But do not punish those whose only transgression was that they did what you would not, took me into their hearts and gave me love. Surely that would be unworthy of you, General Hua Wei, for it would also be unjust."

My arm still around Min Xian, I turned to go.

"Mulan."

It was the first time I had ever heard my father speak my name. In spite of my best effort it stopped me in my tracks. Slowly I turned around.

"Yes, Father," I said. But I did not kneel down. I would meet my fate standing on my own two feet.

He will pronounce my punishment now, I thought. Perhaps I

would be beaten, locked away without food, or, worst of all, forbidden to see Li Po. But it seemed the surprises of the day were not over yet.

"I will spare your friends if you answer me one question," my father said.

"What would you like to know?"

"If you could have anything you wished for, anything in all the world, what would it be?" my father asked.

If he had told me I was the loveliest girl in all of China and that he loved me, I could not have been more astonished.

Oh, Father, you are half an hour too late, I thought.

Unbeknownst to my father, he had already granted one of my wishes. He had come home. But the very arrival that had granted one wish had deprived me of another. It was clear that I could never make him proud of me. I could never earn his love. My heart had only one wish left.

"I would like to know my mother's name," I said.

Then I turned and left the courtyard.

Six

FOLLOWING THE DRAMATIC EVENTS OF MY FATHER'S HOME-coming, an uneasy peace settled over our household. Somewhat to my surprise, there was no more talk of punishment. But then there wasn't much talk of anything, in fact. For we all quickly learned that one of my father's most formidable attributes was his ability to hold his tongue.

When someone refuses to speak, those around him are left to imagine what his thoughts might be, and all too often the pos-sibilities conjured up are not pleasant ones. It made no sense to me that my father did not back up his stern words with equally stern actions. Surely this was part of being a soldier. And so I did not trust the uneasy peace that came with this current silence.

But at least my outburst had taught me a lesson. Sometimes, no matter how much you wish to proclaim them, it is better to keep your thoughts to yourself. Speaking out when someone else is silent puts the speaker at a disadvantage. And so I learned to hold my tongue.

It's difficult to know how things would have resolved themselves without the help of two unexpected elements: my skill with a sewing needle and my father's traveling companion, General Yuwen Huaji.

"You must not take your father's long absence so much to heart, Mulan," he said to me one day several weeks after their arrival.

General Yuwen was my father's oldest and closest friend. They had served together for many years, commanding troops that had fought side by side as they'd battled the Huns. It was General Yuwen who had been with my father when word of my mother's death had arrived.

And my father had been in battle at General Yuwen's side not two months before we met, when his old friend had seen his only son cut down by the leader of the Huns. The fact that General Yuwen had slain the Hun leader, thereby avenging his son's death and securing a great victory for China, had not softened the blow of his loss. After a great victory celebration members of the army were given permission to go home. General Yuwen decided to accompany my father.

For some reason I could not account for, General Yuwen

had taken a liking to me, which was just as well, since my father was doing his best to ignore me. The two men had just returned from spending a week touring the far corners of my father's estate, making sure everything was being run properly.

"And you must not mind that it takes him a while to grow re-accustomed to the peace and quiet of the countryside," General Yuwen continued as we walked along. "Returning here was . . . not his first choice."

I had not been permitted to see Li Po since my father's homecoming. In Li Po's absence I often took walks with General Yuwen. He quickly came to enjoy walking by the stream, and this was the route he had chosen for us this afternoon, saying he needed to stretch his legs after so many hours in the saddle. My father did not accompany us.

"Then why did he come home at all?" I asked now. "You will be returning to the emperor's service, will you not? Why should my father stay in the country?"

Surely he isn't staying because of me, I thought.

"Your father is growing older, as we all are," General Yuwen said. His words were reasonable, but I had the sense he was temporizing, working up to something else. "This is his boyhood home. He has many happy memories of this place."

"And many unhappy ones," I countered. Though perhaps they could not precisely be called memories, as my father had not physically been here on the day that I was born. "This is where my mother died."

General Yuwen was silent for several moments, reaching out to help me over a patch of uneven ground. One of my father's first edicts had been that my wardrobe had to be improved. My tunics and pants had been banished and silk dresses put in their place. They were not as fine as if I'd lived in the city, but they still took some getting used to. They were awkward and slowed me down.

"This was a lot easier when I could dress like a boy," I said.

General Yuwen smiled. "I'm sure it was, and I sympathize. Unfortunately, you are not a boy."

"I'm sure my father would agree with that sentiment," I said, the words flying from my mouth before I could stop them.

General Yuwen was quiet for several moments.

"It may not be my place to say this, Mulan," he said at last, gesturing to a fallen log. We sat down upon it, and the general stretched his long legs out in front of him. "But not all is as it seems with your father. He sustained a serious wound in our last battle with the Huns—"

"It's his right leg, isn't it?" I interrupted. General Yuwen's head turned toward me swiftly, as if in surprise, and I felt my face coloring.

"My father favors his right leg," I said. "His gait is not smooth and easy, as yours is, when he walks. Mounting and dismounting his horse seems to give him pain, and he always has more trouble walking after a ride."

"You have keen eyes," said General Yuwen. "And what's more, you use them well. Your father took a deep wound to his right thigh. The doctors stitched it up, but still it will not heal properly.

"Now that the leader of the Huns is dead and peace has been established . . ." General Yuwen paused and took a deep breath. "The emperor has given your father permission to retire to his estates."

"Retire to his estates," I echoed. "You mean the Son of Heaven sent my father home? After all those years of service, he sent him packing, just like that?"

"There is something more," General Yuwen acknowledged. "It is true that the leader of the Huns is dead. But he has a son who escaped, a son who is old enough to raise an army and return to fight us.

"The emperor believes such a possibility is unlikely. He believes the Huns have been crushed. Your father does not agree."

"Don't tell me," I said suddenly. "My father spoke his mind."

"He did." General Yuwen nodded. "The trouble is that your father gave his opinion when the emperor did not ask for it. This has made the Son of Heaven very angry, so he gave your father *permission to retire* to the country."

"I see," I said softly.

"You must not pity him," General Yuwen said quickly. "And you must be careful not to reveal what I have told you.

That, I think, would make things even more tense between the two of you than they already are."

"What should I do, then?" I asked, genuinely interested.

General Yuwen clapped his palms down against his knees, a signal that we'd been sitting long enough.

"The same thing I tell him he must do for you," he said. "You must give each other time."

General Yuwen stood and reached down a hand to help me to my feet. "Now tell me about this friend of yours, Li Po."

"Why do you want to know about Li Po?" I asked, surprised.

"Answer my question first," the general said. "Then I will answer yours."

"Li Po is smart," I said. "His family wants him to be a scholar, but I told him he could be the finest archer in all of China."

"It was he who taught you to shoot?" General Yuwen inquired.

I nodded. "And to read and write, to ride, and use a sword. I offered to teach him how to embroider, but he declined."

General Yuwen smiled. "But surely you knew that for him to teach you such things, and for you to learn, was risky for you both."

"We made a pact of friendship," I said slowly. "We promised to be true to each other for the rest of our lives. Li Po wanted to share what he was being taught, and I wished to learn. I—"

I broke off, wondering how I could make him understand. "I am not like other girls, General Yuwen. I never have been, not from the day I was born. Min Xian says it's because my parents loved each other. That it's because I am a child created by true love when my parents were granted their hearts' desires. So it only makes sense that I would wish to follow my heart too."

"And what does your heart desire, Mulan?" General Yuwen asked quietly.

"To be allowed to be itself," I answered at once. "I wish to be neither more nor less than Hua Mulan. But I must be allowed to discover what that means. I think that is all Li Po wants. That's what we were talking about in the tree that day. We were trying to figure out the way to know who we are, to be true to ourselves."

"You would miss him if he went away, then?" the general asked, and I felt a band of ice close around my heart.

"I knew it. Li Po's going to be punished, isn't he?" I said. "My father is going to make sure he's sent away."

"It's not quite like that," General Yuwen said. He came to a halt again. Abruptly I realized we had walked all the way to the plum tree. We stood for a moment, gazing at its ancient boughs. The plums were long gone now. Autumn was on its way. Soon the leaves would change color and fall. The tree would change, as all living things do.

How will I change, without Li Po?

"Your father may be retired, but I am not," General Yuwen went on. "Though the country is at peace, someone must still keep a watchful eye, to safeguard China. The emperor has given me this honor."

"I congratulate you," I said.

"Thank you," General Yuwen said with a faint smile. He paused for a moment, his eyes on the plum tree. "If my son were still alive," he went on, "I would rely on him to help me. I need someone to be my aide, someone quick-witted whom I can trust, who I know is loyal.

"My son is dead," General Yuwen said softly. "But I have been thinking of your friend, Li Po."

"Li Po is all the things you describe," I said, both moved and astonished. "But you would do that? You would take Li Po into your household? Give him such an important position even though you barely know him?"

"I would," General Yuwen said. "If you thought he might wish it. The friendship of which you speak, the one the two of you share, is a very rare gift, Mulan. Someone willing to bestow such a gift should not be punished for it, nor should he be left to languish in the countryside.

"As for my trust, that is something he must earn, of course, as I must earn his devotion. But from all you have told me, I think we would both be equal to the task."

"You would never regret it," I said. "Li Po would serve you well. And I think that what you offer would make him happy."

"And what about you? Would this make you happy?"

"Yes," I answered honestly. "And no. There are times when

I think I don't want anything to change. Then I remind myself they changed forever the day my father came home. But even if he had not, I am not so young and foolish that I believe Li Po and I could have gone on as we were forever. And since I am not, then I must learn to put the wishes of his heart before those of mine."

"You are most certainly not young and foolish, in that case," the general answered. "You have just given me a fine and true definition of love. I will speak to his family, then, and if all goes well, Li Po will accompany me when I depart."

"When will that be?" I inquired.

"In about a week's time. Now that your father has toured all his estate, I have helped him as he needed. It is time for me to return to the emperor's service, to the court at Chang'an."

"My father will be sorry to see you go," I said. "Though I don't think he'll say so."

"And what about you?" General Yuwen asked with a smile.

"I'll be sorry to see you go too," I said. And I meant it. "May I write to Li Po?"

"Of course you may," General Yuwen said as we turned our steps toward home. "And I'll make sure he has time to answer."

We walked in silence for several moments.

"I would like to ask you something," I said. "Though I'll understand if you don't want to tell me."

"What would you like to know?"

"Did you know my mother?" I asked in a rush. "I'm not

asking you to tell me her name," I hurried on. "I'm just wondering if you knew her, if you would be willing to tell me something of what she was like."

"I did know your mother," General Yuwen said quietly. All of a sudden he stopped. I saw him look up and down the stream, as if searching for something. "Ah, there it is," he said. "Come with me, Mulan. Don't worry. I'll tell your father this was all my idea if you come home wet and muddy."

I followed General Yuwen down the bank to the stream. I thought I knew where he was going. There was a place just ahead where the stream cut into the earth to form a deep, still pool. The banks rose up steeply on either side. A narrow path led down to a shelf overhanging the pool. From it a person could kneel and look down into the water.

General Yuwen knelt and then leaned out, gesturing for me to do the same. I gazed down and saw our faces reflected below us.

"If you want to know what your mother looked like, you have only to gaze at your own face," General Yuwen told me.

Startled, I lifted a hand to my cheek, and saw my reflection do the same.

"Has no one told you?"

"No," I replied. I stared at my face. The girl in the water had high, sweeping cheekbones, a determined chin, dark and wide-spaced eyes. *It is not a beautiful face,* I thought. But it was a face that others would remember. Without vanity, I thought I could determine that much.

"Min Xian used to tell me I reminded her of my mother," I said after a moment. "But she usually did this when I was upset about something, so I thought she was just trying to offer comfort."

"I'm sure she was," replied General Yuwen. "She was also telling you the truth. The resemblance is . . . startling."

"That explains it," I said as I sat back.

"Explains what?" asked General Yuwen.

"The day you and my father arrived," I said. "My father asked me to show my face, to look up. When I did, there was this odd silence, one I couldn't explain. But I think I understand it now. It's because you both were looking into my face and seeing my mother's."

"It was a shock, let me tell you," General Yuwen acknowledged. "Particularly since I'm pretty sure your father and I both thought you were a boy from your dress and defiance, until that moment."

General Yuwen reached out, disturbing the calm surface of the water in order to pick out a stone. He turned it over between his hands and then passed it to me. It was shaped like an egg, made smooth by the water, the perfect size to fit in the center of my palm. I closed my fingers around it, feeling its cool strength.

"Is that why my father dislikes me so much?" I asked. "Because I look just like my mother?"

"It's nothing so simple," General Yuwen said. "And I don't

believe that your father dislikes you, Mulan. But looking at your face does remind him of what he has lost. I don't think that can be denied."

"But it could remind him of other things too, couldn't it?" I asked. "It could remind him of happier times."

"It could," acknowledged General Yuwen. "And I hope as he gets to know you better that that's exactly what it will do. But you must give it time, Mulan.

"I know thirteen years must seem like a very long time to grieve, but I was beside your father when word came of your mother's death. I heard his heart break in sorrow. I'm not sure there's enough time in all eternity to mend a wound like that. There is only the will and the discipline to carry on. Your father possesses those qualities in abundance.

"But holding fast to discipline makes it hard to reach for anything else, even if you wake up one day and discover you might want to."

"Why does my daughter always seem to be either in or about to fall into that stream?" I heard a deep voice inquire from behind me.

General Yuwen and I both gave a start and turned.

Hands on hips, looking as tall as a monolith, my father was standing on the bank above us.

Seven

"It's all my fault," General Yuwen said easily. He got to his feet and helped me to mine. "Just as it's my fault if Mulan has spoiled her fine new clothes. I wanted to show her something, and this was the best place to do it."

"Huh," my father said. This seemed to be his favorite remark. But he did not ask what General Yuwen had wanted me to see, and for this I was grateful. I hadn't yet decided how I felt about looking so much like my mother.

"You should come home to dinner," my father said now. "Min Xian wondered where you two had gone. I was afraid she would start fussing."

"By all means, let's return, then," General Yuwen said. He

glanced in my direction, and I thought I saw him wink. Could my father have actually been worried about me?

"I don't know about you, Mulan, but all of a sudden I'm starving."

"Min Xian's food is always excellent," I said.

"Huh," my father said again. He turned to go. But then something unexpected happened. The bank was wet, the result of the recent rains, and as my father put his weight onto his back leg, he slipped. His leg gave way and my father fell heavily to the ground. Before either General Yuwen or I could take a step, my father was rolling down directly toward us.

General Yuwen moved swiftly, placing himself between my father and the water. There was a grunt of impact as their bodies connected, followed by a moment of silence as the two friends lay sprawled on the shelf above the water. At General Yuwen's motion I had scrambled back, out of the way. Now I moved swiftly to kneel down beside the two men. General Yuwen was the first to sit up.

"Are you all right?" I asked anxiously. My father still lay upon his back. "You're not hurt, are you?"

"Of course I'm not hurt," my father said gruffly. "It will take more than a fall to wound an old campaigner like me." He frowned suddenly, and I followed the direction of his eyes. To my shock I saw that I was holding his hand between both of my own, gripping it tightly.

My father lifted his eyes to mine.

I were ready. I had passed my best sewing needle through a candle flame to sterilize it, and then I'd threaded it with a length of my strongest thread. But as I took my place at my father's side, I began to worry that my hands would shake despite all my brave words.

I stared at the gash across my father's right leg. General Yuwen had been right. The wound was not healing properly. The edges still were angry and red. Though I knew the general had cleaned it carefully, I put a cloth into the steaming water, feeling the way its heat stung my hand. Then I pressed it to my father's wound, testing his strength and mine. The flesh of his leg quivered as if in protest to my touch, but my father never made a sound.

Just get on with it, Mulan, I thought. I set the cloth back into the dish of water and took up my needle and thread. *This is a seam, just like any other.*

Straight seams I had always been good at. Straight seams I understood. I appreciated them; they were the best way to get from here to there. It was the fancy stitches that served no purpose.

"I will hold a light for you," General Yuwen said.

"Thank you," I answered.

Li Po brought a cushion. "For your knees," he said.

I shifted back so that he could slip the cushion beneath them.

"I will begin now, if you are ready," I told my father.

"I am ready," he said.

I pulled in one deep, fortifying breath, set the needle to the edge of the wound, and began to stitch.

Afterward I was not certain how long it had taken, for time seemed first to slow and then to stop altogether. There was only the sound of my father's breathing, quick and light. General Yuwen shifted position once or twice, ever so slightly, so that my hands never worked in shadow but always in clear, bright light. And so I came to the end of the wound and knotted off the thread, snipping the extra with my embroidery scissors. I got to my feet, trying to convince myself that my knees weren't shaking.

"There. That's done," I said.

My father sat perfectly still for a moment, looking at the stitches I had made.

"It is *well* done," he said, correcting my words and praising me at the same time. Then he lifted his eyes to mine. "I thank you, my daughter."

For the first time since the day we'd met, I looked straight into my father's eyes.

"I am glad to have been of service to you," I said. "And I am happy to have pleased you, Father."

"It would please *me*," General Yuwen put in, "if you'd stay off that leg for a while. Give Mulan's fine stitches a chance to do their work."

"Why is everyone so bossy all of a sudden?" my father asked. "I'm hungry."

General Yuwen laughed, and set the lamp down. "So are we all. Let Mulan wash her hands, and then we will eat."

The four of us ate together right there in the kitchen, gathered around the fire, General Yuwen, Li Po, my father, and I. The light of the fire played over all our faces as we devoured Min Xian's good food.

It was the happiest moment of my life.

General Yuwen left at the end of the week with Li Po riding beside him. Li Po promised he would write as soon as he was settled in Chang'an. I was eager to know all about the city and the duties he would perform there.

That day I awoke early, as soon as the red streaks of dawn began to mark the sky. I lit a stick of incense and said a prayer to the Hua family ancestors, asking them to watch over Li Po and General Yuwen, to keep them safe from harm. Then I put on my best dress in honor of their departure, vowing silently that I would keep it clean. I was out in the courtyard watching the sun come up when General Yuwen found me.

"Good day to you, Hua Mulan," he said. "Are you making the sun rise?"

"You are the one doing that, I think," I answered with a smile. "For she wants to keep an eye on you, to see you safely back to Chang'an."

"Thank you for your kind words," the general said. "Will you walk with me to the stables, Mulan? There is a gift I would like to give you, if you will accept it."

"With pleasure," I said.

We walked to the stables in companionable silence.

General Yuwen's horse gave a whicker of greeting at the sight of us. The general produced a slice of apple from a hidden fold in his garments, offering it on a flat palm. Then he went to where his saddlebags lay ready to be strapped to the horse's sides. General Yuwen took something from among them and then turned back to me. I caught my breath.

It was a bow. The finest I had ever seen, the wood so smooth it seemed to glow. He held it out.

"Let me see you try it," the general said.

I took it from him, feeling the weight of it in my hands. *He did not have this made for me,* I thought. I could tell that this bow had been designed for someone taller and stronger than I was. But I had no doubt I would be able to make it shoot true, if I practiced enough. Li Po had taught me to shoot using his own bow.

I set my feet, as Li Po had taught me, lifted the bow, and pulled the string back, taut. I held it there until my shoulders sang with the effort it took to hold the string straight and still. Then I eased it forward again, lowering the bow.

"That was well done," General Yuwen said. "I knew I had made a good choice." He turned back to the saddlebags and produced a quiver of fine-tooled leather filled with arrows. "These belonged to my son."

My mouth dropped open before I could stop it. "Oh, but," I stammered. "Surely Li Po . . ."

"Li Po is as fine an archer as I have seen," the general agreed. "You were absolutely right on that point. Nevertheless, I am giving this to you, Mulan. I would like you to have something to remember me by. But more than that . . ."

He paused, and took a breath. "I would like to give you something to help you to remember yourself. To remember the dreams that you hold in your heart. I will be taking Li Po far away from here, and as a result you will be lonely. Perhaps this will help."

"It is a wonderful gift," I said. "I will take good care of it, I promise. But I don't have anything to give you in return."

"You are giving me your best friend," the general said. "I think that's more than gift enough. Now let's go inside for breakfast before your father begins to fear that I intend to take you with me as well."

And so on a fine autumn morning I watched my oldest friend and my newest friend ride away together. And I wondered what would happen to those of us who stayed behind.

Eight

My days with my father soon fell into a rhythm. While he spoke no more than he had before, his silence no longer stung me with imagined comparisons between the daughter he had envisioned and the daughter he had actually found. This new silence felt gentler, more companionable somehow. As if my ability and determination to restitch his wound had enabled more than just the healing of his leg. It had created the possibility for us to heal as well.

I caught my father watching me from time to time when he thought I wouldn't notice. He did this mostly in the mornings while I worked dutifully at my sewing. Sometimes I wondered if it was because I looked like my mother once had, hard at work with her own needle and thread. But although my father and I were slowly drawing closer, we both avoided the subject of my mother.

My days were not all given over to traditional tasks, as I had once feared they might be. My father suggested I continue with my reading and writing. He set me a series of tests during our first days together, as if to judge my progress.

"Your friend Li Po taught you well," he commented after reviewing my work. "You have a fine and steady hand with a calligraphy brush."

"Thank you, Father," I answered, both astonished and pleased by the compliment.

My father gazed at the characters I had made, as if reading something there I had not written that only he could decipher.

"You must miss him very much," he finally said.

"Yes, I do," I said. "But I . . ." I broke off, hesitating.

My father looked up from his study of my work. "But what, Mulan?"

"I am glad that General Yuwen wanted to make Li Po his aide," I said. "It is a wonderful opportunity. It is perfect for him. I would not have you think—I wouldn't wish Li Po back just because I miss him. I am not jealous of his good fortune or his happiness."

My father regarded me steadily for several moments. It was long enough for me to curl my toes inside my shoes, the closest I could come to squirming without giving myself away.

"Your feelings do you credit, Mulan," my father said at last. "I think . . ." Now he was the one to pause, as if he wished to use the perfect words or none at all.

"I think that you would be a good friend to have."

Before I could think of an answer, my father tapped the sheet of paper in front of me with the end of his brush.

"Now," he said, "let us see if we can pick up where you and Li Po left off."

And so my father became my new teacher, teaching me even more characters than Li Po had. Surely there was not a girl in all of China with my skills, and not simply because I could read and write.

It took some time for me to decide what to do about General Yuwen's gift of his son's bow, quiver, and arrows. But I finally came to the conclusion that he had not bestowed such a gift only to have it collect dust. And so late one afternoon, as my father was following his usual custom of quiet contemplation out in the sunlight, I took General Yuwen's gift from its hiding place and changed from one of my new dresses back into my tunic and pants. Then I headed to the old plum tree.

There were no plums at this time of year, but there were still plenty of leaves to use for targets. The fact that I had learned to shoot on one of Li Po's bows now came in handy, as it meant I was accustomed to handling a bow made for someone larger than I am. I made myself string and unstring the bow half a dozen times, testing my strength against its weight before I so much as looked at an arrow. And even then I tested the tension of the string first, pulling it back, holding it steady, easing it forward another half a dozen times. Only when I felt certain that the bow and I understood each other did I select an arrow and put it to the string.

I set my feet the way Li Po had always shown me, feeling the power of the ground beneath my feet. I pulled back the string, sighted, and then let the arrow fly. By a hand's breadth it missed my intended target, a fat cluster of autumn-colored leaves at the end of one of the plum tree's branches. Annoyed with myself, I made a rude sound. I took a second arrow and tried again. This one just tickled the leaves as it whisked by. My third arrow passed straight through the target, scattering greenery as it went. I lowered the bow and rolled my aching shoulders.

"That is fine shooting," I heard my father say. Startled, I spun around. I had been so engrossed in mastering my new bow that I hadn't heard my father approach. We stood for a moment, gazing at each other. I was just opening my mouth to apologize for both acting and looking so unladylike, when my father spoke first.

"May I see the bow?" he inquired.

Wordlessly I brought it to him. He took it in both hands and examined it closely. "I know this bow," he said at last. "It belonged to Yuwen Zhu, General Yuwen's son."

"General Yuwen gave it to me as a parting gift," I said.

"Huh," my father said, and I felt my heart plummet. In my

experience this was the reply he gave when he wished to keep his feelings a secret.

"Today is the first day you have used this?" my father asked.

I nodded. "Yes, *Baba*."

Without warning my father lifted the bow as if to shoot it himself, pulling back the string.

"Huh," he said once more. He lowered the bow and turned to look at me. "And you shot only twice before you found your mark?"

"I shot three times," I said, "and found my mark on the third try. The bow and I are still becoming acquainted."

"Hmm," my father said. I wasn't quite sure what to make of this new comment.

"I suppose it was your friend Li Po who taught you to shoot as well."

"Yes, Father," I said again, and then I decided it might be better to get it all over with at once. "And to ride a horse, and to use a sword, though I'm better at riding and archery than at swordsmanship."

"Is that so?" said my father.

"I'm sorry to have deceived you," I began, "but I—"

My father held up a hand, and I fell silent. "I don't think 'deception' is quite the right word," he said quietly. "I never asked if you could do such things, for it never occurred to me that you might be able to. When I was away, I didn't think much at all about what you might or might not do, to tell you the truth."

An expression I had never seen before came and went in his eyes, too quickly for me to be able to identify it.

"Is there anything else that I should know about?"

"No," I answered as steadily as I could. "At least, I don't think so."

"So let me see if I have this right," my father went on. "I have a daughter who can read, write, ride a horse, wield a sword, and accurately shoot an arrow with a bow that would make a strong young man work hard. She can also weave, sew as fine a seam as I have ever seen, and embroider."

"Yes," I said, "but I hate the embroidery."

"I am glad to hear it," my father answered without missing a beat. "In my experience those who are good at everything usually are also good at being insufferable."

I opened my mouth, and then closed it without making a sound. "I don't know what to say," I confessed.

At this my father laughed aloud. And suddenly the expression on his face that I had been unable to read before made perfect sense. It was amusement.

He handed me back my bow. "That makes two of us, Mulan. I don't know what to say to you most of the time. That's the plain truth." He made a gesture. "Come, let's walk and retrieve your arrows."

"What about the bank?" I asked. It had been a tumble down the stream bank that had reopened his wound.

"I believe I have mended well enough to risk the stream

CAMERON DOKEY

bank," my father answered, with just the glimmer of a smile. "Mending me is something else you did well, my daughter."

We crossed the stream and retrieved my arrows in silence. My father turned and looked up into the branches of the plum tree.

"You like this place, don't you?" he asked. "You come here often."

"It's my favorite place," I answered. "It has been ever since I was a child. I don't know quite why."

My father was silent, his eyes on the tree. The leaves were turning color. Soon they would begin to fall. In less than a month I would turn fourteen. Within the following year I would be considered a young woman, old enough to marry, no longer a child.

"Your mother loved this place." My father finally spoke, his tone quiet. The gentlest breath of wind could have knocked me over in surprise.

"When your mother and I were first married, it was early spring and there was still snow on the ground. But when it melted and the plum trees began to bloom, your mother went out every day to cut branches and bring the blossoms indoors. If ever there was a moment when I could not find her, I knew right where to look. This tree was the one she loved best of all."

"It's always the first to bloom," I heard my own voice say. "Every year. I know because I watch for it." I went on, before I lost my nerve, "I'm sorry for what I said before. When you asked me what my wish might be. I was angry."

486

"Perhaps you had a right to be," said my father.

"That doesn't make any difference," I replied. "In my anger I spoke with disrespect. It was wrong, and I apologize."

My father pulled in a very deep breath, and expended it in a long sigh. Then, at last, he took his eyes from the tree and looked at me.

"Thank you, Mulan. You have spoken the truth to me, even though you were afraid to, I think. In return I would like to tell you a truth of my own. It is a truth that may not be easy for you to hear."

"I will listen to your words with patience, Father," I said.

My father's gaze returned to the plum tree.

"I thought that I would never return to this place," he said quietly. "I did not wish to, after your mother died. I have been a soldier almost all of my life. I have seen death. I have taken away life. Death on the battlefield is something I understand. It may not be easy, but if one dies performing his duty, a soldier dies an honorable death."

He paused, falling silent for so long I thought perhaps he did not mean to continue.

"But your mother's death, the fact that she should lose her life bringing a new one into the world . . . *That* I could not find a way to reconcile," my father went on. "I could not even find a way to honor your mother in my memory. Every thought of what we had once shared and what I had lost was like a knife twisting in my heart. I even . . ."

His voice sank so low that I had to strain to hear it. "I even wondered whether or not I might have been to blame."

"But how can that be?" I protested at once. "You never meant her harm. You loved each other."

"But that's just it," my father said, his voice anguished now, an anguish that came from deep within him. It seemed to cause him physical pain to bring it forth. His voice sounded as if it was being wrenched from his body against his will.

"Perhaps there is a reason our people marry first and hope love will come later, rejoicing if it comes at all. Perhaps to love as strongly as your mother and I did was unnatural. Her untimely death has always seemed so."

"No," I objected. "I don't think that can be right, *Baba*. As long as you act with honor in her memory, isn't love honored also?"

"But what if I did not act with honor?" asked my father. "I locked away my feelings for your mother. I deliberately put from my mind all thoughts of this place, our lives together, and the child we had created. I told myself that I was doing what a soldier should, that I was being strong.

"But the truth is, I was doing just the opposite. I took the coward's way out, because to deny my past with your mother meant that I denied you as well. It was many years before I saw the truth of this, and by the time I did . . ."

My father broke off, shaking his head. "By the time I did, it seemed it had to be too late, as you were nearly grown."

"And then you were wounded, and you had to return here," I said, filling in the rest of the story. "And the daughter you weren't so sure you wanted fell out of a tree at your feet."

"Yes, but not just any tree," my father said, bringing us full circle. "This one. The tree your mother loved so much. That is the reason Huaji and I rode along the streambed. I wanted to see this plum tree before anything else, and you cannot see it from the road.

"And it isn't true that I did not want you, Mulan. I just didn't understand how much I did until I came home."

"Then you aren't disappointed in me?" I asked, trying to ignore the sudden quaver in my voice. "You don't . . ." I paused and took a moment to steady myself. If my father could speak of things that pained him, then so could I.

"You don't mind that I'm not like other girls too much? You don't think I will bring the family dishonor?"

"Of course not," said my father at once, and so swiftly that I knew he spoke from his heart. "I will admit you surprised me, at first."

He smiled again, ruefully this time, so I knew he was smiling at himself.

"Actually, you surprise me all the time. But being different is not necessarily a bad thing, though it can be . . . uncomfortable. When you are different, you carry a burden others may not. All of us carry the burden of our actions, since that is how we ensure that we act with honor. But when you are different, you also carry the burden of others' judgments. And many are quick to judge, and judge harshly, Mulan. You would do well to remember that."

"I will do my best, *Baba,*" I promised.

"Well, then," my father said, "that is all that I can ask." He handed me back the arrows he had retrieved. "It's getting late. Let's go back to the house."

In that moment the question of my mother's name quivered on the tip of my tongue. I took my tongue firmly between my teeth and bit down. My father had shared things today I had never imagined he would. It had not been easy for him. If my father could do something difficult, then so could I. And so I did not ask the question that still burned in my heart. Instead I matched my footsteps to my father's.

We were about halfway home when we saw a figure running toward us.

"What on earth?" my father exclaimed.

"That is Old Lao," I said, beginning to feel alarmed. Never, in all the years that I had known him, had I seen Old Lao move so quickly. "Something must be wrong."

We quickened our pace, as much as my father's stiff leg would allow. When he saw us hurrying toward him, Old Lao paused. He bent over, hands on his knees, in an effort to catch his breath.

"Master and young mistress, come quickly," he gasped out as we approached. "There has been an accident. You are needed at the house."

"Run ahead and find out what it is, Mulan," my father instructed, laying a reassuring hand on my shoulder. "Old Lao and I will follow, together. We will come as quickly as our legs allow."

I handed my father the bow and then took off at a dead run. And suddenly, even in the midst of my concern, I was glad to be just as I was. Glad to be different from other girls. For my father had sent me on ahead. He had given me his trust.

Nine

WHEN I GOT TO THE HOUSE, MIN XIAN WAS FUSSING LIKE A mother hen. A young noblewoman's transport had overturned in the road. One of her bearers had a broken arm. And though the lady herself was not injured, she was distressed and shaken. Min Xian sent me to comfort the young woman while Min Xian herself prepared to set the servant's broken arm.

"You be nice now," Min Xian instructed. "No frightening her with your sudden ways. She's a real lady, and she's had a tough time."

"Of course I'll be nice," I answered, stung. "You don't need to remind me about the courtesy due a guest."

Annoyed, I stomped off. Outside the door to the great room,

the one where my father and I did our lessons, I took a moment to compose myself. Coming into the room with a scowl on my face would hardly be the way to comfort a guest in distress.

"Good evening to you, mistress," I said as I entered.

The young woman was sitting at the window, but her eyes were focused downward, at the hands clasped tightly in her lap. She lifted her head at the sound of my voice, and I caught my breath.

She was the loveliest woman I had ever seen, no more than a few years older than I was. I had a swift impression of delicate features, gorgeous and elaborate clothes. I bowed low in welcome, and it was only as I did this that I realized I was wearing my old tunic and pants.

No wonder Min Xian had warned me not to frighten her, I thought. Our guest would probably think I was a boy.

"I am sorry for your troubles," I said in what I hoped was a quiet and soothing voice, resisting the impulse to smooth out my well-worn garments. "I hope you will find peace in our home. My father will be here in a moment. In the meantime, how may I see to your comfort?"

The young woman cleared her throat. "My servant," she said in a light, musical voice.

"He is being attended to as we speak," I replied. I gave her what I hoped was a reassuring smile. "You must not worry. Nobody sets bones better than Min Xian. She's getting on in years—she'd admit to this herself—but she's still strong. She'll have your servant's arm set right and bandaged in no time, just you wait and see."

The young woman's face became pale, as if just the thought of what it might take to set an arm was more than she could bear to contemplate. She had the finest skin that I had ever seen. In her bright silks she reminded me of some exotic bird that would be painted on a piece of porcelain.

"May I bring you some tea?" I asked. "Or something else that you might like? My name is Hua Mulan, by the way," I added.

"Hua Mulan?" she echoed, a faint frown appearing between her brows. "Oh, but I thought . . ." She broke off, a blush spreading across her cheeks so that now she looked like a rosebud that was just about to open. I felt a corresponding heat in my cheeks, but doubted I resembled a flower in any way.

"I'm sorry my clothes are so deceiving," I said, deciding an explanation might help. "I've been practicing my archery, and I can't wear a dress, you know, because of the sleeves . . ."

My voice trailed off as I watched our guest's eyes widen. It could have been in surprise, but it looked an awful lot like alarm.

Shut up, Mulan, I told myself. I felt like a clumsy oaf before this elegant stranger. *You're not helping things at all. When will you learn that when in doubt, it's better to hold your tongue?*

Fortunately for all concerned I was saved by the sound of approaching voices and footsteps.

"That will be my father," I said quickly. "Hua Wei. I'm sure he'll want to make sure you have everything you need."

The young woman rose gracefully to her feet just as my father came into the room.

"I am sorry for your misfortune," my father said as he bowed in greeting. "Please make use of our humble home."

"Thank you for your kindness," the young woman answered, executing a bow of her own.

How graceful she is, I thought. *Like a willow bending in the breeze.*

"Your servant is resting," my father continued as he gestured for the young woman to resume her seat. "He will be sore for many days, but he will mend well. No one sets bones better than Min Xian."

"So your . . . daughter has told me," she replied. I felt my cheeks flush once more at the slight hesitation before the word "daughter."

"I will go and change, Father, if I may," I said.

"Of course, Mulan," my father answered without turning his head. All his attention was for the young noblewoman.

"If you will excuse me, mistress," I went on.

She did not speak, but inclined her head.

"My distress has made me forget my manners," I heard her tell my father as I made my way across the room. "I apologize. I have not introduced myself. I am Chun Zao Xing."

I tripped over the threshold and turned to stare.

"Mulan," my father said, "are you all right? Is something wrong?"

"Nothing but my own clumsiness," I answered. "Please forgive me." Then I turned and fled.

Our visitor had the same name I had given to my mother so long ago: Morning Star.

Ten

AS QUICKLY AS IT HAD ARRIVED, THE NEWFOUND CLOSENESS between my father and me departed—for Zao Xing's presence changed everything in our house. My father and I no longer had our calligraphy lessons together. He paid me no additional visits while I practiced target shooting. Instead his time was given over to caring for Zao Xing's comfort. Even Min Xian seemed to think this was the proper thing to do.

"Poor thing," she remarked one morning about a week after Zao Xing's arrival.

Her servant was healing just as he should, but mending a broken arm takes time. My father had sent a message to Zao Xing's family, explaining what had transpired. In it he'd told them that their daughter would be well cared for in our home for as long as she and her family wished her to stay.

"I doubt they'll be in any hurry to have her back," Min Xian went on with a click of her tongue.

We were sitting in the kitchen working on a pile of mending. I was happy to have something to keep my hands busy, even if the task did keep me indoors.

"Why do you say that?" I asked, curious in spite of myself.

I could not decide how I felt about Zao Xing. It wasn't quite accurate to say that I disliked her. But I did feel very keenly when I was in her company all the ways that we were different, and the contrast made me uncomfortable.

Zao Xing had the finest dresses I had ever seen. Her hair was always elaborately styled. Her slippers were covered with embroidery stitches so tiny that just looking at them made my fingers ache. Beside her I felt like a simple country girl. Which, I suppose, is precisely what I was.

"Has your father not told you?" asked Min Xian. She went on before I could tell her what we both already knew she knew: My father had told me nothing. "Zao Xing is a young widow."

Min Xian made a sympathetic sound. "Just barely married, poor thing, when her husband's horse threw him and he broke his neck before she could conceive a child. Zao Xing's *popo*, her mother-in-law, does not love her, and a daughter-in-law who can produce no son is no use to anyone. So her husband's family was sending her back to her parents when the accident happened, right outside our door."

"That is terrible," I agreed.

To be passed around like a piece of fruit on a plate—one last, spoiled piece that nobody wanted. No wonder Zao Xing always seemed so sad, in spite of her luxurious clothes. No wonder she seemed to start at even the slightest sound, something I had found both perplexing and irritating about her. No doubt Zao Xing feared any new noise was a fresh disaster headed her way.

"Your father has his eye on her. You mark my words," Min Xian said.

"What?" I asked, my attention snapping back to Min Xian. "What did you just say?"

"I'm saying you should keep your own eyes open, that's all," said Min Xian. "Your father has been alone a long time, and a lovely young woman like that . . . You can tell he feels for her. You can see it in his face."

"I don't want to talk about this," I said.

Min Xian put down the shirt she'd been mending and regarded me steadily for several moments. She extended her hands. I placed mine into them, and she gripped me tightly.

"I know you don't, my little one. But you'll thank me for these words later. This much I have learned, in my long life. It's better to be prepared."

Then she let me go and made her favorite shooing motion. "Now go on outdoors before the sun goes down. Being in the fresh air will do you good. Don't stay out too long, though. It's turning cold."

For once I went somewhere other than the plum tree, choosing instead to walk through one of the great stands of bamboo that grew near our home. A bamboo grove is an eerie place because it always seems that the long and supple stalks speak to one another. Even when I can barely feel the breeze upon my face, the bamboo quivers. Its papery leaves hiss and rustle. Usually, I find this lack of peace unsettling. That night it was precisely what I wanted.

Could Min Xian be right? I wondered. *Does my father, who so mourned my mother that he forbade anyone to speak her name aloud, now intend to replace her with a new wife, with Zao Xing? Am I, who have been motherless all my life, about to acquire a stepmother?*

I paused before a thick stalk of bamboo and placed my hand upon it. It was smooth and cool to the touch. And suddenly, almost before my mind knew what my body intended, I leapt upward, wrapping both hands around the stalk. My weight carried us back down to earth. The leaves hissed as if in protest, the stalk strained against my hands, longing to spring free, to be upright once more. I set my feet and held on tight.

I must learn to be like this bamboo, I thought. I must learn to be stronger than I looked, so strong that I could bear a weight greater than any I had previously imagined upon my back, upon my shoulders, and in my heart. *I must learn to bend beneath my burden like the bamboo does.*

Unlike the brittle branches of a plum tree, a stalk of bamboo will not snap. The only way to break it is with the blade of a knife. That's how strong, how flexible, it is. *And I must learn to be just like it,* I thought once more. *I must learn to bend, not break.*

I let go of my hold, stepping back quickly as the stalk of bamboo whipped upright and then seesawed from side to side before settling into its own rhythm once more.

I do not want my father to marry Zao Xing, I thought.

If he did, surely any chance he and I might have to truly come to know and understand each other would be lost. My father would have a new life, begin a new family, and it seemed all too likely there would be little room in it for me.

"There you are, Mulan," came my father's voice.

I took a moment to compose myself before turning to face him, for I did not want my father to read the conflict in my face, the worry and unhappiness in my eyes.

"I went to the plum tree," my father continued when I did not reply. An awkward silence fell. *It must be settled between them, then,* I thought. I had come to know my father's silences well.

There was the silence that spoke of his displeasure, the absentminded silence, the silence that told me he was so deep in thought that he hadn't even noticed me at all. But never before had any of my father's silences told me he was uncertain, unsure of what to do next. I listened to the great dry whisper as the wind moved through the leaves of the bamboo.

"What is it, *Baba*?" I asked quietly.

My father sighed, adding his breath to the air that stirred the great green stalks around us.

"You are absolutely right, Mulan. I did come to tell you something, and now that I'm here, I don't know how to do it."

"Then let me guess," I said, never feeling more grateful to Min Xian than I did at that moment. Thanks to her, I would not be taken by surprise. "You are going to marry Zao Xing."

"That's right," my father said, surprise and relief both plain in his face. "How did you know?"

"I didn't," I confessed. "It was Min Xian. She was the one who said she could see how things would go."

"But you can see it does make sense," my father said, as if trying to convince us both. "To be sent back to her family like that . . ."

"I can see why any man would wish to marry Zao Xing," I answered honestly. "Just as I can see why she would wish to be your wife. It will be a fine thing for her, to become a member of the Hua family."

The only thing I could not see was where I would fit in, but this information I kept to myself.

"You will not mind too much, then?" my father asked, and here, at last, he did take me by surprise.

He is trying to break this news as gently as he can, I thought. It was a far cry from our first meeting.

"No, Father," I said. "I will not mind too much."

"Then you have made my happiness complete, Mulan." My

father gave me a great surprise then, moving toward me to lay a hand upon my shoulder. It was the closest we had ever come to an embrace.

"Come," he said. "Let us return. I know Zao Xing is waiting anxiously."

My father dropped his arm but stayed beside me all the way back to the house. And so before the month was out, my life changed yet again. I turned fourteen, one year shy of being an adult myself, and Zao Xing became my stepmother.

We tried to get along, the two of us. Honestly we did. I often thought things might have been easier if we hadn't been trying quite so hard to like each other. But nothing Zao Xing and I did quite closed the gap between us. Nothing could erase how very different we were. It was as if we were speaking the same language but the words meant something different in her mouth than they did in mine. Try as we both might, we simply could not understand each other.

"We've got to do something about your clothes, Mulan," Zao Xing said after she and my father had been married for several months. "And it's high time you began to wear your hair up. You'll be married yourself in just another year."

"I sincerely hope not," I said before I could help myself.

Zao Xing turned from where she had been fussing with the contents of my wardrobe, surprise clear on her face.

"Oh, but I thought . . . your friend, the one to whom you

write . . . the one General Yuwen took into his household."

"You mean Li Po?" I inquired. I had had several letters from my friend by now. Life in Chang'an was so full that Li Po claimed he worked from morning till night, but I could tell that he was enjoying himself. Serving General Yuwen was a great honor.

Lately, though, Li Po had written that there were disturbing rumors of a new threat from the Huns. It seemed that my father had been right after all. The son of the previous leader was rousing his people, claiming he had had a vision that his destiny was to avenge his father's death by leading an army to destroy China. It was said he meant to attack soon, despite the fact that winter was fast approaching.

The Emperor has called his advisers together, Li Po had written, *trying to decide on a course of action, to determine which of the whispers racing through the city are true and which are false.*

Not even the Huns had yet tried to attack when the winter snows were this close, but it was said that the Hun leader's vision had portrayed him and his warriors lifting their swords in victory over a field of snow stained red with Chinese blood.

The peace my father and General Yuwen had spent so many years trying to achieve could end at any time.

"Li Po's mother hates me," I said simply, pulling my attention back to the conversation with my stepmother. "I think I would rather die an old maid than have her for a mother-in-law."

I watched as Zao Xing digested this information. "Oh," she said after a moment. "That is very unfortunate."

"Oh, I don't know," I answered with a sigh. "I don't particularly want to get married, to tell you the truth. I'd rather stay at home."

"Do you really mean that?" Zao Xing asked, a tone in her voice I couldn't quite read. "You would rather stay here than have a household of your own to run someday?"

"I think I do mean it," I answered slowly. "I think I would rather stay in my father's house, if I cannot do what my parents did and marry for love."

I had not intended to speak of this, for such thoughts had only begun to take shape in my mind. But now that I had said the words, I recognized them for the truth. I would rather stay alone than marry as Zao Xing once had.

"But of course I will do as my father wishes," I said. The decision of my marriage would be his, not mine.

"But if we could convince him," Zao Xing said, abandoning my clothing to move to my side. "Together, you and I. If you stayed . . . If you and I could learn to be friends. I would so like to have a true friend, Mulan. Someone who could be with me when . . ."

She blushed and broke off.

"You're going to have a baby, aren't you?" I said.

Zao Xing nodded. "I only became certain a few days ago. I haven't even told your father yet. It's my plan to do so after dinner, tonight."

She reached out and took my hands. The color in her face

was bright, and her dark eyes were shining. *She is truly happy,* I thought.

"You love him, don't you?" I asked suddenly. "That's the real reason you married him."

"Of course I wanted to marry your father," Zao Xing said. "Any woman would be honored to become a member of the family of Hua."

"That's not what I mean," I said. "You *love* my father, Zao Xing. Don't deny it."

To my astonishment tears filled my stepmother's eyes. "I suppose you think that's ridiculous, don't you?" she said. "That I'm not worthy, not after the way he felt about your mother."

"Of course I don't think that," I said at once, and watched her tears spill down her cheeks. "And I know less about my mother than I do about you. I've never even heard her name."

Zao Xing let go of my hands to wipe her cheeks with an embroidered handkerchief. "So it's true. Your father forbade anyone from speaking your mother's name aloud."

"Yes, it's true," I answered quietly. "From the day of her death to this one, no one has spoken my mother's name, not even Min Xian, who nursed her when she was a child."

"Your father must have loved her very much," Zao Xing said.

"I believe he did," I answered honestly. "But I also think . . ." I paused and took a breath. "I think that he loves *you* now."

"Do you really think so?" Zao Xing asked, and I heard the

yearning in her voice, the hope. "Why? I tell myself he does one minute, and then I tell myself I'm being foolish the next. Your father and I have been married only a few months. We barely know each other."

"But that's the way love is supposed to happen, isn't it?" I asked. "Out of nothing, growing over time."

I took a moment to consider why I thought my assessment of my father's feelings was correct.

"My father's face grows peaceful when he looks at you," I finally continued. "When he speaks, his voice sounds more gentle than it did before. I've never had anyone love me, not in the way we're talking about, but if someone were to offer me these gifts, I would think they were given out of love."

Zao Xing was silent for many moments, gazing at me with dark and thoughtful eyes.

"I wasn't sure that I would like you at first," she confided. "You seemed so different, so strong. I thought you would despise me for not being more like you."

"No," I said. "That's not the way things are at all. In fact, you've got it turned around. I thought you'd dislike me because we seem so unalike. I'm not pretty, and I don't know the first thing about dressing well."

"Outside things are easy to learn," my stepmother said at once. "And as for not being pretty . . ." She cocked her head to one side. Then, to my surprise, she reached out to lay a gentle palm against my cheek. "I think you have more beauty than you know. The right eyes will see your strength for the beauty that it is."

I lifted one of my hands to cover hers. "Stop it," I said. "Or you'll make me cry."

"So we're agreed, then?" Zao Xing asked. She gave my cheek a pinch that made us both smile.

"I'll tell your father about the baby tonight. And I'll say that you confided in me, that you asked me to tell your father you have no wish to be married, to leave home. Instead you'd rather remain here with us."

I nodded, to show that I agreed with this plan.

"You can help with the children, ride and shoot that enormous bow as often as you want," my stepmother went on, describing my future life. "You can give the children lessons, even the girls, when the time comes. It won't be quite like having a household of your own, Mulan, but it would not be a bad life."

"No," I answered. "Not a bad life."

I wouldn't have the respect a well-married woman would enjoy. And the children I would watch grow up would not be my own. But I would be free to be myself, loved for who I was. Wasn't that what both Li Po and I had wanted, right before I fell out of the plum tree at my father's feet? Right before my father's sudden appearance had changed all our lives?

"I gave my mother a name once," I said. "Right after my seventh birthday, when Li Po first offered to teach me to read and write. Li Po said I should give her a name I chose myself, since no one could tell me what her true one was.

"So I chose the most beautiful name I could imagine. A name that I could whisper before I fell asleep at night and when I woke up first thing in the morning. A name that could belong to any hour of the day or night, that would always bring me joy and comfort."

"What name did you choose?" my stepmother asked.

"Your name, Zao Xing," I answered softly. "I will be content to stay here if you will be content to have me."

"With all my heart," Zao Xing replied. "I will learn to be both mother and friend if you will let me. Someday I hope we may both speak the name of the woman who gave birth to you."

"I hope so too," I said.

And for the first time since I had heard the sound of horses beneath the plum tree, I felt like I was home.

Eleven

LESS THAN A WEEK LATER MESSENGERS SENT BY THE EMPEROR RODE though the countryside. The rumors of a Hun attack were true. Our ancient enemy was massing in great number. In response the Son of Heaven was assembling a force to resolve the matter once and for all. A force so strong no invading army would be able to stand against it. A force that would free China from the threat of the Huns for all time.

To achieve this the emperor had commanded that every household in China send a man to fight. Recruits would meet in a great valley near the mountain pass through which it was believed the Huns would attack.

The muster would occur in one week's time.

I do not think I will ever forget the look on Zao Xing's face when the messenger arrived at our door. Never did I respect or love her more. I could see Zao Xing's body quiver with the effort it took to not cling to my father, to keep her fear and despair to herself. Not once did she beg my father to stay with her and the unborn child she carried. Not once did she plead with him to not allow history to repeat itself.

Instead she, Min Xian, and I worked together to make sure my father would have everything he needed when he rode away to war. We sewed a fur lining inside his cloak, for he was heading north and the weather would be cold.

We made sure the leather of his armor was waterproof and supple. My father cared for his weapons and his horse himself. And all of us waited for special word from the emperor calling my father to return to his duties as a general. Surely, after all Hua Wei had done to defend China, the Son of Heaven would request my father's experience once more.

But the days came and went, and no message from the emperor arrived. And though he tried to hide his pain at this, it seemed to me that with every day that passed my father grew older before my eyes. Until finally the night before he had to depart arrived. By then we all knew the truth: There would be no special summons. When my father went to fight, it would be as a common soldier. This increased the chance that he would not come back alive.

We ate a quiet dinner the night before my father's departure.

Zao Xing's eyes were red, signaling she had been crying in private. But she sat at my father's side and served him his dinner with her customary grace.

From across the table I watched the two of them together. I saw the way my father angled his body toward her as he sat, a gesture I think he made without knowing it. I saw the way their fingers met as she passed him dishes, lingered for a few moments before moving on to their next task.

They are showing their love for each other without words, I realized suddenly. And though I was sure they would do so later in the privacy of their own apartments, it seemed they were also saying good-bye. As I watched them demonstrate their love, I felt a resolution harden in my heart. It was one that had been taking shape there for many days, ever since word of the muster had come, but that I had allowed myself to clearly acknowledge only that night.

I cannot let him go, I thought.

My father had as quick and agile a mind as ever, a mind that could have been used against the Huns. But his body was growing old. The wound that had sent him home in the first place had been slow to heal. There was every reason to suppose my father would not survive another injury. Against all odds he had found happiness. My father had a new, young wife who would give him a child, perhaps even a son.

If I had been a son, I could have gone to fight in my father's place. My father could have remained home and our family could still have kept its honor. But I was not a boy; I was a girl. A girl who could ride a horse, with or without a saddle. A girl who could shoot an arrow from a bow made for a tall, strong man and still hit her target. A girl who had never wanted what other girls want. A girl unlike any other girl in China.

I must not let my father go to fight, I thought. *I will not.*

I would not watch my father ride away, and then stay behind to comfort my stepmother as she cried herself to sleep at night. I loved them both too much. And I had waited too long for my father to come home in the first place to stand in the door of our home now and watch him ride away to die.

And so I would do the only thing I could to protect both my father's life and our family's honor: I would go to fight in his place. I would prove myself to be my father's child, even if I was a daughter.

I waited until the house was quiet and then waited a little longer. I had no way to make certain the others were asleep. If I'd had to make a guess, it would have been that none of us would get much sleep that night. But finally the walls themselves seemed to fall into a fitful doze, as if acknowledging that the future was set and there was nothing to be changed by keeping watch through the night.

I threw back my covers and slipped out of bed, dressing quickly in my oldest clothes, the ones that made me look the most like a boy. My ears strained against the silence, alert for even the slightest sound. But the house stayed peaceful all around me. Whispering a prayer of thanks, I gathered the few belongings I had decided to take and tied them into my winter cloak. It was not as warm as my father's because it had no fur lining. But it would have to do. I took my bow and quiver full of arrows and slung them across my shoulders.

I tiptoed to the kitchen, wrapped some food in a knapsack, and retrieved a water skin. I would not risk filling it here but would do so from the stream. Then I let myself out of the house and walked quickly to the stables. I did not look back. I feared that if I did, I would lose my nerve, in spite of all my resolve.

It was fortunate that my father's great stallion and I were well acquainted with each other. Otherwise, my plan would have been over even before it had started. I fed the horse a bit of apple, and he let me saddle him without protest. I was just leading him from the stall when the door to the stable slid open. I stopped dead in my tracks.

"I thought so," Min Xian said as she poked her head around the door.

"Min Xian," I breathed. "Be quiet. Come in and close the door."

"What's the point in doing that when you'll only open it right back up again?" she asked, but she did lower her voice. "You didn't think I was going to let you go without saying good-bye, did you?"

"You knew I would do this?" I asked, suddenly feeling the hot sting of tears behind my eyes.

"Of course I did, little one," my nurse said. She crossed to where I stood, my hand on the horse's neck, and she placed her hand on my arm. "I saw you watching them at dinner, and saw into your heart, my Mulan. I should stop you."

"No. You shouldn't," I said. "It's the only way. You know it too, Min Xian."

"I don't know that," she answered crossly. But I knew Min Xian too well to be deceived. The longer she sounded cross, the longer she could postpone crying.

"But even these old eyes can see that it may be the best way," Min Xian went on. "Now turn around. You can't go off with all that hair. It'll give you away for sure. If I cut it and then tie it back, you'll at least stand a chance of looking like other peasant boys."

"Oh, thank you, Min Xian," I said, for I had worried about my hair.

I turned my head and felt her strong fingers grasp my braid. A moment later there was a tug and a rasping sound as Min Xian moved the knife blade back and forth. And then my head felt strange and light. Min Xian tucked the thick braid of hair into her sash. Then she quickly rebraided what was left on my head, tying the end with a leather thong.

"That's better," she said. "Now take this." She turned me back around and thrust a bundle into my hands.

"I packed food," I protested.

Min Xian gave a grunt. "Take more. It's a two-day journey to the muster place, and you've never ridden as hard as you must to make it there in time. If you faint from hunger as soon as you arrive, you'll be no use to anyone."

"Only girls faint from hunger," I said. "And I'm no longer a girl, remember?"

Min Xian gave a snort. "Hold your tongue unless you're spoken to," she said. "Go quickly. Don't stop to make friends on the road. It will be full of many such as you, going to do their duty."

She stepped back. "Get along with you now. And remember that no matter what you show on the outside, inside you have a tiger's heart."

"I will," I promised. "Please tell my father and Zao Xing that I love them."

Min Xian nodded. "I'll hardly need to do that," she said. "They already know it, and they'll feel it all the more strongly once you are gone. Hurry now. Before I change my mind and wake them up instead."

"Help me, then," I said. Together we carefully lifted each of the horse's hooves and wrapped them in cloth. This would keep the noise from giving us away as we crossed our courtyard. Once I reached the hard-packed earth of the road, I would take them off. There would no longer be a need for silence.

Min Xian went with me as far as our gate, helping me to

ease it open. I led the horse through and stopped to free his feet. Min Xian took the cloths from me, clutching them to her chest.

"Mulan."

I swung myself up into the saddle, heart pounding. I was really going to do this. I was going off to war.

"What is it?" I asked. "Speak quickly, Min Xian."

"There is something you should know before you go," she said. "Something that I should have had the courage to tell you long ago."

"What is it?" I asked again.

"Your mother's name was Xiao Lizi."

Before I could answer, Min Xian stepped back through the gate and shut it fast behind her.

I put my heels to the horse's flanks, urging him out into the road. I was glad he was sure-footed, even in the dark, because I could see nothing through the tears that filled my eyes.

My mother's name was "Little Plum."

Twelve

I ARRIVED AT THE ASSEMBLY PLACE FOR THE SON OF HEAVEN'S great army after two days of hard riding. Along the way I had plenty of opportunities to be grateful for Min Xian's advice. Two long days in the saddle is not the same as an afternoon's ride for pleasure. By the time I reached the place of muster, my whole body was aching and sore. But I had done it, becoming one of the steady stream of men and boys traveling to do their duty.

I moved as swiftly as I could, and I spoke to as few people as possible.

The longer I traveled, the colder it became, for I was moving almost due north. More than once I wished for my father's fur-lined cloak.

For as long as I live, I will never forget my first sight of the great encampment and the army that the Son of Heaven had called together to defend China. It was a large valley at the mouth of the mountain pass through which the emperor's spies had said the Huns planned to attack. As I approached, it seemed to me that the land itself had come alive, for it moved with men and horses. The air above it was filled with the smoke of cooking fires. A long line of recruits clogged the road that was the only access. As we waited, word of what was happening began to move down the line.

Each new recruit was being asked a series of questions before he was given his assignment and permitted to enter the valley. The army would be divided into three large companies, each one led by one of the princes.

"As for me, I hope to fight with Prince Jian," said the man beside me. He was not quite my father's age. Though, with his face lined from the sun it was difficult to tell.

"You'd do better to fight for the middle son, Prince Guang. He's the better fighter, or so they say," commented another.

"That may be," the first man answered. "But I've heard that General Yuwen is commanding Prince Jian's forces. He's an old campaigner. I've fought with him before. And the young prince is the emperor's favorite, or so they say."

"That must make things happy at home," a voice behind me remarked.

The older man beside me snorted. "I know nothing of court

intrigues," he replied. "But I do know this: Many things can happen in the heat of battle."

After that there was no more talking, as each of us stayed busy with our own thoughts. Soon enough I came to the head of the line.

Where the road ended and the encampment began, the land widened out. There a group of experienced soldiers were interviewing the recruits and handing out assignments. Those of us on horseback now dismounted. I reached to thread my fingers through the horse's mane, and he turned his head, blowing softly into my face through his large nostrils, as if to offer reassurance.

"You, boy, what is your name?" the official barked.

I had given this a lot of thought and had decided to stick to the truth as much as possible. I could hardly say my name was Hua Mulan, for there wasn't a boy on earth who was named orchid. But I thought that I might risk my family name.

"Hua Gong-shi," I answered as boldly as I could.

"Huh," the soldier said, and I bit the inside of my cheek to hold back a smile. He sounded exactly like my father.

"You are young to have such a fine horse," the soldier said. All of a sudden he thrust his face right into mine. "Unless, of course, you stole it."

"I am not a thief," I said, feeling my cheeks warm with the insult. My heart began to pound in fear and anger combined. But even then my mind was racing faster.

Think, Mulan, I told myself. If I could think, and act, quickly enough, perhaps I could turn this situation to my advantage.

"The horse was a gift," I said now. "From General Yuwen Huaji himself. Go and ask him, if you don't believe me."

The soldier made a sound of disgust. But he did step back. I had managed to sow a seed of doubt.

"You expect me to disturb a general on your behalf?" the soldier inquired, his tone sarcastic. "Perhaps I should just turn you over to his aide right here and now. He'll soon get to the bottom of this."

"Perhaps you should," I said at once.

"You," the soldier said, pointing to a boy even younger than I who stood nearby. "Go and get General Yuwen's aide and bring him back here. I can't remember his name, but the one who's always with him. You know the one."

"His name," I said firmly, "is Li Po."

"I can't believe it," Li Po said some time later. The fact that I had not stolen my remarkable horse had been established once and for all. I was now assigned to Prince Jian's forces—specifically, to an elite archer corps. I had Li Po to thank for both these things, just as I had him to thank for my first hot meal since leaving home.

"Which part?" I asked now.

"Any part," Li Po said as he handed me a cup of steaming tea. Though our conversation was impassioned, we were both careful to keep our voices low.

"When I realized it was you, I thought my heart would

stop. You shouldn't be here. This is not a game, Mulan. What on earth were you thinking?" Li Po frowned. Before I could answer these questions, he posed another. "What did you say you were calling yourself?"

"Hua Gong-shi," I answered, taking the tea from him just in time. At my reply Li Po dropped his head down into his hands, though not before I thought I saw his lips begin to curve into a reluctant smile.

"You told them your name was Bow-and-Arrow?"

"It was a better choice than Wood Orchid, don't you think?" I said.

Li Po sighed. "I am happy to see you. Don't misunderstand me," he said, lifting his head, "but . . ."

"My stepmother is going to have a baby," I said before he could go on. "The emperor sent no word to my father. Instead we received the same summons as everyone else—that every household in China must send a man to fight."

"Every household must send one *man*," Li Po said. "That's precisely my point."

"Tell me something, Li Po," I said. "How long do you think my father would have lasted as a foot soldier? What do you think it would do to him to ride away to war leaving yet another pregnant wife behind?"

Li Po's face looked pinched, as if he hated to speak his arguments aloud. "Your father is not the only older man to answer the emperor's call."

"You're absolutely right," I answered. "He is not. But I saw an opportunity to spare him, and I took it. It is done. Hua Gong-shi is not the only lad to answer the summons either. And I have skills many other *boys* do not. You ought to know that. You saw to it yourself."

"I'll have to tell General Yuwen. You realize that, don't you?" Li Po said. "He'll recognize the bow on your back, not to mention the horse."

"You must do what you think is best," I replied. "That's what I've done, and all your fine arguments will not make me sorry for it."

I sat back, and we eyed each other for a moment.

"You look well, Li Po."

"Stop trying to flatter me," he said. "It won't get you anywhere, not for the rest of the day, anyhow. I'm going to stay mad at you for at least that long."

Without warning he leaned forward and pulled me into his arms. "If you die, I'm never going to forgive you, or myself. But I am glad to see you, Mulan."

"Gong-shi," I mumbled against his chest as I wrapped my own arms around him and held on tight. "I'm surprised the general trusts you if you can't remember even the simplest details."

Li Po gave a strangled laugh, and we released each other. It was just in time, for in the next moment the flap of the tent whipped back. General Yuwen stood in the opening.

"I heard we had an interesting new recruit," he said. He moved forward, letting the tent flap fall closed behind him.

I got to my feet, prepared to bow. "Stop that," the general said. He caught me to him, much as Li Po had, and then held me at arm's length while he studied me.

"I ought to take you out behind the tents and thrash you," he said.

I managed a shaky laugh. "You'll have to get in line behind Li Po."

"You should listen to her . . . him," Li Po said, making an exasperated sound as he corrected himself. "I may not agree with everything your new recruit has to say, but he does make several interesting points."

"My stepmother is going to have a child," I told General Yuwen. "The emperor sent no word for my father, no call to return to his previous duties. It seems he is not to be forgiven, even now, when the wisdom of his words has been proved beyond a doubt."

General Yuwen nodded, his lips forming a thin line as if he were holding something bitter in his mouth.

"My father and stepmother, they love each other," I said softly, and suddenly my voice caught at the back of my throat. "You know what it is like to lose someone you love. You watched your own son die. Once I saw the way my father and stepmother felt about each other, I could not let him respond to the emperor's summons. *I could not.* So I took the horse and came in his place."

I gave a watery laugh. "And the funny thing is, I didn't even like her at first."

"Mulan," General Yuwen said gently. "Mulan."

Then, just as swiftly as the tears had come, they vanished. I was through with crying. I steadied my feet, put my hands on my hips, and lifted my chin, just as I had on a day that seemed a very long time ago. The day when I had knelt, soaking wet, in a stream and seen two men on horseback for the very first time.

"No," I said. "I am no longer Mulan. I stopped being Mulan two days ago. Take me out behind the tents and thrash me if you must, but you won't make me return home. I'm staying, whether you like it or not."

"She told them her name was Hua Gong-shi," Li Po spoke up. "So I assigned her to the prince's new corps of archers. She shoots almost as well as I do."

"I am well aware of that," General Yuwen said. "Did I not give her my own son's bow?" He passed a hand across his face, and for the first time I saw how tired he was. "Well," he said.

He moved farther into the tent and sat down. Li Po poured him a cup of tea.

"My heart may wish you safe at home, Mulan, but the heart is not always granted what it desires. This much all three of us know. Given the circumstances, I think Li Po's choice makes good sense. Now I will drink my tea, with no further discussion."

We all drank in silence for several moments.

"The prince has asked to meet you," General Yuwen finally said.

"To meet me?" I echoed, astonished. "Why?"

"He meets as many of his new recruits as he can. But he pays particular attention to his archers. He is a fine bowman himself. And then there was the . . . somewhat unusual manner of your arrival. Did you really think a boy leading a war horse was going to go unnoticed?"

"Apparently, I didn't think at all," I said.

Li Po gave a snort. "I could have told you that much."

"I told the one who questioned me that the horse was a gift from you," I said to General Yuwen.

"We will let the story stand," the general said, and nodded. "I have told the prince that you are a distant relation who once did my son a service, and that the bow you carry and the horse you ride were your rewards. I think he wonders at it, a little, but he hardly has the time to ask questions. There are many more important things to think about and do."

"What of the Huns?" I inquired.

"All in good time," General Yuwen replied. He got to his feet. "First I must take you to meet Prince Jian. After that I will take you to be with the rest of the archers. Li Po is their captain. Did he tell you that?"

"No," I said. "He was full of other information, but he left that out."

General Yuwen gave a quick smile. "I have decided it would

be wise for my young relative to share Li Po's tent," he said. "So that he has someone to guide him during his first experience of war."

"Let us hope that it will also be the last," I said.

"We shall all hope that," said the general. "Now come. I will take you to Prince Jian."

Thirteen

"The truth is, you've arrived just in time," General Yuwen said as he walked beside me.

All around us men snapped to attention as the general strode by. Everywhere I looked it seemed to me that I saw men tending to equipment and horses. An uneasy alertness seemed to lie over men and animals alike, as if they understood that all too soon the battle would commence.

"Our scouts report that the Huns are closer than we thought. They will be here by the end of the week. How best to meet them has been the cause of much discussion."

"Oh, but surely . . . ," I began. I'd been in camp less than an hour. It was hardly up to me to voice an opinion as to how the battle should be fought.

"No, tell me," General Yuwen said, as if he had read my thoughts. "You should hold your tongue before others but not before Li Po or me, at least not when we are alone."

"I thought the way to meet them had already been decided," I said. "The Huns must come through the mountain pass just beyond this valley or not at all."

"That is true enough," General Yuwen agreed, "but there is more. There is also a second, smaller pass less than a day's ride from here. It is so narrow no more than two men can ride abreast. Prince Jian thinks this pass should be protected as well."

"But his brothers do not agree?" I asked.

"Not entirely, no. Prince Ying is cautious to express his opinions. That is his way. But Prince Guang has openly ridiculed his younger brother. We may be far from the imperial palace, but court intrigue is still very much with us, I'm sorry to say. And that is a thing of which Prince Guang is a master.

"There," General Yuwen said, pointing. "Those are the princes' tents. The one flying the green banner is Prince Jian's."

The princes' tents stood in the very center of the camp, arranged so that they formed a great triangle. Each had a pennant of a different color flying from its center roof pole. The red designated the eldest, Prince Ying, General Yuwen told me, and the blue the middle brother, Prince Guang. Each banner displayed the same symbol, the mark of the princes: the figure of a dragon with four claws. Only the emperor could display the figure of the powerful five-clawed dragon. Even from a distance I could hear the sound the banners made as they snapped in the cold afternoon wind.

I was curious to see Prince Jian, the young man whose life my father had once saved, and whose fate was so closely tied to that of all China. *Was it a blessing or a curse to bear the weight of such a prophecy?* I wondered.

"What is he like?" I inquired.

"Prince Jian?" General Yuwen asked.

I nodded.

"He is unlike anyone else I have ever met," the general said honestly. "Of course he pays attention to protocol. He is a prince. But he is also . . . approachable. The common soldiers love him, because he lets them speak."

"And his brothers?"

"Prince Ying is the oldest, as you know," General Yuwen said. "He has many talents. But I think that sometimes Prince Ying is misunderstood—especially by his father. The prince is a scholar, not a soldier. He has a deep and subtle mind. He will make a great statesman someday, a great emperor during peacetime."

"And the middle son, Prince Guang?"

"He is the one to watch with both eyes open," General Yuwen replied. "He is a courtier through and through. To turn your back on him is to risk exposing it to a knife. He resents being the second son very much, I think."

"Is it true what the men say? That the emperor favors Prince Jian?"

"It is not my place," the general answered, "to claim to know what is in the Son of Heaven's heart." He glanced over at me. "But to speak my own mind . . . I believe the emperor does favor Jian over the others, and that they all suffer as a result. To promote the youngest over the eldest disrupts the proper order of things. Only strife can come of it.

"Besides, I do not believe that Prince Jian seeks out his father's special favor. Though, like all dutiful sons, he desires his love."

"What does Prince Jian want, then?" I asked.

"To be allowed to be himself more than anything, I think," General Yuwen answered, his tone thoughtful. "Not an easy task for a prince. But even more than that, I believe Prince Jian wants what is best for China."

"Determining what that is cannot be an easy thing either, I should think," I observed, remembering my father.

General Yuwen gave a short bark of laughter. "And I think you are right."

We reached the princes' tents. A sentry snapped to attention at our approach. The general announced that we had come at Prince Jian's request, and the sentry gestured to one of the guards stationed on either side of the prince's tent flap. The flap was closed to keep out the cold and to provide privacy. The guard ducked inside to inform the prince of our arrival.

"No more talking," General Yuwen said in a low voice. "But remember what I have spoken. Use your ears, not your tongue, and keep your eyes open."

"I will," I promised.

The guard reappeared and gestured us forward. The prince's tent was much larger than General Yuwen's, as befitted his rank. There were tables for maps, and chairs for the prince and his advisers. Rich rugs covered the hard-packed earth of the tent floor. General Yuwen and I entered and made our obeisance, kneeling and pressing our foreheads to the ground.

"Ah, Huaji," I heard a voice above my head say. "There you are. So this is the lad whose name is Bow-and-Arrow. Stand up, both of you. I would like to take a look at you, boy."

I got to my feet, though I was careful to keep my eyes lowered. My heart was pounding so loud it seemed to me all those in the tent must be able to hear it.

"Let me see your face," instructed Prince Jian.

Gong-shi. My name is Gong-shi, I told myself over and over. But Gong-shi was like Mulan in one important respect. Like her, he possessed the heart of a tiger.

I lifted my head and gazed directly into Prince Jian's eyes.

They were dark, like my own. Glittering like onyx beads, they narrowed ever so slightly as he studied me.

Those eyes will not miss much, I thought.

Prince Jian's face was striking. Taken feature by feature, I

could not have described it as a handsome one. His forehead
was, perhaps, too high and wide, his chin too strong. And even
though at that moment I thought I detected the hint of a smile,
if I'd had to make a guess, it would have been that all too often
and particularly of late his mouth had been pressed into a thin,
determined line.

But, taken all together, it was a face that commanded attention. Prince Jian had a face that, once seen, would be hard to look
away from, a face that would inspire others to fight for his cause.

Though his clothing was made of rich fabrics, the prince was
as simply dressed as I was. His clothing was practical, ready for
action. This fit with the man General Yuwen had described, one
who did not stand on ceremony. A man who commanded respect
not just because of what he was, but because of *who* he was.

And I found myself wondering, as if from out of nowhere,
what it would take to make him truly smile.

"You are very young, are you not?" the prince asked softly.
During the moments in which I had been studying his face, he
had been making just as thorough a perusal of mine. I dropped
to one knee, once more looking at the ground.

"I am old enough to dedicate myself to your service, and to
that of China, sire," I replied. It was true that I had promised
General Yuwen that I would use my ears and eyes rather than
my tongue. But the prince's question called for a response.

You are not all that much older than I am, I thought, even as I
focused my eyes on the rich carpets.

It had been my father's rescue of this prince that had earned him the right to marry my mother. Both events had occurred when Prince Jian was not yet ten years old. He would be in his early twenties now.

"That is well spoken," Prince Jian remarked, "but it will take more than fine words to defeat the Huns."

He stepped away, and I felt my heart beat a little easier. I had not offended him by speaking, after all.

"That is your son's bow he carries, is it not?" the prince continued, addressing General Yuwen now.

"It is, my lord."

"An interesting present. Though I am sure you would have bestowed such a gift only on one who was worthy," Prince Jian remarked.

"I am utterly unworthy, sire," I said, and then bit my tongue. For now I *had* spoken out of turn, since the prince had not been speaking to me at all. "I can only seek to repay General Yuwen's generosity by proving my worthiness by fighting in China's cause."

"Well spoken once more," the prince replied. "What do you think, Huaji? This one has a monkey's tongue. I'm beginning to think there is more to him than meets the eye."

You have no idea, I thought, grateful that protocol allowed me to keep my eyes upon the floor. I feared that if I looked at Prince Jian, I would give myself away. There was something about him that seemed to draw the truth from those around him. I wondered what he would think if he knew the truth about me.

"I am tired of being inside," the prince suddenly announced. "I've been in one tent or another poring over maps and arguing with my brothers since early this morning. I could use a little target practice myself, and I would like to see you shoot, boy. Let us go out, before the light fades."

"It shall be as it pleases Your Highness," I said.

The prince's boots came into my view, and then he briefly rested the fingers of one hand on the top of my bowed head.

"I doubt that very much," he said softly, "but let us see what a little target practice can do to improve my mood."

With the prince leading the way, we went outside.

Word spread quickly through the camp that Prince Jian intended to match shots with the youngest and newest member of his elite corps of archers. By the time we arrived at the target range, a large crowd had already gathered. All the soldiers fell to their knees at Prince Jian's approach, but neither their presence nor the way they paid him honor seemed to improve the prince's mood. He made a curt gesture to General Yuwen, who commanded the men to stand up.

It might have been easy for the prince to ignore the crowd. He was royalty, after all, and had grown up amid the bustle of a palace. As for me, the crowd at the target range seemed enormous. And the army of which I was now a part constituted more people than I'd seen assembled in one place in my entire life. As I thought of all of these people who would be watching my every move, I felt a hard fist of fear form in the pit of my stomach.

"I will set Your Highness's arrows, if I may," General Yuwen offered as we approached the line from which we would shoot. A series of straw targets had been set up some distance away. With a jolt I saw that they were in the shapes of men.

Of course they are, I thought. *That is why we are all here, Mulan. To protect China, at our enemies' cost.*

Though the targets I now faced were larger than any Li Po and I had practiced on, I still wondered whether or not I would be able to hit one, for I had never shot at anything like this before. *But that is what you will be doing,* I thought. *Soon enough.* And when it came time to aim then, it would not be at men of straw but at men of flesh and blood. I fought down a sudden wave of dizziness.

"I accept your offer, Huaji," replied Prince Jian. "Three arrows, I think, to start. That should be enough to see what this small one is made of, don't you think?"

And then, without warning, Prince Jian smiled. It lit up his features, making the spirit within him blaze forth. Prince Jian clearly enjoyed a challenge.

With this realization I felt the fist in my stomach relax just a little. While there were many differences between us, in this the prince and I were exactly alike. I, too, loved a challenge, so much so that I had yet to find one that could make me back down. I was not about to start today, no matter how out of my league I felt.

Very well, Highness, I thought. *Let us see what an unknown archer and a prince may do, side by side.*

"And Gong-shi?" the prince asked. "What of him?"

"I will aid him, with your permission," said a voice I recognized.

"Ah, Li Po," Prince Jian said with a nod. "That is well. What do you say? Shall we give Gong-shi one shot extra, to let him test the wind?"

"No, Highness." I spoke before Li Po could reply. A sudden hush fell over the crowd. In it I realized that perhaps the words "no" and "Highness" did not belong together, at least not in a statement by themselves.

"With respect," I blundered on. "You have shaped your targets like the enemies of China, and they will show me no such kindness."

Again I felt Prince Jian's keen eyes roam my face. "The lad makes a good point," he acknowledged, lifting up his voice. "It shall be as he says." And now the silence of the crowd was broken by murmurs of astonishment or respect, I could not tell.

Concentrating fiercely, trying to shut out all but the task at hand, I took the quiver from around my neck and handed it to Li Po. General Yuwen was already in possession of Prince Jian's arrows. The prince and I took our positions, sighting toward one of the targets. Behind us Li Po and General Yuwen knelt and thrust two arrows each, points first, into the cold ground.

Without looking back Prince Jian extended a hand. General Yuwen placed an arrow into the flat of his palm. The prince wasted no time. With swift, sure motions he set his arrow to the bow, pulled back the string, and let the arrow fly.

Straight and true toward the target it went, embedding itself not in the straw man's chest but through its throat. A cheer went up from the soldiers, even as I felt my body tingle in shock.

I might not have thought of that, I realized. If I had shot first, chances were good I would have aimed for the target's heart. But a true warrior would be wearing armor. Though a common soldier might not, his body would be protected. This was why Prince Jian had shot through the neck. It was one of the few unprotected places on a warrior's body.

I swallowed, feeling my throat constrict. It seemed to me that I could feel the gaze of every single eye in the crowd. The bow, which I had so carefully and proudly trained myself to use, felt heavy and awkward in my hands. If I failed, I would be a laughingstock. And worse, my failure could reflect on Prince Jian.

I extended my arm back, as the prince had done.

"Remember to plant your feet," Li Po murmured for my ears alone as he placed the shaft of the arrow into my palm. "Remember to breathe. Above all, remember who you are, for there is no one like you in all China, not even the royal prince who stands at your side."

At his words I felt my fear pass away. I returned to my true self. It did not matter that I now was called by a boy's name. Even Prince Jian ceased to be important. All that was important was that in my heart I knew what I could do. I knew who I was.

I was the only child of the great general Hua Wei. I had come here so that he might have a long and happy life, and to give him a gift he had not asked for, that of holding his second child on the day that child was born.

I had come because, as strange and unusual as I was, I thought I could accomplish one unusual feat more. One that had been inside my heart from the moment it had begun to beat, or so it seemed to me in that moment. I had come to make my father as proud of me, his daughter, as he would have been of any son.

Or, barring any of these fine things, I wished, quite profoundly, that I might not make a complete and utter fool of myself.

I widened my stance and pulled back on the bow. I sighted along the shaft of the arrow, picturing in my mind where I wished it to go. The cold evening breeze tugged at my sleeves, as if urging me to let go. But I did not listen. For once in my life I remembered to be patient.

The wind died away, and I let the arrow fly.

My shot was not as perfect as Prince Jian's. His had pierced the target straight through the middle of its throat, while mine passed through just to the right. But it was a good shot nevertheless. A killing shot, had that distant figure been alive. As my arrow found its mark, a second cheer went up.

"The boy can shoot. Perhaps he's got the right name after all," I heard one of the soldiers remark.

"Move the targets back," Prince Jian commanded. Once again he flashed me that smile. "And turn them to the side." A man in profile offered less of a target than one facing front.

"And my young friend here will shoot first this time."

Taking this second shot was more difficult than the first. One good shot can be made by even the worst of archers. And this time I let my nervousness get the best of me, my arrow passing not through the target's neck but embedding itself in the target's upper arm.

"The shot is still a good one," the prince said over the murmur of the crowd. "For now that arm is useless and cannot be raised against China."

He accepted an arrow from General Yuwen and let it fly. Like the first, the prince's second arrow passed cleanly through the target's neck, piercing it from side to side. Again a cheer went up from the crowd. Then it was cut off abruptly as, with one body, the assembled spectators dropped to their knees.

"Entertaining the troops, I see," remarked an unfamiliar voice.

Belatedly I knelt myself, with Li Po at my side. Even General Yuwen and Prince Jian made obeisance, though the prince merely bowed.

"So this is the boy who carries a warrior's bow," the voice went on. "I hope you can do more than just carry it on your back."

I could not have answered, even if I'd thought a response was necessary. My tongue seemed glued to the roof of my mouth.

"How many shots?"

"Three, Brother," Prince Jian said. "Two are accomplished. There is one to go."

"Why not shoot together?" the newcomer asked. "Prince and commoner, standing side by side. Such an inspiration, wouldn't you agree?"

This must be Prince Guang, I realized. Though surely he would never have performed the act he was urging on Prince Jian. For if a prince and commoner performed the same action but only the commoner prevailed . . .

Oh, be careful, I thought. Then I wondered if I was cautioning myself or Prince Jian.

"An excellent suggestion," Prince Jian answered. "For surely we all carry the same desire in our hearts to rid China of her enemies, prince and commoner alike."

"Get up, boy," Prince Guang instructed in a curt tone. I stood, praying that my trembling legs would hold me up, and was careful to keep my face lowered. With a gloved hand Prince Guang grasped my chin and forced my face upward.

"This one has a soft face, like a girl's," he scoffed.

His words made my blood run cold even as it rushed to my face. Though, in truth, I did not think Prince Guang had the slightest idea that he'd guessed my secret. He was simply looking to add further insult to his younger brother, should I outshoot him.

Prince Guang released my chin and stepped away, wiping his hand against his overcoat as if the touch of my skin had soiled the leather of his glove.

"I look forward to the contest."

At a signal from Prince Jian the final target was moved into position and placed so that it was an equal distance between us both. The prince held out a hand for his arrow and nodded to me to do the same.

"Listen to me, Gong-shi," he said so quietly that I thought his voice carried no farther than General Yuwen and Li Po standing directly behind us.

"Nothing is more important than defeating the enemies of China. When you let your arrow fly, remember that."

"Sire, I will," I promised.

Together we took our positions, sighting the target. As I looked down the shaft of my arrow, the world dropped away. I did not feel the tension of the crowd or Prince Guang's clever malice. There was only the feel of the bow and arrow in my hands, the tug of wind, the sight of the target. A great stillness seemed to settle over me. The whole world seemed sharp and clear and calm. I pulled in a single breath and held it.

Prince Jian is right, I thought. *Nothing is more important than defeating the enemies of China.*

I released the breath, and with it the arrow. For better or worse, the deed was done.

I was barely aware of Prince Jian beside me, mirroring my

actions. The arrows flew so quickly that I could hardly mark their flights with my eyes. As if from a great remove I heard the sounds they made as they struck home. For several seconds not a single person reacted. And now the only sound that I could hear was that of my own thundering heart.

Then, suddenly, it did not beat alone.

For it seemed to me that I could hear a second heartbeat, pounding out a rhythm a perfect match to my own. Its beat had been there all the time, I realized, shoring mine up, urging it on.

Prince Jian, I thought.

Then every other thought was driven from me as the crowd of soldiers surrounding me and the prince erupted in a great roar of sound.

Now, at last, I realized what my eyes had been trying to tell me all this time. The prince's arrow and my own had found precisely the same mark, passing directly through the target's throat. It was the best shot I had ever made, and I had done it with my heart beating in time to that of Prince Jian.

He moved to stand beside me then, clapping me on the back as he threw back his head and laughed in delight. I staggered a little under the gesture, for, abruptly, I was dizzy.

"Well done," Prince Jian said, his hand resting on my shoulder. "You come by your name honestly, Gong-shi, and I think you are more than worthy of that bow.

"Bring me the arrows," he instructed Li Po.

Li Po took off running, returning a moment later with the

arrows in both hands. At a nod from Prince Jian, Li Po held the arrows up for all to see.

The points were joined. Prince Jian and I had each shot so true that the points of our arrows had pierced each other and the target both.

"That is fine shooting," I heard the voice I knew was Prince Guang's say. I would have knelt, but for the sudden tightening of Prince Jian's grip on my shoulder. I stood still but trained my eyes on the rough stubble of grass that covered the ground of the target range.

"I will remember it, and you, Little Archer."

Without another word Prince Guang turned and walked away. I swayed, my legs threatening to give out under me. I thought I heard Prince Jian murmur something beneath his breath.

"This lad is ready to drop, Huaji," he said to General Yuwen. "Where do you lodge him?"

"With Li Po," General Yuwen said.

"Good." Prince Jian nodded. "Have Li Po get him something to eat, and then let him rest. But have Gong-shi at the ready, in case I should call."

Prince Jian gave my shoulder one last squeeze and let me go. "You have keen eyes and a strong heart, Little Archer," he said before he turned away. "I have need of both. I will not forget you either."

Fourteen

"I WISH THEY'D STOP STARING," I MURMURED TO LI PO AS WE crossed the camp the next morning.

I had gotten my first full night's sleep since leaving home, and had enjoyed the first hot breakfast, besides. Though General Yuwen had stayed with him long into the night, Prince Jian had not sent for Li Po or me after all. But shortly after breakfast we received word that the last of the scouts had returned. Now a meeting was being held in Prince Ying's tent, and we had been summoned. General Yuwen was already there.

"You'd do well to get used to it," Li Po replied. "You are famous." He glanced down, mischief briefly dancing in his eyes. "Little Archer."

I made a face. If we'd been alone, I'd have stuck out my tongue. But I knew better than to do that when the entire camp seemed to have their eyes on me, watching to see what impossible deed I'd perform next.

"And I wish they'd stop that, too," I said.

At this Li Po grinned outright. "I know. But you can't really blame them, any of them. You *are* famous now, and you *aren't* very tall, not for a boy."

"Especially not after you've done your best to whittle me down to size," I remarked. We walked in silence for several moments. "Why should the princes summon us to this council?"

"I am included because I am the captain of Prince Jian's archers," Li Po answered. "You, because he has asked for you, I suppose."

"Prince Guang will be there too, won't he?"

Li Po nodded. "It's a pity that he seems to have taken a dislike to you. Prince Guang is not a good adversary to have."

We walked in silence for a moment while I digested this fact.

"Why should he bother with me at all?" I asked finally. "I'm only a common boy. Surely I'm not worth his time."

"Under ordinary circumstances, I'd say you were right," Li Po replied. "But our present situation is far from ordinary." He turned his head to look at me. "You really *did* make an extraordinary shot yesterday, you know."

I had told no one what had happened in the moments after I'd let my final arrow fly, not even Li Po. I wasn't certain that he would understand. I wasn't all that sure I did myself. I was closer to Li Po than to anyone else, but never had I felt as close to another human being as I had when I'd felt my heart beat in time to that of Prince Jian. It was as if we had become the same person, our two hearts beating as one.

"It's not only your shooting, of course," Li Po went on. I recalled my wandering thoughts. "There's also the fact that Prince Jian has taken a liking to you. That alone would be enough to bring you to both his brothers' attention."

"Let's hope the oldest, Prince Ying, doesn't decide to dislike me on sight too," I remarked.

"That is not his way," Li Po replied. "But if you will listen to some advice . . ."

I nodded my head, to show I would, and Li Po continued.

"It might be a good idea for you to do a little noticing of your own. General Yuwen says you can tell much about a man by studying those whose company he chooses. It's always a good idea to know who the favorites are."

"That is good advice," I said.

"As long as you don't let anyone see that you are watching," Li Po added after a moment. "The trick is—"

"I know what the trick is," I interrupted, struggling to push back a sudden surge of annoyance. "The trick is to watch without looking like you're doing it. What makes you so bossy all of a sudden? All of this is new to me, I admit, but I'm not completely without brains, you know."

Li Po stopped walking and seized me by one arm.

"If I'm bossy, it's because I'm worried about you," he said, speaking in a low, intense voice. "Is that so wrong? In a matter of days target practice will be over and we will all be going to war. And you are not like other people. You are unpredictable. You always have been, Mulan. If I'm warning you, it's only for your own good."

"My name is Gong-shi," I corrected. "And since when are you always careful and wise?"

Li Po gave my arm a shake. "That is not the point."

"Then, what is?" I cried.

"The point," Li Po said through clenched teeth. "The point is that I don't want you to die. I don't want to ride home and have to explain to your father why I didn't take one look at you and send you right back home where you belong. It's what I should have done. I never should have let things come this far."

"You didn't have a choice," I answered. "And neither did I. Not once Prince Jian asked me to shoot at his side. Before that, even, when the guard accused me of stealing my father's horse. It's done. Let it go, Li Po. I can't change things and neither can you.

"Besides, we went over this yesterday, when I first arrived. Let us not spend the hours we have together arguing like children."

Li Po let go of my arm. "You're right," he said, his voice still strained. "I know you're right. But I can't help but feel afraid for us both. When this is over, I still plan to shake you until your teeth rattle."

"Yesterday it was thrashing me behind the tents. Today it's shaking me until my teeth rattle," I said. "Make up your mind."

"I'm giving serious consideration to both," Li Po said, but now I heard a hint of laughter in his tone.

"Well," I answered, "at least you'll have a while to make up your mind. Any thrashing you mete out will have to wait until after we've defeated the Huns. Now come on. Let's go."

We walked in silence the rest of the way. Arriving at Prince Ying's tent, we identified ourselves to the guards outside. A moment later General Yuwen appeared in the flap opening.

"Good. You are here," he said. "Come inside, but do so quietly, and keep your wits about you."

We ducked inside the tent. General Yuwen made a gesture, showing us our places. The center of the room was dominated by several tables filled with charts and maps. The princes and their advisers were bent over them, talking quietly. Servants and lesser soldiers stood along the perimeter. Li Po and I took our place among them. I was glad that Li Po had warned me about what to expect, though I still had to struggle to control my surprise.

Everyone—even the servants—was standing up.

It was Prince Jian's doing, Li Po had explained. The prince had made his position clear at the very first council of war and had refused to back down. He would not discuss battle strategy with men on their knees. A man should be able to stand on his own two feet when deciding the best way to send others into battle—when weighing the options on which his own life might hang, and the lives of his soldiers.

But Prince Jian had not stopped with insisting the generals be allowed to stand in his presence. He insisted the soldiers called to the councils should be allowed to do so as well, for it was their fate that was under discussion. It was an unheard-of change in protocol. Prince Guang had been furious, but Prince Jian had not budged. He would not ask any man to kneel before him when they were both doing the same thing: trying to determine the best way to safeguard China.

Prince Ying had agreed to his brother's terms first. Prince Guang had held out longer. But word of Prince Jian's actions had spread quickly through the camp. His popularity had skyrocketed. It was said that even those soldiers not directly assigned to Prince Jian's service would willingly die for him. For he treated them not like pieces on a game board but like men. In the end Prince Guang had given in.

The result was that all those who would plan strategy with the princes were allowed to move around the room as they wished, though I soon noted how careful everyone was to keep a respectful distance from the princes. But even this much freedom was a drastic change from years of tradition.

Like me, it seemed that Prince Jian was different.

"You still insist on ignoring the smaller pass," he was saying now, his tone heated. It seemed that Li Po and I had arrived in the midst of an argument.

"And you still insist on wasting resources where there is no danger," Prince Guang shot right back.

I let my eyes flicker to Prince Guang's face before returning to the spot on the wall of the tent I had chosen as my focus point. I had selected this spot with care, in an attempt to follow Li Po's instructions to keep my eyes open without appearing to do so. By choosing a spot about midway up the side of the tent opposite where I stood, I could see anyone in the room simply by shifting my eyes.

Prince Guang was the most handsome man that I had ever seen, a fact I had not been able to appreciate the day before. But it was not a kind of good looks that I found compelling. Instead the prince's smooth features made the gooseflesh rise along my arms. Prince Guang possessed the cold, smooth beauty of a snake.

This one loves himself more than he loves anything else around him, I thought. I wondered if that included China.

"It is not a waste of resources to protect China," Prince Jian began.

"Oh, spare me your sanctimonious proclamations about China," Prince Guang interrupted. "We all know about the prophecies and how important they make you, little brother. Perhaps you feel you are too important to fight. That is why you insist on guarding something that needs no protection."

"Enough!" the oldest brother, Prince Ying, cried. "You bicker like children, and it solves nothing."

It was the first time that he had spoken since Li Po and I had arrived. Following Prince Ying's outburst, a humming silence filled the tent. In it I could hear the dragon banner snapping in the wind high above me. I snuck a second look, at Prince Ying this time.

The Son of Heaven's firstborn was not as compelling as his brothers. He was not obviously handsome like Prince Guang. Nor did his features command a second look, as Prince Jian's did. But he was finely made, his voice and expression both more than a little stern. There was a crease permanently etched between his brows, as if from long hours of studying.

I remembered what General Yuwen had said, that Prince Ying possessed a fine and subtle mind. I wondered if it could maneuver through the rivalry between his brothers.

"We have been circling this matter for days," Prince Ying went on. "Both of you make good points." He frowned at Prince Guang. "Therefore, there is no need to cast doubts on anyone's honor. Just as there is no question of Jian leading an expedition to the smaller pass himself, assuming we decide to mount one. He is needed here, as we all are."

I half expected one or the other of the younger brothers to protest Prince Ying's words, but both stayed silent.

They respect him, then, I thought.

"Whose scouts were the last to return?" Prince Ying asked now.

"If it pleases Your Highness," said a voice I did not know, "those belonging to Prince Guang."

"And what do they tell us?" Prince Ying asked.

"The same thing all the other scouts have." Prince Guang spoke for himself this time. "That the Hun army is fast approaching, but there is nothing to show that they intend to divide their forces. They have no reason to. The second pass is simply too small."

"But you cannot *know* that," Prince Jian said, his voice impassioned. Almost against my will my eyes moved toward the sound of his voice. As he made his case, the color in his face was high. His dark eyes sparkled.

"We cannot afford to leave the smaller pass unguarded. Even a small force coming through it could do damage. It could attack the forces we have here from behind, or, even worse, the enemy could sweep on, into China."

He stepped to the table, stabbing a finger onto the map. "We have concentrated the majority of our forces here, in this valley, at *your* insistence, Brother."

His eyes were on Prince Guang as he spoke. "Only a small contingent of men remains to protect our father and Chang'an."

"We all agreed this valley was the clear choice," Prince Guang replied, his voice stiff.

"It *is* the clear choice," Prince Ying agreed. "Make your point, Jian."

"My point is that the Huns are not stupid," Prince Jian

exclaimed. "And we should stop pretending that they are."

Once again he stabbed a finger against the map. "If we leave that pass unguarded, we leave China unprotected. A small force coming through it could ride unchallenged to Chang'an."

"Who do you propose we send to protect it?" Prince Ying asked. "Surely we need every man here. We cannot afford to divide our forces."

I know! I thought.

It was only as absolute silence filled the tent that I realized I had done the unthinkable: I had spoken aloud.

You are in for it now, Gong-shi, I thought.

Prince Guang was the first to recover.

"If it isn't the Little Archer," he said, his voice as cold and as smooth as a lacquer bowl. "Don't be afraid. Come forward, boy. Tell us what great plan you have devised in just one morning that the great generals of China have been unable to find after days of discussion."

"Guang, enough," Prince Ying said, his own tone mild. "You'll give the boy a heart attack. He already looks half-dead from fright."

"I beg Your Excellencies' pardons," I said, and now I did kneel, pressing my forehead to the ground. "I am presumptuous. I did not mean to speak aloud."

"But speak you did," Prince Ying replied. "And I agree with my brother, at least in part. Such an exclamation must have come straight from the heart. I would like to know what you think you've figured out."

"Stand up and speak, Gong-shi," Prince Jian instructed. "My brothers sound ferocious, but not even Guang will bite you."

I wouldn't be too sure about that, I thought.

Slowly I got to my feet. I could see General Yuwen standing just behind Prince Jian. Carefully I avoided his eyes.

"Now, then," Prince Jian said when I had risen. "What is so clear to you that the rest of us have failed to notice?"

"I do not claim that you have failed to notice it," I said, choosing my words with great care. "Only that I have not heard anyone speak of it this morning. But if the pass is truly so narrow that only two may ride abreast . . ."

All of a sudden Prince Jian laughed. "I think I see where he is going," he said. He shook his head ruefully, as if chastising himself. "The truth is, I should have thought of it."

"What?" Prince Guang barked, the single syllable like the crack of a whip.

Prince Jian turned to face his middle brother, a smile still lingering on his face.

"Archers."

By the time the hour for the midday meal arrived, the plan was in place. Rather than sending troops to try to block the pass, Prince Jian would send a division of his corps of archers. We would be accompanied by a small company of foot soldiers and several of the prince's swiftest runners. If the Huns did come through the pass, the archers and soldiers would hold them off. The runners would alert the main body of the army that reinforcements were needed. In this way a larger force would not be dispatched until the need had been proved beyond a doubt.

Nevertheless, it was a dangerous assignment. The Chinese force would be a small one, because although Prince Jian's brothers had finally agreed that such a force was necessary, they would agree to no more. We would have no experienced general to lead us. Instead that duty would fall upon Li Po as captain of the archers.

"Let those whom you send be volunteers," General Yuwen proposed. "For men will face even the greatest danger bravely if they choose it for themselves."

"That is a sound suggestion," Prince Ying agreed. "And, save for Jian's archers, let the men come from all our forces. Let anyone who wishes to volunteer be given permission to go. That way all will know there is no hidden favoritism. All have equal value."

"Be careful," Prince Guang warned. "You're starting to sound just like our unconventional younger brother. Father may not be pleased."

"Father is not here," Prince Ying replied, his voice calm. "A prince may have a costlier funeral, but his bones rot at the same rate as anyone else's. You might do well to remember that, Guang."

Prince Guang's face was suddenly suffused with color. "Is that a threat?" he demanded, stepping forward.

"Don't be ridiculous," Prince Jian said mildly. But I noticed that as he spoke he moved to place himself between his two brothers. "Ying simply reminds you of an obvious fact. In death, all men are alike."

The color still high in his face, Prince Guang pivoted on one heel, snapped his fingers for his advisers and attendants to follow, and strode from the tent. It seemed the council of war was over. Prince Jian had won the day, but not by much.

As soon as Prince Guang departed, Prince Jian came toward me.

"Highness, forgive me," I said, falling to my knees as he approached.

"No," he said simply. "I will not. You have helped to provide the solution to a problem that has troubled me for many days now. I am in your debt."

He reached down and placed a hand on my shoulder to urge me to my feet.

"Highness, if I may," Li Po spoke.

The prince nodded. "What is it, Li Po?"

"Perhaps Gong-shi should lead the archers," Li Po said. "Though he is young, the other men admire and respect him. I believe that they would follow him, even into great danger."

"No!" I cried out, appalled. "I am not experienced enough, and I . . ." I swallowed past a sudden lump in my throat. "I am not sure that I wish to command others."

"One cannot always choose whether to command or not," Prince Jian observed quietly. He reached to grip Li Po's shoulder. "Your suggestion does you credit, and I think I understand why you make it. Even I have heard the men murmur of the young archer whose aim is as true as a prince. But I think I will leave things as they are, Li Po. Gong-shi makes a good point too. Your own experience will be needed."

"It shall be as you wish," Li Po vowed.

"Good," the prince said. "Then make ready, for you will go first thing in the morning. The Huns are close, and I do not like surprises."

He turned away. Together Li Po and I left Prince Ying's tent and made our way to our own in silence. This time I did not notice the stares as we walked through the camp. I was too busy wondering how Prince Jian would react if he knew the greatest surprise of all.

How would he feel if he learned that the archer who had fulfilled his desire to leave no portion of China unprotected was not a young lad named Gong-shi but a girl named Mulan?

Fifteen

I DID NOT SEE PRINCE JIAN FOR THE REST OF THAT DAY. BOTH Li Po and I were busy making preparations for our departure. After some discussion between Li Po and General Yuwen, it had been decided that half of our company of archers would go to the narrow pass.

"I would send all of you if I thought I could," General Yuwen said as we took our evening meal of rice and seasoned meat. He could have too, for every single member of the archer corps had volunteered to go. But a consultation between General Yuwen and his fellow commanders had determined that no more than half of the archers could be spared. The men had drawn lots to see who would accompany Li Po and me and who would remain with the main army.

"Do not wait, but send your runners as soon as you can if you need reinforcements," General Yuwen continued his instructions. "Once you have spent your arrows, you'll be down to hand-to-hand fighting, and if it comes to that, even a small force of Huns may overpower you."

"It shall be as you say," said Li Po.

General Yuwen sighed. "I wish your father were here, Mulan," he said. "It would be good to fight once more with my old friend at my side."

"You do him honor," I said. "And I will do my best to do the same."

"Well," General Yuwen said. He stood up. "I have a final meeting with the other generals, and then to bed. Make sure to get a good night's sleep. There is no telling when the next one will be."

With that, he left the tent.

"I am going to bid the horse good night," I said. "Do you want to come?"

"I think I will stay here," Li Po answered. "I want to write a letter to my parents."

"I should have thought of that," I said as an image of my father and Zao Xing rose in my mind.

"I will write something for you, if you wish," Li Po offered.

"Thank you. I would like that," I replied.

All of a sudden Li Po grinned. "I could say hello to my mother for you," he said. "I could tell her she missed having a hero for a daughter-in-law."

"I'm sure she'd be delighted to hear the news," I answered with a chuckle, even as I felt my heart give a funny little squeeze inside my chest. "But I am not a hero."

"You mean, not yet," said Li Po.

I left our tent and made my way to the far edge of camp, where the horses were picketed all together. Dark came early at this time of year. The campfires were already lit.

The mood is different tonight, I thought. There was no raucous conversation. Instead all around me men were quietly and seriously attending to their tasks. Soon the true test of all our courage would come.

My father's horse was pleased to see me, particularly when I shared the carrot I had brought along. Even the horses seemed to sense that something was different. My father's stallion tossed his head and pawed the ground, as if eager to set off for the pass.

"Do not be impatient," I whispered against his dark, smooth neck. "The morning will come soon enough." It was only as I began to step away from the horse that I realized I was not alone. A figure stood in the shadows at the edge of camp, in the place where the light of the campfires did not quite reach. I gave a gasp, and the figure stepped forward.

It was Prince Jian.

"I did not mean to startle you—," he began, but he interrupted himself. "No, don't *do* that," he exclaimed as I began to kneel down. To my astonishment Prince Jian reached out and hauled me upright.

"I get so tired of staring at the tops of people's heads all day long. Stand up."

"It shall be—"

"Yes, yes," Prince Jian said impatiently. "I know. It shall be as My Highness wishes. Shall I tell you what I wish? Sometimes I wish I were not a prince at all."

"You should not say so!" I exclaimed, shocked and surprised. "If the men heard you, they would lose heart. They do not fight simply for China. They fight for you, because they love you."

As I do, I realized suddenly. And not just as a comrade in arms but as a soul mate. I could feel how Prince Jian's heart was made differently from all others, just as my own was. It wanted different things, things it didn't always know how to explain to itself. In this way it called out to mine.

But this was a secret my heart had to keep forever. For my heart was not just Gong-shi's. It was also Mulan's.

"I know the men love me," Prince Jian answered simply. "I know it. But sometimes I think it makes what I must do twice as hard. It is not easy to know you are sending some men to their deaths, even if they face death willingly, with love in their hearts."

I chose my words carefully, as if walking through thorns. "I cannot say 'I know,'" I said. "We both know that would be a lie. But I think, I hope—that an act done out of love has the power to wipe the slate clean, to absolve. You may not always wish to be a prince, but nothing, not even your own will, can change the fact that that is who you are.

"How much better, then, for you to send your soldiers into battle understanding their true value, acknowledging that their loss will be mourned. We may not have a choice but to fight, yet surely there is still a right way to send men into battle, and a wrong one."

Prince Jian took a step closer. He was so close I could have reached out and touched him, though I did not.

"Who are you?" he asked in a strange, hoarse voice. "How can you say such things to me? How can one so young, a stranger I've just met, see so clearly the conflicts of my heart?"

My own heart was roaring in my ears, so loudly that it threatened to drown out any other sound.

Tell him, I thought. *Tell him that your heart understands his because his heart is like your own. Tell him you are as different as he is. Tell him his older brother is right. There is much more to you than meets the eye.*

I didn't, of course. Even as my heart urged my tongue to speak, my mind won the struggle. If I told this prince the truth, he would surely prove himself to be like all other men in one respect: He would judge what I could do on the basis of my sex. If he knew I was a girl, not only would he feel betrayed that I had deceived him, he would make me stay behind. And that was a risk I would not take. I had not come so far only to sit in my tent. I had come to help save China.

"I cannot answer that," I said, and thought I felt my own heart break a little at my response. "I am sorry."

"Don't be," said Prince Jian. "I think I know what you would say. I felt it yesterday as we stood side by side before the archery targets. Our hearts are joined; they are the same somehow. I don't pretend to understand it, but I believe it to be true."

"I do not claim to have the heart of a prince," I protested. Even in the darkness I caught the flash of his smile.

"No? Then maybe you've just proven my point, Little Archer. My brothers would tell you soon enough that my heart is not as royal as it should be."

"If they say that, then they are wrong," I answered confidently. "I believe you would do whatever it took to make China safe, even if it went against your own heart's desire. Surely that is what it means to be truly royal."

"Do you have no fear of what tomorrow may bring, then?" Prince Jian asked.

"Of course I do," I replied. "I have as much fear as any of your soldiers on this night, but my fear will not save China."

Prince Jian put a hand to his neck, to where the tunic that he wore parted to expose his throat. He made a motion I did not immediately comprehend. Then, as I watched, he lifted something from around his neck and extended it toward me. From his outstretched fingers hung a length of fine gold chain. At its end dangled a medallion.

"Take this," Prince Jian said.

"Highness," I protested, "I cannot. You do me too much honor."

"Take it," Prince Jian repeated. "Do not make me command you."

Slowly I reached for the chain, the tips of my fingers just barely brushing Prince Jian's. I held the medallion up so that it could catch the faint firelight. There was a raised symbol on the medallion's smooth, round surface.

"Can you see what is there?" asked Prince Jian.

I nodded. "It is a dragonfly."

"And what does the dragonfly symbolize?"

"Courage," I said.

"Courage," Prince Jian echoed. "Let me see you put it on."

I slipped the chain over my head, letting both chain and medallion slide down to hide beneath my tunic, just as the prince had worn it.

"That medallion was given to me many years ago," the prince said quietly. "When I was just a boy. It was a gift from Hua Wei, who was once my father's greatest general. He presented it to me when he returned me to my father, after rescuing me from the Huns.

"General Hua said that if ever I feared my courage might fail, I should remember our ancient symbol. I should remember the courage embodied by the strength of the fragile wings of the dragonfly."

"He sounds like a wise man," I said, battling with a fierce

and sudden impulse to cry. I could almost hear my father speak the words, as if he stood beside me.

"My father's greatest general," Prince Jian had said.

"I believe he is a wise man," Prince Jian answered softly. "He helped me to remember that those who seem invincible are sometimes not so very strong. While those who seem small and fragile may carry great things inside them. Think of this tomorrow, Gong-shi, when you face the Huns."

"Sire, I will," I promised. And now I did kneel down, and Prince Jian did not stop me. "I have no gift of gold to give you in return, but I swear that I will give you all the courage in my heart. When that is spent, I will find the way to give you more."

"In that case," Prince Jian replied, "your gift is more valuable than gold. Whatever the future brings, I will always honor the strength of your heart. It reminds me to stay true to what I hold in mine.

"Now stand up, and don't think I didn't notice that you knelt down after all."

"Indeed it is true what they say," I said as I stood. "'Prince Jian has keen eyes.'"

"And his archers are impudent," the prince replied. "And now I will say good night. Think of me when you face the Huns, and fight well, Little Archer."

"I will," I promised.

Without another word he turned and was gone.

Sixteen

OUR COMPANY DEPARTED AT DAYBREAK, THOUGH WE COULD
not see the sun. Dark clouds lowered in the sky, and the wind
had the raw sting to it that always meant snow. Li Po called the
archers together; General Yuwen assembled the foot soldiers.
Those of us on horseback would ride ahead, and half a day's
swift march would bring us all to the second pass.

Once there we would await the Huns.

All three princes came to speed us on our way. Prince Guang's
handsome face was impassive. If he was unhappy to have been
overruled by his brothers, he did not show it in public.

"Take this," Prince Jian said, suddenly materializing at my
side as I sat upon my horse awaiting orders. In his outstretched

hands he held a war horn made of polished bone.

"This horn has been in my family for countless generations," the prince said. "It is said that its voice is that of China. Though the throats of a million enemies cry out for our blood, the voice of this horn will always be heard above them. If your need becomes dire and all else fails, sound the horn and I will come."

"My lord," I said, reaching down and taking the war horn. "I will do so."

The horn felt cool beneath my fingers. Its surface was elaborately carved; its mouthpiece, gold. As I tucked it beneath my shirt, I felt a moment of dizziness, as if I could feel the earth turning beneath my horse's feet as the prophecies about this prince began to come full circle.

Though, as Li Po gave the signal and our company began to move out, it seemed to me suddenly that the fate of China no longer lay in Prince Jian's hands or even in his heart. Now China's fate lay in mine.

We were cold and tired by the time we reached the small pass that was our destination, for the way was rocky and the riding hard. Though a fire and a hot meal would have been most welcome, we had neither. Even the best-tended fire will smoke a little, and we would risk nothing that might give away our location to the Huns.

After we had rested and eaten a cold meal, Li Po took a group of archers to reconnoiter the cliffs on the right side of the pass, while I led a second group to explore the left one. At the same time, Li Po sent scouts through the pass itself, that we might learn more of its terrain and determine if any additional information could be gathered about the whereabouts of the Huns.

"There is this much in our favor," Li Po said late that afternoon, after we had finished our reconnaissance. We were having our own small council session, just the two of us. The rest of the men were checking their equipment. The scouts had not yet returned, but we had posted a guard at the head of the pass. Our force might be small, but we would not be caught unawares.

"The cliffs are steep and rocky. They will provide us with good cover," Li Po continued.

"Now if only I knew whether to hope that Prince Jian is right about what the Hun leader intends, or that he is wrong," I replied.

"Try hoping that we are strong enough to meet whatever challenge comes our way," Li Po suggested.

"Captain!" I heard a voice call.

Quickly Li Po got to his feet. "Keep your voice down!"

"Apologies, Captain," the soldier, a man whose name I did not know, said in a quieter voice. "The scouts have returned. They have sighted the Huns."

"You are sure it was the Hun commander that you saw?" Li Po asked several moments later.

The scout leader stood bent over with his hands on his

knees, breathing hard. The news he and his comrades carried back to camp was dire. A large Hun force was headed our way. It was commanded by the Hun leader himself.

"As sure as I can be," our scout leader said. He pulled in one more deep breath and then straightened up. "I saw their standard with my own eyes. A great horse, galloping."

"Perhaps it is a ruse," another scout suggested. "Meant to trick us."

"They have no need to do that," I said. "They believe the pass is unguarded."

"How large is their force?" Li Po asked. "Could you tell?"

"So large that we could not see them all," the scout leader replied. "We stayed as long as we dared, but we left before we could be seen, lest we give all of us away."

"You did well," Li Po answered at once. "You made the right choice. Go get some rest and what you can to eat. The rest of you, return to your posts. Gong-shi and I will confer about what to do next."

"We will never be able to hold them," Li Po said in a tense voice after the others had departed. "Even a small force would have tested our strength, but to face the Huns in such numbers . . ."

He eyed the war horn I wore slung around my neck. "Perhaps it is time to hear the voice of the war horn."

"No," I said decisively. "Not yet. That will only bring them on. They'll overwhelm us before we even have the chance to fight."

"You are up to something," Li Po said. "I can always tell. What is in your mind?"

"Give your fastest rider my father's horse," I said. "And have him ride for reinforcements. We have but two things in our favor: the narrowness of the pass and the element of surprise. Let us put them both to work for us."

"If only there were some way to block the pass completely," Li Po cried.

"I have been thinking about that," I said. "First send the messenger to Prince Jian. Then come with me. I have seen a place where we might attempt such a thing."

By the time the sun plunged behind the mountain, our plans were set. In addition to the man on horseback, Li Po had also sent his two swiftest runners to Prince Jian. No more horses could be spared, but it did not seem prudent to trust our information, or our fate, to just one man.

Shortly after sundown Li Po and I led the archers up into the cliffs. There, as silently as we could, we worked feverishly on the plan we hoped would ensure both our survival and China's.

Though the pass was never wide enough for more than two men to ride abreast, there was one spot where the passage grew so narrow that the legs of the riders seemed sure to brush against the sheer stone walls as the men rode side by side. This was the narrowest point of all, and it was here that Li Po and I hoped to create a rock slide. A rock slide big enough to block the passage so that no men could come through the gap afterward. Even if we didn't close the pass completely, we hoped to slow down the Hun army long enough for our own reinforcements to arrive.

It was exhausting work, cruel to the hands we would need later to ply our bows. We labored through the night. At least the work took such concentration that none of us had much room to spare for thoughts about what would happen once the sun rose. We could only hope our plan would work and that word of the Huns' true intentions had reached the princes' camp.

We could only hope that some of us would survive.

Li Po called a halt several hours before daylight, sending the men back down the mountain for food and what sleep could be managed before dawn. After much discussion the two of us had decided that we must allow a great enough number of Hun soldiers to come through the pass to maintain the illusion that they remained undetected, that their plan was succeeding and they would catch the Chinese army by surprise. And here, at last, something about what the Huns were planning worked in our favor, for our scouts had reported that the Hun leader rode at the head of his column of soldiers.

Once we triggered the rock slide, the Hun leader would be cut off. He would be unable to turn back, and the main body of his forces would be rendered incapable of moving forward to join him. This would leave the Hun leader and his smaller group of soldiers with just one choice: to move forward, into China. There they would be confronted first with our force and then, if all went well, with reinforcements from the main Chinese army.

And the signal to trigger the avalanche, to set the whole plan in motion, would be one last warning to our own troops: the sounding of the war horn.

The first of the Hun soldiers entered the pass just as the sun rose in an angry, sullen sky. The wind had more bite to it than it had the day before. Now it was too cold to snow. I kept the fingers of my right hand, the one I would use to pull the bowstring, tucked into my armpit in an attempt to keep them warm. We could hear the Huns long before we could see them. The narrow gorge seemed to push the sound of the horses' hooves ahead of the animals themselves.

As had been the case for our reconnaissance the day before, I took my archers into the cliffs on the left of the pass while Li Po led his into the right. The pass was so narrow that I could actually see Li Po from where I crouched. I felt the dragonfly medallion the prince had given me, warm against my skin.

Courage, Mulan, I thought.

The sound of the Hun horses echoed against the stone walls, so loud that it seemed impossible that we could not see the horses and riders themselves. The sound seemed to rise to a fever pitch. As I watched from the far side of the pass, Li Po rose from his crouch. At this signal all our archers set the arrows to their bows, but they did not fire. Li Po held up one hand, palm facing outward.

Hold.

Now, finally, the first group of men and horses began to pass beneath us in a relentless, endless tide. My arms and shoulders ached with the effort it took to hold the bow steady, and still Li Po did not give the order to fire. I saw the archer closest to me pull his lips back from his teeth in a grimace of determination and pain. Still, Li Po's hand never wavered.

Hold. Do not fire.

And then, suddenly, I saw it: a rider bearing a banner with the figure of a galloping horse, the standard of the Huns. Beside him rode a soldier with a great round shield. And just behind them was a single rider, alone. His horse was the most magnificent I had ever seen, his coat like burnished copper. The soldier's long, black hair was not tied back but streamed freely over his shoulders.

Surely this had to be the leader of the Huns.

Even from a distance it seemed to me that I could feel this man's restless energy, the determination that possessed him, propelling him forward. And I understood why others would follow such a man, even into these impossible conditions. There was something about his confidence and assurance that made the impossible seem possible.

I could feel my shoulders start to tremble with the strain of holding the bow taut. More than anything in the world I longed to let my arrow fly. Now the dragonfly medallion felt like a burning brand against my skin.

Lend me your strength and your determination, I thought. *Help me find the courage to hold on, to do what I must.*

The Hun leader and his standard-bearer were directly beneath us now. And finally, with one swift decisive motion, Li Po brought his hand down, giving the signal to fire. The air around me sang with the sound of bowstrings being released, the hiss of arrows as they sought their targets. The sound of men crying out in surprise and pain and the almost human screams of the horses rose up as if to surround us.

The Hun leader urged his troops forward, only to encounter the resistance of our own soldiers. The narrow pass seemed to roil like boiling water as men and horses jockeyed for position. Hun archers began to return our fire. The Hun standard-bearer lifted his face toward the cliffs as he screamed out his defiance. At that moment Li Po rose to his full height and sent an arrow straight toward him.

As the arrow hurtled downward, the standard-bearer sat hard in the saddle, trying to force his horse forward. But there was no room for him to maneuver. The way ahead was blocked by soldiers. Li Po's arrow pierced the banner and then buried itself deep into the standard-bearer's shoulder. Screaming in fury and pain, the bearer released the standard. It tumbled to the ground and was trampled by the feet of the horses.

Now the Hun leader rose in his stirrups, calling out to his soldiers in a great and terrible voice. He set an arrow to the string of his own bow, turned his horse to one side, and fired upward. I felt my heart leap into my throat. In his determination to see the Hun standard fall, Li Po had forgotten to take cover. He was still standing, and because he was visible, he made the perfect target.

"Li Po!" I cried.

But even as I shouted, I knew it was too late. As if guided by an evil demon, the Hun leader's arrow found its mark. As Li Po toppled backward, I rose to my own feet and fired.

This was the shot that I had missed not three days before, through the neck, from side to side. As if he heard my cry of pain and despair over every other voice around him, the Hun leader swiveled his head in my direction.

My arrow caught him beneath the chin, piercing his throat clean through from one side to the other. With tears that threatened to blind my eyes, I dropped to my knees, letting go of my bow and reaching for the war horn. I put it to my lips, drew in a single breath, and sent forth its call. Into it I poured all the pain and courage that lay within my heart.

I made the war horn sing with the voice of China.

At once, the Chinese soldiers below me began to retreat down the pass, drawing a portion of the Hun troops after them. I waited as long as I dared, praying that as many of our men as possible were clear.

I put the horn to my lips and again made it bellow. This was the signal the archers had been waiting for. On both sides of the pass, they dropped their weapons and put their shoulders to the rocks we had labored so long and hard to loosen the night before. The very air seemed to quake and shudder as, with a great groan, the rocks gave way and the walls of the pass began to tumble downward toward the Hun soldiers below. A cloud of dust rose, thick and choking. For the third and final time, I blew into the war horn's mouth.

And then, without warning, the earth gave a great crack beneath my feet and I, too, was tumbling down. My last thought, before the world turned black, was that even if I would be crushed myself, at least I had helped to crush the enemies of China.

Seventeen

I RETURNED TO MYSELF SLOWLY, AS IF TRUDGING UPHILL through a long and narrow tunnel. It was dimly lit, yet not entirely dark, because it seemed to me that I saw faces of companions I had known and loved, passing in and out of focus as I walked.

I saw General Yuwen's face most often. Next came an ancient, wrinkled face I did not recognize. And every once in a while, when the tunnel seemed most steep and endless, when it seemed to me I could not take another step, I thought I saw the face of Prince Jian. He gazed down at me with an expression I could not read save for the sorrow in his eyes.

Once I thought I opened my eyes to see him sitting beside

me, head bowed down, cradling in his hands the dragonfly medallion he had given me the night before the battle with the Huns. Another time I felt the medallion against my skin once more, and the tight hold of Prince Jian's hand on mine.

And finally there came a series of days when the tunnel proved too dark and steep to travel at all. It was then that I was seized by a great fire in all my limbs, when my ears grew deaf and my eyes grew blind. And in those days I could not even wonder whether my journey had, at last, reached its end. I could form no questions, for I was lost, even to myself.

When I opened my eyes at last, it was to light that was the color of a pearl, a color that I recognized, and I knew I had awakened just before dawn. For several moments I lay absolutely still, searching for some clue to my surroundings, staring upward as the light grew stronger. The answer came almost at once. I was in my own tent, the one I had once shared with Li Po. I was lying on the pallet that had once been my bed. My body felt ... unfamiliar. Light as a seedpod spinning through the air, heavy as a stone, all at the same time.

I shifted, and felt pain shoot through my shoulder. *I have been injured,* I thought.

And at this the memories came flooding back. Memories of blood and pain, the screams of men and horses. I made a sound of protest, and in an instant Prince Jian was there, kneeling beside me. He took my hands in one of his and pressed his other hand against my brow.

"Your skin is cool to the touch," he said. "Praise all the gods, your fever has broken." His eyes roamed over me, his expression unreadable.

"I believe that you will live, Little Archer."

I tried to speak but managed only a croak because my mouth and throat were parched. As if he understood, Prince Jian released me, stepped away briefly, and then returned with a cup of cool water. He eased me upright, helping me to drink. I could take no more than a little, for in all my thirst I was weak and clumsy. Water dribbled down my chin and down onto my neck.

"Li Po," I managed to get out.

Prince Jian laid me back down. "Perhaps it would be better to wait . . . ," he began.

"No," I said. "No, tell me."

His eyes steady on mine, Prince Jian shook his head, and I knew the thing I feared had come to pass.

"I am sorry. I am told he died bravely," the prince said.

I nodded, blinking against the tears that filled my eyes. "He took down the standard. We were victorious?"

"Yes, we were victorious," Prince Jian replied. He fell silent, as if deciding what to say next.

He has grown older, I thought. There were lines around his mouth I didn't recognize, and his face looked pale and drawn. His shoulders, though still straight, now looked as though they carried some impossibly heavy burden.

"But the archers who fought beside you say that it was you who made our victory possible," the prince finally said. "They say you killed the Hun leader with a single shot. Is this so?"

"It is," I said, my voice a little stronger now. "But it was Li Po who made it possible. When the standard went down, the Hun leader turned his head toward me. It was . . ." I paused and took a breath. "It was the shot I missed that day when we practiced at targets."

"I see," Prince Jian said. "This bears out what I was told." His mouth twisted into a strange smile. "It would seem you are now a great hero, Little Archer."

He knows, I thought. *He knows that I'm a girl and not a boy.*

I had no idea how long I had been lying there, but I must have been tended by a physician. My true gender would have been discovered at once.

And now, for the first time, I felt my courage falter. I could not imagine how this prince, who had shared the innermost workings of his heart with me, could forgive the fact that I had kept something so important as my true identity from him.

"Highness," I said. "I—"

Prince Jian stood up. "I will bring General Yuwen to you," he said, speaking over my words. "He has been concerned about your welfare, spending many hours beside you. He will wish to know you are once more yourself."

At his choice of phrase I winced, for I had not truly been myself before. The difference was that now we both knew it.

He will never forgive me, I thought.

More than anything else in the world, I longed to call Prince Jian back, to explain all the reasons for what I had done. But I did not. I had betrayed his trust. And where there is no trust, it does no good to explain.

"Thank you," I said finally. "I would like to see General Yuwen to thank him for all his care."

"I will go, then," said Prince Jian. He moved to the tent flap, lifted a hand to push it back, and then paused.

"I am sorry for the loss of your friend," he said. Then he stepped through the opening and was gone.

General Yuwen came in several moments later. He strode at once to where I lay and knelt down beside me. Gently he took my hand in his.

"Mulan," he said simply. "My little hero of China."

At the sound of my true name the floodgates opened. I did not behave like a hero of China, brave at all costs. Instead I threw my good arm around General Yuwen as I would have liked to with my own father, burying my face in the crook of his neck, and I wept like a child for everything I had lost.

It was from General Yuwen that I learned the full story of the events of that day, and its aftermath. Now that my fever had broken, I began to make a speedy recovery. It was true that I was covered from head to feet in scrapes and cuts, in bruises that would have made Min Xian hiss like a steam kettle in sympathy.

My right arm was in a sling. In my tumble down the mountain I had broken my collarbone. I had been so buried in rubble that it was a miracle I didn't have more broken bones. It was Prince Jian who had found me.

By the time I had made the war horn cry, a relief force had already been sent on its way to provide reinforcements. The messengers Li Po and I had sent had reached Prince Jian safely. The prince himself had led the relief force, an honor that, as the eldest, Prince Ying could have claimed as his own. But he had been gracious, acknowledging his youngest brother's wisdom in insisting that the second, smaller pass be protected—even over the objections of his brothers and their councilors.

"Never have I seen anyone fight as Prince Jian did that day," General Yuwen confided one night.

I was now well enough to be up for long periods of time. The general and I were sitting outside the tent before the bright blaze of a campfire. General Yuwen often came to spend his evenings with me, and he was not alone. Word that Gong-shi— the young archer whose shot had helped to save all China—was in fact a girl had spread quickly through the camp. Many of the soldiers came to pay their respects, but also, I suspected, to relieve their curiosity. Only Prince Jian stayed away. I had not seen him since the day I first awakened.

"The prince was like a tiger," General Yuwen continued now. "When the battle was over and we began to take stock of our wounded . . . When Li Po's body had been discovered but you could not be found . . ."

The general broke off, shaking his head. "Never have I seen anyone more determined," he went on. "One of the archers who had fought beside you was brought before him to explain what he thought had befallen you. It was long after nightfall. Prince Jian had had no rest and little food. Still he took a torch and went to search for you himself. He would not rest until he found you, he said."

"And after all that, I turned out to be a girl," I said quietly.

"Not just any girl," General Yuwen said. "Hua Wei's own daughter. Like your father before you, you are a hero, Mulan."

"You called me that before," I said. "But I don't feel very much like one, and I never set out to win that title."

"Perhaps that's why it fits you so well," the general answered quietly. "You thought not of yourself, of your own glory, but of China. The emperor is eager to meet you. He has even sent for your father."

Though winter was almost upon us, the emperor wished to celebrate China's great victory over her ancient enemy not in the capital but here, in the mountains where the battle had been fought. He was already on his way, with a great cavalcade of retainers. And my father was to be among them.

"So he is forgiven, then," I said.

"It would appear so," General Yuwen replied. "But, then, he was right after all. The Huns did present a danger, as long as the son of their former leader was alive. Now that he is dead, the Huns have no one to lead them. The next in line is an infant. It will be many years before he is grown.

"But the arrow that turned the tide in China's favor was fired by none other than Hua Wei's own child. It is your actions that have restored your father to favor."

"Even though I'm a girl?" I said.

General Yuwen smiled.

"And Prince Jian?" I asked. "Can I win back his favor by my actions, do you think?"

"Ah, Mulan," General Yuwen exhaled my name on a sigh. "There I think you must be patient. Give him time."

"I don't think there's enough of it," I said simply. "I hear what the men say around the fires at night. The Son of Heaven intends to make Prince Jian his heir, passing over Ying and Guang. A prince and a general's daughter might have found a way to bridge the gap between them, assuming I might be forgiven in the first place, but now . . ."

My voice trailed off. "Even if I am patient for the rest of my life, I think the gulf between us will be too great to cross."

General Yuwen remained silent. In spite of the warmth of the fire, I shivered, for I discovered that I was cold. And it seemed I might never be warm again, because this cold came not from the air around me but from the depths of my own heart.

I want to go home, I thought. I longed for the familiar branches of the plum tree, Min Xian's face. Most of all I longed for Li Po.

But even when I returned, nothing would be quite the same. Li Po was gone, and the Mulan who would return was not a child anymore.

In the weeks since I had made the decision to leave my father's house, I had grown up. And I had learned that not every battle can be fought by firing an arrow from a bow. But I would have to face whatever new challenges came my way as bravely as I had faced the Huns. I could not wallow in self-pity, thinking about what might have been. I had to do my duty. It was the only way to stay true to myself.

I wonder if this is how Jian feels about the possibility of becoming emperor, I thought. Despite the rift between us, I believed I still understood what was in his heart, because it was just like mine. And what Prince Jian's heart wanted was to run free, to command no other than itself. But like my own heart would, Prince Jian's would accept his responsibilities. He would do his duty with his head held high. He would bring himself and his family honor.

I must learn to do the same, I thought.

I had to cease to mourn what could never be and learn to make the most of what was possible. And I would begin by trying to mend the hurts of the past.

Asking General Yuwen to bring me paper, brush, and ink, I sat up late, composing a letter of sympathy to Li Po's mother.

Eighteen

THE VERY NEXT MORNING THE OUTRIDERS APPEARED, GIVING us warning that the Son of Heaven would soon arrive. A great space had been prepared in the middle of the camp for his tent, with those of the princes flanking it on the left side, the side of the heart.

As soon as word reached him of his father's approach, Prince Ying sent soldiers to line the roadway, so many that they stood six deep. Not only would this give many men who had fought bravely the chance to see the emperor, it meant that the Son of Heaven would be welcomed by those who had fought for China's cause.

The minor court officials appeared first, followed by the

members of the emperor's own household. The silk of their elaborate robes seemed to dazzle my eyes.

"There are so many of them," I murmured to General Yuwen.

He smiled. "That is not the half of them," he replied. "Only those most suited to travel. The rest stayed behind in Chang'an."

"No wonder my father found it quiet in the country," I said.

"Look!" General Yuwen said, pointing. "The Son of Heaven arrives!"

There was a flash of gold, like sunlight glancing off a mirror, and suddenly I could see the emperor himself. His horse was the color of sable. The Son of Heaven's cloak spread across the horse's back. Though lined with fur to protect him from the cold, it was also embellished with the figure of a five-clawed dragon embroidered in gold thread. The embroidery was so thick, the stitches so fine, that as the cloak shifted in the wind it seemed as if the dragon would leap from the emperor's back and take to the sky.

Straight to the center of camp the Son of Heaven rode, to where the princes stood in front of his tent to welcome him. As he approached, all those assembled knelt to do him honor. I had practiced kneeling and then standing up again, in the privacy of my tent. It's hard to kneel with only one arm for balance. The last thing I wanted was to humiliate myself and bring dishonor to my family by falling on my face as I paid homage to the Son of Heaven.

The emperor brought his horse to a halt.

"My sons, I come to celebrate your great victory," he said.

"Father," Prince Ying replied. "You are most welcome."

"I give thanks for your safety," the emperor went on, "as I give thanks for the safety of China. Rise now that you may look into my face and see how much I love and honor you."

At their father's instruction the princes stood, even as the emperor dismounted. He embraced each in turn.

"Where is the archer?" the emperor inquired. "Let me see Hua Wei's child."

I felt my heart give a great leap into my throat.

"There, Father," Prince Jian said. "Beside General Yuwen."

"Rise and come forward, child."

I did as the emperor commanded, a simple act that required every bit as much courage as facing down the Huns. Slowly I walked forward until I stood before the Son of Heaven.

"Tell me your name, Little Archer," he commanded, though his voice was not unkind.

"If it pleases Your Majesty," I said, astonished to hear my voice come out calm and steady. "I am Hua Mulan."

"I recognize your father's determination in your face," the emperor said.

"Majesty, you honor me to say so," I replied.

"Hear me now, all of you," the Son of Heaven cried in a great voice. "Once, long ago, in return for a great service I offered to grant Hua Wei the first wish of his heart. Now I offer this same gift to his daughter. For she has given me what I wished for most: the safety and security of China."

A great cheer went up from the soldiers. I stood, frozen in shock. The thought that the emperor might offer me such an honor had never even occurred.

What *was* the first wish of my heart?

Like my father, could I wish for love?

No, Mulan, I realized. *You cannot.* Not because I did not love, but because until this moment I had not recognized that love for what it truly was.

My father had spoken his wish, knowing he loved and was loved in return. But I was not so fortunate.

I cannot wish for love, I thought. *But I can wish because of it.* Prince Jian had given me the gift of courage when I had needed it most. Perhaps now I could give him something he would value just as much.

"Speak, Mulan," the Son of Heaven urged. "Tell me what I may grant you to show my gratitude."

"The Son of Heaven commands me to speak," I said, "and I will do so. This then is my reply: The first wish of my heart would be that you grant the first wish of a heart other than my own. A heart I will name, if you will let me.

"I have served China. I already have my reward."

There was a startled pause.

"Where is Hua Wei?" the emperor finally said. "Let him come forward."

"Here, if it pleases Your Highness," my father said.

"Your daughter speaks well, Hua Wei," the Son of Heaven complimented when my father had come to kneel before him.

"Your Highness honors us both to say so," my father replied.

The Son of Heaven frowned. "You are sure that is your final answer?" he asked me. "You will give away your own wish to someone else? Who is this person whose heart you value so much?"

I took the deepest breath of my entire life. *Do it, Mulan,* I thought. *Show courage. Be true to yourself.*

Though the emperor had given me permission to stand, I knelt once more, at my father's side.

"I cannot answer that question, Majesty," I said.

"Why not?"

"Until I know that Your Majesty agrees to my request, I cannot speak the name aloud. For if I speak too soon, I throw away my wish."

At this, Prince Guang could contain himself no more.

"Father," his outraged voice rang out. "Surely this has gone on long enough. Much as I respect your wish to honor Hua Wei's daughter, I must—"

"What you must do"—the emperor's voice sliced through that of his son's—"is to show your respect by holding your tongue. I gave the girl leave to speak from her heart and she has done so. She displays great wisdom in also speaking her mind. I cannot ask for the first and then fault her for the second.

"Very well, Hua Mulan. You shall have what you desire. Name who you will, and he shall have the first wish of his heart. This I swear to you from my own. Now stand up and tell me who it is."

"The Son of Heaven is gracious and bountiful," I answered as I stood. "With all my heart I ask that you bestow your gift on Prince Jian. For it was he who first saw the way our enemies would try to defeat us. He is the true hero of China, not I."

"Jian, step forward," the emperor said.

"Father," Prince Jian said, even as he obeyed, "I cannot—"

"Why are all my sons suddenly so determined to tell me what I can and cannot do?" the Son of Heaven inquired. "Do you think that I am in my dotage? That I don't know my own mind?"

"Of course not, Father," Prince Jian protested.

"I am glad to hear it," the Son of Heaven answered. "Now do as I command." All of a sudden the emperor's tone softened. "Do not be afraid. No matter what it is, I will make the first wish of your heart the first desire of mine. I have sworn it. Therefore speak, my son."

"I will obey you in this, as in all things," Prince Jian said. I was grateful that he was standing next to me, for it meant I could not look at him. Instead I kept my eyes straight ahead, gazing at the emperor's elaborately embroidered cloak.

"This, then, is what I would ask of you, Father. Do not make me return to court. Instead let me stay in these wild lands. Let me dedicate my life to keeping China safe in her remotest places, for there I will be free to be myself."

"What you ask for is difficult to grant," the Son of Heaven said, his voice heavy. "For it runs counter to my hopes. But I have sworn to give you what you wish, and I will honor my word. So be it, Jian, my son. You may serve China in the way that is closest to your heart.

"Come now." The emperor made a gesture, calling all his sons to his side. "Let us go inside and we will speak further of these things."

"Father," Prince Jian said, "I will do your bidding with all my heart."

As the Son of Heaven and his sons passed by me, I knelt once more. When he reached me, the emperor stopped.

"Hua Mulan."

"Yes, Mighty Emperor," I said.

"It seems I owe you a second round of thanks. You saw what was in my son's heart, while I saw only what was in my own. I will make sure to ask him how this might be so."

With that he strode past me and was gone. His sons followed in his wake. When they were safely inside the tent, I got to my feet and turned directly into my own father's waiting arms.

Nineteen

"WHEN I REALIZED THAT YOU HAD GONE, WHEN I REALIZED what you had done, I thought that I had lost you forever," my father told me later that night.

Though my father had feasted with the emperor, the princes, and the generals, he had left the celebrations early so that we might have some time alone. I had not gone to the celebration at all. Instead I had pleaded weariness and the pain of my wounds. General Yuwen had secured the emperor's permission for me to remain quietly in my tent. I did not think I would be missed, at least not by the Son of Heaven himself.

He had made good his promise. He would grant his best-loved son the first wish of his heart, but the emperor would not thank me for it. It robbed him of his own wish that Prince Jian succeed him. I wondered if his father might see the wisdom of Prince Jian's choice, in time.

There would be several days of celebration and ceremonies yet before the emperor's great army would disband and before my father and I would ride for home. Chances were good I would never see Prince Jian again. I tried to tell myself that it was for the best. I didn't get very far.

"I am sorry I went away without saying good-bye." I brought my thoughts back to the present and my father. "But I could hardly tell you what I wanted to do. You would never have let me go."

"Of course I wouldn't," my father said. "What kind of father would I have been, then?"

I smiled. "The same kind you are now, I hope. One who loves his daughter well enough to forgive her." Without warning I felt the tears well up in my eyes. "Oh, *Baba*," I said. "I just want to see Zao Xing and Min Xian. I want to see the plum trees bloom in the spring. I want to go home."

"And so we shall, my Mulan. Zao Xing will be pleased to see you. I was afraid she'd worry herself sick the whole time you were away."

"How is the baby?" I asked.

"Growing strong. Zao Xing complains she will grow as great as a house before the baby arrives. Min Xian takes good care of them both."

"I'm glad to hear it," I said. "Keeping Zao Xing and the

baby safe was part of the reason I went away in the first place. I could not bear . . . I did not wish . . ."

"My daughter," my father said as he gathered me close. "I know. I am so proud of you, and not just for your ability to sneak off with my horse or for your skills with a bow. I am proud of your generous heart. Someday I hope you will have the reward it longs for."

"I hope so too," I said.

"Mulan," my father went on, "there is something that I would like to tell you, a thing I should have spoken to you long before now."

I burrowed a little deeper in my father's arms. "I think I know what you want to say," I said. "You wish to tell me the name of my mother. Min Xian told me before I rode away. Please don't be angry with her. She said I should not ride without knowing."

"She was absolutely right," my father replied. "And I am not angry for it. Her heart was more generous than mine in this." My father kissed the top of my head, the first such affection I had ever known him to show.

"Come now," he went on. "Let's get you a good night's sleep."

"Baba," I said suddenly, "do we have to wait until the end of the week? Couldn't we go home tomorrow? I'm well enough to travel. Honestly I am."

"Let me see what Huaji has to say," said my father. "If you are well enough, and there is no other reason to stay, perhaps we

may go. The emperor has already honored you. But if it is the
Son of Heaven's pleasure, we must stay."

"I understand," I promised. "But you'll ask General Yuwen
first thing tomorrow?"

"Why not ask me now?"

My father and I turned as General Yuwen made his way
through the tent flap. He and my father greeted each other
warmly. Then the general turned to me.

"Perhaps it is not my place to say this with your father sitting right beside you, but I have never been more proud of
anyone than I was of you today, Mulan. You have saved China
twice, I think. Once by taking a life. Today by giving Prince Jian
the opportunity to ask for the life he truly desires.

"He will serve China, and himself, far better living the life
of his heart than he would have in the life his father had chosen
for him."

"And Prince Ying will become emperor someday?" I asked,
remembering the general's belief that Prince Ying would be a
fine emperor during peace.

General Yuwen nodded. "Now there is no reason for anything else to occur. This has been a good day for China."

"Then I have done my duty and am content," I said.

The general regarded me quietly for a moment. "I think," he
finally said, "that you have one more duty to perform. Prince Jian
has asked to speak with you. He is waiting nearby. He did not
wish to intrude on you and your father."

"The prince wishes to speak with me?" I said, trying to ignore the way my heart quickened. "Why?"

"I think that must be for him to say," General Yuwen replied. "Shall I tell him to come?"

"No," I replied. "There is no need. I will go myself. Instead stay here with my father. I'm sure the two of you have many things to discuss. But if I feel my ears burning, I will know you talked of me, so be warned."

"We promise not to mention your name at all," my father said as he bundled me into a cloak. I didn't believe him for a moment.

And so I was smiling as I stepped out into the night. I stood for a moment, letting my eyes adjust. The tent had been bright with lantern light, but now a full moon hung in the clear night sky, wrapping everything around me in the embrace of its cool white glow. I had taken no more than half a dozen steps toward Prince Jian's tent when he materialized by my side.

"You came," Prince Jian said. "I wasn't sure you would."

"Of course I would," I answered, and now my heart was impossible to ignore. It beat painfully inside my chest for all the things that it desired, now out of reach.

Do not fool yourself, Mulan, I thought. *They were always out of reach.* I might as well have stretched out my arms to touch the moon in the sky.

"If only to say good-bye," I went on.

"Will you walk with me?" Prince Jian said. "The sky is bright tonight."

"Just so long as you watch out for any holes," I replied. "It will never do for me to fall and lose the use of both my arms."

In the moonlight I caught the flash of his smile. He stepped to my left side, and taking me lightly by my good arm, we began to walk together.

"That sounds more like you," Prince Jian said. "I thought . . ." He paused, and then began again. "I thought I might have lost you."

My pride put up a brief struggle and then went down in flames. *Why shouldn't I tell the truth?* I wondered. *I'll never see him again after tonight.*

"No," I answered quietly. "You could never lose me. It simply isn't possible."

"Why?" Prince Jian suddenly burst out. "Why did you do it?"

I didn't even pretend to not know what he was talking about. Still, I paused. I wanted to choose my words with care, with more care than I had chosen any others in my life.

"When your father made his offer, I looked into my heart to see what it might wish for above all else," I replied. "But I discovered that, as powerful as he is, what I desired most lay beyond even the Son of Heaven's power to bestow.

"So I looked into my heart again, and I thought . . ." My voice choked off as, just for a moment, my nerve faltered.

Remember the dragonfly, Mulan, I thought.

"I thought—I hoped I saw the way to make things right between us," I said after a moment. "I never meant to deceive you."

I broke off again, and made a wry face.

"Or at least no more than I deceived everyone else by pretending to be a boy. That night, before I went away to fight, I wanted to speak, to tell you the truth, but I could not. I could not tell you who I really was.

"In spite of all the ways that you are unique, in this you would have been like everybody else. All you would have seen was that I was a girl. You would have made me stay behind."

"I think that you are right," Prince Jian said slowly. "But is this all?"

"I don't know what you mean," I said.

Prince Jian stopped walking, though he kept his hand on my arm. "Mulan. Today you gave me the chance to speak the truth of my heart. Will you not tell me the truth of yours? If the only reason you spoke to my father as you did was to settle a debt between us, it is more than paid. If that is all there is between us, then tell me so. I will go, and we will never speak of our hearts again, for we will never see each other.

"But before I let this happen, I ask you again: Is this all? Did your heart bestow its great gift for no other reason? Does it want nothing else from me?"

"I might ask you the same question," I replied, making a bold answer lest my heart read too much into his words and begin to hope too much. "You are a great prince. Why should you care what my heart wants?"

"The answer to that is simple enough," Prince Jian said.

"Though discovering it was hard. It is because I love you."

How brave he is! I thought. For with that simple declaration, he had set all defenses aside and laid bare his heart. He had been unwilling to risk China, but it seemed that he would risk himself.

You must be no less brave, Mulan, I told myself.

"In that case, you are more powerful than the Son of Heaven," I said aloud. "You have done what he could not. You have given me the first wish of my heart."

"And what was that wish?" Prince Jian asked. "Please—I would like to hear you say it out loud."

"That you love me as I love you," I said. "But this was a gift that only you could bestow."

Jian turned me to him then, mindful of my injury, and took me in his arms. "Mulan," he murmured against my hair. "Mulan."

"I know my name," I murmured back.

I felt a bubble of laughter rise up within him, heard it burst forth before he could stop it.

"Yes, but I'm still getting used to it," he replied. "You must give me a little time yet."

"I will give you all the time I have," I vowed, and felt his arms tighten.

"What?" he asked, his voice light and teasing even as he held me close. "No more?"

"Even this great hero of China has her limits, Majesty," I answered.

He tilted my face up and looked down into my eyes. "No," he said softly. "I really don't think so. That is one of the reasons I love you so much."

I reached up and laid a palm against his cheek.

"You have to stop this," I replied. "You'll make my head swell as well as make it spin."

As our lips met, we were both smiling. Our first kiss was full of the promise of both our hearts. A kiss of true love.

"I cannot promise you an easy life," the prince said when at last we broke apart. "But I hope that you will choose to share it with me anyway."

"Tell me something, Your Highness," I said. "Does anything about me tell you that I want an easy life?"

He laughed then, the cold night air ringing with the sound.

"No," he answered honestly. "Nothing does. Will you marry me, Mulan? Will you make your life with me in China's wild places, where our hearts may run as free as they desire?"

"I will," I promised. "But first I must return to my father's house. My stepmother is going to have a child. I would like to be there when it arrives."

"I will come with you," Prince Jian said. "I would like to meet Li Po's family."

"I love you," I said as the tears filled my eyes. "I love you with all my heart."

"I am glad to hear it," Prince Jian answered. "For I love you with all of mine. Though I suppose I should have asked your father's permission first."

"I believe that he will give it," I said. "For if there is one thing my father understands, it's marrying for love."

We were married in the spring, beneath the plum tree. Its blossoms were just beginning to fade and loosen their hold. Each time the wind moved through the branches, fragrant petals showered down around us. Neither the emperor nor either of Jian's brothers came to the ceremony. But General Yuwen was there, and Zao Xing, holding my baby brother in her arms. He had made his appearance early, causing us all alarm. But he soon proved the rightness of his choice, for he was growing fat and strong. In honor of my recent exploits, and to encourage him to grow up big and strong, my parents named him *Gao Shan,* High Mountain.

The night before Jian and I exchanged our vows, I could not sleep. I lay awake for many hours gazing out the window at the stars. I heard a soft whisper of sound and turned from the window to discover that my stepmother had entered my room, my baby brother in her arms.

"I wondered if I would find you awake," she said. "I don't think I slept a wink the night before I married your father."

"My own marriage will be all right, then," I said as I patted the bed beside me. "Look how well yours turned out."

Zao Xing chuckled as she sat. I held out my arms for the baby, and she placed Gao Shan into my arms.

"I won't be here to watch him grow up after all," I said.

"No," my stepmother said softly. "It appears that you will not. But I hope you won't stay away forever. Who knows? Perhaps you will return to have your own child."

"For goodness' sake, I'm not even married yet," I exclaimed. Zao Xing clapped a hand over her mouth to keep from laughing as the baby squirmed in my arms.

"Here, take him back," I said. "I want to give him something."

Zao Xing took the baby back. He settled peacefully in the crook of her arm. I reached around my neck and lifted the dragonfly medallion over my head. I held it out in one palm.

"Prince Jian gave me this," I said, "the night before I rode away to fight the Huns. He said my father had given it to him when he was just a boy. I would like Gao Shan to have it, to remind him of Jian and me when we are far from home."

"It's a wonderful gift," Zao Xing said, her eyes shining. "Thank you, Mulan. He is too young to wear it yet, I think, but I will save it for him. And I will tell him of his famous sister's exploits. They will make fine bedtime stories."

"I'm not so sure that's a good idea," I said. "He'll grow up getting into trouble."

"No," Zao Xing replied. "He will grow up to bring the Hua family honor." She leaned over and kissed me on the cheek. "Your father and I are both glad to see you so happy, but we will miss you, Mulan."

"I'll miss you, too," I said. I returned her embrace.

"Now," Zao Xing said. "You lie back down. Gao Shan seems happy. I think we'll just sit beside you awhile."

The last thing I saw before I closed my eyes was my stepmother cradling my baby brother in her arms. I fell asleep to the sound of her gentle voice singing a lullaby.

My father gave me his horse as a wedding gift.

"Ride up the streambed," he said when at last the day arrived for Jian and me to depart. "It will take you through the woods to where our land ends and the rest of China begins, and you will understand why I chose that path to return home."

"We will do so," I promised. I swung up into the saddle. "Make sure you teach my little brother how to use a bow."

"Come back and teach him yourself," my father said.

"I will do that also," I answered with a smile.

"Take good care of my daughter," my father said to Jian.

"As you once cared for me," he vowed. Then he grinned. "Though, truly, I think you may have things backward."

The sound of laughter filled our ears at our departure. Jian and I rode up the streambed as my father had requested, the horses picking their way carefully among the stones.

"I wonder why your father wanted us to go this way," Jian mused as we rode along.

"I can't say for certain," I said. "Though I think I'm beginning to guess. Wait until we reach the woods. Then we will know."

Half an hour's travel farther brought us to the first of the trees. Soon we had passed beneath their boughs.

"Look," I said, pointing. "Oh, look, Jian."

Here and there on the forest floor, now hidden, now revealing themselves, tiny white blossoms lifted up their heads.

Wild orchids.

Turn the page for a sneak peek

at another magical tale. . . .

THE WORLD ABOVE

Cameron Dokey

Prologue

CONFESSION: I NEVER INTENDED TO GO LOOKING FOR ADVENTURE.
One came looking for me anyhow. And not just any old adventure. A really, really big one. The kind of adventure that changes your life. It certainly changed mine. Though, for the record, it was all Jack's fault.

Most things are.

Don't get me wrong. Jack is my brother, my twin, in fact, and I love him with all my heart. But if ever there was a magnet for adventure, or rather, *mis*adventure, Jack would be it. All during our childhood, he was forever getting into what our mother called "scrapes," most likely because a lot of scrapes (and also scratches) were actually involved.

Jack is my fraternal twin, not my identical twin, by the way. I'm a girl, not a boy. And before you leap to any conclusions, my name is not Jackie. It's Gen, short for Gentian, a wildflower that grows on the hills near the farm that is our home. Mama says she named me this because the gentian blossom is the exact same color blue as my eyes. Also the color of Jack's. Our hair, as long as I'm taking a moment to provide some physical description, is blond.

But here a difference arises. Jack's hair is a color that can only be described as golden. You know, like the sun. Mine is more like clover honey, a little darker and more serious. Just like the rest of me, my hair calls a little bit less attention to itself than Jack's does.

And this external feature, so easy to dismiss, actually reveals quite a lot about us. It provides a glimpse of who we are inside. Jack is the dreamer. I'm the planner. Jack is happiest when he's the center of attention. Me, I much prefer to stay in the background.

Which actually leads me back to where I started. Adventure. My having to go on one.

I began by climbing up a beanstalk.

I'm sure you're familiar with the story. Or at least you think you are. "Jack and the Beanstalk." That's what our tale is usually called. But there's a problem with that title. Actually, there's more than one. Whose name do you see there? Just Jack's. It doesn't mention me at all.

Not only that, it gives the impression there was only one beanstalk involved, when in fact there were many.

I'm thinking it's time to set the record straight. To share the true story. Not because I want to be the center of attention, but because the longer version of the tale is actually a whole lot more interesting than the shorter one.

My family, which consisted of Jack, our mother, and me, lived on a small farm. In good times we grew enough to feed ourselves and have some left to sell on market days in the nearest town. But we had not had a good year for several years running. The truth is that we were poor. So poor that one day we made a bitter decision: We had no choice but to sell our cow.

The cow's name was Agapanthus, something else most versions of our story leave out. And this is a shame, as Agapanthus is a pretty great name, as names for cows go. It's also a blue flower, just in case you were wondering. Agapanthus produced the sweetest milk for miles around. This made selling the cow herself a pretty good plan, even if none of us cared for it much. Jack cared for it least of all.

"But I don't want to sell her," he said. He, Mama, and I were standing in the barn. It had once contained several cows and an old horse to help pull the plow. Now only Agapanthus was left.

"I don't see why we have to," Jack went on now.

"Because it's the only option we have left," I said as patiently as I could. We'd been going over the same ground for what felt like hours. "We have to be able to plant, Jack. It's either that, or leave the farm. The money Agapanthus will bring should be enough to buy some clover seeds to help keep the fields healthy this winter, with enough left over to buy the seeds we need in spring as well. Then, if the weather will just cooperate and the crops do well—"

"Now who's being a dreamer?" Jack cut me off. "Neither of those things happened this year, not to mention last year, or the year before."

"Which isn't the same as saying they won't next year," I said, trying not to let my voice rise. "And *if they do,* we'll have enough to feed ourselves and take to market to sell besides, just like we used to. We might even earn enough money to buy Agapanthus back."

"Not very likely," Jack scoffed. He moved to throw an arm around the cow's neck, as if to protect her. Agapanthus butted her head against his shoulder. "Only a fool would let her go."

"Or someone desperate," I answered steadily. "A person brave enough to face the fact that they're out of options."

Jack opened his mouth to speak, but before he could, our mother intervened. "My children," she said. "Enough."

Jack shut his mouth with a snap, but he still glared at me. As far as he was concerned, the decision to sell the cow was all my doing. Hence, my fault.

"I don't like it any better than you do, Jack, but I think Gen is right," our mother went on. "We have to sell the cow. We can't afford to lose the farm. There is nowhere else for us to go."

There was a moment's silence while my mother's words hung in the air like dust. We all knew she was right. But knowing a difficult truth inside your head and hearing it spoken are two very different things.

"Then let me be the one to take her," Jack said, speaking up first and thereby foiling the plan I was about to propose: I should be the one to take the cow to market. Of the three of us, I would be able to obtain the most money for her. I drove the hardest bargains.

But now that Jack had spoken, I knew what our mother would decide. Though our outlook and temperaments were very different, Jack and I didn't actually argue all that often. Something about us being twins, I suppose. When we did disagree, however, our mother almost always took Jack's side.

"Very well," she said, agreeing to his proposal. "But be ready to take the cow to market first thing tomorrow morning."

And so, early the next day, still scowling to show how much he disapproved, Jack set off with Agapanthus. I probably don't have to tell you what happened next. Jack and the cow never made it to market. They didn't even make it all the way to town. Because along the way, Jack encountered an old woman who made him an offer he couldn't refuse: seven beans with mysterious and magical properties in exchange for our cow.

It's usually at this point that the storyteller pauses, allowing two things to happen: The storyteller gets to catch his or her breath, and the listeners have an opportunity to share their opinions about Jack's decision.

The general consensus is that my brother was an idiot. Quite literally, a bean-brain. And it is most certainly true that when Jack came home that afternoon and revealed what he had done, our mother wept. This cannot be denied.

Tears of rage. Tears of despair. That's what most versions of our story tell you. But I'm here to tell you the truth. My mother's tears were neither of those things. Instead they were tears of joy.

My mother recognized those beans. She had waited a long time for them. Sixteen years to be precise, as long as Jack and I had been alive. She knew those beans were magic. Why? Because my mother had once planted a bean just like them herself, to grow a beanstalk of her own, a beanstalk that had saved all our lives.

You know those bedtime stories your parents told you when you were little? The ones populated by fairies and dragons, by damsels in distress and knights in shining armor? I hope you're sitting down. Because I'm here to tell you that they're all true. They just didn't happen in this world, the one where you and I were born and raised, the one my mother always called "the World Below." They happened in the land of my mother's birth, which should have been the land of Jack's and mine. A land of countless possibilities, including the ones that only magic can provide. A land that hovers out of sight, floating just above the clouds.

A land called the World Above.

My mother told bedtime stories too, of all shapes, sizes, and varieties. But the one she told most often was the tale of how and why the first magic bean was planted, how its beanstalk came to grow, and why it was cut down. The tale of how we'd stopped being sky dwellers and had become residents of the World Below.

It begins the way all good tales do. With *Once upon a time . . .*

One

Once upon a time, a royal duke ruled over a small but prosperous kingdom. His name was Roland des Jardins. He was a wise and generous ruler, and his people flourished under his stewardship. There was only one cloud on the kingdom's horizon. Duke Roland was childless.

His duchess had died in childbirth many years before. The infant had perished also. Heartbroken by these events, Duke Roland had never remarried. By the time this story came to pass, the duke was getting on in years, though he was still hale and hearty. Still, it was a problem that he had no son to carry on the family name, no daughter to be the apple of her father's eye. You've probably heard enough stories like this to understand the reason why.

Without a child, girl or boy, the duke had no heir. No one to succeed him and rule when he was gone. And when there's no clear contender for a throne, the less than clear ones always, well, *contend*. They compete and argue with one another. It's part of what the word means, after all. And all this uncertainty, this *contention*, meant that, although the duke's kingdom was at peace with its neighbors, it bore within it the spark to be at war with itself.

Now, there resided in Roland des Jardins' household a young nobleman named Guy de Trabant. Guy's father, Horace de Trabant, had been Duke Roland's closest childhood friend. He was also a duke, a ruler in his own right. His lands and those of Duke Roland bordered each other. It had been the two dukes' fondest hope that one day they would have children who would grow up to marry, thereby uniting the two kingdoms. Sadly, this dream had not come true.

First Roland des Jardins' wife died, and their infant child shortly thereafter. Then Horace de Trabant perished of the sweating sickness when his own son, Guy, was little more than a boy. As was the custom at that time, Duke Horace's widow sent her son to live with his father's friend, so that he might be raised in a duke's household and learn how to govern.

Many years went by. Guy de Trabant flourished under Duke Roland's care. He was everything a young nobleman should be. He was strong and handsome, brave in the face of his adversaries, generous to those less fortunate. He was, in fact, the old duke's successor in all but name. No one doubted that Duke Roland would name Guy de Trabant his heir. The two kingdoms would thereby be united, though admittedly not quite in the way that the two fathers had originally hoped.

Then something completely unexpected occurred. Roland des Jardins fell in love.

It happened at Guy de Trabant's wedding. Among the guests was a young woman named Celine Marchand. She was of good but minor birth, her father being a somewhat impoverished nobleman whose estate lay near the border of the de Trabant lands. Under ordinary circumstances, she might never have come to Duke Roland's attention at all. But the lady Celine was special. She had what they call "a way" about her. It didn't hurt, of course, that she was absolutely lovely.

Her hair was as blond as corn silk, her eyes as blue as a summer sky. She had one dimple in her chin and one in each of her cheeks when she smiled, which she did often. Her lips were full and red as ripe strawberries. Nor was this all. Lady Celine was also well-spoken, intelligent, and kind. Duke Roland fell in love at first sight, and the wonder of it was that Celine loved the duke as well.

So bright and shining was the love between them that not even the most cynical courtiers whispered that Celine Marchand had used artful wiles to snare a powerful older man in order to better her position in the world. All it took was one look at the couple to see that they were meant for each other.

Duke Roland and Lady Celine were married three months after Guy de Trabant. Then Roland des Jardins' subjects held their collective breath, praying for nature to take its course. For it seemed impossible that, after waiting so long for a second chance at happiness, the fates would not grant Duke Roland a child.

There was one person, of course, who, in his heart, could not bring himself to wish the old duke joy. Naturally, that person was Guy de Trabant. For if the new duchess bore a child, Guy's chance to become Duke Roland's heir would be over and done with forever.

If I'm to remain true to the way my mother always told the tale, this is where I must pause. I must gaze into space, as she always did, as though I can actually see events unfolding before my eyes. When I do this, I am using my imagination. But when my mother did it, she was looking back onto the scenes from her own life.

When she spoke of Celine Marchand, my mother was talking about herself.

It was always Jack who broke the silence, who brought my mother back to the here and now.

"What happened then, Mama?" he would ask, even though, by the time Jack was old enough to do this, we both knew the story by heart.

"What happened next?" my mother always echoed, as she pulled her attention back to the World Below. Sometimes her eyes held the sheen of tears, though never once did Jack and I see them fall.

"Injustice," my mother said. "That is what happened next, my son. Ingratitude begetting sorrow. I feel the wrongness of what happened as clearly today as I did long ago."

Desperate to obtain that which he had spent a lifetime believing would one day be his, Guy de Trabant had rallied the most contentious of Duke Roland's nobles in an attempt to seize the duke's crown. The battle for possession of the palace was brief but bloody. When it was over, the old duke lay dead, and the young man he had loved like a son was on his throne. But Guy de Trabant's rule could not yet be considered secure, for though the castle was searched from top to bottom not once, not twice, but three times, the duchess was nowhere to be found.

As it happened, she was less than a day's journey away. Duchess Celine had left early in the morning to visit her childhood nurse, an old wise woman named Rowan. The duchess had told no one but her husband of her plans. She had made the journey in the hope of confirming a suspicion that had recently taken root in her mind.

Duchess Celine believed she was with child.

By the time the duchess reached the wise woman's cottage, long shadows had begun to fall. Rowan helped the duchess tend to her horse, and then the two women went inside the cottage. They shared the evening meal together, and afterward the duchess insisted on doing all the washing up. Then, at long last, the two sat down before a bright and cheery fire, for although the day had been fine, the nights were beginning to turn cold.

"So," Rowan said after a few moments of contented silence. "How long have you known?"

At this the duchess gave a quick laugh. "I didn't *know*," she confessed. "Not for sure. Not until just now. It's why I came to see you. But I've suspected for almost a month."

"Your news will bring great happiness," Rowan said.

To which the duchess answered, "I hope so."

"Did I mention that it's twins?" the old wise woman asked. At which the duchess laughed once more.

"You know perfectly well you didn't," she replied. She rested a hand on her belly, as if she could already distinguish between the two children growing there. "Two," she said, her face thoughtful. "I hope it's one of each, a girl and a boy."

"Have you told Duke Roland yet?" the wise woman asked.

Celine shook her head. "No. I wanted to wait until I had seen you. I didn't want to raise false hopes."

It was at precisely that moment that a gust of wind blew down the chimney, sending out a shower of sparks. Startled, the two women leaped to their feet to stamp them out. But even when the sparks were extinguished, the wind was not. It prowled through the branches of the trees outside the house, making a noise that was a lament and warning all at once. The old wise woman cocked her head, as if the wind were speaking a language she could understand.

"What is it?" Celine asked, for the voice of the wind was making her anxious. "What is wrong?"

"We must wait for the morning to know for sure, I think," her old nurse said. But she moved to take Celine's face between her hands and gazed into her eyes for a very long time. So long that the young woman began to tremble. For it seemed to her that, though her old nurse's hands were warm, and though the fire still burned in the grate, the room had suddenly grown cold. A cold that was finding a way inside her, burrowing straight toward her heart.

"No," she whispered. *"No."*

"Let us wait and see," the wise woman counseled. "By its very nature, wind is impetuous. Sometimes it exaggerates things or misunderstands."

But by the morning, the voice of the wind was not alone. Word of what had happened in the palace began to spread through the countryside, told by the hushed and fearful voices of Duke Roland's former subjects. In this way, the duchess learned that her worst fears had been realized. Her husband was dead. She herself was in great danger. Her unborn children were Duke Roland's true heirs. They must be protected at all costs.

"Ah, Roland! I should have told you," Celine whispered, as the tears streamed down her cheeks. "I wish I had. At least then you could have died with this joy in your heart."

"His heart was full of joy already," Rowan said. "For he loved you well."

"As I loved him," Celine replied.

At this the old woman gave a brisk nod. "Even so. Dry your eyes. You must not pour this love away in grief. You will need it to sustain you in what is to come. There is only one place where you and your children will be safe. You know that, don't you?"

Celine took the deepest breath of her life. She could feel it expanding her lungs, then streaming throughout her body, all the way down to the tips of her fingers and toes. She let it out and did a very unduchess-like thing. She wiped the sleeve of her dress across her face to dry her eyes. She squared her shoulders and lifted her chin.

"I know what must be done," Duchess Celine said. "Show me how to reach the World Below."

About the Author

CAMERON DOKEY is the author of more than thirty young adult novels. Her most recent titles include *The World Above* and *Winter's Child*. She is also the author of *How NOT to Spend Your Senior Year*. Cameron lives in Seattle, Washington.

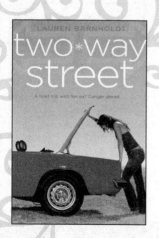  

The Kingdom has strict rules about class and etiquette. But rules are made to be broken.

JACKAROO   ON FORTUNE'S WHEEL   ELSKE

Cynthia Voigt

The Newbery Award-winning author of

Dicey's Song

From Simon Pulse · Published by Simon & Schuster

Love. Heartbreak. Friendship. Trust.

Fall head over heels for Terra Elan McVoy.

LOOKING FOR THE PERFECT BEACH READ?

FROM SIMON PULSE
PUBLISHED BY SIMON & SCHUSTER

From **WILD** to **ROMANTIC,** don't miss these **PROM** stories from Simon Pulse!

A Really Nice Prom Mess

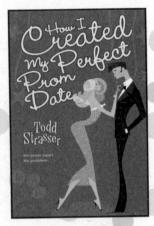

How I Created My Perfect Prom Date

Prom Crashers

Prama

From Simon Pulse

• • •

Published by Simon & Schuster

SiMONTeeN

Simon & Schuster's **Simon Teen** e-newsletter delivers current updates on the hottest titles, exciting sweepstakes, and exclusive content from your favorite authors.

Visit **TEEN.SimonandSchuster.com** to sign up, post your thoughts, and find out what every avid reader is talking about!

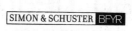